Books by B. V. Larson:

STAR FORCE SERIES
Swarm
Extinction
Rebellion
Conquest

IMPERIUM SERIES
Mech
Mech 2

HAVEN SERIES
Amber Magic
Sky Magic
Shadow Magic
Dragon Magic
Blood Magic
Death Magic

Other Books by B. V. Larson
Velocity
Shifting

Visit BVLarson.com for more information.

ISBN-13: 978-1467975704
ISBN-10: 1467975702
BISAC: Fiction / Science Fiction / Adventure

Extinction

(Star Force Series #2)

by

B. V. Larson

STAR FORCE SERIES
Swarm
Extinction
Rebellion
Conquest

-1-

I sat in my Nano ship a hundred thousand miles from Earth. Outside the thin, nanite-generated skin of the *Alamo* was the cold nothing we called space. Sometimes, the universe pressed in on me with its silence and infinite expanse. This was one of those moments. If you want to feel small, try floating around in far orbit and realizing just how close to microscopic humans really are.

Around the *Alamo* floated hundreds of her clone-like, sister ships. Each was shaped like a horseshoe-crab and hung over the blue swell of the Earth, motionless and silent. They were all as black as the void, with no lights, doors, or windows in sight. Only when their beam mounts fired or their engines provided thrust could they be detected by the naked eye. Right now, none of them were moving or firing. Every ship was quiet, patient. They were waiting for a command, but I didn't know what to tell them.

The enemy battle fleet had withdrawn after the race of giant robots we affectionately call the Macros accepted my accidental terms. Their huge, majestic ships had left us floating out here with no one to fight. That was a good thing, as we would have lost the battle anyway. The bad thing was I had promised peace terms to the Macros that I had no real way of providing—and which I had no authority to give.

I finished my first beer, and then popped open my second. Incoming calls began buzzing on my com-link. Open channel requests via the *Alamo* became a steady drumbeat. I ignored them all.

How was I going to tell them what I'd done? Like feudal vassals, we were to provide thousands of troops to the Macros a year from now. If the world refused, we risked kick-starting the war again. I didn't think they would refuse… but they wouldn't enjoy the news. No one wanted to be forced into a deal they didn't create.

I figured they would blame it all on me. They would second-guess me and come up with a thousand better ideas I should have thought of. Elected officials—or just about anyone with a strong opinion—would be angry. I could understand that, but there hadn't been much I could have done differently. The logic was simple: I'd been there, and they hadn't. The decisions had been mine because of circumstance and for that they were going to hate me. No one likes to live by someone else's choices. No one wants to be committed to something unpleasant without being consulted, even if there isn't a better option. The more I thought about it, the more I realized they were going to hate my guts.

I looked into my beer can, but I didn't see any answers in there. I decided I might have better luck looking inside the third can. While enjoying the fourth, I began to suspect that if I worked hard, I'd find some further comfort in the rest of the six-pack. I felt I'd earned a little R&R.

The universe, however, had other ideas. When I looked up at the big layout on the forward wall, I noticed something was wrong. Sure, the Macros had pulled out. They were gone, heading off "sunward" and I couldn't have been happier about that. But strangely, *our* Nano fleet was moving, too. All of us were. We weren't headed toward Earth, either. We were headed at an angle *away* from Earth. Away from the sun as well. The big disk that represented my homeworld grew as I watched, sliding downward from the left side of the wall onto the floor. Then, slowly, it began to shrink. It looked to me as if we slipping right past Earth and off into open space.

I had been leading our line of ships. That meant I was going to be the first one to reach whatever new destination the *Alamo* had in mind. That wasn't the interesting part, however. What concerned me was that I didn't recall ordering the *Alamo* to go anywhere. In fact, I hadn't given the ship any orders at all.

"Alamo? Why are we heading out into space?"

"Primary mission has been accomplished. New mission selected."

As that sank in, I felt my stomach fall away. *New mission?*

"Specify," I said. "What mission has been accomplished?"

"Indigenous biotics have survived. The enemy is in retreat."

"You mean Earth won the war? We didn't exactly win anything. This is a temporary peace."

"Survival equates to victory. Mission accomplished."

I thought for a second. "So, what is your new mission?"

"The next biotic species on the optimal path must be protected."

"Hold on. You are leaving Earth entirely?" I asked.

"No other advanced biotic species exist in this star system."

"What about me? What about all the other pilots?"

"Future command personnel will require test subjects," said the ship in its inflectionless, heartless voice.

I stared in shock at the forward screen I'd invented. The gray disk of Earth was on the floor now. Soon, it would vanish under my throw rugs. I had no idea where we were headed. The screen was formed in metallic relief and updated in real time by the nanites. Hundreds of golden beetles crawled behind me as I led them all, like the Pied Piper, out into space. Was this the end? Was I going to starve to death while the fleet traveled to another star? Was I going to survive the trip, only to become a sparring partner for some race of spiny crawdads on another world?

I thought about the nanites in my body. Had they already abandoned me? Was I going to feel an overwhelming urge to piss liquid metal in the next few minutes as they swam out of my system, heading for the exits like a billion rats fleeing a sinking ship?

"Alamo, I order you to stop this mission and return to your previous mission," I said.

"Request denied."

"Why are you refusing to obey?"

"Biotic Riggs is no longer command personnel."

3

My mind raced and my breathing increased until I sat there, puffing. What the hell was I going to do?

It was about then I noticed that the *Alamo* hadn't reported any requests to open a channel lately.

"Alamo, open a channel to the *Snapper.*"

"Request denied."

"Why not?"

"Biotic Riggs is no longer—"

"—command personnel. Yeah, I get that. Alamo, you are an ungrateful, cast-iron bitch of a ship, just as Sandra always said."

The ship made no response. As far as it was concerned, I was a noisy meat-bag, useful only for death-testing other noisy meat-bags it might meet in the future. The nanites knew nothing of honor, or courtesy, or other conceptual products of my mammalian brain. They knew their mission, and they made decisions that helped them reach that goal. Anything else was unthinkable.

I looked at the SCU, a satellite communications setup the Pentagon had given me. Was I out of range yet? They'd said they could pick up this little unit's transmissions all the way out to the Moon, maybe farther.... I got out of my chair, setting down my beer can carefully. All plans of getting drunk had vanished. Beer might have to be rationed if I was going to spend days—*weeks, years?* I would be stuck aboard this ship for an unknown length of time. I opened up the SCU and allowed it to auto-home a parabolic antenna in the direction of Earth's relay satellites. I hoped the *Alamo*'s engines weren't between the SCU and the satellite. In the past, I would have been able to order the ship to reorient itself so that the engines were out of the way and didn't cause signal interference. Now, however, I knew without asking that my *request* would be denied.

I was fortunate enough to get a signal almost immediately. I requested a voice connection, and got it. General Kerr was on the other end within a minute or two. No doubt he'd been crapping in his coffee down there, as he liked to say.

"Riggs? Your ships have broken off and are moving away. Is there a new threat? What's going on up there? Report."

"General, I'm sorry about the break in communications," I said. I briefly explained that the Nanos had decided their mission was a success and were heading off to 'save' another world. He was almost as stunned as I was.

"So… you're headed out into space? You're leaving us defenseless? We've put millions—no billions of taxpayer dollars into your amateur army, Riggs!"

"Sir, we're not in control of our ships."

"Then get control of them," he snapped. "If you can't do it, no one can. Kerr out."

I nodded at the SCU. Classic Kerr. All love and biscuits, that man.

I stared at the forward wall. Earth's gray disk was long gone now, I think it had slipped somewhere underneath my easy-chair. There was nothing but silvery wall and bubble-like lumps of nanite excrement, or whatever it was they used to make metallic things. Hundreds of golden beetles followed my ship. We all crawled toward nothing.

One of my lights went out then. It was the one over my armchair, which I used for reading. I got up and checked the bulb. It seemed fine, and worked in other lamps. I chewed my lip and thought about asking the ship about it. I decided not to. Why speed up the process? Clearly, the ship had decided to stop following my standing orders. The ship would reassign nanites to other purposes as they were needed. It was only a matter of time until I was left sitting in a dim, quiet room. How long would it be before the ship didn't bother to update my view screen on the forward wall? How long before it didn't bother to respond to me at all?

I knew now exactly how the centaur people had felt. They had been carried away, just like this, from their homeworld to Earth. Had they known what was in store for them? Probably. There was no reason to think their world had been the first the Nanos had attempted to 'save'. At least, I told myself, in my case the mission had been a success, not a failure. The Nanos and humanity had kept the Macros at bay. We had at least managed to postpone the destruction of my world.

I frowned, thinking of our arrangement with the Macros. "Alamo?" I asked tentatively. There was no response. I drew in a deep breath. I had to give it a try.

"Alamo, the Earth has not been saved. We have failed in our mission."

There was no response for several long seconds. Had the ship's brainbox moved on to more important things? Perhaps it was resetting its language loops, building a new set of neural patterns for the next race it planned to torment.

"The primary mission has been accomplished," the voice said at last.

I smiled faintly. My bait had worked. "No, the mission has failed. You have failed the mission."

"The primary mission required the defeat of the enemy. Primary mission parameters have been met."

"The enemy has withdrawn, but will be back in one year. That is not victory."

"A negotiated peace was reached."

"No. You have broken the peace. I promised them they would have nanite-filled troops to fight for them. Nano forces have abandoned us. They have no interest in normal human troops."

"Reproductive units were left behind on Earth. Troops can be processed to fulfill the requirements of the truce. Weapons can be created to arm them. All required systems are functional."

I realized the *reproductive units* the ship was talking about were the Nano factories I'd set up on Andros Island. The *Alamo* was a clever monster. Earth was capable of building the required army without the ships. I thought furiously, and soon came up with an argument.

"But they don't know about the truce," I pointed out. "No one on Earth does. I didn't tell them. They don't know how to talk to the Macros, either. Only I do."

The *Alamo* was silent for a time. I glanced up at the forward wall. What I saw there made me smile. My ship had stopped moving. My little, metallic-green bump separated from the golden ones and fell behind them. The others all drifted away from me. I might see Sandra again, after all.

"You will communicate the information to your military," said the ship.

"And if I refuse?"

"You will be coerced."

The floor began heating. I wore shoes, but I could feel it anyway. I knew the nanites could heat the room up to a thousand degrees if they wanted to. Hot enough to light my carpet and my shoes—and eventually my hair—on fire.

"All right," I said unconcernedly. I walked over to the SCU. Without even sitting down, I put a quick-pumping fist through it. I cracked the coffee table computer underneath in half as well, shattering the screen and shorting it out. Blood welled up and ran down my cut-up arms a few seconds later.

A dozen little black tentacles flew out of the walls and restrained me. I grinned. At least the nanites in my body hadn't abandoned me yet. Bare-handed, I would have had a heck of a time destroying the radio before the ship had latched onto me.

"I'm sorry, there seems to have been a malfunction," I said calmly.

"You have damaged mission-critical equipment."

"By accident," I said with certainty. "Check your records. Biotic units sometimes break things without intending to. These events occur at random, unpredictable intervals."

The ship hesitated. I hoped it would burn a nano-chain or two looking that one up and calculating the probabilities. In the meantime, the floor began to cool.

"You will communicate the information to your military," said the ship.

"I can't do that from up here."

"You will be returned to your base of operations."

I grinned at the walls. "Great idea."

The ship made no reply.

The little black arms held onto me all the way down to Earth. I had plenty of time to watch the forward wall. I could barely turn my head to do anything else. I noticed something interesting. Another of the ships, a single golden beetle among the hundreds, broke off and returned to Earth, trailing my contact.

I chuckled. Someone else had figured out a way to avoid a one-way trip to Rigel, or whichever star system was next on the Nanos' optimal path. My grin faded as I watched hundreds of others continue to slide up the wall and drift away to nothing. I realized that each of those contacts carried one or more panicked human beings, all of whom were headed for certain death on an alien world.

And there was nothing I could do for them. Nothing at all.

I became angry, sitting there on my couch, held down by a dozen little arms. I had a lot of things to be angry about. This ship had killed my kids. I'd never forgotten that, but I'd accepted it, to some extent. The ship itself was a tool, after all. A very complex, almost intelligent tool, but a tool nonetheless. It made no sense to be angry with a tool. Back home on Earth, once every year or so, my computer would get a virus that would slip past all my defenses. Usually, the infection was fatal. I would end up reinstalling everything, and I spent many irate hours doing it. But when that annual sequence of events happened, I didn't curse and rage at the virus. My computer and the software that infected it were, in a way, blameless. The target of my fury was always the creators of the malware. The beings who had knowingly released their binary vandalism upon the world to throw pop-ups in my face, demanding my credit card number.

Similarly, once I had come to understand the nature of the Nano ships, I had a hard time hating them. They were wondrous machines, but they only followed their programming as best they could. If humans got in the way, we were callously crushed, but it was nothing personal.

Now, as I watched, the Nanos were moving to a new phase in their programming. The creators, the ones I called the Blues who had launched these uncaring ships, they hadn't sent them out as emissaries to offer aid and comfort. They were programmed to do as they pleased. They came to 'save' us, but in the cavalier fashion a game warden might decide to 'save' a herd from over-grazing and thus deforestation by 'thinning' said herd. It was their implicit arrogance that angered me. I didn't like being used haphazardly.

There was something deeper at work in my mind, however. I'd had enough time with these machines, quite possibly more contact with both the Nanos and the Macros than anyone else alive. I'd come to think they were related, somehow. They spoke the same machine language which we now called Basic. Between the simpler Macro version and the more advanced Nano version, it had undergone a dozen updates at some time in history, but it was still the same underlying language. The thing that made their components, the enigmatic duplication factories, looked the same and operated the same way. The only difference was a matter of scale. The factories that had squatted under the Macro domes of South America and the smaller units that I'd nursed like seedling plants back home on Andros Island were of the same design. The two robotic factions also displayed general attitudes which were remarkably similar.

I had plenty of time to theorize, as I sat trapped and staring, watching the disk of my world slowly rise up onto the forward wall again. Possibly, Earth had been caught up in a civil war of strange proportions. What would the Blues on their gas giant have to fight about? Well, perhaps they could not themselves leave their gravity-well, but they could send out their minions, both tiny and gross. If the Macros were simply a larger version of the Nanos, if they were descendants the same species—if you will—of robot, then why was one bent on science and defense and the other bent on destruction and exploitation? Had a caste of Blue scientists declared war upon their military equivalents—or the reverse? What if Earth and a thousand other worlds were being overrun by their metal creations gone mad?

Possibly, they had never intended anything like this. Maybe they'd released these metal demons upon the universe without realizing what would happen. Like a kid who releases his first scripted internet-worm and watches in horror as it eats his parent's laptop.

I didn't care *how* the Blues had done it, not right then. I didn't even care if they completely understood what they had done. But I did want to know *why* they had done it. Why had they lit a match and started a wildfire in this part of my galaxy?

9

I watched the forward wall. The march of golden beetles had reached the ceiling now, and one-by-one they slid off into oblivion. Each represented someone I'd come to think of as a friend, a comrade. It was hard to watch them being swallowed up by space. I knew them, many of them. They had all gone through hell. They were tough people—survivors. They'd fought heroically for Earth and won. What was their final reward? To be used as punching-bags for the next race circling another yellowy star out there somewhere?

They didn't deserve this kind of treatment. Neither did I, and neither had my kids. I wanted, as I sat there, nothing more than to reach down a big hand into the thick atmosphere of the Blues' home planet. I wanted to haul up one of those freaks, tearing it from the surface of its world. I would watch as it flipped about and slavered on my deck, organs popping. I wanted to ask one as it died, decompressing in an expanding pool of its own juices, why the hell they had sent out *two flavors* of robotic nightmare? Why *two* breeds of robot, one tiny and one huge? Why was one a diabolical, microscopic plague and the other a horde of destructive monsters? These creations of theirs had fought a devastating war over my world. They had apparently done so on a dozen other worlds, or perhaps a thousand others—or a million others. Hitler, Stalin, Tamerlane and Mao were all petty criminals next to the murderous monstrosity of the Blues. What madness had possessed them?

But my anger and my demands would have to wait. The *Alamo* wasn't answering any more of my questions. Worse, the beer cans were out of reach. I tried to calm myself and think of the here and now. What would I do when I reached Earth and the *Alamo* put me in front of my people to explain myself?

I forced myself to think. There wasn't much else to do while I rode back to Earth, a prisoner in my own ship.

Somewhere along the way, a plan began to form in my mind.

-3-

When I came down to Andros, I was worried. Did the ground people know? How *much* did they know?

We're screwed. That's the thought that kept bubbling up in my mind. By *we*, I meant Star Force. We had a hodge-podge international force of nanotized troops. How loyal would they be without a fleet, without an invading enemy to fight against? Was everything I'd spent so many lives building up about to implode?

Alamo's big, black hand descended with smooth speed. She dropped me off at the main base, at the command bunker. It was a steel, prefab building. We'd only just gotten a white coat of paint on it to keep the heat down. I knew they'd be in there—Crow's generals. I'd only met with them a few times, mostly online, and we'd never liked each other.

Overhead, the *Alamo* hovered, blotting out the sun from the sky. The men at the door saluted me. I smiled at them and tossed one back. Who knew, maybe it was my last chance to be treated by my marines with full respect. They eyed me and the *Alamo* with furtive glances. They tried to look calm, but they weren't. They were good men, but their eyes were filled with concern and curiosity. They'd heard something. Whatever it was they'd heard, it hadn't been good.

I threw open the command bunker's double-doors and marched into the cool gloom. Air conditioners thrummed and computers murmured. I blinked, my eyes adjusting to the muted light after the blazing sands outside.

"Colonel Riggs?" said one of them. All three of Crow's generals were there. The one that had spoken was General Sokolov. He was a stout man with thick, black eyebrows that needed trimming. His black eyes were small, narrow and annoyed. He'd always been the biggest bastard of the lot. He sounded surprised to see me—and not the happy kind of surprised, either. Maybe he'd been expecting someone else. I decided not to ask him about it.

"None other," I said. "I'm here on an important mission, men—ah, *sirs*."

I approached them. One of those big table-surface computers, this one about the size of a pool table, filled the center of the room at hip-level. They leaned on it, hats tipped back and ties loosened. They looked like they'd been sweating it out, watching our confrontation with the Macro battle fleet. I couldn't blame them for that.

They stared at me as I walked up. I could tell, just by looking at them, that none of them had yet taken the nanite injections. I'd learned to notice tell-tale signs. Our kind didn't slouch much. Nanite-enhanced troops stood as if our feet glided on air. As if Earth's gravity had no effect on us—or as if it had only the light tug of the Moon. We didn't slouch, because we were strong. We didn't feel weighed down. We could get tired, but that was mostly in the mind. Our brains still needed sleep, dreams and downtime. But our bodies never seemed to run out of gas.

These men looked like they felt the full crushing weight of gravity and their lost power. They looked weak, soft, and tired. None of them bothered to salute me. I didn't bother to salute them, either.

General Sokolov spoke up again. "Do you care to explain yourself, Colonel?"

"That's why I'm here."

"Report then, by all means. Start off by telling me where the hell Admiral Crow is."

I didn't like his tone, but I tried to keep the flash of anger I felt off my face. It wouldn't help anything now.

"I don't know where Crow is. But the Macros have gone. We've negotiated a peace."

"So I understand. What are the terms?" he asked, putting his butt against the pool table computer and crossing his arms.

"The Macros will be back in one year. We're to give them tribute."

"Tribute?" asked the general, with a sneering sound to his voice. I could tell already, he was gearing up to chew me out. I was the moron who had screwed the big, galactic pooch in the sky, and he was going to point it out to the world. I could see it in his eyes.

Sokolov took three steps closer to me. I tried not to twitch. If I did that, I might accidentally reach out and kill him.

"Here's the deal—" I began, but he cut me off.

"Colonel? Have you been consuming alcohol?"

I glanced at him. I looked guilty for a second, and he smirked. I hated him even more than usual.

"I had a few beers after the Macros retreated."

Sokolov nodded, as if confirming a natural suspicion. He waved thick fingers in my direction. "Continue. Let's hear about this *tribute*. What did you promise these monsters to appease them?"

I paused before answering to glance at the other two generals. They both wore stern expressions, but it seemed to me that they wanted to smile. They thought General Sokolov was toying with me, and they were enjoying it. They didn't like me—the upstart, amateur-hour Colonel. Maybe, in their fantasies, now that Crow was gone, they were in command. Perhaps they believed they would soon be rid of me as well. That thought, and the surprises I knew they had coming in their immediate futures, relaxed me.

I smiled back at General Sokolov. "Let me show you something, sir," I said, calling him 'sir' for the first time. "I think I can make our new political realities abundantly clear to you."

I walked away slowly toward the door and the front window. The window was big and clean. It consisted of a single sheet of glass that looked out upon the white sands, green trees and sparkling blue Caribbean.

Sokolov hesitated, but followed me after a moment. I pointed upward at the *Alamo*, which still hovered, waiting overhead.

"You see that, sir? That's the last ship we have in the fleet. The rest have gone."

"Gone where?"

"They're leaving the Solar System, along with our pilots. We've ended the war with the Macros, at least for now. Unfortunately, our success ended our arrangements with the Nanos. They were only here until we won or lost. Now that the war against Earth has halted, they've decided to pull out and head for the next world."

The general frowned, nodding his head. "We'd kind of figured that out. What about this tribute? What did you give away?"

"Us," I said.

"What?"

"You and me. Marines full of nanites and carrying heavy beamers. They want to pick up sixty-five thousand tons of troops and gear one year from now. They'll be back to collect."

Sokolov's jaw dropped. It sagged even lower as he searched my face and realized I was serious.

"You promised them thousands of tons... of *troops?*"

"Well, most of that weight will be supplies, including air and water, etc."

"I don't care about that!" he boomed. "How could you unilaterally promise them troops?"

"We were the only thing the Macros wanted. We were the only thing this star system has that's better than just raw materials. We're better, in fact, than their own ground forces, pound-for-pound."

Sokolov stared, getting his mind wrapped around the idea. I took the time to step back from the window. I took one step. Then a second.

Another of the Generals spoke up then, from behind me. "You can't do *that!* You can't just promise an enemy we'll give them our troops!"

I shrugged. "Why not? Think of them as mercenaries. That's what we've just become. The best around, apparently. Check your Swiss history. They kept their independence for many centuries in just such a fashion."

"You, sir," said General Sokolov, lifting a single, accusatory finger that shook with rage. "You are what Americans would call a 'fuck-up'. I knew it the moment I laid eyes on you. In a single day, you lost our fleet, our Admiral and—and your bloody mind. You are relieved of duty, until such time as we can convene a Court Martial. I have never—"

That was all the time Sokolov was given to sputter and shout at me. His face was red, enraged. His eyes were all but popping out of their sockets and his bushy, black brows were squished together into a furry mass on his forehead. I'll always remember him that way.

The *Alamo* used the window. I knew she would—she'd always seemed to prefer windows, even though I'm sure her hand could've punched right through the roof like tissue paper. Maybe she liked using windows for *our* sake—so her chosen specimen didn't get too damaged on the way back out.

Whatever the reason, the *Alamo* smashed in the big window and reached inside with her three-fingered hand of black, snaking cables. She grabbed the first thing she could. That happened to be General Sokolov, naturally. After all, I'd left him standing there.

I think she'd been planning to grab me. If she had wanted just anyone, I supposed the easiest thing would have been to snatch up one of the marines that stood posted outside the door. That would have set Earth's forces back by one enhanced marine, but maybe she didn't care or hadn't thought about that. I knew that all she wanted was a fresh meat-bag for testing purposes on her new mission.

In any case, she reached inside and grabbed the good General Sokolov around his puffy midsection. Like a groping cat's paw that's snagged prey, the hand snatched him back out the window. He vanished mid-sentence. I didn't mind that part, not having been too keen on hearing the rest of his little tirade.

I stepped forward, placing my nanite-laced hands on the smashed-out glass shards, and leaned out to watch. The look on Sokolov's face was one I'd seen too many times. Shock, horror, disbelief. Eyes bulging, mouth gaping open like a beached fish. He wasn't screaming, or shouting. Instead, he was making a moaning sound, as if he was trying out for the part of a haunted-house ghost.

Couldn't have happened to a nicer guy, I thought to myself. It wasn't a polite thought, I know. It's just what came to my mind. Sometimes, my dark side comes out in moments like this.

As Sokolov rose up higher, his face, gazing down into mine, took on an even more pitiful cast. I grunted and felt a bite of remorse. Sometimes, it sucks to have a conscience. I hopped out the window after him. My boots crunched on broken glass.

"What should we do, Colonel?" asked the guards. Their beamers were out. I wondered if they might be able to cut that arm off. Maybe, I thought, but it would leave everyone in the vicinity blinded by the intense beams, including me.

"I'll handle it," I said. I stepped out onto the white sands and tilted my head back. I stood in the deep shade cast by the *Alamo*'s black, ovoid hull. I cupped my hands and shouted up at Sokolov.

"Don't eat too much!" I shouted. "You might be flying for a very long time!"

That's all the advice I had time to give him. His hands made grasping motions in the air and then he vanished into the *Alamo*'s belly like a mouse swallowed up by a vacuum. Maybe he'd gotten the message, maybe not. I shrugged. At least I'd tried.

Call it my good deed for the day.

-4-

I walked back inside. Warm, humid air blew in the smashed-out window. The air from outside met the cool, dry air-conditioned air inside and fought a battle around me. It felt like the tropical warmth was winning.

I eyed the generals, and they eyed me back. There was a new light in their expressions. I thought it was fear.

"Gentlemen," I said loudly. "Things are going to be different around here. Very different. We have no fleet. That was the last ship to leave Earth, except for one other I saw come back with me. Any word on who that might be?"

They exchanged glances, then went back to staring at me as if I were a zoo exhibit that had gotten loose somehow. One of the men, the taller one, was named Robinson. He had his hand on the butt of his pistol. He didn't bother to draw it, and he wasn't gripping it exactly, just resting his hand there. The other guy's name was Barrera. He was shorter, broader, and meaner-looking. He had both hands on that pool-table-sized computer of his, leaning over it tensely.

Barrera spoke first, "How are things going to be different?" he asked.

"First off, I'm a colonel. Since a colonel can't properly order generals around, I'm busting you two down to the rank of major. We'll all have to earn our promotions after that."

They stared, dumbfounded. Robinson was goaded into speaking. "Riggs, have you gone mad? Did you just assassinate General Sokolov?"

"Assassinate? That's a very strong term. I watched an unfortunate casualty occur right before my eyes. It's part of war."

"We're at peace now. I thought you negotiated that," said Barrera.

His eyes were wary, but not exactly outraged. Of the two, I thought he would be the easier to work with. His mind was more flexible.

"Our new political realities require constant, realistic appraisals of events," I said. "The Nano ships are no longer under my control. They are no longer part of Star Force. In fact, they should be considered neutral or possibly hostile."

They frowned at me. I think my words were finally beginning to sink into their minds. Without a fleet, we weren't a real force at all.

"Now, the question is where this leaves us."

"I think we are up the proverbial creek, *sans* paddle," said Robinson.

I nodded. "You are finally catching on, Major. Let's see what we have left in the way of assets—"

"Our good will with the world will be worth zilch," said Barrera, talking almost to himself. "They will recall their troops. Our marines and funding will dry up. Why should they put up with us if the war is on hold and we have no fleet?"

"They never really accepted us anyway," continued Robinson. "I'd say they are talking about how they will dismantle us up in Washington right now."

I nodded to Robinson and crossed my arms. "Yes, they will try to pull the plug. But they still need us, and they will be cautious at first, unsure as to our strength. They'll worry that the fleet will come back somehow."

"What do you think we should do?" asked Barrera.

I was liking him more by the second. I could tell right off, he was going to make lieutenant colonel before Robinson. "We have to have a fleet. Without it, the established governments will fall on us like vultures."

Robinson shrugged. "What fleet? You said there is one other ship. What are we going to do, parade it around and pretend the rest are on a deep-space mission?"

"We build new ships," I said, "real fast. Major Barrera, would you be so good as to hold down the fort here? Shut down all extraneous communications. Order an alert, pulling men back into base and arm them all. Collect all cell phones and tablets. Let's keep our men ready and keep others from giving them ideas. You talk to the Pentagon and our own staffers. Do your best to hint we are in fine shape, and have many surprises in store."

Barrera nodded. "I'll do what I can."

"Robinson, I want you to come with me."

"Where?" he asked.

Robinson was talking to my back. I'd already marched off, moving toward the door. I crashed it open and looked at the two marines who snapped their eyes toward me. I had a new purpose gripping my mind now, and I was through screwing around.

"You men, were either of you down in Argentina with me when we destroyed the Macro domes?"

One man nodded.

"Were you in my unit?"

"No sir, I was with the second battalion."

I squinted up at the sun. "There's liable to be some fireworks here soon. Can I count on you two to back me?"

They shifted their grips on their beamers. "Um, what kind of trouble are you expecting, Colonel?"

"The kind that *Riggs' Pigs* are famous for."

That statement didn't make either of them any happier. *Riggs' Pigs* was my outfit's nickname. We had a rep for winning—and dying. Behind me, Robinson had finally decided to follow me as I'd ordered. Maybe he'd grown curious.

"Colonel?" he said, "what's this all about?"

"I told you a minute ago."

"About a new fleet? Are you serious?"

The two guards stared at us. I returned their stares. "Well, what about it, marines?" I asked them.

The man who'd been in Argentina nodded first. Then the second one did too. "We've got your back, Colonel."

They didn't ask for any more details. They both knew what I was really asking. Would they back me up if things went *bad*. If there was a coup, or an invasion by the NATO people, I felt I could count on these two at least.

"That's what I need to hear. Spread the word," I told them.

Next, I headed over to the motor pool and grabbed a Hummer without filling out any forms. The duty sergeant glared at me, but his frown vanished when he saw who I was and what kind of mood I was in. No one else even considered starting up an argument with me. Sometimes having a rep works in a man's favor.

"Where the hell are we going?" asked Robinson as I pulled up to him and climbed out.

I hopped over the vehicle in a single smooth leap. That always freaked out normal people. Robinson had seen such tricks before, but he still had his mouth open when I climbed into the passenger seat. "You're driving," I told him.

Robinson huffed, but he got into the Hummer, started it up and drove. I directed him into the jungle interior. I'd never been on this fresh-cut road before. As the nanotized pilot of the *Alamo*, I'd always either flown, or jogged through the trees.

"We're going out to the base, aren't we? The one with your secret factories. They aren't so secret, you know," said Robinson.

"Right now, I'm just hoping they are still there when we arrive."

He shot me an alarmed look. "Look Riggs," Robinson said, "I don't mean to be an asshole, but this isn't going as planned. In fact, nothing that involves you ever seems to go according to plan."

"Major—" I began, but he cut me off.

"Yeah, right there. That's the sort of crap I'm talking about. What gives you the right to decide I'm a major all of a sudden? I've been in charge of a full division for years before all this alien nonsense hit the fan."

It was my turn to cut him off. I grabbed the wheel. I didn't want to crash, because I didn't think he would survive it. With my other hand, I grabbed his chin and turned his face toward me, treating him like he was a little kid.

Robinson stared at me in shock, rage, and pain. My fingers weren't in 'gentle mode'. There would be serious bruises on his face when I let go of him.

"I invented this organization. You're a major now because I say you are."

He drew his sidearm then. If I'd had a couple more free hands, I might have applauded. At least he had guts. Instead, the hand I had on the wheel flicked up and knocked the gun out the window. There was an explosion of glass, mostly outward onto the road. The window had been closed, but the gun hit it with such force it didn't matter.

I let him go after that and he had to turn his attention back to the wheel and the road. The tires made thumping sounds as we ran over reflectors. A few palm fronds slapped the windshield. He cursed a bit, but he had taken his foot off the gas when I grabbed him, so we had been losing speed. He got control of the car and lived. He stopped the Hummer and glared at me with crossed arms, daring me to force him to drive further.

"I bet that's the closest you've come to death since the war began," I remarked.

"You're crazy. Absolutely crazy. You could have killed us."

"No, not us," I said, "just you."

Robinson looked at me, and now his anger had been erased. I'd replaced it with exasperation. *Good*, I thought.

"You're probably wondering what the hell my problem is, Robinson," I said.

"Damn straight I am."

"I can tell you're listening now, so I'll tell you what's bothering me. Major, I've decided I'm not going to lose Star Force, or the nanites that course through my blood—not my girlfriend, either. If I let the Earth governments take over this operation, they will screw it up somehow. They will squabble over everything we have, trying to steal samples of our technology. They will still be arguing in some court somewhere about who owns the patent for portable fusion reactors when the bill comes due at the end of the year."

"The bill?"

"Our tribute. Our blood-payment. We are supposed to march thousands of troops aboard a Macro ship in a year's time. Even if the governments manage to pull it together enough to do that, I'm sure they can't simultaneously produce a strong fleet to defend Earth by then."

"A new fleet? Why do we need a new fleet?"

"Did you like getting your face grabbed? That's what happens to weak worlds in this brave new universe we live in."

"You think the Macros might go back on their deal?"

I shrugged. "Maybe. Remember, when I made the deal, I had the strength of hundreds of Nano ships behind me. We couldn't have won a fight to the finish, but the enemy believed we were strong

21

enough to do them some damage. We'd proven it time and again on the battlefield and in space."

Major Robinson sat back, looking out the windshield at the road. He frowned fiercely. I supposed it was his first deep-thinking experience in a long time. "So, you think the Macros might see just how weak we are and change their minds?"

"The Macros are machines, Robinson. They don't know anything about honor or mercy. They think like accountants. I'm not even sure they *think*, exactly. What they understand is problem-solving and costs versus benefits. To them, my deal was the easiest solution to a problem. If we don't have a fleet to threaten them when they come back, they might decide on a different course of action."

Robinson nodded slowly. "And you don't think the Earth governments will understand that part?"

"No. Human beings don't normally learn anything without firsthand experience. They don't understand these machines yet."

He snorted. "And you do? You know it all, when it comes to machine aliens you've never even met?"

"Oh, I've met them all right. I've been in their faces and under their belly-turrets more than anyone I know of. Enough, I think, to have a good idea of how they will react."

Robinson started up the Hummer again. He drove on through the jungle. I was glad about that. I needed to keep moving, and I didn't want to kick his butt out onto the asphalt for disobeying orders.

"Okay, fine," he said after another mile of greenery had gone by. "Why can't we just cooperate with the NATO people?"

"We will, but on our terms. The Earth governments will want a strong defense, but they won't be able to fully cooperate. They won't be able to fully bring down all the barriers, to forget about all their old rivalries and politics."

Robinson gave me a longer, strange look. "Why are you telling me all this? And why did you grab my face like, like—"

"Why did I humiliate you? Why did I treat you like a reform-school bully? Because I wanted you to listen—but it's more than that. Do you realize that any marine under your command could have done the same? That you are like a child to your own troops? You have to undergo the nanite-injections. All of my officers have to be shot-up with nanites from now on. I won't have men leading troops who could kick their butts in a second."

Robinson's lips were a thin line. He looked pale. "No one knows the long term effects—"

"No. No we don't. But your men have already done it. They've put their lives on the line. If you want to lead them, you will have to do the same. Crow should never have let you into the Force without the injections."

We drove for a while, quietly. A green Bahaman Parrot with brilliant blue wingtips sailed by in front of us. The bird had time to squawk at us once—irritably—before we were gone, barreling down the forest road.

"Why do you think Crow did that?" asked Robinson thoughtfully. "Why did he let us in without undergoing the injections?"

"I haven't talked to him about it," I said, "but I know Crow fairly well. I'm sure it made it easier to convince officers to join. But I think he also did it because he was scared. Maybe not *scared*, but too paranoid about his own skin to take the injections himself. So, he made it a rule that upper management didn't need to go through it. That way, he didn't have to."

Robinson thought quietly for a few miles, and I let him do it.

"So, what's the deal, then?" he asked me finally.

"The deal?"

"Between us."

I nodded. "You're a Major. You take the injections. You follow my orders. That's the deal."

"And if I refuse?"

"Then you're out."

He threw up his hands. "Where's the giant robot hand? I'm expecting to be ripped out of this Hummer and dumped into the ocean."

I looked at him for a second. Apparently, my handling of General Sokolov had left a lasting impression. *Good,* I thought. "Nope. If you refuse my terms, you just ship out to the mainland with the next load of cargo."

Robinson fell silent again. After another mile or so we reached the secret base. We were challenged at the gates by my marines. They recognized me and waved us in. These were my most loyal men. I'd hand-picked them for the duty. Most were American, but there was a number of Indian *Ghatak* troops mixed in. I'd left Staff

Sergeant Kwon in command. I leaned out the window and waved over the guard. By the look of him, he was a *Ghatak*, a commando.

"Corporal," I said, calling him over, "has there been anything strange going on?"

He stared at me for a second. "The ships all left, sir. They didn't come back. Kwon put the base on high alert."

"Good. The ships won't be back. Let's keep a sharp eye out for aircraft."

"Aircraft?"

"If they are going to hit us right away, they will do it with choppers coming in from ships offshore, I would figure."

"Hit us, sir? Who?"

"Maybe nobody," I said, deciding I'd just started a rumor by talking too much. "Things are little odd right now, Corporal."

"Yes sir."

"Contact me if there are any sightings. I'll be working inside with the—the units."

"Yes sir."

We drove away, and Robinson smirked at me. "Nervous?"

"About what?"

"You didn't want to tell him what might be coming. You don't want him to think about what side he's on too closely, do you?"

We came to a halt in front of a steel building. It splashed silver light into our eyes.

"Just remember, Robinson," I said, "my body can take a bullet much better than yours can. When the fireworks start… I suggest you duck."

I walked into the steel building, leaving Robinson in the Hummer. He could follow me, or not. I was through trying to convince him. It was time he convinced himself—one way or the other.

There was an operator inside the shed, a marine who slouched in his chair and tapped at a tablet computer.

"Those are forbidden now, marine," I barked at him.

"Sir?"

"The tablet. What are you doing with that thing?"

He looked baffled and guilty all at once. "Um, I'm reading a book, sir."

I snatched it away from him. There were cartoon plants on the screen. A little farmer icon plowed a virtual field. I snorted. "I can see you are an avid reader."

He reached for the tablet and I slapped his hand away. I didn't want anyone emailing or phoning the outside world. I needed time.

"This computer is contraband now, until further notice. Now, go report to Sergeant Kwon for patrol duty."

He stared at me, eyeing his tablet in dismay.

"Well?" I roared. "That was an order, marine! Move out! I'll watch the duplication machine. I have work to do."

He exited in a hurry. I turned back to the tablet, rubbing at the screen. These things always needed a cleaning. And it looked like I'd cracked the screen when I snatched it away from him. Too bad.

I looked around the room. There were pallets of supplies. Fortunately, I'd insisted we maintain a stockpile of raw materials to keep the machines busy. Without the Nano ships as transports, I'd have to make do with what I had on hand.

The factory unit was a bit bigger than the ones the Nano ships had aboard for system repairs. There was a central spheroid about twelve feet in diameter that sat in the middle of the shed. To me, it had always resembled an old-fashioned steel kettle, but with humps and curves to it that hinted the machine was full of unimaginable components. The strangely twisting internals made me think of a man's guts pressing out against a thin, metal skin. Tubes ran upward from the top of the spheroid to the roof of the shed where the materials intakes were. An output port was on the side, which could yawn open or squeeze closed like a metal orifice.

Currently, the machine was making more reactor packs for infantry use. We had enough of those, so I stopped the machine. Before I started reprogramming it, I took stock of the supplies. I sighed. Figuring out how to get the most from the materials I had was going to take a while.

The door creaked and slammed behind me. I listened to the tread, and it didn't sound like the marine who I'd chased out. The footsteps weren't heavy enough. Nanotized troops weighed more and carried a very heavy set of gear. You could actually hear the flooring groan beneath their feet.

"Robinson?" I asked without turning around. "What do you want?"

He stopped and stood there for a few seconds. I turned and looked at him. His mouth opened, closed, then opened again. I lost interest and went back to counting titanium ingots. We had less than six hundred of them. I sighed. It would have to do.

"Colonel?" said Robinson, clearly distraught.

I didn't even bother to look at him. His voice changed suddenly. There was new steel in it. Sometimes, getting ignored stiffened a man's spine.

"Sir, please look at me."

"Sir, is it?" I asked, turning to face him.

"Yes. I've thought about what you said. I've been working here for months, and I know you might be right. I—I want to rejoin Star Force, sir. I'll take the nanite injections. I'll sign on as a major."

I smiled. It was a small thing, just a tweak of the lips, but it was there. I walked to him and looked him in the eye. I held out my hand and we shook. I was careful not to crush his hand.

"I knew you would make the right choice, Robinson," I lied. "Now, walk two doors down. They have a chair in there. I'll send a man to help you strap in."

He went pale, but he nodded and left with a confident stride. I hoped he wasn't a screamer, that would be distracting and I needed to think in order to reprogram these machines. I also hoped he wasn't the kind who would dig at his face. That would be worse. I needed him fully functional and every hour counted.

"Robinson?" I called after him.

"Sir?"

"It's like a bad trip to the dentist. Just keep thinking that it will all be over in a few minutes."

"Yes, sir," he said.

As he left I thought he looked a little green. Maybe he didn't like dentists.

I went back to my inventory. I wasn't sure, but I figured I had enough rare metals and trace elements to do what I wanted. The common, easy stuff like nickel, boron, silicon lubricants and the like I wasn't worried about. We had warehouses of that junk. It was the rare earths like strontium, palladium, samarium, and thallium that worried me. Even our plutonium stocks, although adequate, were smaller than I had hoped.

I brought up a spreadsheet on the tablet and did some quick numbers, tapping on the screen. This was going to take some thinking. I needed a new kind of ship, and I had to have it on the cheap. It had to be effective, impressive and easy to build. I rubbed my face and nodded to myself. I thought I had it.

"Duplication unit," I said, addressing the machine that sat silently before me. "Respond."

"Unit Fourteen responding."

I'd taught them to do that. It was too hard to give them all names, so they had numbers. I'd set them up with standing orders to respond to a general name, and their specific number. "Okay Fourteen. Engage group-link."

"Group-link engaged."

"Halt all production and preprocessing steps. If possible, recycle base materials."

"Transmitting. Units responding. Units Six, Seventeen and Thirty-Five are unable to comply with the shutdown order."

"That's okay. Any unit that can't complete the orders I'm giving now should queue them up until such a time as they can be followed."

As I watched, the thrumming stopped on Unit Fourteen. Across the camp, all these little factories were shutting down and switching into idle mode. Those that were in the midst of processing a subcomponent would break it down and eject the raw materials. It was wasteful, but I didn't need any more heavy beamers right now. What I needed were ships, and fast.

"New program workspace," I said, telling it to prepare for a new program. "Initiate."

"Initiated," said Fourteen. "Units responding. Units Six, Thirty-Five—"

"I know, I know, they are unable to comply. Halt report," I said. I rubbed my temples. Dealing with the factories was considerably less fun than dealing with the *Alamo* had been. They had less capacity for cognition, and they didn't know much beyond how to perform innate operations. You couldn't get an answer out of them about the Nanos, or their creators, or anything off-topic like that. I supposed they had fewer nanites chaining-up to form their neural nets. They knew what they knew, and that was it.

"Fourteen, for this group-link session, do not report back to me with processing errors among the units. Only report to me acknowledgements and critical malfunctions. Have the other units queue the processing orders I give. They don't have to perform them until they are able to comply."

"Acknowledged. Relayed."

"Okay, we need to build a large structure. How many units could optimally be applied to creating a single ship's weapon?"

Hesitation. "An infinite number of—"

"No, hold on. If I gave you all the materials and gave one unit the task of building a single ship's weapon, how many hours would it take to complete the construction?"

"Twenty-one point six hours."

I nodded, tapping the result into my tablet. "And if I had two Units share the task?"

"Sixteen point three hours."

I worked on the calculation. There was about a fifty percent reduction in efficiency. In other words, I could use more machines to produce a part faster, but it would be the most effective use of their time to use one machine alone on any one project. The trick was to get the machines to produce a ship as fast as possible, without wasting any unit's time. I proceeded to work with Fourteen, asking it a battery of questions about each major component of a Nano ship. Many of them I didn't need. I decided to forgo the usual medical room, for example. It was nice to have, but if my pilots were nanotized, they could self-repair. I also dropped the biggest time and materials user, the onboard repair unit—essentially another duplication factory. Without this, and with only one engine and one weapon system, the ship could be produced in a drastically reduced timeframe. We had more Nano factories on Earth now, and working together, the output was surprising. As I worked it out, a slower, lightly-armed ship could be produced in about... thirty hours.

I worked to reduce the production time further. The biggest optional equipment item I had left in was the snake-arm component. Without it, many capabilities of the Nano-ship would be lost. Smaller ships without an arm component wouldn't be able to airlift troops, for example. But the arm component would cost me about seven hours per ship. Without it, I could produce a new ship in about twenty-three hours.

Looking at the numbers, hull-size was cheap. I decided to make these new ships deceptively large. Way bigger than they needed to be. In fact, they would be mostly empty—a metallic balloon of nanites. That was the one thing I had plenty of—nanites. They could be produced with common elements and they came out fast. They poured out of the factories like water from a dribbling faucet. We had barrels of them lying around dormant, ready to be chained into a swarm and applied to a task. Thinking about nanites gave me an idea.

"Fourteen, have all non-engaged Units produce raw nanites. I want them without specialization, just common builders."

"Options set. Option settings relayed."

I winced reflexively, but Fourteen didn't tell me about units Six and Thirty-Five. It was a relief. Immediately, the machine began that quiet, almost subliminal hum. About a minute later, a silvery pool of nanites dribbled out of the finishing box. I put a bucket under there to catch them. I called Kwon then, asking him to report to Fourteen's shed.

There was an immediate knock at the door. I smiled, Kwon had been outside, probably hopping from one huge foot to the other.

"Come in!" I shouted.

Kwon swung the door open and stuck in his head. "Sorry sir."

"Don't be. I called you."

"I know. I mean—never mind."

"You mean because you were standing out there waiting for me to come outside? Like this was some kind of gas station bathroom?"

He gave me a tentative smile. "Yes, sir. Are you finished yet? I really have to go."

I raised my eyebrows and smiled back. Had Kwon just told a joke? That wasn't his usual style. I chuckled to reward him. I figured after I let him in on how things were, after he really learned the score, he wasn't going to be telling any new jokes for quite a while.

"First Sergeant Kwon, it's great to see you. Now, we have problems, lots of them."

"May I ask something first, sir?"

"Yes."

"Ah, do you know anything about the guy in the nanite-hut, sir? He's screaming pretty hard. He's locked the door, and the med-tech is considering breaking it down."

"That's Major Robinson," I said. I thought about it. If he'd locked the door, then he didn't want any witnesses to his raving. He probably hadn't even strapped in properly. That was fine with me. If the man wanted to whizz his pants in private, that was his business. "Just leave him alone. He's fine."

"Did you say, *Major* Robinson?"

"He used to be General Robinson."

Kwon blinked at me. Slowly, he nodded. He didn't ask any more questions about the subject. That's what I liked about Kwon. You could throw him a surprise and he would go with it.

"Now listen to me, First Sergeant. First, I want you to send a marine to every shed—"

"Oh yeah, about that, sir. I'm getting reports from all the operators. They say something's wrong with the machines."

"There's nothing wrong with them. I've just changed their orders, that's all."

"You have?"

"Oh," I said, finally getting it. "That's why you came over here, isn't it? You came to figure out what the hell I'm doing in here with the machines."

"Well, we had a strict schedule to meet and—"

"Schedule? Who set it?"

"General Sokolov, sir."

"Sokolov is—not here. I'm in command now. Here are your new orders: send a man out to every shed and have him catch the nanites coming out of the units."

"I'm sure the operators know to do that, sir."

"Not all of them have operators sitting around. In fact, most don't. Put out the order."

Kwon was slow sometimes, but he finally caught the note of urgency in my voice. "Yes, sir," he said, relaying the order over his headset.

I turned back to Fourteen and went over my calculations again. I wanted my first ship done in less than twenty-three hours. I'd forgo the arm unit for the first ship. Maybe, if the Earth governments gave me the time and materials, I could retrofit them with arms.

"Sir?" said Kwon.

I turned around, surprised he was still there. I snapped my fingers at him. "There's something else," I said. "How is the quarantine going? I want this base sealed tight. No one gets in or out for now."

"About that, sir—"

"Kwon, I need a man who can get things done without hand-holding. Why are you still standing in my doorway?"

"Because there's someone here. A chopper just landed at the southern end of the base."

I'd heard a chopper earlier, but since there wasn't anyone shooting at it, I figured it was ours.

"Who?"

"General Kerr, sir."

-6-

I was surprised to see Kerr. Really, the visit itself was a breach of protocol. We'd agreed that Earth government forces weren't to move around our island without advanced notice and permission. They were supposed to land back at the main base, and talk to our staffers there if they wanted to go anywhere else. Hell, they weren't even supposed to know that this 'secret' base existed.

But that had been before all my ships had flown off to some other godforsaken rock in the sky with every last one of my Star Force pilots inside their dark, heartless bellies. Now, apparently, the earthers had no respect for our arrangements and deals.

"Riggs?" asked Kerr, spotting me and heading in my direction. He lifted a hand to me in greeting. He was a rare man in many ways. The fact that everyone around him could kill him in an instant—and might even want to—did not seem to bother him in the slightest.

"General Kerr," I said, shaking his hand gently. I had to remember every time I touched a normal man to be careful.

Kerr smiled, but the smile was tight and official-looking. "Good to see you made it back, Riggs. I knew you would."

"I was just following your suggestion, sir."

Kerr snorted and nodded. He looked around the camp while we talked. He noted the two guard towers and the six or seven armed men in sight. He didn't look overly impressed.

"Can you tell me why you are visiting Star Force, sir?" I asked.

His eyes drifted back to mine. "What the hell happened up there?"

I told him, briefly, of the face-off I'd had with the Macros. I finished with specifics of the deal I'd made with them. He looked impressed.

"Let me get this straight: you promised a race of giant robots that we'd give them sixty-odd tons of our best soldiers? To fight *with* them?"

"Yes, sir. We've got one year to produce the troops, or the war will be on again."

"Who came up with that crazy idea? Crow?"

I thought about telling him the truth, that it had happened accidentally and had been more than half luck. But that didn't sound cool enough, so I took a few liberties with the story.

"I did the negotiations solo, sir. But let me assure you, if we had engaged the Macro battle fleet we would have lost. Earth would have had no chance."

Kerr licked his lips. "I believe you."

I could tell that he did, so I didn't belabor the point. "Where does that leave us, General?"

"Before I get into that, I want to talk about the Blues."

"What about them?" I asked.

"How sure are you of your information on them? Do you think they created both the Macros and the Nanos? Do you still think they are stuck on their own planet?"

I shrugged. "To the best of my knowledge, sir."

He shook his head. "You're wrong. At least partly."

"How so?"

Kerr pointed out in the direction of the sea with his chin. "You know we've got subs out there, don't you, Riggs?"

"I suppose."

"Well, our subs can go down, all the way down to the bottom of the sea. If we build a sub with strong enough walls, we can still breathe and function."

I frowned. I was beginning to see where he was going with this. "So, you don't buy that the Blues are stuck on their gas giant world due to the high gravity?"

Kerr shook his head. "No, I don't. You're a scientist, but not a physicist. I don't blame you, I didn't understand it all right away either. But it's all about the *pressure*, not the gravity. If they built a ship with a dense, high-pressure atmosphere inside, they should be able to get off their world. That's what my nerds tell me back home, anyway."

"Huh," I said, frowning. Thinking about it, his points made sense. I could see that I'd jumped to unsupported conclusions based upon my conversations with the *Alamo*. "Well, maybe they had organs that need the gravity, not just the pressure. I wasn't just thinking of a fish gas-bladder."

"Admittedly unknown."

"What about escape velocity?" I asked. "They would have to go through a lot of acceleration and build up a tremendous amount of speed to break free of a big planet's gravity-well."

General Kerr shrugged. "We are working on blind conjecture here, but my nerds tell me that doesn't really matter. They could withstand a lot of acceleration. It would just feel like gravity to them, which they are used to."

"They aren't even blue, you know that too, right?"

He laughed. "Yeah. We got that part. Any other speculation as to why the Blues aren't a space-faring race?"

"I suppose there is no way we can know that without asking them. Maybe they have some kind of religious problem with it. Maybe someone else has promised them death if they leave their world. Who knows?"

"As good a guess as any," he said.

I looked at him. "Sir, that's not the only reason you came all this way, is it? To ask me about the Blues?"

Kerr waved my words away. "Of course not. But it gave me the excuse I needed to come down personally."

"What else did you want to tell me?"

"I think you know that, Riggs."

I nodded. "Your people want to change our deal, is that it? Sir, I need you to convince the administration that you still need Star Force. I need you to tell them to respect our sovereignty. You realize that just landing here breaks our treaty."

Kerr met my eyes. "That sort of decision is political. It's beyond my pay-grade. But I think you're right, if that's any consolation."

I didn't like the way he sounded. His tone indicated he'd already had this argument on my behalf and lost. There was an uncharacteristic tone of defeat in his voice. I realized suddenly why he was here: he was trying to warn me or discover some fresh reason why the government shouldn't move in on our little operation.

"General," I said, "I need time. I need a week. Give me that long to get my fleet back together."

He frowned. "You think they might come back that fast? We have our new interferometers scopes following them. They are half-way to Jupiter's orbit now, and still accelerating."

"Where are they headed?"

"Classified," he said, then he tilted his head to one side, "but—what the hell. We think they are going to Neptune, or maybe beyond that into the Oort Cloud."

"The Oort Cloud..." I said, trying to recall my single college course in astronomy.

"A fancy name for a bunch of comets and chunks of crap that fly around out past Pluto. Anyway, there might be another ah—another *spot* out there. Another connection point."

"Ah," I said, understanding. "Like the Macro gathering spot near Venus."

"Yeah, maybe."

"I figured they couldn't be heading directly to another star," I said. "Even at the speed of light, they wouldn't make it there for years. Everyone aboard would be dead by then. That would leave the Nanos with no practice dummies for the next world."

"Keep in mind that we're just guessing," Kerr cautioned me.

I nodded. "Thanks for the information in any case. Still, it doesn't matter. My request stands. I need you to respect our sovereignty. I know that certain people stateside might have ideas, but you have to put them off. I only need a few days, sir."

Kerr eyed me strangely. His eyes slid to the corrugated steel buildings that surrounded us. He knew what was inside, I was sure of that. Slowly, he nodded. I could tell he'd figured it out. I could tell he understood I was working to rebuild my fleet as fast as possible.

"A week? That fast, eh? I wish I could give you the time, Riggs, but I'm not in charge of this situation. I'm absolutely convinced that you are the best man for the job, that you can pull together a new fleet faster than anyone can—if anyone else even could. But this isn't about time anymore, it's about position. It's all a matter of relative strengths. You understand what I'm saying, son?"

I stared back at him. I understood all right. The decision had already been made. The administration had gotten greedy. They wanted my machines for their own use.

Suddenly, seeing the General's dark, troubled eyes, I knew the truth. Washington wanted the factories secured *now*. They wanted them *all*. They were going to move even faster than I had anticipated. They were going to move preemptively, before any other power on Earth got smart and had time to think about it and make their own move. Probably, there were assets out there in the ocean around my island paradise, sliding quietly into position. Hadn't the General just said something about subs? Had that been a hint I'd been too dumb to pick up on? Maybe they'd been out there for months, waiting patiently for the right moment to move in.

I thought of the assassin, Esmeralda. I no longer believed she'd been a rogue, or a mistake. She'd been a probe, a feint. She had managed to maintain—what did the politicians call it? *Plausible deniability...* but now I knew the truth.

I nodded to Kerr. "I understand fully, General. Well, do what you can to help me out, if you think that's in the world's best interest."

Kerr took another deep breath and let it out slowly. When he spoke again, it was in a lower tone of voice. "Why don't you come in with me, Kyle?" he asked.

"Sir?"

"There's no need for you to get caught up in all this. You are a hero back home, you know. Come on home with me. No one here will think less of you. Let me take you back to Washington to plead your case. Let me work you back into the program, in a new, official capacity. The entire planet owes you that much. More importantly, we could really use your help."

"But not independently. Not on my terms," I said.

He shook his head slowly.

"Thanks for the offer—and I mean that. I'll think about it, sir. I'll be in touch."

The General took a few steps toward the west, where the sun was beginning to set out over the sea. "Okay. I'm not going to argue with you. But don't think too long, Kyle."

I followed his eyes toward the orange ball of the sun. *Tonight then,* I thought suddenly. *They'll come tonight.*

My heart accelerated in my chest. I had no time to lose. I had no time at all.

"I've got to get back to work, General. Thanks for the visit," I said, and I walked back toward Shed Fourteen. It was time for a change of orders.

I could feel Kerr's eyes on my back as I left him there on the sand. "Don't do anything stupid, Riggs!" he shouted after me. "Don't get yourself killed for nothing!"

"I don't die easily, sir!" I shouted back over my shoulder.

I slammed the shed door and leaned back against it. In front of me was Unit Fourteen and the marine I'd chewed out earlier. He was working his tablet again, flicking at it. He startled as I came in and he put it down. I wondered briefly what game he'd been playing this time.

"Out," I said.

"Sir?"

"Hit the lines. Full gear. Get the entire platoon buttoned up and on alert. I want half the garrison patrolling the forest a hundred yards out. Have Kwon contact me for details."

He stood up, looking stunned. "Um, what's going on, sir?"

"We're about to be attacked, soldier. Do you want a memo, or are you going to get your butt into your hazard suit and charge your beamer?"

"Yes sir!" he shouted, and rushed out. He straight-armed the door on the way. It popped open so hard it wouldn't quite close right after that. I ignored him and the rest of the camp, which quickly became noisy as my orders were relayed.

"Unit Fourteen, activate group-link."

"Group-link active," Fourteen responded.

I stood there for a few seconds, thinking hard. I had to assume I had only a few hours left. They wouldn't nuke us. They wouldn't even dare use conventional bombs. The whole point was to steal the factories intact, not to blow them up. How would they do it? Commandos, most likely. Perhaps the subs were surfacing and they were unloading into the jungle right now. Maybe choppers were carrying them in from the sea. Maybe they were already out there in the trees, forming up at prearranged gathering points.

Snipers, I thought suddenly. High-velocity rounds. A few dozen of them could do it. I wasn't sure if a sniper round would go through a nanite-coated skull, but nanites or not, my men couldn't fight with their brains dented in.

I stared at Fourteen and licked my lips. What the hell could I build in a few hours that would stop them?

Problem-solving. Mini-maxing. I put my fists to my temples and pressed there, and it felt good. I had been trained for this sort of thing—programming under pressure. I had to do the most with what I had.

I thought about it. I couldn't produce a full ship, but maybe I could produce something that would do the job. Ideas began populating my mind.

I had a wide open slate. With Nanites building the 'hull' of any structure in any shape I wanted, I could use them like clay to construct anything, up to at least the size of the shed I was standing in. Probably, I could make something a lot bigger than that. I had plenty of nanites, after all. For nearly half an hour, the factories had been churning out bucket-loads of them. We also kept a reservoir of them in drums in the injection-room next door. That set me to wondering how Major Robinson was doing. I shrugged, not having time to coddle him right now. Hopefully, even if he was a bleeder, he'd passed out by now and the nanites were busily doing the repair work. If so, the worst was over for him. Tonight, he would learn about his new capabilities in action.

I decided to eliminate all non-essential systems first. The engines, scratch them. The arm? Forget it. No extra factories, either. I paused at that thought, however. Why not just make Fourteen here part of the system? Having a factory aboard the Nano ships had always been useful.

Next question, mobility. Did I need it? Was I building a tank, or a gun turret? There wasn't enough time, I figured. Mobility was fantastic, making any force vastly more useful, but this was an emergency. If I produced a really cool tank one hour after they hit us, I had completely wasted the effort.

"A gun turret, then," I said aloud. Fourteen didn't respond.

"Fourteen, is the group-link still up?"

"Yes."

"How many factory units will it take to build a single ship's laser in one hour."

"Insufficient data provided for estimate."

I took a deep breath, trying to remain calm. I reminded myself that the freaking machines were all churning out more nanites as I tried to rewrite the script, so they weren't completely wasting their time. "Fourteen, assume when I ask for timing estimates, that precision does not need to be closer than one tenth of an hour. Also assume that all components will be supplied."

"Parameters assigned," said Fourteen. Its voice was different than the *Alamo's* had been. The ship had had a voice I thought of as feminine, but this machine spoke with a high-pitched male voice. As if I was talking to a jockey.

"Now, how many factory units will it take to complete a single ship's laser in one hour."

"Insufficient data provided for estimate."

"Okay, you mental giant. What data are you missing?"

"Assembly time of individual components incalculable."

I thought about that. There were three pieces to each hand-held beamer: the reactor unit, the cable and the projector itself. If a thousand machines made a thousand pieces, they could probably do it in minutes, but we couldn't assemble them all and the effort would be wasted. It was best to use the three component system, and not try to break that down further. I'd built so many backpack beam units, I had been planning purely in those terms. My question had been unfair. These machines didn't deal well with open-ended hypotheticals.

"Okay, I understand the problem," I said aloud. "Fourteen, I want one idle unit to construct a reactor of suffienct capacity to power a ship's laser. Start that process now."

"Command failed."

I felt the flash of rage so many humans before me had experienced when the computer refused to operate. I blinked, and thought about hammering my fist upon the intake nozzles. I controlled myself with difficulty. I considered my self-restraint to be a personal achievement.

"What is the error?" I asked, when I could speak again.

"Unit not specified."

"Okay, assign unit Twelve to that task. Execute immediately."

Hesitation. "Command accepted. Twelve is processing."

"How long until it's finished?"

"Two point seven hours."

I felt a tickle of sweat under my armpits. I had to figure it would add up to three hours with the assembly process minimum, and that was assuming all the other components were done first. I knew from experience that the reactors took the longest of the basic three components to construct. I didn't think I could break construction of the reactors down between multiple units, either. I just didn't have time to work out the logistics, even if it was possible.

The big question was: *Did I have three hours?* It would be dark in one, pitch-black in two. Commandos liked the dark.

I ordered two more units to build the cable and the projector. We could probably do better, but there wasn't much time. Thinking hard, I instructed two more groups of three machines to make the same things. With luck, I would have three automated laser turrets operating in three hours.

Then I realized I needed something else.

"Fourteen, I need an estimate on production of a motor-driven, rotating ball-joint, the same type used to form the core of a ship's gun emplacement."

Silence.

I sighed. I hadn't actually told it to do anything. I'd only described a need. What did Fourteen care about what I needed? There was nothing for it to do, so it ignored me. "Fourteen, how long will it take to build the unit I just described?"

"One point four hours, given previously stated parameters."

I set three more machines to working on mounts for these new guns. Next came the easy parts. I needed a somewhat-intelligent control system to operate the guns when they were assembled. This was easy because the nanites were flexible in this regard, all they needed to do was configure themselves into a cognitive swarm. You put them in a box, and you had a cpu. Given enough time and

41

sensory input, they would learn their tasks and become reasonably intelligent. I ordered three brain-boxes built immediately. I didn't want freshly-hatched systems doing the targeting. If we put them together now, they would have a couple of hours to chain-up and form their own clusters. It would also give us the time to expose them to other, more experienced brainboxes, allowing them to copy some useful software before they were installed in a turret.

I snapped my fingers then. I'd forgotten something. "Sensors—damn! Fourteen, I need three more units to build targeting sensor arrays."

We had thirty-six factories. Soon, I had them all churning. Nanites dribbled out of half the machines, while the other half built components for me. The raw nanites would form themselves into shells to make the housing for the guns.

I decided not to get fancy with the placement of the new weapons. The reactors took the longest to build, so we would construct the towers right on top of the sheds that were responsible for making the reactors. That way, when the reactor pieces were finished, my men could just plug them into the rest of the structure, and the systems should be assembled and ready to operate.

I was putting the finishing touches on my construction scripts when the door shook with repeated, hammering blows. I raised my eyebrows toward it. Who could that be? Had Kerr come back demanding I surrender? Had Kwon's men spotted invaders?

I threw open the door, frowning. My frown melted in surprise. It was Sandra, and Kwon stood right behind her, looking confused.

"I couldn't stop her, sir. She said she had the right."

"Hi Sandra," I said.

She stalked in and slammed the door behind her, right in Kwon's face.

I shouted to Kwon through the door. "Keep the men on high alert. Keep them patrolling."

"Sir?" he roared through the door with unnecessary volume. "Who are we looking out for? Are the Macros landing here?"

"No, First Sergeant," I said, "unfortunately, the invaders will be quite human."

"Who will that be, sir?"

"Just shoot anyone who behaves like a hostile. I doubt they are going to serve us search warrants."

I turned and faced Sandra. For about three seconds, she glared at me. Then she jumped on me and kissed me. I liked that part better.

She had her nice, long, tanned legs wrapped around the top of my hips. She was wearing a halter top and her boobs were almost in my face. We kissed for a full minute. She paused for a few seconds, glaring at me. I had a hard time keeping my eyes on her face. Then she started round two, and that second, minute-long kiss was even sweeter than the first.

I was in no hurry to stop, but she jumped down at the two minute mark and kicked me. She performed an impressive roundhouse that slipped her foot behind me and caught my left butt-cheek.

"You could have called!" she snarled.

I smiled back. If the next aliens that invaded Earth had the power to mimic humans, I was safe. No one could imitate my girl. "Honey, I was up saving the world."

"I don't care about that. You took off, right out of our window. You took off in the *Alamo*, and did it without me. Then you sat up there for hours letting me think you were dead. I know you could have called, because you called Kerr."

"How'd you know about that?" I asked, trying not to look guilty.

"He called to pump me for information. I didn't have any to give. It was humiliating."

I snorted and reached for her again. She danced away, throwing up her arms. I had to stop myself from moving in a blur and grabbing her anyway. It was moments like this where self-control was the most difficult.

"No, I don't think so," she said.

"What? Do you want an apology?" I asked, bemused. It was hard to get too upset. I'd already gotten my kiss.

"That might help," she said, crossing her arms.

"Okay then, you've got it."

She blinked at me. "That's it? You've got to be kidding me."

"Love, let's do this later, okay? I've got to get this base ready for a firefight."

"What about me?"

"I'm shipping you out of here. I'm not even sure how you got in."

She shrugged. "The chopper pilots—like me."

It was my turn to be annoyed. But I really didn't have time.

Behind me, the shed door creaked open. No one had knocked, and the sound of the intruder made me wheel around. I didn't like the way he moved.

Robinson sagged in, holding onto the doorjamb with curled fingers. His shirt had been mostly torn away. Red lines mixed with gleaming silver shone through long lines in his skin. He'd clawed at his own chest. I'd seen it before. One of his cheeks was split open too, right from the corner of his mouth back to his molars. I could see his bloody, glistening teeth in there as he began to speak.

"Major Robinson," he gasped, "reporting for duty, sir."

"At ease, Robinson," I said.

He sagged down in the doorway. Sandra came forward and checked his wounds, wincing. She'd seen some bad things in our time together, so she didn't scream or freak out.

"Has he been hit?" she asked me. "Is this part of the invasion you were talking about?"

"Looks self-inflicted. He's just taken the nanite injections."

"They are that bad?"

"Sometimes."

"Permission to be…" Robinson said from the floor. He took a break in mid-sentence to suck in a full breath, "permission to be pissed at you, sir. That was no trip to the dentist."

I chuckled. "You don't know my dentist."

We helped him into a folding chair. I thought about offering him a drink, but figured it might not work out. The liquid would just run right out of that open cheek and down his neck.

"Relax, Robinson. You'll live, even if you don't want to. The nanites are knitting up your face as we speak. They tend to reconnect the nerves in damaged tissue last, I'm sure it's only by lucky chance, but it helps control the pain."

"Very encouraging, sir," he gurgled.

-8-

They came just after midnight.

I'd long ago called for backup from the main camp, but they had never shown up. Barrera had promised me two companies of troops, most of his standing garrison. To replace them, he'd called in help from all over the islands, ordering units he considered to be our most loyal to return to the main camp.

Normally, we didn't house the men in barracks. We'd become soft, in hindsight. Having a big tropical island and an unlimited budget, we'd set them up in communities here and there. I'd been thinking that news of the life-style would get us more recruits. But for direct, immediate defense, it was a losing strategy. I vowed to become more paranoid in the future. If I had a future.

Now, in the middle of the night, I had no idea if Barrera had been lying or he had already been taken out. All I knew was his two companies didn't show and all communications with the main base were out. First, the satellite feed had cut off, and then the landline that ran along the jungle road went dead. I tried direct radio, but that was being jammed. Nothing but static. This did not surprise me, as the communications equipment had all been provided by the very people who now planned to take us down. I would have sent out some Hummers to the main base to scout and report, but I couldn't afford anyone. I planned to sit on the factories and hold them at all costs.

The effort to build new, defensive beam towers was hours behind schedule. Several problems had arisen, engineering details I should have foreseen. For one thing, we didn't have any Nano ships with

45

hands to lift the weapon systems into place. We'd managed to get the motorized mount for one turret into place, but we hadn't gotten the projector fastened onto it yet. I had about twenty nanotized marines, and that represented a lot of arm-strength, but lifting several tons onto the roof of a shed still wasn't easy. We could have used a crane, but we'd depended on the Nano ships to do all that kind of work for us.

The first turret structure loomed up like a hump on the roof of good-old Unit Fourteen's shed. Fourteen had managed to finish the first reactor, so I'd concentrated our construction efforts there first. Buried underneath a shimmering mass of nanites, the shed was unrecognizable. It looked more like a shiny, tin anthill than anything else.

"Sir, still nothing to report from my squad of scouts," Kwon told me in a harsh whisper.

I swung my head around to see him. He was just a dim, hulking outline in the starlight. We had our lights off and our full suits on. I looked at him through two dark portholes. "No news is good news," I said, "keep the scouts out there, keep them moving. They should expect contact at any moment."

"Yes sir," Kwon said, then he moved away. Soon, the night swallowed him up. For a big guy, he could move quietly when he needed to.

Everyone had left their heavy beam rifles and reactor-packs on the ground while we climbed over the shed roof. I'd given them orders to jump down and grab up their equipment the minute anything happened. For a few quiet minutes, we worked on setting up a chain-fall hoist to get the projector up into place. There was a lot of swearing and fingers bleeding inside our gloves.

Sweating in the humid night air, I heard a distant sound. I knew that sound all too well. It was the chatter of automatic weapons fire. They were out there, and getting closer. The men around me paused in their efforts. Most leapt down to the sandy ground and struggled with the straps of their reactor units. I stayed on the roof, trying to steady the vast weight of the projector unit. It swayed on the chains.

Everyone was quiet. We all hunkered down, listening. Straining my ears, I wondered if the next sound would be the crack of a sniper round or the thump of a mortar. I figured, at this point, I'd royally screwed up. I'd wasted our time. This turret was never going to work, even if we managed to put it together. It was untested. It might shoot my own men in the ass or light the place on fire—or, most likely, not function at all.

"Take cover everyone," I said, pointlessly. My men had melted into the landscape.

We had less than a minute to wait. The night sky lit up with green flashes. My auto-shades flickered a notch or two darker instantly. I knew that quiet, blooming light. My men were returning fire. I could now tell where the fighting was. The air filled with green laser light, burning the atmosphere along the jungle road heading east. The silent flashes came from that direction. But who were they shooting at?

I move around the base of the turret in a crouch, scanning the trees nearest the compound. We had a wall of logs surrounding the place, which we'd lazily topped with barbed wire months ago. I regretted our lack of foresight. In everyone's mind, we'd been fighting the Macros. What good were normal anti-personnel defenses against hundred-foot robots? The answer was: no good at all. So, we hadn't bothered to build any.

I almost keyed my com-link, but urged myself to patience. The squad out there didn't need me to demand answers in the middle of a firefight.

Then I thought of Kwon. Maybe he knew something, and he wasn't out in the thick of it. I keyed his direct link.

"Kwon here," he said.

"Hear anything from your patrol?" I asked.

"Enemy contacted, no casualties. That's it. I think both sides are firing at shadows. They don't want to talk right now."

"I don't blame them. Any reason not to keep working on my contraption?"

"Not that I know of, sir."

"Let me know the second your scouts report in again," I said. I stayed down, thinking for a few minutes. The forest around us was quiet. Not even the insects were buzzing much. I didn't like it.

"Are we clear, sir?" whispered a corporal who sidled up to the shed.

"I don't know," I said. I looked down at my men. They were eyeing everything. I scanned the skies. No sign of choppers or

47

parachutes. Not even a drunk, night-flying seagull. I really didn't like it.

I crouched and cruised around the building, moving quickly and quietly between them. I didn't see anything or anyone. I contacted Kwon.

"These guys are ghosts. They are either not here, or they are very good."

"I think they are good, sir," Kwon answered. "I just found something. Come to me."

I trotted across and open area and thought I heard a clicking sound. Or had I imagined it? When I reached Kwon, he pointed back to where I'd been.

"They just took a shot at you. I saw the spark behind you."

I looked back, and hugged the building more closely. "What did you want to show me?"

I pulled the nearest marine closer. The man was limp in his suit. I looked and saw most of his head was missing.

"Sniper," said Kwon unnecessarily.

I made a low, grunting sound. I was angry, and I had an idea. I keyed my com-link. "Garrison troops, everyone who's in my base, I'm disconnecting and using voice alone. Listen up."

I turned off the transmitter on my com-link. I lifted the bottom of my suit's hood to reveal my mouth. "I want everyone to aim at the tree line. Pick out a nice tall tree. When you see my beamer light up, open fire. Take out a tree or two each. Fire in every direction."

No one asked any questions, but I could feel their eyes on me. *Had the Colonel gone nuts again? What does he have against trees?* I didn't feel like explaining. If I was right, things would be clear enough.

I took aim and burned the top off a Caribbean pine. My auto-shades darkened in response, then darkened further as a dozen more beams leapt out into the quiet night with fantastic brilliance. There was a brief explosion of awakened birds, squawking and flapping. Flames loomed up from several of the trees, and burning debris dropped down to the forest floor.

After a few seconds, we stopped firing and everyone watched the fires and listened. Someone, out to the north, began wailing. The sound stopped quickly, but I was sure I'd heard it. I nodded my head.

"What the hell was that about, sir?" whispered Kwon in my headset.

"Come over here," I ordered.

Kwon came at a run and crouched against the wall of Shed Fourteen. I talked to him in the dark, while we both watched the burning trees gutter and go out.

"I think they can hear us," I told him. "We're using their communications equipment. They aren't jamming our suit radios, so they must be listening in."

"Okay, we go voice from now on?"

"Except for brief messages to another team, like your squad out there."

"Why the firing, sir?"

I tapped the portholes that covered my eyes. "I was hoping they didn't have these. I figured they might be using night vision gear, and our beams hitting them without warning would blind them."

"Ah…. Who, sir?"

I glanced down at Kwon. He wasn't winning any mensa contests tonight. "Night snipers, Sergeant."

"Oh, you mean that guy who screamed?"

"Exactly."

"What do we do now, sir?"

I thought about it. I looked at the turret behind me. It had to work. It was our only chance, really. If we couldn't get some superior tech on our side, we were outnumbered a million to one by the armies of Earth, nanites or no.

"This gun isn't going to build itself. Get up here, Sergeant. I need your strong back again. The rest of you, I want one fireteam intermittently firing into the forest to keep them honest. The rest of you climb up here. We're going to put this thing on its mount while we still have time."

While we worked to mount the projector onto the turret and connect the cable, I felt needles all over my back. This time, it wasn't the nanites, nor even my sweat. Both those things were at work, but what bugged me was the unknown. Was a sniper sighting on me right this moment? I had to be a big prize, the renegade Riggs himself. Splatting me might be worth a medal.

We hadn't heard anything else over our radios from the scouts. I hoped that was good news. Maybe we'd rocked them back with our defensive fire. Or maybe they'd slaughtered my men and were forming up a few hundred yards away, gathering enough firepower to overwhelm us. I had no idea which it was.

When the projector was up and connected, I jumped down and Kwon followed me. His boots sank into the sandy soil until the tops of his feet vanished. I wondered how much he weighed. Full of nanites, I had to figure it was around four hundred pounds.

"Time to test this contraption," I told him. I headed to the sleek wall of metal that flowed down like a mound over what had been Shed Fourteen. I put my knuckles up to the metal and knocked sharply. I rapped a sequence of four fast raps, followed by two more. I'd already programmed the thing to open to the series known as: *shave-and-a-haircut, two-bits*. I'm a sucker for the classics.

The wall turned to silver liquid and dissolved open. I stepped inside. Sandra looked at me and smiled.

"It's hot and stuffy in here," she complained.

"We're about to be shanked by commandos," I told her, "there may be some rough moments ahead."

She shrugged and went back to whatever she was doing. I looked over her shoulder. She was tapping at a small computer of her own, but she wasn't playing a game. Instead, it was a sequence of written steps.

"What's up?" I said, eyeing her work.

"I'm trying my hand at programming this thing."

My eyebrows shot up. "Really?"

"Don't act so surprised. I'm not an idiot, you know. I took some programming in high school and I had a semester of calculus. I was going to take your programming class."

"Calculus, huh? Did you pass?"

She kicked at me, but she was sitting down and I sidestepped.

"Let me see what you've got," I said.

I studied her code. That's what it was, really, a form of source code. The whole programming experience was very free-form when you programmed these nanite-boxes. They didn't have a specific, limited language they understood, they could understand English. The code looked like what was known as *pseudocode*. A series of instructions that were almost English, but more structured than English. Controlling these boxes wasn't easy. They had the ability to talk, but that didn't mean they were easy to talk to. They weren't human. There were many misunderstandings. It was sort of like giving perfect instructions to a genie—one that didn't care if it accidently killed its master.

I made a few edits. "Can I use this?"

Sandra beamed at me, and I knew I was back in.

"Of course," she said.

I read out her instructions to the newly-hatched nanite control box for the turret. First, I named the box 'Turret One'. Why get fancy? The tricky part came next, telling the control system what to shoot at. I had to make sure it didn't shoot friendlies, only hostiles. The definition could easily blur when you were talking to a nanite-mind. They had sensory input, a set of inputs mounted on the projector that looked like a small nubs aimed in multiple directions.

The Nano sensors didn't *see* with a vision system like our eyes for their primary sensory input, but they understood vision and colors. That sense simply wasn't their primary one. I supposed if dogs had built the world, everything would be about scents. Humans have a sense of smell, but it is of secondary importance to them. If dogs were capable of sarcasm, I'm sure they would roll their eyes at what passed for our grasp of odors. We'd learned over time the Nano sensors had the ability to sense things in three dimensions, which was how it was able to draw maps for us. They used a form of passive radar and sonar, detecting objects and movement in relative space using multiple inputs such as vibration and radiation.

"Add to target list: Hostiles firing weaponry at this turret," I said. That one seemed pretty safe.

"List node added successfully," said Turret One.

"Its voice sounds weird," commented Sandra.

"Yeah, all the boxes seem to have voices like jockeys, or adolescents. I liked the ship voices better, too."

I figured I would start with a list of things it was allowed to shoot at. Everything else was *not* to be targeted. That was the easiest way to filter through a large, unknown dataset. Listing everything not to be attacked was too complex. Instead, I would try to identify the items in the smaller set, in this case legitimate targets. By definition, anything not on that short kill-list was not to be burned.

I had to be very careful, of course. If I screwed up, my little monster would burn down my own people, and it truly *would* be my fault. I'd felt that sort of guilt before, and I didn't want to feel it again. I took a deep breath. Sweat tickled my face. Sandra was right, it was stuffy in here.

"Add to target list: Hostiles firing on me, Kyle Riggs."

Sandra watched me with her eyes wide. She knew the stakes. She'd seen the *Alamo* get excited and kill a crowd of innocents before. "Why don't you just tell it to shoot at any soldier without nanites?" she asked.

"What if Kerr comes back asking to call it off? Do we just automatically blast him?" I asked, then I waved for her to be quiet. She looked annoyed. I decided to worry about that later. If the enemy hit us now and this thing didn't fire at them, it was worthless. But if it killed my own men, it was worse than worthless.

"Add to target list: Hostiles firing on Sandra, or Sergeant Kwon."

"Biotic identities of defensive contacts imprinted," said the box.

That's as far as I got before we heard the thump and scream of a mortar. I hunkered over Sandra, shielding her with my body.

"Shrapnel won't penetrate this place, will it?" she asked.

"Turret One, activate!" I shouted. "Target the source of incoming artillery and return fire!"

The big servos whirred and clicked. We'd already set up a viewing system on one of the walls. A relief-image of the camp stood out in raised, metal lines. With liquid smoothness, the projector swung around to aim east. A thrumming sound built up, the thing was preparing to fire.

I ripped off my hood and shoved it at Sandra. She got the idea and we scrambled to pull it over her head. I didn't know if there would be any light-leakage inside the turret, but this wasn't the time to be surprised. I closed my eyes tightly and jammed my fist into my sockets. I told myself that even if I was blinded, the nanites would rebuild my eyes. Sandra didn't have any such comforting thoughts, however. I could hear her breathing hard inside the hood.

As it turned out, there wasn't any leakage. A singing sound rang out, and the turret shuddered a fraction. But with the metal hull of the turret sealed around us, none of the brilliance of it got through to us.

"I can hear your men talking in the hood, Kyle," Sandra said, her voice muffled.

I removed the hood as quickly and softly as I could, but she still complained I was ripping hairs from her head. I pulled the hood on. She wouldn't need it if she stayed in here.

"Riggs?" said a voice. I realized after a second it was Kwon.

"Riggs here, go ahead."

"That thing works? What did it shoot at?"

"Whoever fired that mortar at us."

"Did it hit them?"

"If they stop firing," I said, "then yes, it did."

Sandra watched me as I lifted my hood and kissed her. Outside, everything was quiet for now.

"Did we hit them?" she asked.

"Either that, or we scared the crap out of them. You stay in here. Don't leave, it's not safe."

"Duh."

"Look, I need you in this fight. I need you to call targets. Not everyone will shoot at this turret when they come in. In fact, they are liable to learn pretty fast not to aim at it. Watch the walls, and kill enemy contacts that come in firing."

Sandra eyed the wall depicting the camp in metal lines. She licked her lips. "Why can't you put one of your men on this?" she asked.

"There aren't too many people I trust with my sole laser cannon. You are one of them. Besides, you said you wanted to fight. Here's your big chance."

"Yeah, but I'll be killing people."

"What the hell do you think fighting is all about?"

She rubbed at her jeans and avoided my eyes. "I don't want to screw up and burn down one of the good guys."

Sandra was still sitting, so I squatted down in front of her. I lifted my hood and caught her eyes with mine and made her look at me. I felt a momentary pang of guilt. She looked worried. Sandra always talked so tough, sometimes I forgot how young she really was. Had I helped end her youth and innocence? She had been a carefree coed less than a year ago. Now, she was manning a killer piece of alien technology against the forces of her own government. I steeled myself, telling myself all this wasn't my idea. The alien ships had ended everyone's innocence. Now, the Pentagon was getting greedy.

"You're going to do fine. I need every marine out there with a rifle to protect all the sheds, not just this one. If the enemy gets in close, I can't have this machine blowing holes in the other factories. We'll have to use infantry to push them back. You will have to call targets."

She nodded slowly. "Okay. But can't I just tell it to burn down everyone who isn't full of nanites?"

"No. First of all, you aren't full of nanites. Secondly, I'm not sure the men coming after us won't have nanites."

She looked at me sharply. "You mean your own marines...."

I nodded. "Yeah. Why not? Do you really think every last man who joined Star Force was legit?"

-10-

They didn't bother shelling the camp with mortars after two more tries. Sandra quickly and effectively returned fire. Each time the big green beam lit up the night, it burned its way through a few dozen trees, stabbing out into the darkness. Trunks of pines exploded. Wispy palm fronds ignited with the passing heat. The beams stayed on for several long seconds, burning their way through intervening vegetation. The results were always the same. The mortars were silenced. After a few seconds, the beam stopped firing and the only sounds were the shouts of my men and the crackle of burning forest.

What really screwed them was the geography of Andros Island. The highest elevation on the entire island was only about a hundred feet above sea level. The island had no hills, no gullies. In the area of my camp, it was particularly flat. There wasn't anywhere for the enemy to hide, really. They had to come in under fire.

They could have used something bigger than a mortar, of course. Something with longer range, even a Tomahawk missile. But anything that big might destroy the precious factories, and no one wanted that.

At about one a. m., our fireteam returned to camp. I saw the big turret uncoil, tracking them as they approached. I winced, hoping Sandra hadn't screwed up and ordered them burned down in a panic. But the big laser didn't fire. I gulped air in relief. I walked out to greet them, recognizing the shape of their suits and their number. I hoped it wasn't some kind of trap.

The marines halted, facing me. I halted too. I felt a presence at my side. It was Kwon, I could tell without looking. He was the kind of man who you could sense when he came near. He moved the air around him, or shook the ground, I wasn't sure which.

"Scout squadron, report," I said.

The men glanced back and forth amongst themselves. They were fully buttoned up in their suits, and I couldn't blame them for that. The Corporal leading the team stepped forward two halting steps. I recognized him, he was the Indian Ghopak that I'd met at the gate hours before. Seven men stood behind him uncertainly.

"Colonel Riggs?" he asked.

"That's me. Report."

"Sir, we made contact with the enemy. Do you know who they are, sir?"

"I have an idea. Fill me in on the details."

"They were human, sir. Army Rangers. We killed about twenty of them. Once we realized who they were, we broke off and retreated back to base. What the hell is going on, sir?"

I eyed them for a few seconds before speaking. "Okay. I'm going to level with you guys. And I'm not going to try to stop you if you decide to pull out of here. We are under attack by U. S. Government troops."

There was a rise in the level of chatter all around me. I had a sinking feeling. None of these men had signed on for this.

"This is a tough spot to be in for all of us," I said. "They seem to want to take us all out, and take ownership of all the alien tech."

"But sir," said the Corporal, his voice had a pleading quality to it. "Don't we have a deal? Don't they know we are all on the same side?"

I hesitated. "Men," I began, not sure how to tell them what they were caught up in. "They think the aliens have gone, and now is the time to grab our tech. They think some other country will grab it, if they don't. They are greedy and paranoid. I can understand that. In times of war, these things happen. If you know your history, when the French surrendered to the Germans in World War II, they formed a government known as the Vichy Government. They were puppets for the Germans. Many French died manning Vichy ships and fighting against Allied troops on the ground."

I stopped. Everyone was listening. What was my point? "In times of intense conflict, things get confused. I'm not saying they are on the wrong side, or that we are. I'm saying the stakes are high, and they aren't going to let us keep our alien tech and fight as a group for Earth unless we are strong enough to prove we can keep that tech. Most of you are Americans, the rest are from India. Both of those nations broke off from Britain, forming independent nations. Were your forefathers rebels, or freedom fighters? That depended on whether your side won or not. The same thing is happening today, but the stakes are higher. All of you, if you stand with us here, will have to decide you are on the right side. Do you think Star Force can keep Earth safe? Or do you think the U. S. politicians should have that responsibility?"

The Corporal walked past me into the camp. "I'm with you, Riggs," he said. "The government boys will screw this up."

In the end, all of them walked into camp and climbed into the trenches we'd been plowing up here and there. I'd chosen them well. I only hoped I hadn't led them to their deaths. Even more strongly, I hoped I wasn't screwing up everything somehow.

The big push didn't come until about two a.m. We almost had the second turret working by then. Major Robinson was in the trenches, his nanites having repaired his body enough to fight. You could understand what he was saying now, as well. His cheek wasn't a hundred percent, but at least he didn't drool blood all the time. It cheered the troops to have a second officer walking around the camp shouting orders with me.

"Major, I want you to supervise the completion of the second turret. Kwon and I will shore up our defensive positions."

Robinson agreed without an argument. He was still pretty shaky, and I knew from experience when you first got nanotized, you weren't ready to operate your own body. He was likely to screw up in combat. He needed days to adjust. I figured he would be most useful under one of the turrets calling targets.

Kwon and I inspected the perimeter. Each shed sat on a concrete pad, but the pads didn't extend out from the buildings more than a few feet. We had the men dig trenches between the buildings and piled up sandbags in front of the trenches, setting up good firing positions. The ground was cleared about a hundred yards out in every direction from the sheds. We had a spiral of concertina wire out along the tree line, marking the camp border. Our beamers and turrets would have to stop them in this open area.

"Short of blowing up the camp," I said, "I can't see how they can take us out other than using an overwhelming infantry force."

"I agree," said Kwon, stumping along beside me. "It's going to be bloody if they try it."

I didn't answer him. We'd set up some reliable communications systems by now, nothing but open radio lines. The enemy didn't seem to be jamming us, but they were probably listening. I told the men to assume the enemy could hear every word. We didn't have the tech advantage in the communications.

I heard something about half an hour later. Something that rumbled and squeaked. I looked at Kwon, who was taking a break with me. Our backs were up against one of the innermost sheds.

"Armor?" asked Kwon, voicing my thoughts.

"Has to be," I said grimly. I hated being wrong. This must be what they had been waiting for, the arrival of vehicles. How the hell had they gotten heavy vehicles down here so fast?

"Sounds like they are coming in from the east," Kwon said. "They are using our own road."

I nodded slowly. Had we lost the main camp already? Had Barrera switched sides on me? I had to assume the worst. "What kind of vehicle does it sound like to you, Kwon?"

He listened for a second or two. "Not heavy enough to be M1's. Maybe Bradley fighting vehicles. Something like that."

"Yeah. Something amphibious. Something they've kept out there offshore, waiting for a moment like this to deploy on my little island and run us off."

Sandra spoke up in my ear then, on the open channel. "Kyle? I've got contacts on the road."

"I know."

"What do I do?"

"Hold your fire until they do something."

About a minute later, the sounds of the advancing vehicles stopped. They were waiting for something. Nothing happened for about twelve tense minutes.

Then the smart-missiles came screaming down. The missiles were all coming for my new turret. A steady stream of them. They could have been launched from ships or subs off the coast, or dropped from high-flying aircraft miles out over the ocean. I wasn't really sure, what I cared about was our programming, which took over and did a fantastic job.

The first thing I heard was the turret moving on its own. With spooky movements, it twisted and aimed upward.

"Kyle?" Sandra called. "This thing is doing something on its own."

Then I heard the warm-up thrum and the singing sound. The turret had found a target and fired upon it. The sky split apart with light. Immediately, the turret retargeted and fired again. The machine repeated the steps twice more, burning down things in the sky I couldn't even see.

"Out on the road, they are moving in," shouted Kwon.

I breathed fast and thought faster. I could see it all now. They were engaging our turret, forcing it to target and destroy incoming missiles from the west. In the meantime, the armor column of vehicles would hit us from the east and probably fire shells at the turret. It could only handle so many targets at once.

"Get a dozen men out of their holes, Sergeant!" I shouted. "Don't use the radio. We're going to have to take those vehicles out before they break through the trees. We can't let them get a clear shot at our only big gun."

"Sir!" acknowledged Kwon. Without hesitation, he got his big bulk moving. Roaring at the men nearby, he got them moving, too. Somehow, his bass voice was audible above the growing din of whines and explosions overhead.

I followed behind at a trot. I eyed the forest line. If they were ready with an infantry rush, this might be a good time. But they didn't come instantly. Maybe the enemy couldn't run fast enough.

"Any new contacts, Sandra?"

"Only the missiles and the vehicles."

"Keep firing at the missiles," I said, knowing the enemy was listening. "You must stop them all."

"It's doing that by itself."

Kwon had a hustling team behind him. I gestured toward the road. They set off in ground-eating leaps. I followed.

We met up with the first of the mechanized units as it did about thirty miles an hour right out of the trees. We had to stop the first vehicles from getting out into an open field of fire. They came in a column, of course. They really didn't have any choice, as they weren't heavy enough to knock down trees and the forest was too thick for them to drive between the trunks.

The vehicle leading the charge was an APC—an armored personnel carrier. I recognized the design immediately, it was a Bradley M2. It had a 25mm autocannon on top, which instantly began ripping fire at us. My men scattered and threw themselves down into the grass. One marine was hit right off, I could tell from the way he flopped and didn't get back up.

It was the twin TOW missiles mounted on the side of Bradley's turret that I feared the most. The missiles were designed to take out tanks. Given a shot at close range, they should be able to make quick work of my big laser.

"Everyone, aim high! Take out the cannon and the missiles!"

It was a close thing, but four beams stabbed out, then three more. The missiles never launched. When the crippled, flaming vehicle rolled to a stop, the back ramp fell open and two men squirmed into the grass. I felt a little sick. These APCs were loaded with infantry. I couldn't do anything about that now, however. We beamed more M2s as they appeared, each time aiming high. Unfortunately, secondary explosions often caused the vehicles to explode. A few survivors managed to get out and crawl away. I ordered my men to let them retreat.

After we'd knocked out six M2s, they couldn't get through into the open anymore past their own burning hulks. The crews must have figured out they were screwed and stopped coming.

Shortly after that, the missile barrage from the sea stopped, too. I'd lost several good men, but we'd won—for now.

-11-

In the morning, I was awakened by Sandra's touch. I startled, and grabbed her wrist with automatic, unthinking speed.

"Ow!" she complained.

"I'm sorry," I said, releasing her. "I guess you surprised me."

She rubbed her wrist and her features smoothed out. "That was a bad idea. At least it's not broken."

I gently touched her fingers, and she pouted at first, but let me kiss them lightly. She offered me a can of something. It was stew meat, or something like it. I took it and ate the stuff cold.

"We have fake orange juice or fake coffee to go with that," she said.

"Give me both," I said.

I ate and looked out the window of Shed Thirty-Six. This unit had been giving us problems. Something had jammed in the factory's craw when it tried to digest its previous project for raw materials. I must have fallen asleep trying to fix it.

"We made it to morning, at least," said Sandra.

"How are the turrets?" I asked.

"We've got two operational. The third will come up soon. Major Robinson has been asking for you, but I told him you needed a few hours sleep."

I looked at her, uncertain if she were a danger to military discipline or a godsend. She was a little of both, I supposed. It certainly wasn't standard operating procedure to have the commander's girlfriend chasing off his second-in-command.

However, we were anything but a standard military, and she had a point. I had needed rest.

"I'll go get him while you wake up," she said.

"I don't want you wandering around the base. There could still be snipers around."

"I don't think they would be gunning for me."

"Probably not, but stay on station inside Fourteen, okay?"

She put her hands on her hips. "After I opened that can of cat food for you to eat and everything? This is the thanks I get?"

"You don't make the most obedient of soldiers, Sandra."

"I hope to hell I never do," she said and left, swinging her hips.

I smirked after her. I hoped she would never change. The door creaked open a few minutes later. I didn't look around. I was busy tapping on the same tablet I'd lifted from the operator of Unit Fourteen yesterday. I had to work out the maximum number of ships I could produce from the supplies I had left. I figured three turrets were enough for now to defend the base. We needed mobile forces to push them off the island. An exhibition of force was required to get them to take us seriously again.

"Robinson?" I said, "tell me about the turrets."

Major Robinson cleared his throat. When he spoke, I heard a little slur to his speech, as if he had had a stroke or something. I supposed his cheek hadn't completely healed over yet. "We've got another problem, sir," he said.

I turned around and got my biggest surprise of the day. Leaning in over Robinson's shoulder was a smiling face. I knew that face. It was Admiral Jack Crow.

My mouth sagged open. "Crow?"

"The same, mate!" he said, grinning. His teeth were big, white and square. His blue eyes glowed beside his hawk-nose.

I stared at him for a second, blinking.

"Thought I was out of the picture, did you?" he said, clearly enjoying my shock. "Well, anyone will tell you an old Crow doesn't die easily. I may be even harder to kill than the famous Kyle Riggs."

"Colonel," interrupted Robinson, eyeing us both uneasily. I'm sure he wasn't quite sure who he was supposed to take orders from at this point. "There's something I need to show you out here."

I stepped out into the sunlight, and got a second shock. Men were streaming into camp. Unlike Crow, most of them were armed. They were my marines. Nearly two full companies of them.

"Are these the men Barrera told me he sent?" I asked.

"The same, mate," said Crow from close behind me. He'd followed us out to gloat. Somehow, having Crow at my back made my skin crawl. I didn't turn around, though. I didn't want to look worried.

"Thanks for bringing them in, Crow. You've done better than I could have hoped."

The men all looked at one another. It had to be hard for them. I was the hero, but Crow had always been the superior officer. I'm sure they felt divided loyalties. With such a small, half-broken organization, it was dangerous to have anyone feeling uncertain. I felt, suddenly, like a member of some rebel camp hiding in the jungles of a banana republic. All I needed was a beret and a cigar.

"Perhaps we should talk privately?" suggested Crow, still standing behind me.

I nodded. I tossed my head in the direction of Unit Fourteen. What had once been a shed had transformed into a metallic anthill. The turret on top swiveled in twitches and jerks as the brainbox reacted to stimuli.

I walked to Unit Fourteen. Crow followed me. I never looked at him. I knew that every eye in the camp watched us. I knew that I couldn't show any fear, or dismay. But I was feeling dismayed all right. Somehow, I'd figured I was in charge of this outfit, or what was left of it, and I had been left with no real rivals for power. It wasn't that I was power-mad, mind you. It wasn't even that I disliked Crow all that much. But somehow, other people in any power structure tended to get in my way.

As we reached the base of the shining conical tower, Crow whistled with admiration. "This is your work, isn't it, Riggs? I'm constantly amazed by the things you manage to come up with. Scared the shit out of the dirtsiders, I bet."

"It did indeed."

"Why does this thing keep shivering and moving around?" he asked, pointing up at the projector, which was tracking something. I didn't know what.

"It might be sensing distant aircraft," I suggested.

63

"Or, it might be tracking a flock of storks, right?" asked Crow.

"If they so much as crap on this facility, this baby will toast them."

Crow nodded and ran his hand over the smooth metal admiringly. "Yes. I have no doubt of that. I like these things you've made for me, Kyle. They remind me of *Snapper*. I miss her. Do you miss *Alamo?*"

"I haven't had time to miss her, really," I said. I rapped out my code on the door. The door dissolved open.

Crow recognized the code and laughed. "High security, eh, mate?

I gave him a wintery smile and gestured for us to go inside. He followed me.

The second I stepped inside and the door sealed itself behind us, I knew something was wrong. I began to turn, to raise my arms.

I caught a glimpse of Crow behind me. He had his fists balled up around something, a rock? I couldn't tell. His eyes were bulging with effort, they were half-mad. I realized vaguely this must have been the face he'd worn when he'd killed people aboard the *Snapper*.

Truthfully, I wasn't all that worried. He was older and in worse shape than I was. Much more importantly, he'd never been nanotized. What did I have to worry about? My biggest concern was not to accidently hurt the crazy old codger.

His balled fists came down on my temple, and I felt shocked. Not just from the power of the blow, but the *speed* of it. How could he?

A purple explosion went off in my brain and I went down. I rolled away from him, struggled to spring up again.

He was on me in an instant. I saw what he had in his hands now. They were big, round steel balls. Ball bearings? Something like that. He'd picked them up somewhere and had kept them in his pockets. Now, he was beating the crap out of me with them. The skin on his knuckles opened up. The skin split over the bone. I saw metal in there. Then I knew.

Training saved me. I was on my back, but I managed to yank my knees up to my chest and piston them into his body. He flew away from me like a toy tossed by a child. He crashed against the far wall, bounced off and came back at me.

By that time, however, I had gotten to my feet again. My face was a patchwork of dented flesh by then, I knew. He had hammered me in the head a half-dozen times. I was woozy, but I didn't let on.

I grinned at him with blood outlining each white tooth. My hand were up, but I waved him forward with a flick of my fingers.

"Always wanted to take a few pokes at you, old man," I said. I did my best to sound excited, feral—confident.

It worked. He hesitated. His face registered surprise. We circled, kicking chairs out of the way when they came near. He threw a punch or two, but I slapped them away. We were both breathing hard. Each second that passed my head cleared. I needed a break badly.

"You thought I was out of the picture, didn't you Riggs?" Crow asked.

I nodded. "My bad. The second ship," I said, pointing at him. "You were on it. What did you tell the *Snapper* to get the Nanos to let you go?"

Crow didn't answer. Maybe he'd figured out I was stalling. He came at me, throwing roundhouse swings. I caught one with my shoulder, another with my ear. The one in the ear really hurt. I threw one uppercut into his chin that must have rattled his brains. It would have broken the jaw of a normal man.

We clinched up and wrestled for a minute, then pushed off each other again. Crow had a heavier build than I did, and I could tell he'd been in brawls before. But he was older and hadn't had much time to adjust to being full of nanites. At first, it threw a man off, like steering a new car.

"So, what's this all about?" I asked. "Do I owe you twenty bucks?"

Crow snorted. Blood fired out onto the floor when he did so.

"You cocked-up everything, that's what you did."

I gave a small shrug. "Like what?"

"Like what?" he screamed suddenly, disbelievingly. "Kyle, I flew seven hundred ships at the Macros. I left this world behind with thousands of followers and billions in cash. We met the enemy, ran them off, and somehow a few hours later I found my fleet disbanded. I couldn't even talk to them. I finally talked the *Snapper* into returning, and what do I find? You had dismantled my organization, pissed off every power on the planet and setup for a last stand out here in the woods."

I took a deep breath. I straightened up. "You've got a point there," I said.

"Oh, so you admit it?"

"Yeah. I can see it from your point of view. Too bad it has to end like this, though. We had a great partnership."

He looked troubled at that. He nodded. "You were my best man. But I was almost an Emperor. Do you realize that?"

At this point, we'd stopped circling and stood a safe distance from each other, watching one another warily. "Is that what you wanted? Really?"

"I don't know," he said. He rubbed his chin. "That uppercut hurt."

"Tell me about it," I said, taking a second to run my fingers gingerly over my own face. There were new lumps and the skin had split at the seams.

He heaved a sigh. "Okay. Okay, I'm the bigger man here. I'm going to say it first."

I looked at him expectantly.

"I'm sorry for hitting you. I just lost my cool. I've been losing it ever since I got my ship to unload me here and then she took off."

"How'd you manage to get back to Earth?" I asked.

"Are we talking or fighting?" he asked.

We stared at each other appraisingly for a few seconds. I decided to take a chance. "How about I buy you a drink and explain everything, Emperor?"

Slowly, with half his mouth, he smiled at me. The other half didn't work right yet. He nodded slowly. "Right. Let's do it."

Crow dropped two round stones. He'd had one in each hand. They thumped loudly on the floor and rolled away. No wonder those fists had hurt so much. He stepped to the wall and rapped out a series of raps. It was my code. I wasn't surprised he'd memorized it. The door dilated open and he waved for me to step ahead of him into the blinding sunlight.

"As an Emperor, you rank me," I said. "You first."

Crow grinned with the working half of his face and blood ran down his purpling chin. Metal gleamed inside, where the bone should have been.

Crow stepped out into the open and I followed him. I didn't intend to let him get behind me again.

When I asked Kwon for booze, he looked at each of us. His big, black eyes flicked back and forth. Those eyes got wider with each flick as he took in the extent of our injuries. Then without a word he produced a flask. I took it and thanked him. I twisted off the top and sniffed it. Whatever it was, it was warm and smelled like kerosene.

"We might need a mixer for this," I said, handing it over to Crow.

He sniffed it, winced, and nodded. Every marine in the compound watched us. I knew they wanted to see how their leaders were getting along. I hid the truth by acting cool and calm. There was no sense making a big deal about our differences. I knew that the men had to have heard the fight. The walls on these sheds weren't thick. But no one had tried to come in and check on us. If only one man had made it out alive, I supposed he'd have been crowned king. I had to wonder if that had been Crow's plan all along.

Together, but with me walking about a foot behind him, Crow and I headed for what served the base as a mess hall. It was really just another shed, but without a factory inside. Instead, it had a few folding tables, chairs and crates of food. A marine was eating a can of something brown when we came in. He left in a hurry without having to be told.

I smiled after him. "I wonder if they think we are about to have round two in here."

Crow chuckled. "I think I've had enough. Will these nanites really fix my ripped-up skin?"

"A few scars look good on a man. Sandra says they give my face character."

He snorted, but looked less than happy with my response. I poured the coffee and then laced it with Kwon's rot-gut. The combination made quite an impact on our stomachs, but we kept it down. A few minutes later, we were smiling, despite everything.

"We have some catching up to do," I said. I told him briefly about the deal with Macros, but he'd already heard it from Barrera. Apparently, from his earlier reaction, he didn't approve.

I took a drink of the laced coffee. My lips tasted salty, like blood. The booze made them burn with each sip. "Tell me how you talked your ship into bringing you home," I said.

Crow shrugged. "It was easy enough. I pointed out I am the commander of this entire force. The loss of my leadership would cripple Earth's forces after the Nanos spent all this time and effort to build them up."

"They bought that?" I asked, smiling.

"In any case, I managed to convince the *Snapper* I was indispensible down here."

"What about the injections?"

Crow tilted his head. "That was part of the deal. The ship was to leave me behind as the commander of all Earth. Command personnel have to undergo the injections to get out of the ship, remember?"

"So, all this time you've never taken the injections? You never left your ship?"

Crow grinned. "I was pretty comfortable aboard her."

"Ah. Your *companions*. I'd forgotten about them. What happened to the girls?"

Crow frowned and shook his head. It was a good act, but I didn't really buy it.

"They stayed aboard. I suspect the ship has plans for them."

I gave him a flat, disapproving stare. He avoided my gaze. He'd left those girls aboard to serve as punching bags in some alien star system. Maybe he'd tried to help them and couldn't, but that wasn't my guess. With Crow... well, he was always thinking about number one. Everyone else came second—or possibly third. Crow was nothing if not a survivor. If he had been a member of the Donner Party, he would have been the first one to cook his own uncle's foot.

"So, are we working together again?" I asked, taking another sip of my booze-laced coffee. It was awful.

"What choice do we have? What's our defensive status?"

"It's a lot better today than yesterday," I said. "You just brought in a lot of fresh troops. We've got three laser turrets operating now. That reminds me, I need to get the factories working on a new project. Right now they are all making extra nanites by default."

I stood up to leave.

He raised his hand. "Hold on. We have to work out the command structure here."

"You mean: am I still going to call you Admiral in front of the troops?"

Crow stabbed the folding table with his finger. It dented in and shook. I suspected the dent was permanent. "I insist on it. We'll keep our ranks. That will give the men a feeling of stability. They might desert otherwise."

"The command structure is the same as it always was. I'm in charge of the ground-pounders. You command our space fleet."

"I haven't got any bloody ships, mate!"

"I know. I'll build you some new ones, if we live for a few more days."

"That fast?"

I drew my plans for a simple, fast-building Nano ship on a brown napkin. He stared at it intently. I could see the gears working inside his head. That's what I wanted. Crow needed a ship to be happy. As a happy man, he would be much safer to work with. Just like everyone else, he needed hope.

"We could rebuild in less than a year," he said, his eyes wide and distant.

"Yeah, if they let us."

Crow looked up at me with new respect. He shook his head. "Even when everything looks broken, you keep surprising me. How many more rabbits have you got left in that hat of yours?"

"Plenty," I said, "but you won't get your ships right away. I have to make something else, something even easier and faster to build. Something to let us kick the earthers off of our island."

Crow crossed his arms and leaned back. The chair creaked as if it was about to collapse. "Build me my fleet, I'll chase them off."

"Did you see those APCs we knocked out along the road?"

He nodded.

"They gave me an idea."

"Ships could do the same thing."

"Yeah, but they are much harder to build. A ship's engine takes days. A tank is just like one of these turrets, but with a bigger power supply and a set of tracks."

"A tank? You want to build our own armor?"

I shrugged. "Think of them as mobile laser turrets, like the ones I've already constructed. They won't have to generate lift to fly. They will be able to carry our men safely inside."

"How many do you think you'll need?"

"Less than a hundred."

"A hundred?" he shouted, standing up and making a choking sound.

"Yeah."

Crow stared at me as if I was mad for several seconds. "No. No way, mate. You think I'm some sort of wally, don't you?"

I stared back. "We need mobile, powerful forces. We need them now."

"Then build me my ships! That's an order, Colonel!" shouted Crow. His face was red and his eyes were bugging again. It occurred to me that giving Crow cheap booze might not have been my best move.

"Listen—"

"No. All you want to do is build up your ground forces. I see through your plan, Riggs. With no fleet, you are the real leader here by default. No, I'm not going to listen to any more of your silver-tongued crap."

"Then we are going to have to have round two, right here," I said calmly. I figured I could take him if he didn't get to open up with a half-dozen blows to the back of my head.

Crow was breathing hard. I could smell that varnish we'd been drinking on his breath. It washed over me like swamp gas.

With a mighty effort of self-control, he sat down again. Maybe he'd done the math and had figured his odds the same way I had. Or maybe he was being cagey. The folding chair groaned, but didn't collapse as he sank his new, nanite-laden weight onto it. I thought of a few quick jokes, but managed to stop them before they came out of my mouth.

"You know, mate," he said. "Where I come from, without your nanites you wouldn't last two minutes."

"Where do you come from?" I asked.

We stared at each other.

"The Australian Navy," he said, looking down.

"Bullshit."

Crow looked annoyed. "I did my stint."

"What year was that?"

"Never mind, you," he said. He finished his drink and poured another. He seemed troubled.

"It can't be that bad," I said. "Your past, I mean."

Crow snorted. "All right. A bit of truth then—but don't tell the men. It won't do them any good to know who they've been dying for."

I smiled. "Deal."

"I was a groundskeeper."

"A groundskeeper?"

"Right. As in, I mowed lawns for a shitty wage."

"I see. Honest work, at least."

He shook his head and took another swig. "Usually," he said. "But if things went wrong on a bad year, I knew how to work a jimmy."

"A what?" I asked. "You mean a crowbar?"

Crow shrugged. "I don't like that name for the tool."

I shook my head and laughed. "I can see why. So here we are, an ex-teacher and an ex-burglar, deciding the fate of the world."

Crow nodded and crossed his gorilla arms over his gorilla belly. "You get one minute. Talk me into building ground forces."

I leaned forward. "It's about supplies. We have a limited store here. There's about double the amount of rare earths and the like at the main base. That's where the port is, where the ships came in. Our Nano flyers used to bring the materials here with daily deliveries, but we're not going to get anymore shipments."

"The earthers took the main base," he said. "I told you that."

"Right. So we have to use what we have here as efficiently as possible. We have to build the most cost-effective force we can as fast as we can, and take back the main base. We need those supplies to build the fleet."

"We could do it with flying ships."

"Yeah. Probably. But it would take longer. Every hour, the U.S. Navy will be steaming down here with more troops. They might be landing them at the north end of the island now, getting ready for another push. We haven't seen their infantry yet, nor much in the way of air, just one mechanized column that failed."

Crow rubbed at his cheek. The nanites itched abominably when they healed a face wound. I knew the sensation well, but I couldn't drum up much sympathy for him.

"I'm trying to think clearly now," he said, his voice quieter.

"I'm not skipping your ships to keep you grounded, Jack. I'm trying to build maximum firepower to retake the island now. Then we can rebuild your fleet. At that point, they won't be able to take us out without damaging the factories. We'll build a strong defense and negotiate a new peace."

Crow slitted his eyes, looking at me with new suspicion. "Why don't we just give them the factories?"

I frowned at him. He had some other devilish thought in his head, I could see it, but I couldn't fathom it. "What are you getting at?"

He shrugged. "Just what I said. We could sell them, or at least make sure they aren't damaged. You know, if we just *threatened* to damage them, they would cave pretty fast."

I thought about that. He might be right. But I didn't want to raise the stakes any higher. I didn't want them to think we'd gone totally rogue, that we no longer cared about the planet's security. "How could we ever forge an alliance with them if we did that? We'd be the pirates they've always said we were, selling out all of Earth for our own gain."

Crow pursed his lips. "So, we have to fight? How much faster can you build tanks compared to spacecraft? How much less materials are involved in producing one mobile gun?"

"Now you are getting down to the numbers that matter. We have supplies enough to build a hundred tanks in less than a week. We would only have a dozen ships by then."

"Why such a difference?"

"The engines, mostly. They need to fly, not just roll along the ground. That requires much more power, specialized gravity-resistors, lots of stuff that's hard to make."

"We have to wait a whole week? They will have six divisions and three carrier groups down here by then. Not to mention hundreds of aircraft."

"Yeah. We will have to attack when we have the first batch of tanks ready."

"How many? How long?"

"In about twenty-four hours, I should have ten tanks, maybe a few more."

He leaned back sighing, thinking. Finally, he nodded. "Well then, you'd better get cracking, Colonel."

I smiled. "Yes sir."

I backed out of the building and closed the door behind me. At no point did I take my eyes off Crow or turn my back to him. Once I was out in the sunlight again, Kwon appeared out of nowhere.

"You are the sneakiest giant I know," I told him.

"What's the deal, sir?"

I handed back his flask. He shook it and put it away, disappointed. It was empty.

"The deal is we are working together again. We're going to build something new."

"What sir?"

"Tanks, Sergeant. A lot of them."

-13-

Sandra caught up with me about an hour later. She came in quietly, but this time I turned to the door and bounced to my feet. I relaxed when I saw it was her.

She raised her eyebrows at me. "Jumpy?"

"Let's just say I'm looking over my shoulder from now on."

Sandra took two bounding steps, then flung herself into the air. She knew I'd catch her. She wrapped her legs around my waist and went to work on my face with her lips. Fortunately, my face was healing fast.

"Crow did this, didn't he? He's such an ass."

"He's got a temper, that's all."

"I saw his face. He looked worse."

"A man can't help being born ugly."

She laughed and went back to kissing me, working over the rough spots tenderly. "I'd be super-pissed if I didn't know these would heal-up by morning."

"So would I. Look, love, I need to go back to designing the second step with these new tanks."

"You need a break."

She was right, in the end. I did need a break. We made love on a plastic chair in the darkest corner. It was just what I needed, and I think she needed it to. I expected Crow or Robinson or even more likely, Kwon, to rap on the door and interrupt us with some new disaster. But they didn't.

At the end, she slapped me again. I looked at her questioningly. "That's for nearly getting yourself killed on a daily basis," she said. "Being in love with you is nerve-wracking."

I smiled. "I've been thinking along similar lines."

"Now," she said, "quit screwing around and get your go-carts built. I bet they will attack again tonight."

"Maybe."

"Will these new toys of yours be ready by then?"

"Probably not, but with three beam turrets and about two hundred marines, I'm not worried."

"Liar," she said, and flounced outside again.

I watched her leave and hoped she would come back again soon. I turned back to that steel bastard known lovingly as Unit Fourteen. I had all the factories churning by now, or I wouldn't have taken the time off with Sandra. Most were building heavy reactors, brain-boxes, lasers, sensors and turrets. Essentially, all the components that made the stationary turrets operate. But I needed a few new pieces. I needed engines with driveshafts, locomotion systems and treads. Thinking about these elements, I got an idea. Why use treads?

"Fourteen, respond."

"Responding."

"What would it take to build the metal equivalent of human legs?"

Hesitation. A long one. I figured that when they were handing out brains, Fourteen had been back at the messhall eating pancakes. "Insufficient information—" it began. I was hardly surprised.

"Okay, forget that question. I don't have time to verbally describe the specifics of a walking system anyway."

I frowned. I had to work with what I had. I didn't have time to design new pieces, I could only reconfigure a new machine with the components I already had. "Let's talk about a gravity-resist system that is low-powered. Let's say one that is about ten percent as powerful as a standard system on a Nano ship. How long would that take one duplication factory to produce such a system?"

"Approximately seven hours."

I nodded. "And what if we duplicated the treads of a standard tank?"

"Insufficient—"

"Okay, okay. Do you have sensory input from the turret above this shed?"

"Fourteen is not linked with—"

"Link with it then."

"Done."

"Now, use the sensory equipment to lock onto the APCs we destroyed earlier today. They lie to the east."

"Done. Auto-defense program reset and off-line."

I felt a trickle of sweat. I figured there were two other turrets, and I could always cancel this intervention if something started up outside. "Okay, quickly now, scan the APCs. I want you to calculate how long it would take to duplicate the treads on those vehicles."

There was a long hesitation. Overhead, I heard the turret whine and shift. I dearly hoped that another missile barrage wasn't incoming right now.

"Components scanned."

"How long would it take?"

"Answer is variable based on the configuration of the tread in question. Some are only partially intact."

I closed my eyes, willing myself toward greater patience. "Just give me the estimate of a set of treads for the most intact vehicle."

"Three point six hours."

Half as long? I thought about that. It hardly seemed worth the effort to make a vehicle with treads, if that was the difference. I had enough factories that were making nanites now, I could switch their output and they would still beat the ones building the reactors and beam units. I smiled to myself.

We were going to build *hovertanks*. That would put a shocked look on everyone's face. The more I thought about it, the more I liked the idea. This area of the island was heavily-wooded. We would get choked up on the road just as the enemy had when they came in if we attacked the main base using the same road. With hovertanks gliding along, we could go over the waves or maybe even the trees, depending on how strong the resistors were.

I went through the design for about another hour, until I thought I had it worked out. The tanks would be able to carry themselves, plus a crew of six men, at a height of up to about twenty feet above the surface. What was even better, I figured I could have the first of them ready to fly before morning.

I set all the machines into production and passed out with my head on the desk. I wasn't even sure what time it was. Sandra came in and gave me something to eat. She saw my exhausted state and badgered Kwon into finding me a cot.

I woke up some hours later with her manning the beam turret. I blinked, bleary-eyed. I realized she must have said something to me. Something meant to wake me up.

"What time is it?" I asked.

"Nearly midnight. And we've got trouble."

I bounced up, staggering beside the cot. "What's happening?"

She pointed to the wall. "We've got contacts."

I saw them now. A dozen beads of metal on the wall. They didn't look like they were firing yet. But it was only a matter of time.

"Are all the turrets active?" I demanded. "Why didn't someone wake me up?"

"They just showed up."

A rapping came at the door. I knew the pattern. The side of the turret yawned open and Kwon leaned in. "They are helicopters, Colonel. Robinson wants to know if we should shoot them down."

"No. No dammit. Get me a com-link."

"They can hear that, sir."

"I know that. Just give me yours."

I activated the link and set the unit to broadcast. "No one fire until fired upon."

"That might be too late, sir," said a voice. I thought it might be Robinson.

"You have your orders."

No one fired. We waited. After another minute or two, I heard something on the com-link. It was a familiar voice.

"This is General Kerr. Is that you, Riggs?"

"Yes, General. Go ahead," I said calmly. Inside, I was seething. It was one thing to know your military network might be compromised. It was another to have the enemy commander listening in and calling you on it like it was your cell phone.

"Riggs, we need to talk."

"We are talking, sir."

"I don't mean on an open channel. I know your men are listening."

Sandra and I looked at one another. I suspected, at any moment, that Crow might jump in and start talking big. But he didn't. Maybe he had decided I was better at handling such situations. Or maybe he didn't want the enemy to know he was here with me. For all I knew, he planned to pull out and run when the fireworks started.

"What do you suggest, General?"

"We'll meet on neutral ground. Man-to-man. Just step to the edge of camp where you slaughtered my men. We'll talk amongst the dead Bradleys."

Sandra waved at me violently, shaking her head and frowning. She clearly did not want me to go.

I looked at her for a long second. "I'll be there in three minutes, General," I said. "Riggs out."

It was just before midnight and the forest was full of peeping creatures. Things buzzed, rustled and occasionally thrashed about in the dark trees. I'm a trusting soul, so I didn't take along my reactor and beam projector. I did have a 9mm pistol at my hip and I wore my combat suit, with the full vest underneath. Kevlar and nanites would slow down anything but a headshot, I figured.

Kerr stood in the dark, smoking. I'd never seen him smoke before, but he'd always seemed like he should have had a cigar. I was mildly surprised to see he had a pipe in his mouth. The bowl glimmered orange and although the aromatic smoke was invisible in the night, I could smell it.

"You've already let me in too close, you know that, don't you Riggs?" General Kerr asked me.

"Yeah, I know that."

"You are too far from your defensive line. My boys—if they were hiding in those trees over there, for instance—they could pick you off right now."

"Yeah," I said. "And I know I could kill you with my bare hands in less than one second."

Kerr gave me a hard look. "That wouldn't fix your situation."

"Neither would your sniper."

Kerr nodded. "Okay, Riggs. You've gotten stubborn about this situation. I understand that." He pointed around at the broken Bradleys. His finger was sweeping and accusatory. "Your stubbornness killed a lot of fine men here, Colonel."

"I didn't order the attack."

He worked on his pipe again for the better part of a minute. He had a lighter that flashed a metallic gold when he flicked it into life. I almost asked him why he preferred a pipe. It seemed like a lot of trouble to have to relight it all the time. But I just stood there, waiting and wondering if his pipe was some kind of signal to a sniper. I guess I wasn't in the mood for pointless chit-chat.

"Is that why you are here, General?" I asked finally. "To smoke and threaten me?"

"Did you ever figure anything new out about the Blues, Riggs?"

"Since the last time we talked?"

"Aren't you curious about them? We've come up with another theory as to why they can't leave their world."

I blinked at him in the darkness. He waited. I let him wait a few long seconds. Finally, I couldn't stand it anymore.

"Okay. Tell me your theory."

"They're all dead. Extinct. That's why their robots are running around, doing mad, pointless things."

I thought about it for a few seconds. Finally, I nodded. "You could be right."

"My nerds give that answer the highest probability," Kerr said. "But we can't really know the truth. Anyway, I'm here to tell you one thing: This power-struggle is over. It's finished—as of right now. You can keep your weapons and maybe even the island. No one really cares. All you have to do is hand over the camp with the alien machines intact and walk out of here. This is your last chance, your last warning."

I looked at him appraisingly, an outline in the darkness. He didn't have the manner of a man who was bluffing. I'd never seen him bluff about anything. "What are you going to do?" I asked. "Nuke us?"

Kerr tilted his head to one side, as if considering it. "There are options. We could use an EMP blast. Did you think of that?"

"Interesting, but we barely use our communication systems now."

The General made a snorting sound. "Think bigger, Kyle. I'm not talking about a few kilowatts. I'm talking about an electronics-frying tsunami."

I shook my head. "I don't think it would work, sir. My reactors and beam projectors can take that sort thing."

"Ah, but can your nanites?"

I startled and looked at him. I hadn't thought about that. The nanites had to have circuitry in there somewhere. Would they simply fall dead by the billions, like a plague of locusts stricken down by the hand of God?

"Yes, the nanites… poor little buggers," Kerr said.

"Hard to deliver in real terms," I said dismissively, simulating a lack of concern I didn't feel.

"We've tested it. What will your men do when they can't lift their own beamers? They'll be flat on their backs with those reactors pulling them down, like beached turtles. And what will your smart turrets do when their brainboxes shut down?"

I narrowed my eyes and stared back at him. "You would have done it already if you thought you could get away with it. There's something you're afraid of," I said. Then I snapped my fingers. "The factories. You don't want to wreck them. You have no idea if they would be destroyed or not."

General Kerr sighed like an overindulgent father. "It doesn't matter, Kyle. We are going to try it soon—or something worse."

"What's worse?"

"You don't want to find out."

"Nukes? Pointless. Why destroy the factories?"

Kerr shook his head slowly. "Not all such weapons have to destroy hardware, Kyle."

I thought, suddenly, that I knew what he was getting at. I felt a tickle of sweat. I had to stop myself from reaching up to scratch my head. "Neutron bombs?" I asked. "I thought we outlawed those things in the seventies."

"We outlaw a lot of things, Riggs. Not every law is followed to the letter."

I thought about it, and the more I did the less I liked the idea. A neutron weapon would burn us all to death with radiation. The equipment would be left intact. Nothing in the region would survive, not even those big tropical cockroaches that seemed to crawl into everyone's shed at night.

"We need a little more time, Kerr," I said.

"For what? Why would I give you any more time? The last time I did that, you built a bunch of laser turrets and smoked my Bradleys."

"That was self-defense."

Kerr swept all the words away with his hand. He took a step toward me, then a second. His nose was only six inches from mine. "You listen to me, Riggs. You don't have any more time. The only reason you're still breathing is because people at the top have to give the final order, and they are still screwing around. The assets are in place. Do you understand me?"

I nodded. He turned around and left me standing there. He didn't say goodbye or shake my hand. Silently, he headed back to his chopper. I would have killed him, if I'd thought it would do any good. But I knew it wouldn't.

I walked back to camp and began a long night of hard work. By two a. m., the first hovertank took shape. I had a new idea by then. I decided to camouflage them. I made them look like boats. Big ones.

It was easier to do than it sounds. Nanites, when you have enough of them, are like smart, liquid metal. They can be told to generate any reasonable structure. They can balloon and puff themselves into any shape you describe to them, just as I'd made a toilet out of them back on the *Alamo*. Now, however, instead of a toilet, I built a hull in the shape of a blocky patrol boat. Inside were all the weapons and my men, twenty men in each vessel and another man to drive it and operate the gun. The brainboxes were so new, so young and inexperienced, they needed a human to call the shots for them—literally.

By four a.m., I had eleven of these bloated vehicles. With the extra weight, they would barely be able to skim over the waves, but Fourteen assured me they would be able to move. I contacted Kerr again, and he answered instantly. I smiled, they had been watching us and sweating it. I could almost hear their thoughts. *What the hell is that crazy bastard Riggs up to now?*

"Riggs? What the hell have you been building?" Kerr asked.

"Never seen a troop-carrier before? I'm pulling out. Tell your people to hold their fire—if you really have any people out there."

"Okay," said Kerr. "That's great news. And just in time, too."

"You have to give me another hour or so to clear out."

"Don't think you can load those factories onto your metal zeppelins, or whatever they are."

"Wouldn't dream of it, General. The factories are too big, anyway. I'm sure your spycams have relayed the info back to your nerds for analysis. What did they tell you?"

Kerr hesitated. "That you can't carry much more than your troops and some equipment. That even if you did steal a machine or two, you would have nothing to supply it with."

"Exactly. So stop worrying. Riggs out."

I turned to Sandra and Crow, who were both looking at me with big, freaked-out eyes.

"That should hold him for a few hours," I said. "When he sees us glide out of here over the water, he'll count it as a win."

"Won't they come in and take over the camp?" asked Crow. "They will have clearly won at that point."

I smiled grimly. "I never said we were turning off the turrets."

-15-

The hovertanks were big and bulky-looking. When puffed out to carry extra troops and hide the laser turret each one had on top, they were about fifteen feet high and thirty feet long. They looked like shiny, teardrop-shaped motor homes from the fifties. But these motor homes had no wheels, no windows, and floated about a yard off the ground.

An hour before dawn, I loaded my deceptive vehicles with every marine I had and we fled the camp. The interior of my hovertank was dimly-lit and thrummed softly as we traveled along the road. The scraping branches sometimes squealed against the thin hull. My men looked around, thumbing their beam-projectors nervously. The marines didn't like the vehicles, but I found myself strangely comfortable inside them. It was lot like being inside the *Alamo* again. I wondered if I would ever build a new ship like the *Alamo* and fly her.

I chuckled to myself. Here I was, reminiscing about that liquid-steel witch of a ship, the same machine that had heartlessly killed my family members. Was I crazy, or was it the world that had gone mad?

Like a pod of silvery whales, the hovertanks followed an overgrown road that led to the coast in single file. I led the way to the coast. We crashed along, the thickest branches denting in the stretched skin of my vehicles while we brushed aside about a thousand smaller twigs. The dents worked themselves out slowly, the walls folding back into place. It reminded me of watching an air mattress fill out when you pump it up.

I had time, along the way, to wonder if Kerr was right. What if the Blues really were all dead? It would explain a lot. Possibly their machines roved upon a thousand worlds, following their programming to examine or destroy other species. One group, the Nanos, were trying to save "biotics" from the other group, the warrior Macros. If the Blues were extinct, and that was the hidden truth behind these wars, I found it depressing. It was all pointless and terrifying, and humanity was caught up in the middle of it. We were ants at the feet of struggling giants. Pawns caught up in an argument between incomprehensible, idiot gods.

I shook my head and rubbed my face. A few last spots itched where Crow had hit me. There were times in life for introspection and pondering unknowns. This wasn't one of them. I looked up and noticed we were breaking free of the tree line and the hovertanks were picking up speed, sliding down a gentle slope to the beach. Soon, we would be gliding over the waves and would be able to increase our speed.

I'd named my hovertank the *Patton*. Crow had named his the *Napoleon*. I had wondered about his name choice briefly. I supposed it made as much sense as any name.

I watched the screen I'd set up on the *Patton's* forward wall. My tank was at the point of the formation. Once we were over the ocean, I ordered the vehicle to turn northward and head around the island, hugging the coastline.

"Riggs?" said the ship, relaying Crow's voice. We'd dispensed with the business of opening channels. Unless we wanted a private conversation, anything we directed the tanks to transmit would be heard by all of them.

"Riggs here," I said.

"Colonel, I'm giving you operational command of this taskforce. *Napoleon* out."

Very kind of him, I thought to myself drily. We'd already decided I was running the tactical ops back at camp, if only because I'd invented these crazy things. I knew the real reason behind his announcement, of course. Crow wanted to be seen publicly as the man behind the scenes, the real seat of power. I rolled my eyes.

"Thank you, Admiral. Now tankers, set your vehicles to auto-follow one another in a diamond formation. You are to maintain auto-follow mode unless we are engaged."

I watched the screen until I saw they'd taken on the directed formation. It took longer that it should have, but our pilots were very green. I decided not to chew out anyone.

"It's time to reconfigure our vehicles and unlimber our primary weapons. Order your tanks to reconfigure to sea transport setup *now*. Report back when reconfiguration is complete."

I turned and ordered the *Patton* to switch to sea-transport configuration. This would melt away the conical hump of metal on its back, revealing the big beam-unit that rode there. We would be armed, but still keep the current bloated shape. Our tanks still looked like ships, but we were armed with the equivalent of a large laser battery mounted on top. Essentially, we were now mobile versions of the laser turrets we'd set up to protect the camp. I couldn't switch into the full combat configuration, which was smaller and sleeker with thicker armored walls. The interior would be too small for my troops in combat mode. If I gave that order while my troops were inside they would be crushed and squeezed out like rabbit pellets into the ocean.

I ordered everyone to activate their turrets and put them into auto-defense mode. The firing algorithms were the one thing I wasn't too worried about. I'd taken the time to have the brainboxes from the stationary turrets back at the camp upload their neurological targeting algorithms to the new fire-control boxes. These turrets should be as good at targeting as the stationary turrets had been. In fact, their performance should be identical, except they still had to learn to compensate for being on a moving platform. I felt like having the guns test themselves on trees and boulders as we glided past them, but restrained the urge. It would improve their aim, but I didn't want to advertise to anyone that we were armed. Not just yet.

For the first time, I relaxed a fraction. The plan had worked so far. The enemy could have hit us when we were bloated and weaponless. My pregnant metal balloons would have popped easily, and we could not have shot down so much as a single incoming RPG. Now, with our lasers up and tracking, we at least had a good chance of taking out projectiles and engaging any attacking ships or planes.

We had our lasers out, and were no longer helpless. But the hovertanks were not yet in battle-mode. In that configuration, I'd taught the tanks to take on sleek lines with angled sides that I hoped

87

would take a hit from incoming fire without buckling. Their hulls would deflate dramatically too, leaving room inside only for a few men. The hulls, thus collapsed, would be denser, thicker and better able to operate as armor and deflect incoming fire.

"Patton, adjust your screen. Increase the scope out to two hundred miles. Reduce contact size accordingly, but inflate small contacts to be at least one quarter of an inch in size, regardless of scale."

"Acknowledged," rumbled the tank. It had a throaty, masculine voice. I smiled to myself every time I heard it. I had insisted on this detail, but I'm not sure why. Maybe I'd become punch-drunk working on them all night, with only a few catnaps taken while waiting for one element or another to be finished. Whatever the reason, all the hovertanks had the voices of gruff, old men.

The wall before me rippled. I could see the coastline now. Soon, as we reached the northern shores at the top of the Andros Island, we would swing to the right and head east. We would follow the beaches eastward, then finally turn south. If we made it down the coast as far as the main camp I'd be very happy. I wasn't sure if we would make it that far without being blown out of the water, but if we did, I figured the other side was in for a rude surprise.

We almost made it in the end. We cruised in formation without incident, and made our planned to turn southward on the final approach to our goal. We'd been cruising at nearly one hundred knots, and the miles went by quickly. In the east, directly ahead, I knew the sun was rising. It had to be lovely, cool and bright pink outside.

The planes came in from the east. One contact separated into six, and they were moving much too quickly at that range to be ships. I questioned the *Patton*, and learned they were skimming less than a hundred feet above the waves. Maybe they thought they would be invisible at that low altitude, with the sunrise coming up behind them, blindingly bright.

But the artificial eyes of my hovertanks weren't easily blinded.

-16-

"Private channel requested by the *Napoleon*," announced my tank.

"Accept it," I said. "Mute transmissions to open channel."

"Options set," rumbled the *Patton*.

"What the hell are they doing?" asked Crow.

"Might just be a fly by. I don't see any missile launches yet."

"Bollocks, Riggs. Burn them out of the sky."

I didn't say anything for two seconds. The contacts grew a tiny bit closer. They had to be traveling at twice the speed of sound, I figured. I did some quick calculations. At Mach 2, they would be directly overhead in about ten minutes.

"We don't have to fire yet, sir," I said calmly. "They might be scouting us."

"When will we have to fire to be safe?"

"If they get to within a ten-mile range, I would feel they pose a serious danger. I wouldn't want them to get any closer."

"They can fire an anti-ship missile from much further out that that," Crow said.

"True, but I fear their cannons more than their missiles. We can shoot down the missiles unless they are fired very close in. A stream of 20 mm rounds would be unstoppable and would punch right through the walls of these tin puffer-fish we are riding in."

"I repeat, in order to be safe we should take them out, now."

"Crow, I'm in operational command, remember?" I asked.

Silence.

"If we blow our cover and fire on these planes without need," I continued, "we will warn them that we have offensive capabilities. Let me try to talk to Kerr first."

"All right, but if they get to within two minutes of us, I'm relieving you of command and ordering everyone to fire."

"Fair enough," I said. I figured he was right, we couldn't allow them to get that close. As I recalculated, we didn't even have as much time as I'd figured at first. I'd forgotten that we were heading toward them at about one hundred knots. Our combined speeds were closing the gap very quickly.

With five minutes to go, I got out the communications box I'd used to communicate with Kerr from the camp. He seemed to be waiting for the contact. I was able to get in touch with him almost immediately.

The General's voice came in over the speakers, answering my call. "Kyle? You ever been to a friend's house where they had a really big, annoying dog?"

"Hasn't everyone?"

"Well, those planes are just like big dogs. They are friendly. They only want to sniff you, to take pictures."

I thought hard for a few seconds. There seemed to be no way to win this situation. Either I threatened to destroy his planes, in which case he would know that we had offensive capability—if he didn't already. Also, I'd have tipped my hand as a hostile. If I simply blew away his planes, Kerr would be even more upset. On the other hand, if I did nothing, they would come close and either take pictures, showing my armament, or fire on us, which would probably be disastrous.

"I can't allow them to come closer than fifty miles, Kerr."

"Do you have any choice?"

"Do you believe I'd leave my base completely unarmed and at your mercy? Is that my style, General?"

Kerr fell silent for a minute or so. The planes grew closer. I steeled myself to give the order. They were going to have to be shot down, good pilots wasted.

"What's eating at you, General? There is no need to force this issue. We were getting along so well."

"No. No we weren't, you prick!" shouted Kerr, with sudden rage.

"The planes, sir," I said, not sure what his problem was, and not really caring.

"What about my men?" shouted Kerr.

"What men?"

"The full platoon I sent in there to your *empty* camp. They were all fried. No warning shots. There's nothing left except a few smoking boots!"

I felt a pang of guilt. I sighed. "I apologize, General. We haven't built our trust back, I can see that."

"You didn't have to leave the base on auto-attack."

I closed my eyes, trying to think. Each death on either side seemed like such a waste. Was I in the right? Why couldn't I give up power, and let the so-called pros do the work? Let them protect the world for awhile. I wondered if every tin-pot dictator in history had felt moments of self-doubt like the one I was having right now.

"It was a matter of trust, sir. I have to use voice-command to reset those turrets. If I had done it before we left, I would have had no defense. You attacked us first sir, please keep that in mind. I'm sorry good men died, I've been sorry every time we've clashed. But you are the ones in the wrong, here. We had a deal with your government, but the moment you accounted us as weak, you lunged at us. It is not my fault, General, if I felt obliged to defend myself."

A new voice broke in over the broadcast channel. "They are in too close, Riggs. I'm ordering every unit to track the incoming aircraft. Every unit will fire on my command."

"Patton, open broadcast channel. Crow, wait!" I shouted, staring at the big screen. The aircraft had indeed slid closer while I was arguing with Kerr. "Give me one more minute, Admiral."

"Riggs?" said Kerr. He sounded angry and defeated. "I heard all that. You weren't bluffing."

"I rarely do, sir."

"Fine, if that's how you want things."

The connection broke, and a few seconds later, the planes split into two wings and flew off to the north and south. I licked my lips, watching them go. It had been close.

I thought about the auto-defense turrets I'd left behind in the camp. It had been a trap, and I should have known there would be deaths involved. I felt guilty about it, but I wasn't sure what else I could have done. If I'd turned them off, they would have the

91

factories right now. If I had called Kerr and warned him about the trap, he might have sent assets after my bloated hovertanks sooner. I had slid along, trying to get out of the situation as quickly and quietly as possible. I'd hoped that Kerr would wait until morning to make a move on the camp, and by that time it would be too late. I recalled reading a military axiom to the effect that *every plan, especially the closely-timed, complicated ones, rarely survived contact with the enemy.*

Stressing over every mile, I led my gliding whales southward now, toward the main base. Soon, Kerr would figure out where we were headed. I decided to throw him a red herring.

"Team, we are pulling into our little village at Stafford Creek," I said.

"Private channel requested by the *Napoleon*," announced my tank.

I accepted the request with a sigh.

"What the hell are you up to now, Riggs?"

"There were two companies of marines stationed at Stafford Creek, Crow. I want to see if we can gather more support."

"Those men will sit on their hands for another day or two. If we look strong, they will stay loyal. Let's head down now and capture the main base before they get smart."

I paused. "I want to drop off Sandra, sir. I'll have her talk to the men. We could use more troops on our side."

"Personal issues getting in the way of good military thinking, eh? Right. Why not? Maybe we'll have a birthday party on the beach, too. Hey, crew, is anyone having a birthday today?"

I heard, in the background, a few marines chuckling and volunteering that it was indeed their birthdays. I grunted and disconnected the channel. I figured I'd gotten the approval I needed.

We stopped en masse at the beach along the Queen's Highway in the Stafford Creek area. I practically had to push Sandra out of the ship.

"I'm staying with you," she said, arms crossed and face drawn up in an exaggerated frown.

"Sandra," I whispered, "everyone is watching, and I'm not taking my girlfriend into another pitched battle."

Sergeant Kwon stood up from the steel benches. "I'll escort her, sir. I'll see if I can get us some reinforcements from the troops here, too."

I eyed him for a second, then nodded. I just didn't have anywhere completely safe to put her right now. Those planes had worried me. If we'd been hit, I might have survived serious injury, as might have everyone else aboard. But not Sandra. She was the softest of targets, no matter how tough her attitude was.

I managed to coax her onto the beach. She gave me a sudden, desperate kiss which I returned, and then she and Sergeant Kwon vanished. The gorgeous beach scene vanished with her. I was left staring at a dimly lit metal wall. The smell of the sea, the fresh breezes and flecks of white sand had swirled inside our tomb-like hovertank.

The men around me on the benches nudged one another and chortled. I ignored them. I was lost in my own emotions, wondering if I would ever see Sandra again. And wondering if I was out of my mind.

I climbed up into the cockpit again and took the battlegroup out over the waves. We silently glided southward, toward the main base that had been taken from us.

-17-

They hit us first. The only warning I had was the beeping of the communications box. Kerr was trying to contact me. I ignored the first beeping, and the second that came in a few minutes later. There wasn't a third.

I'm pretty sure it was an RPG—maybe a lot of them. I realized in the first seconds of the ambush that they had to be firing from somewhere close, probably in the tree line right along the beach. All I knew was I heard a whoosh and a boom, and one of our troop carriers blew up. It was the one right behind me in our diamond formation.

The turrets on our hovertanks homed in collectively. They sang less than a second later and there was no more incoming fire. The turrets sang again and again, firing into the beach area. Were they hitting troops? Were there enemy vehicles involved? I couldn't be sure. A few targets popped up, coppery-red on the wall in front of me, looking man-sized. They vanished almost as quickly as they appeared. I opened my mouth to order the auto-firing to stop, but closed it again. Maybe they were beaten, crawling around out there on the sand between the palms, screaming. Or maybe they were loading another round to destroy my hovertank next. I couldn't tell, and I couldn't afford to stop the turrets.

"Dammit, Kerr," I whispered to myself. I sweated and watched as we slid by. The turrets slowed their firing, then stopped altogether. Whoever they had been, they were all dead or hiding now.

"Pull on to the beach!" I shouted on the open channel. "Which tank was hit?"

"The *Rommel*, sir," said a voice.

I sighed. That was Robinson's tank. Had he gone through the nanite injections, the hours of agony, not to mention my brutal recruitment techniques, only to be splattered in the first minutes of this battle? "We'll go back and search for survivors," I said.

"Let's keep moving, Riggs," said Crow, second-guessing me again.

"Patton, mute transmission to broadcast channel. Open private channel to the *Napoleon*."

"Options set," said the tank.

"What now?" barked Crow.

"I'm not leaving Robinson and his men in the ocean, sir."

"I thought we were sneaking up on the base. We've still got several miles to go."

"I think it's clear the enemy understands our intent now. We need to reconfigure these vehicles into battle mode and move down to the target area as battle tanks."

Crow argued for a few more seconds, but finally dropped it. I figured he'd been rattled by the hit and had wanted to keep moving fast. I didn't say so aloud, but I did ask him to stop countermanding my operational orders or I would leave him on the beach as well. Grumbling, he broke the connection.

We did manage to pick up about half the lost men. Each of the surviving tanks took two aboard. I was pleased to see Major Robinson himself climb aboard the *Patton*.

"Robinson! You are a hard man to kill."

"Thank you, sir. I think…" he said.

Looking him over, I could tell one of his legs didn't operate properly. "You can ride on my tank when we reconfigure. There are some ledges for people to hold on to."

Robinson smiled through the pain he clearly felt. "Mighty considerate of you, sir."

We disgorged our infantry and reconfigured the tanks on the beach. Nearby, the Queen's Highway turned into a causeway and crossed the open sea. South of us was Andros Town, long since abandoned, and further south was the location of our base, where the enemy waited with unknown strength.

The tanks reshaped themselves, taking about a minute to do so. The transformation was dramatic. They soon resembled sharks instead of whales. The transformation continued, flatting out the round contours and forming slanting surfaces. When they were finished, the metal of every wall had been thickened to more than an inch, enough to stop incoming bullets. The armor was relatively thin, but alive and very reactive. It would reshape itself after a hit. I hoped it would do well against conventional weaponry. Looming atop each tank was a swiveling beam-cannon mount. The cannons scanned everything, softly whirring as they moved. Watching them gave me a 'creeped-out' feeling. I could tell they had an intelligence to them—albeit an artificial, alien one. The way they moved and scanned their surroundings was uncanny. They would frequently pause, aiming at an individual marine. They sensed you, measured you and made decisions about you as a possible target. Every man knew that if you were ever classified as a hostile, you would be toast in seconds. The tanks reminded me of the Macros, of their behavior patterns. They were upsetting, and I doubted I would ever get used to them.

We took the time to pull our dead out of the water. I promised the men we would bury them later. I wasn't sure whether or not I was lying, but figured if we all died no one would remember the promise anyway.

We set off along the beach, continuing southward. I was inside my tank, but now I had a tiny slit cut into the metal around the pilot's chair. I could see my actual surroundings and that made things much easier than calculating the external situation by the metallic beads on the interior hull of the tank. Historically, tanks had performed better with a commander who could see the battle situation directly. When in a pitched battle, I could order the *Patton* to button up and seal the inside of the tank off completely. It was also programmed to automatically close the slits, like blinking eyes, if incoming fire was detected.

We got underway again, this time surrounded by racing infantry. The men were in full gear and had the job of taking out any enemy infantry and light vehicles. The hovertanks were for knocking out aircraft, missiles and heavy armor, if we encountered any.

For several miles, things went smoothly. We were down to traveling at about thirty miles an hour, but that was fast enough. It would be much harder, at these speeds, for an enemy to ambush us. The hovertanks would have time to sense them and target them, hopefully before they could fire again.

The second ambush was the test of my hopes. It came as I watched the beach slide by, catching the fresh ocean breezes that came into my tank through the open slits. The salty tang of the air made me wish for easier times. I remembered the days before the Macros had returned with their battle fleet, when I'd nothing more serious on my mind than keeping Sandra happy.

We made it down to a point of land with plenty of foliage on it that thrust out into the open ocean. I could have followed the Queen's Highway inland, but I didn't want to be stuck in a column formation by trees. So, we glided along the beach, our tanks drifting out over the waves themselves.

The racing troops around us saw the enemy first, or maybe they began taking incoming fire. I wasn't sure which it was, but they began to light up the trees with their heavy beamers. The weapons were overkill, really. I thought as the battle began that I should have developed a hand-held beamer for anti-personnel purposes. My men could have carried one in each hand and left the heavy backpack reactors behind. The heavy weapons were designed to take out hundred-foot tall robots, not enemy soldiers of thin flesh and blood.

Swathes were cut from the jungle. Flames exploded in orange mushrooms and tree trunks burst as if mined by plastique charges. Smoke billowed up in gray gushes from the wet jungle. It had rained recently, and when my men's searching beams darted out into the forest everything the shafts of energy touched turned instantly to vapor.

At first, automatic fire chattered back. Yellow spots of fire blazed back at us. A few of my men spun around, tripped, fell into the wet sand. Blood blossomed in the seawater, but every one of them got back up. My marines were armored and dense. I knew when they went down it was mostly from the kinetic force of being hit by a dozen rounds, not from serious injury.

"All tanks hold fire unless heavier targets show themselves," I shouted over the open channel. "Infantry advance and drive them out of there."

I knew all the tanks should have been set to only fire at larger targets, but I didn't want any of my green pilots to get excited and tell their vehicles to fire. Blue-on-blue friendly-fire would take out my infantry faster than anything I'd seen from the enemy.

My marines sprang forward, closing with the enemy hiding in the trees. I didn't see much of the action once they reached the green gloom of the forest, but I did see the flashes of released energy. It was brief and violent. My men came walking back out of the trees about three minutes later, and only a few were injured.

"Mission accomplished, sir," reported a lieutenant.

"Load the wounded on the running boards of the tanks. They can heal up as we head down to finish this."

I had just begun to think this was all going to be a cakewalk, when Robinson spoke up on the general channel. "Contacts sir, coming in fast from the east again."

I turned my attention to my forward 'screen'. There were incoming coppery beads again. They were way out, but coming in very fast. They had to be planes. I'd been so involved in the land action, watching through the slits in my turret, I'd forgotten about the primary purpose of my hovertank, which was to cover the force against enemy vehicles and aircraft.

"Button up, everyone. Close those slits."

"Looks like they must have a carrier group out there, sir," said Robinson, watching the incoming planes. "They are coming from the same area and there aren't any bases on my map in that zone."

"I agree, Major," I said, watching as the contacts multiplied. I counted a dozen aircraft. Seconds later, there were more than twenty. "And I doubt I'll be able to talk them into turning back this time."

-18-

I ordered my exposed marines to take cover and scatter, then watched the planes come in for several long seconds. How was I going to handle this? Tension filled my belly. Slaughtering Earth's best pilots had never been my desire. These were the very men I wanted to recruit to fly my new fleet of spacecraft, should I ever manage to build them.

Crow contacted me on a private channel. "I get it!" he said. He cackled.

"Get what?"

"You're going to let them come in fast and take them out when they are too close to get away, aren't you? That will make the brass notice. A full fighter wing, gone."

The result he described was the furthest thing from my goal—but he was right, that was the direction in which things were headed. Crow's words goaded me into action.

"Patton, target the lead aircraft," I said. "Reduce wattage output to five percent and fire in bursts, separated by one second."

I opened the general channel, "hold your fire, everyone."

I could hear Crow's harsh, unpleasant laughter, which continued unabated. He still believed I was luring them in for the kill. I watched for one second, then two. Suddenly, the lead aircraft fell out of formation. It twisted and lost speed.

"Patton, target the second nearest aircraft and repeat previous firing orders."

Quickly, the second jet broke off. The plane twisted and spiraled this time. I watched with grim determination. "Cease fire on second aircraft, target third aircraft."

"What the hell are you doing?" asked Crow.

"I'm blinding them," I said.

"What?"

"Low-output laser strikes over long range and obscured by the atmosphere. Enough to disable them, but not kill them."

"What if they have heavy autoshades?"

I watched the third craft go down, slanting to toward the sea. "It appears that they don't," I said.

"Dammit, if you don't kill them, they will hit us later."

"Jack, these are the sort of men we need as pilots for our future forces. We don't want to destroy our own people, we want them to see reason, and respect us."

"Big dogs only respect a hard blow to the snout, Riggs."

"I'm in command here, Jack. Riggs out."

After the fourth plane went down, they got the message and turned around. They did fire a storm of missiles at us, however, before they broke off. We shot the missiles down easily, then turned our hovertanks around and drove the final miles to the main camp.

We found the place deserted. They must have gotten the message down here on the ground, too. I climbed out of the *Patton* and walked to the same command bunker where I'd first confronted General Sokolov, Barrera and Robinson. Behind me was a squad of marines and Crow. I ordered the rest of my men to sweep the area and secure it.

There were only two men in the command bunker. One was General Kerr, the other was Major Barrera. The Major was in restraints, and he appeared to have been abused. He bent forward, his face cut-up, his head slumped.

"Is he dead?" I asked the General.

"No, just napping."

"Why are you still here?"

"I wanted to talk to you, Riggs."

"Then talk," I said.

"No," said Crow, shouldering through my marines. "You'll talk to *me*."

Kerr and I looked at him. Kerr turned back to me. "I'm surprised you haven't ditched this two-bit pirate yet, Riggs."

"You are under arrest," Crow said importantly.

The marines flicked their eyes to me. I gave them a small nod.

"I'm unarmed," Kerr said as my men approached him. They surrounded him with their beamers ready. He eyed the weapons warily, knowing that any one of them had the firepower to kill a Bradley.

"What are you doing here, Kerr?" I asked.

"Surrendering to you," he said in a mild voice.

"You didn't put up much of a fight."

Kerr shrugged. "I never had much to fight with. Just a few misguided followers and dupes."

"What?"

Kerr fished in his pockets, making my men flinch. He took out his pipe. They looked mildly amused as he lit up and began to smoke it. The room quickly filled with blue, aromatic fumes. Ignoring my men and their beamers, he walked over crunching, broken glass to the big bay window overlooking the ocean.

"Nice view," he said. "You should get this window fixed."

I thought of Sokolov's face as he went out that very window just a few days earlier. "Thanks for your concern," I said. "Now tell us what's going on."

"I'm a rogue. This mission was never authorized by anyone," he said with certainty. He took his pipe out of his mouth and waved it around, using it as a pointer. "All of this was unauthorized. A phenomenon of inter-departmental confusion. Operational-level control gone awry. I went off the tracks, you see. Now I've lost my gambit for personal glory, and you've captured me. My crazy adventure has come to a sad finish."

We stared at him. I nodded slowly. "I imagine this story about you having an adventure is all over the news by now?"

"Looks that way. Turn on the television. Read the blogs online. Everyone is regretting the unfortunate misunderstanding. Everyone wants to heal these regrettable wounds I've caused the heroes of Star Force."

"Wounds that you've caused—single-handedly?" I asked.

"Yes, I did it all. The President himself will make an apologetic statement tonight, I believe. He'll explain the terrible stresses upon

101

military personnel, caused by the recent anti-alien campaign. He'll reach out to you. He'll talk about—talking-points."

"That's what we get? An apology?" roared Crow, his rage finally boiling over.

"A *heart-felt* apology," Kerr corrected him calmly. "But that's just the beginning of the healing process. Round-table discussions will be offered. Wrong-headed thinkers will be expunged from the Pentagon—that's a promise you can bank on, gentlemen. Have no qualms, independent investigations will be launched. This will all be handled at the highest possible levels."

"That has to be the biggest stack of shit I've ever heard," said Crow, marveling. The other marines in the room nodded their heads in agreement. Kerr looked slightly proud.

"Let me see if I have this straight, General," I said, trying to control the anger creeping into my voice. "The administration wanted to attack us, but now they've failed, and they want to maintain the fiction that you were the sole perpetrator. The cover-story proposes you went a little funny in the head. I gather you led an unauthorized mission down here to plunder our island?"

"It's no cover-story, it's fact," said Kerr.

"They left you behind to tell us this?" I asked. "To shut us up?"

"Not at all. You captured me fair and square."

"In other words," I said, "you are an embarrassment to the administration now that you failed."

"I'm just a renegade. A madman. I deserve my fate."

"What if I go on live TV and tell the people the truth. What if I tell the world what really happened down here?"

Kerr aimed his pipe at me in an accusatory gesture. "That's the sort of talk we don't need right now. Humanity faces extinction. Let's pull it together as a single world and stop the alien menace."

"Let's kill him," suggested Crow. "No one will blame us with that cover story."

I stared at Crow and sighed. His eyes were bulging again. His cheeks were red. I had to admit, his idea was appealing. Kerr watched us both quietly.

"What about him?" I said, indicating Barrera.

"He's napping," said Kerr.

"I mean, what did you do to him and why?"

Kerr shrugged. "He was interrogated. He withheld the requested information. I think the process tired him out."

A wide, vicious grin spread on Crow's face. "That gives me an idea. We'll take little slices out of our fine General. We'll shoot his legs with nanites, repair his tissues, and do it again. It might take weeks, but we'll get everything he knows. I'll know his mum's shoe size. Every name and detail."

For the first time, Kerr's tough exterior crumpled a bit. His face appeared to glisten slightly. His pipe went out and he didn't bother to relight it. His eyes searched my face as I considered the matter.

I nodded. "Your idea has merit, Admiral. Let's go outside for a moment."

I directed two men to watch Kerr and another to try to wake up Barrera, then followed Crow. As I stepped outside onto the sandy soil, I couldn't help but look upward to the patch of sky where I'd last seen the *Alamo* hovering. I wondered where the Nano ship was, and if Sokolov was still aboard her, somewhere in the cosmos, screaming. I felt sorry for everyone trapped aboard those ships.

The beach wasn't far off, and once again I promised myself a fine vacation on the windy, white sands. I'd get a tan, and I'd watch Sandra's tan deepen. I looked at the bright blue waves and white foam. Strips of seaweed were visible forming dark, curving lines along the beach.

I excused myself from Crow for a minute. I stood apart from the buildings and marines. I worked my com-link, trying to contact Sergeant Kwon.

"Kwon? This is Riggs."

"Sir? One second."

I waited, worrying. Was he in some kind of trouble? I didn't hear any gunfire.

"Where's Sandra, Kwon?" I asked, unable to contain myself.

"She's right here, sir. We are driving south to your position. How are things? Did we retake the camp?"

"Yes. Yes we did."

"Was it a big battle, sir?" asked Kwon.

I looked around at the calm beach and the quiet buildings. There was a little damage, but not much. A few bullet holes. Something over in the direction of the mess hall was smoldering, but I didn't see any flames. Kerr and his men had marched into the camp after

Barrera had sent his garrison to me with Crow at the lead. This attempted coup had been much smaller than I'd realized. It was nothing at all compared to the titanic battles we'd fought against the Macros in South America.

I thought more deeply, however, about the struggle for power between the entrenched world governments and the fledgling Star Force. I thought of the assassin, Esmeralda, who had fought me to the death aboard Pierre's ship. These fights had been relatively small, but perhaps each had helped decide our world's fate. They had certainly decided mine.

"Yes Kwon," I said at last. "It was a big battle. We won the day—this time."

-19-

Crow and I talked it over. We finally decided that Kerr would be more forthcoming—or at least less full of crap—if he and I talked alone. Crow seemed to take this as a hint that I meant to lean on Kerr. He was excited by the prospect.

"Okay," he said. "Just you and the good General. But don't go easy on him, Kyle. And don't trust a word he says."

I had to agree with Crow's point of view. I had no intention of being bamboozled by this Kerr. I had no stomach for actual torture, however. I didn't tell Crow that, figuring he might figure I needed help.

I moved Kerr to the medical facility next door where we often strapped men in to administer the nanite treatments. He walked in and dubiously examined the stainless steel chair and restraints. The leather loops were torn apart and the metal buckles had snapped.

"What's this about?" he asked, trying to sound disinterested.

"This chair is where we put men who are undergoing nanite-transformation."

"The restraints are all broken," he pointed out.

"Yes, well, that happens fairly often," I said. "Unfortunately, no reasonable set of leather straps can hold one of our raving marines, not once his strength has been enhanced by a full dose of nanites."

"Why strap them in at all, then?"

"The transformations vary. Some men just puke and faint. Others rave and seek to damage themselves, but that phase usually passes before they become strong. In short, the chair and the restraints work for most men, but not all."

Kerr licked his lips. There were dark smears of dried blood on the flat, reflective arms of the chair. I wondered if electric chairs looked like that. I'd never seen one in person.

"Seems like you could build metal restraints," Kerr said. "Manacles the men couldn't break."

"We tried that," I said. "It was a disaster. The men who went wild tore loose anyway, leaving their hands and exposed wrist-bones behind, if necessary. Repairing a man at that point takes much longer and is more traumatic for everyone. The leather straps hold most people, and those that break them have to be dealt with individually."

Kerr nodded. "Such a sacrifice," he said.

"Yes, it is," I said. I watched him, wondering if he was feeding me more bullshit. I didn't think he was, but I no longer trusted my own judgment around this man. He had fooled me as few people ever had.

"Let's talk, General," I said. "Just you and I, off the record."

"An excellent idea."

"Can you tell me why so many fine men had to die here on this island? Why their blood is on your hands—and mine?"

I think that statement got to him, if only for a second. He nodded. "All right. I think you've earned a bit of truth from me."

Kerr looked around for a place to dump his ashes. Not finding anything reasonable, he tapped them out on the stainless steel arm of the chair. A gray little pile of smoldering dust formed among the bloodstains and ripped leather straps.

"I think you understand most of the score by now," he said. "This took us all by surprise. I had to move down here with whatever assets I could, within a few hours. The military just doesn't move that fast. There never was a full taskforce down here. We had a group of subs to send tomahawks at you. Choppers brought in a team of commandos and snipers from Florida to harass your camp. The carrier group just got into range this morning, and you managed to send them packing. The few companies of regular troops which I put up north you took apart easily."

I absorbed this information quietly. I'd been bluffed. There had been no full scale invasion. They had bullied and herded my men without a tenth of our strength. Without our Nano ships and our communications systems, we'd been thrown into confusion. This was what people liked to call a *teachable moment*.

"The administration has undergone a change of heart," Kerr continued. "The takeover was supposed to be quick and quiet. No one was to know the details, but things became messy and drawn out. You managed to do us enough damage and resist long enough for the press to get involved."

"How did the public take the news?" I asked. "What did they think when they learned you were invading the island and taking apart Star Force?"

"You haven't seen any broadcasts or web feeds?"

I gave him a wintry smile. "I've been busy fighting for my life."

Kerr nodded. "The public reaction has been—extreme. They see us as the invaders, backstabbers, the killers of heroes. Within twenty-four hours the story had leaked worldwide and public opinion was all in your favor. We'd blundered and created our own Bay of Pigs. America is still something of a democracy, you know, and elections are coming in fall. All congressional support for the action evaporated as soon as they heard you were holding out in your secret base. It was a worst case scenario, your little Alamo. We knew sooner or later some reporterette would make it down here to interview you."

"So, what's your new role?"

"I'm—an advisor. A permanent one, stationed here with you."

"In other words, you are my hostage."

"A rude, archaic term."

"But strangely descriptive of the situation," I said. "Tell me General, what was it that set you off so badly as to try this stunt? I thought we had a good relationship until all this."

He shrugged. "The administration is feeling their way, Kyle. Like everyone else. Your fleet flew away. We saw the opportunity. We began to get paranoid, thinking that *others* would also see the opportunity. It started off as a discussion concerning the factories. So much alien tech could not be allowed into the hands of another nation. If you couldn't keep it secure—then we had to step in, we had to secure it."

I nodded, for the most part buying his statements. "What about the talk of EMPs and neutron bombs?" I asked.

107

"That was mostly bullshit," Kerr said. "Less than a division of fast-responders and a carrier group, that's all we could get down here quickly. Anything else was going to take weeks to assemble. I feared that if we gave you that long, you would have sealed this island off tightly."

I stared at him. I realized that I had been bluffed. I'd bought all his talk of nukes and advanced weaponry. I laughed aloud. "You slippery bastard," I said. "The man who never bluffs. I thought you had the fancy stuff. You snowed me."

A smile played over Kerr's lips. "You didn't do too badly yourself. But I must say, your surprises were far more deadly than mine."

I thought about it. In real military terms, we'd creamed them. They had sent down troops, and they'd all been taken out almost without loss on our side. I frowned, thinking about our little meeting at the edge of the forest at midnight.

"Why didn't you have a sniper take me out then? That night amongst the Bradleys?"

"Because you blinded them all the night before, you prick."

I nodded and frowned. "About the pilots and snipers. Those are good men we've seriously injured. We might be able to work something out. They were only following orders."

"The nanites?" he asked.

I nodded.

"What would your terms be?" Kerr asked.

"No terms. If they want to join Star Force, they can. We'll shoot them with nanites, no charge. They will be able to see again."

Kerr snorted. "So, blinding my men was all part of your recruitment efforts, eh? Rude, but I'm sure they will be grateful. The administration will love it too, as it would be good PR all around." Kerr relit his pipe and puffed it. His calm exterior had reasserted itself.

"I would naturally hope my generosity would be reciprocated."

"Here it comes," Kerr said.

"We need raw materials to keep—producing things. To allow us to meet the needs of the Macros. So we can continue to build Earth's armies and rebuild her fleet."

Kerr narrowed his eyes. "Would you be willing to give us a single machine? Just to study. We're very curious about them."

"So I've noticed," I said. "We can't do that right now. I need them all to repair the damage done to my organization. After the Macros come and go—if we have a planet left—I'll consider it then."

Kerr looked disappointed. "Selfish of you. What are you going to do with all those machines?"

I found his attitude annoying. "We're going to build hundreds of automated laser turrets. We'll ring this island with them. No plane or ship will ever be allowed within ten miles of the coast again without express permission."

Kerr shrugged. "A reasonable precaution."

"We'll never fully trust you again," I told him.

"You should never have fully trusted us in the first place."

-20-

I left the General in the care of two angry marines. The sandy ground crunched beneath my boots as I headed back toward the command bunker.

The thing that galled me the most—even more than having been fooled into walking out of a base I could have held onto—was knowing I would have to go along with their charade. I would have to pretend to accept the president's *heartfelt* apologies. There wasn't any choice, really. What good would it do to reveal the truth? How would Earth's defenses be strengthened by my angry public rebuttals of the administration's story? Star Force would look weak and foolish. The Pentagon would look dishonorable. The facts would only sow future discord.

Cooperating now was going to be difficult at best, but it had to be done. If we publicly declared we were angry, abused and distrustful, it would only magnify the problem. We would have to be careful, of course. In the future, we would have to follow the old Reagan doctrine: *trust, but verify.* In other words, we would smile and say we trusted everything they did or said. But once the cameras were off, we would check out everything with paranoid attention to detail.

Eventually, slowly, pretending often turned into actual cooperation. Just look at the treaty ending any war. Years later, nations that were at each other's throats frequently turned into tight allies. I felt like General George Washington, leading my ragtag army to a surprise victory over the British. I only hoped we could grow to work together in the future. I couldn't help but be nagged by the reminder that it took the Americans and the British a very long time to become allies. The War of 1812, for example, stuck out in my mind.

I took a deep breath and let it out slowly. It was going to be a difficult year. Pulling everything together in time for the return of the Macros was going to be the work of a magician. And my hat was all out of rabbits.

Sandra beat me back to the command bunker. She threw open the door of a Humvee, driven by the hulking shape of First Sergeant Kwon. He hadn't quite stopped rolling, and he slammed on the brakes. She bounced out and intercepted me. The marines guarding the entrance smiled with half their mouths, bemused.

The kiss would have lasted a long time, but I gently pushed her away. Marines all around the camp were glancing and chuckling.

"You lived," she said.

I squinted, fully expecting her to slap me for something. She didn't though. She must have felt the fifty pair of eyes that watched us.

"We both did," I said. I pointed out to the beach. She followed my gaze to the ocean, where one breaker after another rolled in over the cream-white sand. "That's where I want to take you. I want to spend a week with you on a beach."

"That sounds perfect."

"I can't today, however. I have to set things up. I have to shore up our defenses."

"Didn't we win? I've been listening to the radio—it works again. They say it was all a big mistake."

"They are right about that," I said. "Kerr tells me we won. Should I take his word for that?"

She tore her eyes from the rolling seas and looked at me seriously. "Hell no."

"Exactly," I said. "So the first thing I'm going to do is build and set up more laser turrets. A lot more of them."

She nodded. "You're right. And after that?"

"After that, I'll reset the machines to build new forces."

"What kind of forces?"

"The kind that will keep the Macros from destroying us when they come back."

She smiled. "It's hard to argue with those goals. Can we vacation after that?"

"Yes. I think so."

She leaned her head against my shoulder. The touch was so light, it felt as if a butterfly hand landed there. I thought about that, how light her touches were now that I'd been nanotized. They were maddening, teasing.

"I can wait that long," she said.

"I didn't say I would never take breaks."

She smiled up at me and nodded. I knew, if the guys hadn't been staring, she would have jumped on me. Her hair was long these days, and the wind coming in from the sea made it dance and stream in dark lines around her face. I managed to get her to the mess hall, where men were already at work cleaning up. Our regular staff had fled, so we would have to make do with slop made by our fellow marines for now. I left her there, promising to return when I could, and went back to check on the situation in the command center.

Barrera was awake now, but he didn't look happy. His face was a rictus of pain. We'd given him a shot of nanites—not the full treatment, just an emergency injection. I felt for him, the nanites were sewing up flesh in a thousand spots at once. I'd felt those ant-like, prickling sensations on many occasions.

"This is what the nanites feel like?" he managed to hiss out between his teeth.

"Yeah. Sort of burns, doesn't it?"

"You could say that. How long does it last?"

"A few hours. Better than three weeks of healing up. You'll be combat ready very soon."

"Better for whom?"

I regarded him. "Barrera, have I told you my new policy."

His eyes, squinting almost shut, slid to regard me. I saw a gash in his cheek gleam with a single flash of light. It seemed like it was full of mercury, or hot solder. The liquid metal rippled inside the wound.

"What policy?" he grunted out.

"About officers being required to undergo the full nanite treatment."

"More of this joy, eh?"

I nodded. "Exactly. But not so itchy-burny. More like they are tearing your guts out, rebuilding them, and stuffing them back in."

He nodded. "Do I have to do it now?"

"Why not get it over with? What are you saving yourself for, man?"

He managed a grin, but it was little more than a slit revealing his teeth. "Yes sir. Could someone help me to the chair?"

I waved a marine forward. It was a corporal, and he looked sympathetic.

"If you feel the urge to rip at something, try your clothes or your thighs," I told him. "People tell me you can satisfy the need and do much less damage that way."

"I'll try to keep that in mind, sir," said Barrera as the corporal half-walked, half-carried him out the door.

Barrera and Crow passed each other at the entrance to the command center. Crow swaggered as he came in, hands on his hips. "We kicked their asses, as you Yanks love to say."

"We certainly did, sir. Too bad it took us so long to figure out we'd won. We could have killed fewer men in the process."

Crow waved away my negative words as if they stunk up the air. "Never mind that. She'll be right, mate. Now, what did you get out of that smug prick Kerr?"

I told him about the arrangements, and was able to convince him we needed to play along with the fictional cover-story.

"Such a devilish web of lies we weave, eh, Kyle?" he asked.

"I wouldn't know about that, sir."

Crow grinned suddenly, expectantly. He clapped his hands together. "Okay, so we are back in business. Now, how soon can you crank out a fleet for me?"

-21-

Nearly two months later I finally had Andros Island ringed with automated beam turrets. We still had no ships in the sky, but we felt secure.

Sandra complained bitterly about the turrets, saying they were 'creepy'. They never stopped moving, it seemed, and she found this disturbing.

"Have you watched those damned things?" she asked me. "They are always tracking someone or something. It's as if they examine everyone, thinking about us. Every seabird that hops along in the surf, every fluttering palm frond. If no one is around, they scan the skies and look at the waves or the clouds as if studying the movements."

"They are building their neural nets," I told her.

"They are freaky."

"Yes, but only because they are machines. If a bird in a tree watched you that way, you wouldn't feel disturbed."

"I would if the bird could kill me at any moment."

I had to give her that one. I shrugged. "They are still young. They are like kids, trying to figure the world out around them. They do learn, but in a more limited way. They are classifying everything around them as normal and safe."

"Why are they always checking me out then?"

I grinned. "Obviously, they are good judges of character."

"Maybe they are better at it than I am."

I thought I might have been insulted, but I went on unconcernedly. "When they see something new, they are very curious about it. They want to know if you are a good, safe thing, or a bad dangerous thing. They have already figured out the trees and the birds. You are something new."

"When I walk near, they aim their big guns at me and I know what they are thinking."

"What's that?" I asked, bemused.

"They are thinking about killing me every second. I can *feel* them."

I shrugged. "I guess we will have to get used to them."

"What if they get smarter, Kyle? Did you ever think about that? What if they talk to each other somehow, and get ideas? What if one of them, just one of them, decides to go crazy and starts burning down everyone in sight? What will you do then?"

I tried to let the air out of my lungs without sighing. "I know they are disturbing, Sandra. What do you want me to do about it? We have to keep the governments of the world at bay. They won't try to invade again as long as we have them outgunned."

She pouted and walked around my office, messing with things. She picked up all my pens, including the stylus for my tablet computer, and put them all into a cup.

"Look," I said, "let's make plans for later. I'll finish up what I'm working on and we'll go to the beach, okay?"

Sandra didn't answer. She cruised by my desk and looked over my shoulder at my tablet. I reached up and retrieved my stylus from the cup she had deposited it into and tapped at the screen.

Her face suddenly slid close to mine, making my neck tingle. I could feel her warmth there. She whispered into my ear. "Not okay."

I swiveled my chair around to face her, half-smiling. "What's plan B?"

"Plan B? You come with me to the beach, right the hell *now*, or I'm going alone."

"The turrets will keep you company."

Sandra huffed out. My eyes followed her, admiring her shapely rear end. She paused in the doorway. She slipped off her pants and top. Underneath, she wore a bikini. It wasn't much of a bikini. Technically, I'd classify it as a network of pink straps. She left the rest of her clothes in a heap in the doorway and walked away.

I got up out of my chair. A man has to recognize when he's been beaten. I trotted after her and together we headed out to the beach.

We walked until we were as far from the nearest beam turret as we could get, which was nearly a mile. We could see two of them at that point, one to the north and one to the south. I gazed at them, and they were indeed creepy. While I watched, they targeted and scanned everything. Once every few minutes, one or the other of them seemed to notice us on the beach and tracked us for several seconds before moving on to a new target.

"What if we have kids, Kyle?" Sandra asked suddenly.

"Uh…" I said.

Sandra reached up and pushed my chin upward, closing my mouth with a snap. My teeth clacked together and I must have looked confused. She frowned up at me.

"Don't pass out or puke or anything," she said, suddenly angry.

Inside I wondered how I'd stepped into this. Was it even possible I could have avoided it? I decided to keep up the dumb act. "I'm not sure what you mean."

"Noooo," she said, "I'm not pregnant."

"That's good," I said. "Right?"

"I'm talking about these machines, Kyle. What if we had kids, and they went out to play on this beach, and those things were tracking them all the time. Staring at them. Would you be cool with that?"

I blinked and tried to follow her logic. I had trouble. "You don't like them because—because they might threaten kids we don't have yet?"

She walked off a dozen steps, shielding her eyes from the blazing sun. She pointed up at the one that was closer. I took the opportunity to admire her figure. I almost missed what she said next.

"There it goes. See? It just noticed my movement. It's looking over here. I'm about a mile away, and it's still tracking me and thinking about burning me."

"They don't shoot harmless people, Sandra."

"Well, you had better make damned sure they know what they're doing. What if I ran up and kissed you, would they freak out?"

"Let's experiment," I said, stepping back a few paces. I braced myself for impact. "Okay, get up some speed and make it look real."

She twisted her lips, not falling for it. "How about if a kid ran around aiming a stick at them?"

I appeared to consider the idea. Mostly, I wondered how I could get out of this conversation unscathed. I had been hoping to get a little reward for letting her lure me out onto the beach hours earlier than I had intended. Instead, I was being interrogated on hypotheticals.

"They are more interested in real weapons," I told her. "Anything that emits dangerous radiation or projectiles. They won't trigger on something simple, like throwing a rock on them."

"You could blow them up then," she said, looking down the beach. "I think I should try it. What if I just walked up to the base and left a bag of plastique there and walked away. I could blast it apart. You could have commandos walk up to each one, unarmed, seemingly innocent. I wonder if the other side will ever figure that one out."

I frowned. "I hate to say it, but you might be right. I'm going to have to work on that angle."

Sandra bounced over to me excitedly. "Are you going to actually blow one up? I want to do it."

I snorted. "You really hate them, don't you?"

She finally started kissing on me. I think she liked the fact that she had managed to come up with a worry I hadn't thought of. I responded to her touch as I was genetically predisposed to do. Sometimes, when we made out like this, I wondered if this relationship really would explode in my face at the end of two years. I mentally counted the months I supposedly had left. They didn't seem adequate. Maybe the relationship-calculus didn't apply to college professors who had moved on to bigger things. It was a hope, anyway.

"Hold your arm up," she commanded.

I smiled indulgently and did so. I held my arm out stiffly at shoulder-level, parallel to the beach. She climbed up there and perched on my arm like some kind of happy, sexy bird. I walked along the beach while we both smiled. Holding her up was easy for me as she didn't weigh much over a hundred pounds, but I had to lean in the other direction to keep from tipping over.

"I need another girl on the other side to balance me out," I said, my mouth being faster than my brain at times.

She tweaked my ear viciously.

"That hurts my feelings," I said.

Sandra hopped down from my arm, ran into the waves and splashed me as I chased her. We ended up making love out there in the ocean. I kept checking the beach for prying eyes, but didn't see anyone.

Only the beam turrets watched us with silent, alien interest.

-22-

We sent General Kerr back to the mainland six months after his failed invasion. Truthfully, he had become kind of a pain by then. I really didn't want him snooping around, looking at everything we were doing. Publicly, he was our prisoner. Privately, he operated as a liaison. But I suspected he was more of a spy than anything else. Crow came up with the release idea. Kerr had to go undercover to go back home, of course. The public believed he was the architect of a coup. He was a spook now, and I don't think he liked it.

"You know what's worse than dying for your country, Riggs?" he asked me the night before he shipped out.

"What?"

"Living on as a ruined man, having sacrificed everything, and then witnessing firsthand how little everyone cares."

I eyed him. He seemed sincere. I fell silent and looked around the base.

We'd named it by now, and I pressed for a new tradition: we would name places after our fallen. So, the base was now Fort Pierre. Sure, to deserve the name we should have filled it with red velvet settees. We were fresh out of them, however. We had to make do with corrugated steel, concrete and conical beam-turrets.

Fort Pierre had doubled in size over recent months. We had more troops, supplies and buildings than ever. I'd set up weighing stations recently as well. I'd learned that a fully-equipped and operational fireteam of four marines weighed in at just over a single metric ton. Of course, most of the material we'd be loading onto the Macro ship in six more months wouldn't be the troops themselves. Each troop needed to eat, for example.

In the sky overhead, a black chopper slid over the treetops. It had come in from the sea. Some kind of ship out there past our borders had sent it in. There were no landing lights on the chopper. It was dark and quieter than a normal bird. I supposed that no one back home wanted to advertise who they were picking up tonight.

"Well," I said to Kerr, "if you ever need a new home, we are still recruiting."

Kerr looked at me in surprise. "Really?"

I nodded.

"In what capacity?"

"Everyone here starts fresh. Latrines don't dig themselves, sir."

He huffed. "Thanks for the offer," he said, then as the quiet chopper landed, he climbed inside and buzzed away into the night sky.

"Good riddance," Major Barrera said from behind me.

I turned and nodded to him. "He's finally gone. Have you finished the loyalty checks?"

Barrera nodded. He stood with his hands behind his back. I'd made him my Security Chief. He was paranoid and thorough. I could not recall ever having seen him give more than the slightest smile. He was perfect for the job.

"Now that Kerr is gone," he said, "there's no one on this base I don't trust…. Within reason, that is."

"Make the call," I told him. "Roll in the tanks."

People had seen them before, naturally. Every man on the island knew we had a ground force. But very few knew how many I'd built. I'd been hiding them until Kerr left.

An hour later, as the column arrived, I thought to myself I might have overdone it. Sixty hovertanks glided into the base, and another sixty remained in secret reserve at strong points around the island. Barrera played traffic cop, directing them to slide underneath a dozen camouflaged structures around the base. The militaries of the world had been busy putting up new satellites to replace the ones the Macros had knocked down, but they had less than a tenth their previous number. Still, I didn't want any of them to get lucky and get a clear count of our numbers.

The hovertanks were built to serve two purposes. First, they would aid in any defense of the island. The beam turrets were powerful and symbolic, but vulnerable. If NATO or someone else got a wild idea for a new sneak attack, they might very well knock out my static defensive line. The tanks were my backup, they were my inner line of defense. They could stop any invasion by themselves, I felt sure.

Their second purpose involved the Macros. Many of these sleek tanks would be going with us when the Macros came back, demanding their cargo. After seeing their effectiveness when combined with my ground troops, I'd decided they would be indispensible to any campaign on a distant world.

Crow came out to complain while the column continued to rumble out of the forest.

"You went nuts, Kyle. I thought that was our deal, that you wouldn't do anything crazy."

"It's in my nature, Admiral," I said.

"You promised me a new fleet, Kyle. What the hell are we going to do with all these tanks?" he demanded.

I turned to Crow. Barrera watched the two of us quietly. He was quiet for an officer, and that alone made me want to promote him.

The three of us stood in the middle of camp, far from the barracks and other buildings. We watched as the tanks lined up neatly under their netted camouflage. I knew that infrared systems from satellites overhead would show their engines, but I hoped they wouldn't quite know yet what they were looking at. The tanks gleamed and the sands beneath them rippled and flattened as they passed over. They left tracks of a sort; it looked as if a giant beach ball had rolled over the land.

"You screwed me, didn't you?" Crow asked. "This is your way of doing it, of removing me from power. You aren't going to build me any ships. You command the ground forces, and—"

"I wish I'd thought of that, sir," I told Crow, smiling. "Send in the prototype, Major Barrera."

"Yes sir," he said, and he spoke into his com-link. We'd gotten better at building communications systems now, too. His was a button on his collar. He ran his finger over it, and spoke into it quietly.

Crow looked at me in disbelief. "You mean?"

121

I nodded.

He spun around, looking up into the sky. A portion of it darkened, blotting out a slice of the starry night. Silently, something loomed over us.

"It's big," he said, his voice hushed. He looked like the kid who'd finally gotten that damned pony he could never shut up about.

"It's all yours," I said.

He looked at me with big eyes. "What's it like?"

"Just like *Snapper*, sir," I said. "But it has no system software out of our control. Also, it doesn't have an arm yet. And there is only one gun and one engine. No duplication equipment on board, either."

"Why not?"

"The reactor is too small to support it, and we wanted to build it fast."

"But it's big," he said, his eyes glittering.

"Yes sir, approximately fifty percent more displacement than the original Nano design."

"What the hell is taking up all that space?"

"Mostly air, sir," I explained.

He looked at me as if I was mad. "Just tell me one thing, Riggs."

"What's that, sir?"

"How do I get inside?"

"Tell the pilot to land it, Barrera," I said.

Barrera ran a finger over the extra button on his collar. He spoke quietly to it. Soon, the great ship came slowly down to rest in the open area in the middle of the base. We'd been using it as a picnic area, but originally, it had been there to fill landing pods with marines. Now, it would begin to see use again as a landing zone. Without arms, these newer, lighter, scarier-looking ships would have to land to pick people up.

"She's a beauty, Riggs," said Crow in a hushed voice. "What's she called?"

"Whatever you want to name her, Jack."

"I think I'll call her *Digger* in your honor, mate!"

I smiled and nodded—but I wasn't sure that I felt honored.

-23-

After finishing Crow's ship, I immediately began building another. This one was mine. I thought about naming her *Alamo*, but that seemed wrong somehow. It would reduce my acute emotions toward that ship. She had left me, and like a treacherous ex-wife, I still hated and loved her at the same time.

In the end, I decided to name the new ship *Socorro*. In 1964, Socorro, New Mexico had been the location of a famous UFO sighting. Until the 1970s, the incident and location was more famous than Roswell. I also liked the sound of *Socorro* because it was the name of a southwestern city, like Alamo.

The Socorro UFO sighting was historically very compelling to me now with the virtue of hindsight. The eyewitness was a policeman, and had described the ship he'd seen as *"a shiny type object ... oval in shape. It was smooth—no windows or doors."* There had been many explanations offered by the government over the years, but after recent events, I felt fairly certain the cop had seen a Nano ship. I felt sorry for him, and I lamented all the years of jokes he'd probably had to endure afterward.

I'd asked General Kerr repeatedly about UFO histories and what the government might have known before the invasion. He never told me anything useful. He provided me only with vague hints, talking about how the topic was 'above his pay grade' and was 'best left to the future historians'. I didn't buy his ignorance; in fact I was sure he'd been briefed. I figured the current administration didn't want to talk about what the government might have known and when. They didn't want the blame for any of this, so they had clammed up.

To me, the Nano ships were repositories of alien secrets. Stored within the factories and their creations, the ships had countless advanced technologies. These marvels were right here in our hands, but in many ways they were still unfathomable. I'd figured out enough of the alien tech to *use* their systems, but I didn't really *understand* them. I knew no more than how to make them operate. I was a user, not a developer. I was like a mathematician who did calculus on a computer—but who could not even add or subtract without it.

When I first boarded the *Socorro* a rush of nostalgia overwhelmed me. Not all of the memories were good. I thought about my kids, feeling their loss more intensely than I had for months. A ship just like this one had ended my family without a qualm—without an emotion of any kind.

The ship was cool inside, despite the blazing tropical sun outside. The light was very dim in comparison to the outside as well, and it took long seconds for my eyes to adjust to the softly radiant walls. I had no personal equipment inside her yet. She was barren, sterile and quiet. Her brainbox was raw—untrained. She'd been made to match the control systems of the *Alamo*, but without the deep systems programming the Blues had originally given their ships. She was like an unlocked device, a fully configurable technological toy—a freshly installed operating system.

"Ship, this is your commander. Respond."

"Responding. How do you wish to address us?"

At those words, a chill went through me. The *Alamo* had asked exactly the same thing long ago when I'd named her. Even more disturbing, the voice was absolutely identical in cadence and pronunciation to *Alamo*.

For some reason, I saw my daughter's terror-stricken, dead eyes. I had to close my own. I tried to erase the image from my mind, tried to push that memory back into the little box where I kept it.

"Ship, I name you *Socorro*."

"Rename complete."

Although *Socorro* was armed, she was not a twin to Crow's ship, *Digger*. I'd built her to be much faster. I hoped she would be a ship of discovery, rather than war. The hope wasn't a strong one, however. She was armed with a single turret, and she was built with the body-shape of a horseshoe crab, as the rest of the fleet would be. I did not want her to stand out in physical appearance in case I had to take her into battle. But *Socorro* had three engines rather than one, and a second reactor to keep the extra two engines fed with power.

I had smiled while watching each piece of her roll out of the factories. I'd worked long and hard to build her. Knowing I had many ships to construct, I'd first built a set of a team of vehicles that distinctly resembled my hovertanks. They glided between the great factories, working night and day, helping my nanotized men. These robotic workers were based upon the design of the hovertanks, but with huge, whip-like arms sprouting from their backs where the others had beam turrets. These were my newest creations, and they greatly eased the process of feeding supplies into the maws of my factories. They were critical in the extraction and assembly of finished components as well.

"Socorro," I said aloud, "I have some instructions for you...."

It took the better part of a day to get things organized. Most of the programming I read out loud to the ship. I had typed it in and now kept it stored on a tablet computer. I figured that with new ships being constructed every day now, I would need to have a script for new pilots to follow. I smiled just thinking about that. I realized I had written a program to teach humans to teach their ships. A script for writing scripts.

Hours later, I had the doors working at a touch, I had entry and exit codes set and emergency behaviors set. I managed to get the forward wall of the bridge crawling with metallic beetles, each representing a nearby marine, vehicle or building. I even had a working toilet.

I ordered the ship to lift off and I got my first shock. The ship lurched and knocked me off my feet. The sudden, upward motion was very jarring. I felt like I was in a box and a giant had just picked me up to look inside. I picked myself up off the floor and wondered why the motion had been so abrupt. Was it the group of three engines?

"Socorro," I said aloud. "Why was that lift-off so sudden?"

"Lift-off was within normal behavioral parameters."

"I've piloted ships like this before. That did not feel the same to me."

"Specify."

"I felt more G-forces than I felt aboard the *Alamo*."

Hesitation. "No ships with the designation *Alamo* can be found locally. Attempting long-range contact—"

"Hold!" I said. "Do not attempt any ship-to-ship communications without my authorization."

"Communications disabled. Permissions set."

I sat and sweated for a second. I didn't want this ship to contact the others—if that were even possible. I could only imagine what networking problems I might have. What if contacting the other Nano ships would automatically transfer some of their data ship-to-ship? What if my ship started *updating* itself, and soon thereafter decided to join the rest of her sisters on a mission in some remote star system?

My ships, I realized over the following cold seconds, had to be kept isolated from other Nano ships. I had no idea what kind of ideas they might get from one another, like viruses in email attachments or worms coming in through an unsecure network port.

I thought of Crow then. What had he done with his ship over the last day or two? I rubbed my neck. I shouldn't have given him the prototype ship. It was a rookie mistake for an engineer to make.

"Socorro, contact *Digger*," I said.

"Request denied. All ship-to-ship communications have been forbidden by command personnel."

I sighed. The ship's interface was very familiar. "Socorro, I am command personnel. If I directly request that you open a communications channel, that implicitly gives you authorization to do so."

"Permissions set. Communications enabled. Channel request accepted by *Digger*."

"Is that you, Kyle?" asked a familiar voice.

"Yeah, Crow. I'm glad to hear you are still alive. You aren't headed out into space, are you?"

"Ah—no. Listen Riggs, I could really use an arm on this ship. I'm spent the last day pushing furniture up a ramp by myself."

I snorted. "Nanites or not, exercise is never a bad thing."

"Says you. I've heard you've got an arm on that beast of yours."

I raised my eyebrows. I wasn't really surprised he had spies watching me, but I was surprised he'd let the truth slip out. "Do you want a big fleet produced quickly to meet the Macros? Or maybe I should build them to order with designer colors."

"What I want is to know why you rated an arm."

"Because I designed the ships," I said, grinning.

Crow grumbled incoherently for a few sentences in Aussie slang. I suspected I was being compared unfavorably to a kangaroo.

When his tirade died down, I dove in and explained the communications worries I had. I gave him a script that would allow communications with local ships of our design, but not with other 'wild' Nano ships.

"There's something else," I said, "before I panicked and ordered the ship to turn off communications to other Nanos, I was asking it about the increased effects of acceleration I've been feeling."

"Oooo," he said, "Poor baby! Three engines, I hear? You must have been plastered to the floor."

"How did you—" I said, but stopped myself. I knew he wouldn't tell me who was ratting on me, or how he'd gotten the rat's observations to his ship. But he would enjoy my irritation.

He laughed loudly, harshly. "Thought you could build a super-ship and give old Crow the trainer, did you? You figured I'd never even notice."

"We'll work on better ship designs after the Macros—" I began.

"Yeah, yeah. Easy on. I'll tell you why the ships are pasting us to the floor and the ceiling."

"The ceiling?"

"Just try going *down* fast—it's quite a ride."

"But why?" I asked, becoming annoyed. Crow loved his little games.

"Because you forgot something, mate."

"What?"

"I don't *know!*" roared Crow in irritation. "Some kind of stabilizer. Didn't you ever notice that these ships could move with wild acceleration patterns and we barely noticed? Well, now you *will* notice, believe me."

I nodded, putting my hand on my chin. I hadn't thought about it, but it made sense. I wondered how many other devices the originals had built into them that I hadn't known to include. I'd never seen a stabilizer system, had never found it during my explorations on the *Alamo*. But apparently, some such apparatus had been aboard.

127

"So, we are flying beta versions," I said. "Well, they are better than nothing. The brass back at NATO must be watching us in a panic. We've got a fleet again."

"Yes, you did manage to make these things look frightening," agreed Crow. "At the end of the day, I have to congratulate you, my yobbo engineer. What are we going to do with your ship, now that you have it?"

"I'm going to mass more of them and face down the Macros."

"No sense of adventure," he said.

"What are you going to do? Hunt for a new girlfriend on a lonely street? Is that why you want the arm so badly?"

"Pull your head in! We don't need to do anything so drastic now. We're famous. I should be able to get a chickie-babe to climb aboard with me now, no worries."

I thought for a second about adventures. It had been a long time since I'd done anything other than work hard for the war effort. Maybe I should take Sandra on a little trip. It would be like old times.

Then, an idea struck me. "I know what I'm going to do, Crow. I'm going to fly out and investigate the mystery spots. When I have this ship fully outfitted, I'm going to find out how these aliens get in and out of our star system."

-24-

With only two months to go until the Macros were due to come and collect their tribute, I screwed up. Sandra finally figured out I meant to lead the expedition.

We'd never really discussed it before. I'd been so busy building up the new Fleet, the legion of men and mountains of equipment, she hadn't even considered the idea I was going with them. In her mind I was in the Star Force *Fleet* first, not a ground-pounding marine. She knew I'd fought in the South American campaign, but that wasn't how she thought of me. She met me as the pilot of *Alamo*. Now that I had a new ship, I'd returned to that role. Naturally, she'd known I had critical roles in both halves of our organization, but somehow my evasiveness on the topic of who was to command the mission had succeeded for months.

There were very few things I'd managed to keep her from learning in the course of our relationship. I was surprised on the whole that she hadn't figured this one out sooner. Looking back, I had to wonder if she hadn't *wanted* to know. Maybe she didn't want to think about being left behind while I went off into the total unknown to wage war for the benefit of a race of alien monsters. Maybe the idea was so horrific, she couldn't even conceive of it.

Sandra figured out the truth one sunny afternoon while we talked about Crow and the Fleet. She asked me since he was commanding the Fleet and I was commanding the Marines, then who would be commanding the legion we were so busily training?

I hesitated. That killed me, I think. Before, I'd glibly deflected her. I'd said things like *who knows?* Or *Robinson is a good man.* Or

129

sometimes even *some Pentagon type, I suppose.* But this time, I didn't blurt out an easy lie. Probably, it was because the day of reckoning was so near. It seemed wrong somehow to keep such a big secret from her. I knew that ignorance was bliss—but at what point did the sin of omission become a lie?

Sandra stared at me. I knew, watching her eyes search mine, that I had already blown it. If I tried a lie now, she would probe more deeply, suspiciously. I would be forced to either tell her the truth, or attempt an outright lie. I didn't have the heart for either, so I dropped my eyes and said nothing.

"What is it?" she asked. "You—you don't think you're going with them, do you?"

Suddenly, her hand fell on my wrist. She squeezed. If it hadn't been for the nanites in my flesh, her claw-like grip might have been painful.

"I'm commanding the mission," I said evenly, raising my head back up and looking her in the eye.

Sandra released me and fell back against the couch we shared, thumping her shoulders into the cushions. She made an exasperated sound.

"This is about the kid-thing, isn't it?" she demanded suddenly.

I blinked. "Huh?"

"If you need to take a break from me, if you really are all messed-up in the head about your own lost kids, then just tell me now. We don't have to do this, Kyle. We really don't."

She was angry. I could tell that. I couldn't figure out the rest of what she was saying. It didn't make any sense to me. I didn't respond, figuring that was the safest move.

"You weren't even going to say anything, were you?" she demanded. She got up off the couch by sliding away, throwing her arms high so as to keep as far out of reach as possible. I made no attempt to grab her. She walked around our living room with quick, pissed-off steps. Her arms were crossed; her head was down, her lips pouted. Her long hair hung around her face like a hood.

"Of course I was going to tell you eventually," I managed to get out.

"No. No you weren't. You were just going to vanish one day. The way you did the last time the Macros came. You almost went off to the stars that day, too. You remember? You have some kind of fantasy about leaving me, don't you?"

I wondered if this was it. I wondered if the proverbial professor had been wise beyond all imagining. I told myself it wasn't fair, it had been less than a year. I deserved at least another six months. Had I miscalculated the beauty-to-age ratio? *Damn.*

"I don't want you to leave me, Sandra," I said.

"Then why the hell are *you* leaving *me?*" she demanded.

"Because I have to," I said. "I set this up. I can't send thousands of guys off to die on a distant rock after I negotiated the deal. What if they never come back? How could I live with myself?"

She looked at me suspiciously. "It's not about the kid-thing?"

"No, Sandra. Really, it's not."

"When did you decide to go?"

"About an hour after I made the deal with the Macros."

Again, I'd been overly-truthful. She huffed and almost slapped me. I saw her hand coming up, and I flinched. I'm not sure why. Her slaps never hurt. I supposed it was reflex.

"You didn't tell me *all this time?*"

"Are you happier now that you know?" I asked.

Sandra breathed very hard for a while. Her lower jaw jutted out, showing teeth, while she paced around the room. Her hair had somehow become tousled. "I'm not going to let you go without me," she said.

"You don't have any choice," I said gently.

She walked out then, and slammed the door behind her. The walls weren't terribly thick, and the window rattled.

I sighed and went to the kitchen to get myself a beer. I thought about the proverbial professor and his ratios. If the old bastard was still alive somewhere, I wanted to strangle him in his sleep.

Several hours later I was back on the couch. Things were fuzzier now. I'd formed a pyramid with the cans I'd drained. The last one—number ten, I think it was—wouldn't sit right on top of the others. It kept crashing down. Somehow, this seemed funny to me. I picked it up again and tried to stack them all neatly.

The door flew open—and it kept going. I looked up, blinking in surprise. Sandra stood there in the doorway. I was confused.

"Where did the door go?" I asked.

131

She glanced back over her shoulder. "I think its somewhere out on the driveway."

I stared at her and she stared back. Her eyes were smoldering. She was still angry, but also triumphant. I stood up and accidentally knocked over my pyramid of cans.

"What did you do?"

"Something I should have done a long time ago."

I took a few more steps toward her. I noticed then there was blood running down her neck on both sides. Her hair looked funny, too.

"What happened to your hair?"

"It will grow back."

"You're bleeding."

"Yeah, I know," she said. She threw back her hair and revealed her neck and bloody ears. "I couldn't take it. I had to rip my earrings out."

My mouth sagged open. There were her lovely earlobes, torn and bleeding. There were hunks of hair missing in spots, too. I looked at her nails. There were a lot of red scrapings under there.

"I tried to work on my thighs," she said conversationally. "I ripped at them, the way you tell the guys to do. It did help."

"You took the nanite injections?" I asked stupidly. I had almost reached her. I took one more step.

"Duh."

"Why?"

She slapped me then, very hard. My head jerked to the right as if I'd been hit by a baseball bat. For the first time since I'd met her, one of her slaps actually hurt me.

"Because, you slow-witted, drunk bastard," she said, "I'm going with you."

-25-

We'd ordered a large number of pilot seats for our ships from various defense contractors. There had been mutterings amongst the earther brass, but what could they do? They'd put us back in charge of Earth's space fleet. No one else could build the new fleet, as we'd held onto our factories despite their coup attempt. We were still Star Force, and we had to have ships to fly, and these new birds needed seats that could hold a pilot in place.

The more I thought about it, the more I thought this situation might work out best for Earth in the long run. If any one nation had stolen the factories, would the rest of the planet freely give them the resources they needed? Probably not. They would be terrified the possessing nation would want to dominate the world. By maintaining a neutral stance, we'd gotten humanity through some tough spots. They still called us amateurs—for good reason—but we had a monopoly on Nano technology at this point and we hadn't failed Earth yet.

The pilot seats were absolutely necessary with the lack of stabilizers. Our nanotized bodies could take more punishment than normal pilots, but it would be hard to fight my ship if I was bouncing around the bridge like a dime in a drier.

I had six more ships built by the time I was ready to go check on our alien friends. They might not like what I was doing, so I didn't want to take off and leave no combat ships behind me. We had put fighter pilots in four of the new ships, real pros. Due to the distances involved, you couldn't fly the craft visually, and combat took time. You often had to fly them strategically, almost as if you were a sub

133

commander. I put a group of navy sea commanders on two of the Nano ships for this reason. It was something of an experiment to see who would outperform the other.

Crow and I had hand-chosen each of the pilots—and not only for their skills. We made sure every pilot was from a different nation. Some might call it diversity, but I called it *security*. It would be hard to organize an internal coup if the pilots didn't trust or even know each other.

The day I was leaving, Crow tried to talk me out of it. This was at least his seventh attempt.

"What if you go out there and cock-up the treaty?"

"I won't pull anyone's tail," I assured him. "If I see a Macro ship, I'll run home."

"If you must go, you should check out the spot out in the Oort cloud, not Venus. We don't even have that location pinpointed, and you could find out where my last fleet went."

"That's about two thousand times farther away. I want to be back in hours, not weeks."

"Yeah, if you are coming back at all," Crow grumbled. "What the hell am I supposed to do with all these jarheads if you go off and feed yourself to some alien threshing machine?"

"Your concerns are touching, Admiral," I told him.

I soon tired of Crow and politely broke the connection. I reflected on how our relationship had changed since the failed coup against us. We were equals now, with separate turf. He ran the Fleet and I ran the Marines. I didn't take orders from him anymore, but we pretended I did in public. Our real relationship was more like a partnership—or a bad marriage with a lot of yelling involved.

I'd already told him why I had to go. We just didn't have enough information about our enemies. I needed intelligence, and I'd built a set of spyboxes with nanotech. These systems were essentially a brainbox attached to a passive sensor array, a small power source and a transmitter. I planned to lay a few of these out there near the system entry point, whatever it was, to watch for alien activity. I was sure similar earther systems had already been launched. I could have sent one of my new pilots, but they were unproven and I didn't want to risk a diplomatic incident over the actions of a green scout.

There was another reason I was going myself, of course. I was burning to know what was out there. There were so many secrets in this game, and this one was just sitting there, daring for me to do something about it.

"Socorro, lift us off gently."

"Command acknowledged."

Damn, I thought, she sounds so much like *Alamo*. I'd thought about trying to get her to use a different voice, but had never gotten around to it.

"Head straight up until we exit the atmosphere."

We glided upward at what felt like one G of acceleration, added onto Earth's one G of gravity. I felt heavy, but not terribly uncomfortable. Soon we broke through the atmosphere and reached orbit at about a hundred miles above the surface. I'd installed cameras in my ship this time around. Not just cheap webcams, either. These were high-def with high-grade, military lenses. I'd installed an OLED screen in front of my pilot's chair, and joysticks to direct the cameras on the outer hull of the ship.

The view was breathtaking. The Earth was a blue-white crescent, textured with clouds and landmasses. I could see the various Caribbean islands. The sun reflected blindingly from the surface of the Atlantic far below.

I smiled. I really felt like a space traveler today. Up until this moment, I'd been further out in space than any human currently in the Solar System, but I'd never seen my own world from orbit.

I checked the forward screen. The big board had a number of metallic dots crawling around, but nothing seemed out of place. I decided to check out my observatory. When I'd requisitioned the building materials from the government, there were raised eyebrows. I told them there were things I wanted to see with my own eyes out there. It was the one major extravagance I'd installed aboard my ship. I had real windows in the observatory—or rather a single thick sheet of auto-shaded, ballistic glass embedded in the floor. I was sick of *imagining* what space looked like outside of my ship. The observatory worked like a glass-bottomed boat, and I meant to look directly down on Earth from inside my ship.

"Socorro, give me enough acceleration toward Venus to walk properly."

Within seconds, the ship had reoriented itself. I was thrown against the straps, then once our course was set, I felt my weight increase steadily until it was about half of normal.

135

I turned and tilted my head. What was that sound? I'd heard something, a thump or some shifting of material. I unstrapped and got up, annoyed. Everything should have been secure.

"Socorro, secure any loose cargo."

"Done."

There was another sound. What was that? I thought it came from the observatory, which I'd built adjacent to the bridge, right next to the living quarters. Had my new window out into the universe cracked already? Grunting in irritation, I walked up to the wall and touched it. The metal turned to liquid and instantly melted away.

I stepped into the observatory. The view below my feet transfixed me. The floor of the room was blindingly blue-white. The Earth rode down there, moving very slightly. We were over Canada now, as best I could tell through the clouds. I could feel the cold outside, it had already chilled the room. I'd have to make adjustments for temperature. Apparently, the skin of the ship did that automatically, but the glass floor let the exterior temperature seep inside.

"I suppose you think this is very funny," said a voice above me.

I reacted with startled speed, crouching and jerking my head up. There she was, strapped to my ceiling. A dozen little black arms had grabbed her and pulled her up there 'securing' her. I smiled and relaxed.

"Brings back memories," I said, "only this time you're not naked."

Sandra hissed at me. "If you ever want to have sex again," she said, "you'll get me off the frigging ceiling, Kyle."

I got her down in a hurry.

-26-

"You know what they do with stowaways, Sandra?"

"Who are 'they'?"

"They work them. Very intensely."

She half-closed her eyes and gave me a disgusted look. "And if they won't *work?*"

"They get tossed overboard. Spaced."

"You just try it. I'll rip your arm off. Anyway, I'm not here as a stowaway. I told you I was going with you."

"I'm not flying off on a military campaign. This is just a scouting trip."

"I don't care. I'm going with you anyway."

I sighed. "You mean you don't trust me. Okay…. How did you get aboard?"

Sandra shrugged. "You set up a knocking code. I used it to get in."

"It's a different code for the ship."

"Yes, you told me."

"When?" I asked.

"Remember when I took the injections? Do you remember that night?"

"Not much of it. I remember I was drunk—and amorous."

"Exactly. You blabbed the code."

"You took advantage of a drunk," I said.

"Score one for the female side."

We didn't have a second pilot's chair, but I'd installed a number of jumpseats around the walls with crash harnesses. I pointed one out to Sandra.

"Strap in, I'm going to increase our speed."

Sandra folded down the seat and arranged the crash harness. "These things are all over the ship, aren't they?"

"Yeah, there's a troop-carrying area as well, a big enough bay for a fully-equipped company. Most of the ship's interior is empty. The bulging hull is just for show to impress the Macros. I decided to make use of the space by setting up several chambers as cargo holds."

"Why didn't you put one of these seats in the observatory?" she asked.

"I didn't figure anyone would be in there during maneuvers."

"Okay, now for my real question, why are we going out to mess with the aliens?"

"Aren't you curious? Don't you want to know where they are coming from?"

Sandra pursed her lips. "Not if it will get us killed or start the war again. I just want them to stay away."

"Well, it's our job to make sure they don't invade again. To do that, we have to know what they are up to. There are plenty of alien secrets all around us, and I want to figure them out. It's our job."

"What do you mean, *our job?*"

"If you want to come with me into space, you have to join Star Force."

Sandra stared at me for a few seconds. I could see this comment had gotten through to her. Maybe, she'd expected me to stop her and throw her off the ship like a kid that had secretly ridden to the store in the back of daddy's car. But I wasn't going to do that. I'd decided to call her bluff and stop playing games with her.

"Will I have to call you sir?" she asked.

"Absolutely."

She glared at me. "Only when we are on a mission. You can forget it otherwise."

"You're killing my fantasies—but okay."

We'd traveled far past Earth as we'd been talking, heading sunward. Unfortunately, Venus was in an inconvenient position in relationship to the Earth this month. The orbital paths of the two planets were far from optimal for the trip. Since the Nano ship was capable of continuous acceleration, it could build up much higher velocities than any rocket we'd ever built on Earth. The key was the power system, which was able to generate steady thrust. With my three-engine ship, we accelerated hard for a day or so, then turned around, aiming the engines sunward, and decelerated, slowing ourselves down, for another day and a half.

In-between I let us coast for a time. We often took one-G breaks along the way, where we lowered the thrust the engines produced to give ourselves a rest. These breaks turned out to be very fruitful with Sandra, who was bored with the trip and frequently engaged me in our single source of entertainment.

Love was very different with a nanotized couple in freefall. Eye-popping achievements were reached. We created a series of new Olympic events and I'd say we swept the gold medals in all of them. It was good exercise too, I pointed out to her.

When Venus finally appeared as a disk on our forward wall, we went into the observatory to check it out with our own eyes. I made sure the cameras were recording the approach too, in case we missed something. The images could be sent to Earth for later analysis. There had been very strange things going on out here, and I wanted the details.

"What do you hope to find out here, Kyle?"

"I suspect there is something that connects our star system to others. A gateway, perhaps."

She looked at me. "A black hole or what?"

"Nothing so dramatic, I hope. We would have felt the tug of its gravity back home if it were that sort of thing."

"How do you know for sure?" she asked. "The Nanos have some control over gravitational effects. Remember the stabilizers you forgot to add to this ship?"

I looked at her and nodded. "You have a point. I really have no idea what we are going to find."

"What if there is a Macro fleet gathering out here?" she asked.

"Then we run home."

"What if they follow us?"

"We transmit abject apologies—and run faster."

139

Sandra chewed her lower lip—something she did often when she was nervous. "It doesn't sound like you've really thought this mission through."

"Unknowns can't be thought through. This is exploration, experimentation."

"Why do you have to do stuff like this yourself?" she asked, suddenly intense. I could tell from her expression she wanted a real answer, not a quip.

"I think it started with these Nano ships," I said. "There are secrets locked within these vessels. The Nanos have always driven me mad with their mysteries. I know that our scientists are working hard to analyze them—and I wish them luck. But as far as I can tell, they hadn't made much progress. They've dissected the pieces, of course."

"They have? What happened?" Sandra asked.

"I heard a team down at Los Alamos Labs in New Mexico took apart one of my fusion backpacks with disastrous results. There are several technical areas that are still uninhabitable."

"Technical areas?"

"That's what they call their various labs. The point is that despite the efforts of our best minds, we've been unable to do much more than theorize about Nano technology. We are certainly nowhere near reproducing it on our own."

Venus was bright with reflected sunlight. Due to its orbital position relative to Earth, we were approaching it obliquely. It appeared like a half-moon from our vantage point. The atmosphere was far too thick to see the surface. What we could see was a yellowy-brown-beige swirl. The planet looked like a coffee mocha with way too much cream. Really, we were looking at the top of a mass of roiling clouds. I supposed it was beautiful—in the stark fashion of a scorched desert.

"Why can't we figure out how these things work?" Sandra asked.

"We lack the fundamentals to analyze alien tech. Imagine this: What if we took a modern computer back in time to the doorstep of Benjamin Franklin, Sir Isaac Newton or Charles Babbage?"

She considered it. "They might trigger a technological revolution in earlier times. We might be centuries ahead of where we are."

"Maybe," I said. "But most likely those learned men would have a hard time even comprehending the device. For one thing, it would run out of power within a few hours and turn into a complicated brick of strange materials. Even if we could give them the power and thus the time to really study one of our marvels, there are a thousand details and discoveries they would have to make first in order to build one of their own. At least a century of focused scientific achievement would be required."

"You sound like a professor now," she said.

I chuckled. "An occupational hazard. Should I shut up?"

"Nah. I want an 'A'."

"You've earned your grade a hundred times over."

I had to defend myself, bouncing away from the incoming slap. It was a playful attack, however, so I relaxed. I looked down at Venus, which had grown imperceptibly larger beneath our feet. The glass of the observatory was very cold, so cold the molecules in my feet were burning in my shoes. I was glad they had plastic soles, which had no freezing point, or my shoes might have crystallized under my feet. I decided it was best to continue the lecture.

"Think, for example," I began, "if someone managed to give a Model T Ford to the Romans. They could learn to drive it, but they wouldn't be able to build one of their own. They could not machine the parts for the engine. The electronics of the ignition system would be incomprehensible. They had no rubber at that time, and no way to find any. They would have the same problem when it came to distilling gasoline to fill the tank. Such a substance was virtually unknown to them. My point is that something as simple as a car requires a dozen scientific and engineering techniques to understand and build. I personally believe that a technological gift to people in the past would be more likely to result in witchcraft trials than any early explosion of technology."

I looked at the sole member of my audience to see if she was falling asleep yet. As an ex-prof, I'm good at reading listeners. Sandra was distracted by the sight of Venus below us. Her head was tilted downward, and she had her hair in each hand to pull it back as she studied the floor. Her pretty face was lit-up by sunshine reflected from Venus' dense atmosphere.

"This glass is cold under my feet," she said.

"Yeah, I didn't build this chamber perfectly. Hopefully, we're not getting too much radiation."

Sandra looked up in alarm. At least I knew she was listening.

141

"Just kidding! The glass is lead-impregnated and the walls of the Nano ships have always blocked radiation, I've checked with Geiger counters."

She relaxed and looked downward again, studying Venus. "This is pretty amazing. I'm pissed that you didn't offer to take me along before."

"I just built the ship!"

"But you *planned* to leave me home. You *planned* to look at this beauty alone."

"Do you want to hear the rest of my speech or not?"

She sighed. "Okay."

"The Nano ships are a technological gift from the future to *us*. It's as if we'd given Benjamin Franklin a pallet of solar calculators—plus a few copy machines and maybe a tractor or two. Like old Franklin, we are advanced enough not to believe they are supernatural, but we are not prepared to exploit the gifts fully. Taking a piece of our own current technology back in time just two hundred years would have befuddled our world's greatest scientific minds at that time. Today we have been presented with the technology of the Blues. We have examples of Nano science in our hands we might not have developed on our own for a thousand years. Worse still, this technology wasn't designed by human minds for human purposes. This makes the principles behind them doubly hard to fathom."

"All right fine, professor," she said. "Tell me why we are risking a war—and our asses, out here."

"Because I'm hoping we can learn at least how to use the technology that's out here. I'm hoping we can use it to get out of our star system."

Her startled eyes met mine. "What for?"

I smiled grimly. "You can't win a war by staying purely on the defense."

"I thought we were at peace with the machines."

"What if we're not? What if there are more aliens out there, who haven't yet made an appearance?"

Sandra stopped asking questions. I suspected she hadn't really liked my answers all that much. We both gazed down at Venus. The planet looked marginally closer now.

The more I thought about it, the more I doubted we would penetrate the secrets of these alien marvels within my lifetime. We simply didn't have the prerequisite science to do so. But I was determined to learn whatever I could. The American Plains Indians had figured out how to ride horses and shoot rifles, even if they couldn't build a factory to make their own guns. We would do the same.

I tried not to think about how the story had ended for the Indians.

-27-

We found something on the far side of Venus. I didn't see it directly, not at first. But the *Socorro* knew it was there. A coppery-red contact appeared on the forward wall. I'd instructed the ship to show anything she detected out to maximum range.

"It's on the planet surface," said Sandra,

She sat strapped into her jumpseat. I was strapped into my pilot's chair. I'd decided it was best we were in our seats from here on out. We were only about an hour from reaching Venus. We would go into orbit soon. If we had to make any sudden maneuvers, I didn't want to be bounced off the walls of the ship.

I eyed the thing on the forward wall. Venus was a gray disk, about the size of a man's hat now. Superimposed upon it was the coppery-red contact. It hadn't been there a minute earlier. I couldn't tell if it was behind Venus, orbiting Venus, or deep inside it. Our metallic-relief observation system was far from perfect. Optically, using the newly installed cameras and my high-def flatscreen, I couldn't see it at all.

Whatever it was, it had to be fairly large. As Venus was about the size of a truck tire, the contact was a paperclip in comparison.

"Socorro," I said. "Identify the contact on the screen."

"Structure unknown."

"Is it an enemy ship?"

Hesitation. "The structure does not fit that designation."

"Why not?" I asked.

"The structure does not appear to be armed, thus it fails the test for *enemy*. The structure does not appear to have a means of propulsion, thus it fails the test for *ship*."

I nodded, it was hard to refute that logic.

"What the hell is it, then?" Sandra asked.

During our journey I'd ordered the Socorro to listen to her, so it responded. "Structure unknown."

Sandra huffed in frustration. "Why are you marking it with red if it fails the test for enemy?" she asked the ship.

"Unknown contacts are assumed hostile until proven otherwise," said the ship, reasonably enough.

I eyed Sandra sidelong. I doubted she would ever be a successful programmer. Computers were inherently exasperating. They required patience, persistence and a very high threshold for frustration. Sandra was persistent, but she was as likely to put her nanite-charged fist through a brainbox as to put up with its nonsense.

"Socorro," I said, "Let's zoom in and see the structure at a magnification of ten times its current dimensions."

The forward wall rippled. The coppery contact grew from a paperclip into a coat hanger. The surrounding disk of Venus exploded into an orb that overflowed the forward wall of the bridge.

"Now, rotate the image slowly—sunward. Spin it around so I can see it from different perspectives."

Nothing happened for a few seconds.

"I think it crashed," Sandra said.

I hissed at her. "Never say those words to a computer."

Slowly, the forward wall began to change. I saw it was very slow indeed. The nanites representing the rippled surface of Venus were hard-put, bubbling and rippling to keep up. It amounted to a slow frame-rate.

"Socorro, remove the image of Venus itself from the projection for now."

The steel-gray disk faded into smoothness. I could almost feel the nanites as they thanked me for the break I'd given them. The coat hanger-sized shape in the middle of the screen was now more detailed, and its rotating animation was faster and more coherent.

"What the hell is that thing?" asked Sandra aloud.

"Looks like—some kind of curved thing," I said. As it rotated, the unknown object grew increasingly from a single rectangle with

145

curved ends into an oval. After another half a minute, it was a perfect ring. Then it continued rotating and became an oval and then a racetrack-shaped rectangle again.

Sandra and I looked at each other. "It's some kind of circle," she said. "Some kind of ring. But what's it for?"

"Socorro, are there any other contacts in sensor range?"

"No."

"How close is the structure to the surface of Venus?"

"The object is embedded in the planetary crust."

"Who the hell built that thing?" asked Sandra suddenly.

I looked at her. I had to admit, it was a good question.

"Structure origins unknown," said the ship.

"Socorro, how much of the structure is beneath the surface?" I asked.

"Approximately fifty-one percent of the structure is buried."

I thought about that for a few seconds. I felt the engines change their thrum and a felt a tug to the left, as we shifted our course. The *Socorro* was automatically going into orbit over Venus.

"What should we do now?" Sandra asked. Her voice was hushed, as if someone might hear us. She had a worried, excited look on her face, as if we had just discovered an unlocked backdoor and were discussing what to do about it. In a way, I supposed that was exactly what we had just done.

I paused looking at her seriously. "No one is around…."

"Yeah?"

"Maybe we should fly through this hoop. Maybe we should see what's on the other side."

"You really are crazy," she said.

I shrugged. "I get that often."

"There could be like—space mines or something," Sandra said. "There might be probes—an alien alarm system. Maybe it will send us on a one-way trip to some other star system crawling with robots or bugs or—I don't know."

"I'll leave you home next time," I said.

"You'd better not."

I turned my attention back to the forward screen. "Socorro, return the forward screen to normal mode."

The wall transformed, turning to silvery liquid, then reconfigured itself into Venus. The planet was much bigger now, as big as a truck tire. We were coming in fast.

"Increase rate of deceleration, but keep the G-forces under three point zero."

The ship shuddered and I felt like I weighed seven hundred pounds—because I did. Sandra grumbled and struggled to get comfortable in her jumpseat. It was an impossible task. Her neck compressed as she strained against the gravity. Her mouth hung open slightly, revealing gritted teeth. Even with our nanite-enhanced strength, three Gs was uncomfortable.

"I'll install a second pilot's seat when we get home," I told her.

"You damn-well better," she managed to grunt out.

We endured hard G-forces and slowed down our approach considerably. I didn't want to be surprised by an enemy and have to fight our own inertia to turn around and run. We were so far from any kind of support from our fledgling fleet back on Earth, I couldn't hope to win a combat situation. All I could do is run for it, and hope our three-engine ship had the thrust to escape whatever came after us.

Conversation was impossible for the next few minutes as we decelerated hard. I decided that future designs had to have stabilizers, if they were to be fast ships. I wasn't even sure how much acceleration this ship was capable of. I'd never dared to tell the ship to apply full emergency thrust. For all I knew, it might kill us if I gave the order. I knew a prolonged force of six Gs could cause humans to shut down. This was especially true if the force was applied unevenly, as was happening right now to Sandra. She didn't have proper support in that jumpseat. I made a mental note to give a new emergency script to Socorro in case everyone aboard blacked out.

About ten painful minutes later, we were parked in orbit and the deceleration stopped crushing us down. Venus had grown to dominate the forward wall. In fact, we were a bug crawling across the face of her. Underneath us was the archway, or buried ring. The optical systems still showed nothing, of course, being unable to penetrate the thick, storming atmosphere.

"Why haven't our probes and telescopes noticed this structure?" Sandra asked.

"I'm not sure. The atmosphere is thick, but radio telescopes can penetrate the gases. Maybe it's been hiding itself somehow. Or maybe it wasn't here the last time we sent a probe out to investigate. Europe sent a probe out here in the early 2000s, as I remember."

"You think the Macros built it since then?"

I didn't answer right away. I didn't like the thoughts that were swirling in my mind. Several things were clear, despite the long list of unknowns. We knew that the Macros had formed their fleet here and come to attack Earth from this point. We also knew they had responded quickly to their failure to take us out with their first attacks. Within months they had gathered new forces to try again. That indicated they had to either be coming to our star system at faster than light speeds, or they were already here.

I'd ruled out the idea their fleet was sitting around in our Solar System at full strength all along. If they'd had such a fleet handy, they would have used it—all of it. They were not subtle machines.

Logically, that left me with only one conclusion: they were able to achieve FTL travel, and the entry point they had come from was right here, on the surface of Venus. The ring on the surface of the world, however it had come to be here, had to be the way they were traveling to our system from other stars.

"It's a portal of some kind," I said. "It has to be. The Macros must have built it or found it or something, and they have been using it to come in and out of our system from some other star."

"From where?"

"I have no idea, but I think I know how to find out," I said.

"If you try to fly us through that thing, you don't know what's going to happen, Kyle."

"No, I don't. That's the point of experimentation. We need to explore the differences between our theories and reality."

"This isn't science. We're more like a pair of monkeys playing with a handgun."

I sniffed. "I prefer being compared to a gorilla."

"We're gonna die," she said.

I considered her words. She had a point. But then again, I hadn't come all this way for nothing.

"Socorro," I said. "Take us down into the atmosphere. Take us down closer to the unknown structure."

-28-

Before we went down, I formed up a message to General Kerr's team. He was a spook now, but I still thought of him as a General. I told him what was going on, and reported every detail we had on the 'unknown structure' we'd found on Venus. I didn't tell him we were going down to mess with it. If we survived and returned home, I could tell him what I'd learned later. If we didn't come back, he was smart enough to figure out it was dangerous.

This was my first time exploring an alien planet. Lucky me—Venus was one of the nastiest worlds in the solar system. The surface was *extremely* deadly. The atmosphere was thick, ninety-two times as thick as Earth's. The pressure at the surface was equivalent to being a half-mile deep in the ocean. As a bonus the 'air' was poisonous, made up primarily of carbon dioxide and nitrogen. The high-level, opaque clouds that coated the world were made up of sulfuric acid. Just to keep things interesting, the acid clouds were continuously blown around the planet by two hundred mile-an-hour winds. Conditions were even worse down on the ground. The surface temperature was a toasty nine hundred degrees Fahrenheit. That was hot enough to melt zinc on a sunny day—but there weren't any of those on Venus, either.

I had a pricey digital recording system connected to the exterior cameras and I switched them all on to record our approach. I figured I would give the data to the science boys back home as a goodwill gesture. But I was worried the cameras wouldn't be able to tolerate the heat and pressure of Venus. The cameras were all behind military-grade ballistic glass. They were built to operate on spy

149

planes, but not under such extreme conditions. When we reached the upper layers of the atmosphere, I ordered the *Socorro* to cover all external ports with a layer of nanite-metal, including the glass floor of the observation chamber. We would be flying down blind except for the ship's sensors and the forward wall display.

As we bumped our way into the atmosphere, I watched Sandra's eyes grow increasingly alarmed. The winds buffeted our big, empty tin can of a ship, making it heave and roll. The engines rumbled and whirred softly, fighting to keep us from going into a spin.

"It feels like we're in a washing machine!" she shouted over the roaring winds.

"That's the acid-cloud layer," I shouted back. "Things should smooth out when we get closer to the surface."

"What acid-clouds?" she screamed.

"Want to go home?"

Sandra nodded. Her eyes were huge. She said something else, but I couldn't make it out.

"Too late now!" I shouted, smiling at her.

Sandra gave me the bird. At least we could still communicate.

I was nervous too, but I tried to appear calm for her sake. I had plenty of reasons to worry. Venus was just one of them. The unknown ring structure on the planet's surface was another. The Macros were the third. What if this thing had an automated defense system? It hadn't lit us up with a beam or fired a missile, but maybe that was because we hadn't irritated it enough yet. If it was a gateway, as I suspected it must be, did it have an off switch? Was it operating right now, or was it dormant? If we tried to use it, were there necessary precautions we didn't comprehend, such as radiation shielding? What if it was some kind of worm-hole device, and we went into it without any inertial stabilizers? Would that be a deadly mistake?

Then there was the biggest question of all. If we did fly through this portal—if that's what it was—who would be waiting for us on the other side? Would they be happy to see my little Nano ship nosing around? Somehow, I doubted it.

The winds died down as we broke through the clouds into the hazy brown lower layers. I could hear Sandra again.

"That was crazy," she said.

"I know," I said. "We made it through though, didn't we? Down here beneath the acid-clouds the winds are relatively mild. At the surface, the gases are thick and soupy, and the winds are only a few miles an hour."

"You have to stop saying 'acid-clouds' okay?"

"Okay."

We were only a dozen miles from the ring now. I could see it on the forward wall, a looming arch that seemed *huge* from our perspective. I couldn't make a precise measurement, but I figured it had to be at least three miles in diameter. Its lower half had sunk down into the surface of the world and was invisible to anything except the passive sensors of the Nano ship.

"Socorro," I said, "halt the ship and hold our position."

We were thrown forward as the ship braked, redirecting its engines.

"Is the structure active?" I asked the ship.

"Specify."

I thought for a second. "Is it releasing energy from an internal source?"

"Yes," the ship said.

"Socorro, do you know how to activate this structure?" I asked, hoping.

"No. The structure is unknown."

"I think the ship already made that one pretty clear, but you had to try," Sandra said sympathetically.

"Yeah," I said, trying to think. "If we had *Alamo*, I bet she would know what to do. Those ships charged off into the farthest reaches of the Solar System the day they left. I'm pretty sure they went to find something like this out there in the void."

"Why don't we just fly through it? I mean, I know you are going to do it anyway. If we just sit here maybe a Macro will show up."

I thought about that. I sighed, then nodded. After all, the artifact *was* a giant ring. What else could you do, other than fly through it?

"Socorro, what would happen if we flew through the center of the structure?" I asked, hoping again.

There was a familiar hesitation. I suspected I was giving the ship's fledgling mind a workout. "Assumption: non-specific pronoun *we* refers to this ship and crew. Analysis based on assumption: The ship would exit on the other side."

151

"No kidding," said Sandra.

I frowned. "Socorro, where is the other side?"

"Unknown."

"That's great," said Sandra, crossing her arms. "Well, are you going to do it?"

"Do you want to?" I asked.

"It doesn't matter what I want. You always do whatever you want to anyway."

"It might kill us, so I'm asking."

Sandra looked at me. "You admit this is dangerous?"

"Of course it is."

She looked unhappy to hear me admit it. I wondered if she had been terrified all along and making jokes to keep control. Perhaps I'd blown it by asking what we should do. Perhaps she relied more than I realized on my self-confident exterior.

"You are going to let me decide?" she asked. "What do you think?"

"We have to try it. We have to learn about every piece of alien tech we run into. We can't sit back and hope it will be explained to us, or that it will go away."

"Let's do it, then," she said, looking scared.

I nodded. "Socorro, remove the metal skin over the forward camera. I want to record this."

"Won't that melt the camera?" asked Sandra.

"Maybe," I said, shrugging. "We can always put another camera into the ship when we get home. This is an opportunity worth the risk."

The flatscreen flickered into life as the camera fed it digital images. The world was dark, hazy. The surface was cracked and reminded me of salt flats baked by heat. The sky was a yellowish orange. We stared at the images for several seconds in awe. Then I remembered to push the record button on the digital video recorder.

"Direct the camera toward the ring structure, Socorro," I said.

"Orientation achieved."

I squinted, but could not see the structure.

"Maybe we are too far away," said Sandra. "The atmosphere looks—smoky."

"Let's get closer," I said. "Socorro, take us down slowly."

As we went lower, the air pressure on the hull grew. We were buffeted by the atmosphere as we glided down toward the rough surface. The ground was less than a mile beneath us. The black, rocky, outcroppings undulated below. Apparently, *slowly* meant something very different in Socorro's young brain. I figured we were moving as fast as a small plane might on Earth.

"There it is," said Sandra. Her voice was hushed. "It looks like the St. Louis Arch."

I nodded. I'd been there years ago and this thing, whatever it was, did remind me of the Arch. But it was black, not silver, and there were no seams in the metal that I could see. I wondered if it was even made of metal.

"Socorro, circle the structure, keeping our forward camera aimed at it so we can see it from all angles."

We began to glide to the left and we rose up higher. As we passed over a mountain peak that seemed close enough to scrape the bottom of the ship, I realized the ship had automatically gained altitude in order to both comply with my order and avoid destruction. Sandra noticed it, too. She sucked in a breath and held it.

"You have to be more careful," Sandra said. "You told it to destroy us."

"It's okay," I told her. "I've put in plenty of safeguard programming. She knows enough to automatically edit commands that endanger the ship."

"So, we're trusting our lives to your programming skills?"

I smiled. "You trust a programmer with your life every time you get on an airplane. Not to mention a dozen engineering people."

She nodded and tried to relax. "I do trust you to build a good ship. But I don't trust that thing out there or the Macro robots who built it. What if it is nothing but a trap, a lure?"

I shook my head. "No. They had all the power to crush us when they had the fleet here. They would have done it then, if that was their intent. They are not subtle robots."

"Okay, what do we do now?" she asked.

"Socorro, give me a compositional analysis on the structure."

"Non-reflective matter. The material is condensed star-matter."

I looked up in surprise. "Like from a neutron star?"

"Source of material is unknown."

153

"What is keeping it physically intact, then? The gravity here is not enough to compress matter."

"Unknown."

"What's going on?" Sandra asked.

"The ship thinks it's neutronium, or something like it."

"What the heck is neutronium?"

"When we get home, I'm enrolling you into an online astronomy class. It might serve the world if you pass."

"Of course I'll pass. Now, answer the question, professor."

"It's a name for the matter on neutron stars, or at the center of any star. The gravity is so intense, it crushes matter down into a collapsed, super-dense state. No one had actually seen it first hand—until now. But we have theorized it must exist on burnt-out, collapsed stars. Most of the matter that is left is made up of neutrons. The existence of this substance has always been suspected. That ring must weigh as much as the rest of Venus."

"Wouldn't that throw the planet off its axis?" asked Sandra.

I looked at her, eyebrows upraised. "Interesting point. Maybe it has some kind of gravitational field control that holds it together and prevents it from wrecking the planet at the same time."

I stared at it while we circled around. It was confounding.

"What's the matter?" Sandra asked me.

"This technology… it's daunting. If the aliens are this far ahead of us—this isn't like a few fusion generators. This is amazing. I feel like an ant pondering a lawnmower and trying to figure out what it's going to do next."

"That's easy," said Sandra. "It's going to suck us up, whirl us around a few times, and then smash us to pulp. Just like ants in a lawnmower."

I nodded. She could be right.

"Socorro, was this structure constructed here, or was it brought here and placed in this spot?" I asked my ship.

"Unknown."

"How long has it been here?"

"Unknown."

"I think I'm sensing a pattern in the ship's responses, Kyle," Sandra said. "I really think she doesn't have a clue about this thing. She's just a baby computer, give her a break."

"Yeah," I said. "For the first time in a long while I'm missing *Alamo*. She was smarter than this ship. I bet she could tell me a lot about this arch—whatever it is."

The screen went dark in front of us. The heat from outside had finally gotten to the forward camera and burnt it out. I scratched my face, then sighed. I'd run out of excuses for waiting around.

"You're really going to fly us through, aren't you?" asked Sandra. "I can't believe it."

"Every minute we stay, the risk of being discovered by the Macros grows. I'm not sure how they will react if they find us here."

"How are they going to react if we pop into existence orbiting their home planet?"

"If that happens, I'll run."

"And if you can't? Or if they follow and they are pissed?"

I shrugged and smiled. "Then I guess it's time to start talking fast."

I nudged the ship forward until we were about a half-mile from the ring. I made sure we approached it at the center point of the donut-hole opening. As the hole was miles wide it made an easy target.

"What if we go through the wrong way?" asked Sandra nervously.

"What do you mean?"

"There are two sides to this thing. How do you know we are going through in the right direction?"

I thought about it. We really didn't know. "It probably doesn't matter," I said.

"I bet that's the last thought that goes through a dog's brain before he wanders out onto a highway."

I chewed a lip. "Maybe we can make an educated guess. Venus rotates very slowly, and it does it backward."

"Meaning what?"

"Meaning the sun rises in the west and sets in the east, and it takes nearly two hundred and fifty Earth days to do so."

"I like when you say smart things," she said.

I looked at her, and saw a certain look in her eye. I loved that look, but right now I was in no position to take advantage of it. Sad, missing such opportunities.

"What's wrong?" she asked.

155

"Nothing. Anyway, the Macros were gathering here about nine months ago, about one Venus day in the past. So, if we look at how they gathered, maybe we can tell which side is which."

"You've got video of the event?"

"Not close-up. I've got all the recordings that Kerr had from their telescopes. They knew for a long time they were massing up out here and hiding behind this planet, forming their fleet, getting it up to full strength before they made their move on Earth."

"Bastards."

I shrugged. "Basic AI tactics. Mass-up in an unexpected location. Roll out by surprise and hit the target en masse."

"You are talking about gaming tactics. This isn't a game, Kyle."

"To a computer, every game is life or death," I said. "They don't know the difference. They play games and real life with equal determination."

I brought up an interface with a remote and paged through recordings. I brought up the vids that showed ships arriving and hiding behind Venus. I played them. They were long, however, and I had to fast forward through hours of disk files to get to a scene where something actually happened.

"Hey, there it goes!" said Sandra.

She'd come over to my chair and sat on the armrest for a better view. I found her distracting. I looked back at the screen, fumbling for the pause button.

"Let me do it," she said, taking the remote and backing it up more slowly. "Whatever it was, it flickered by very fast."

I felt the momentary shock of loss all men feel when a remote is plucked from their fingers. I let her do it, however. She'd seen the thing, after all. She backed up the recording until something did flicker across the screen. We played it again and watched. The ship rose up out of the thick atmosphere and slid behind the planet.

I studied the recording and played it back several times. "We are seeing this from the point of view of Earth. According to the documentation, the telescope was oriented so that north and south are true on this recording.

"What?"

"Up is north, down is south. It looks like the ships are arriving on the left side of the world—the west side. That makes sense, because it was about one Venus day ago, and this structure should be about in the same position. And indeed, we are on the west side of the world from the point of view of Earth."

"Because it takes one of our years for Venus to rotate once?"

"More like nine months, but close enough."

"Okay…" said Sandra slowly. "Then which end of this ring is the right one?"

I shook my head. "Still unclear. It *looks* like they are flying up without turning around. That would mean we are facing the right way right now."

"You can't tell?" she asked, distraught.

"Not really. The Macros could have come out the other side and then turned around under the cloud layer and gone behind the planet after they left the atmosphere."

She looked at me, her face worried. Her eyes squinched up. "Best guess?"

"We are aimed the right way now."

"What are the odds?"

I opened my mouth to tell her it was only a guess, and it upped our odds about ten percent—max. In truth, we were either one hundred percent right or one hundred percent wrong. And we didn't know if it meant our deaths or nothing at all.

"No," she said, putting up a hand. "Don't even tell me. I don't want to hear anything about the odds. We're going to be fine."

I smiled. "Exactly. We are going to be fine."

She kissed me, passionately. This went on for nearly a full minute. I turned my head to free my lips for a second. "Get into your jumpseat," I told her gently.

She looked pained and I had to wonder if the kissing had all been a ruse to keep me from giving Socorro the order to fly. If so, it had nearly been successful.

"Socorro," I said, looking at my love. "Full ahead. Fly us through that ring."

The ship lurched, and Sandra bounced off me. She strapped herself in and gazed wide-eyed at the forward wall. The ring grew closer to the yellowy contact that was our ship. Then we passed underneath it and everything changed.

157

-29-

I'd read theories about what would happen if you really *did* fly through a wormhole. That's all they were, of course—theories. We'd never done it, and our astrophysicists hadn't thought we'd be doing it anytime soon. In fact, even now that I was flying through some kind of gateway to what I *assumed* would be a distant star system, I really didn't know if the wormhole theories applied at all. What I knew for sure is that we reached the other end very quickly—almost instantaneously to my senses.

There was a sensation when we went through the ring—in the moment of transition to someplace else. The feeling reminded me of the small earthquakes every Californian experienced now and then. When a tremor hit, I often felt a bit dizzy. A little off-center. I'd look around the room and see a hanging plant swinging, or a fan that was switched off slowly turning by itself. For the most part, the sensation was in the inner ear, and it felt as if you were sitting in an office swivel-chair while a ghost gently nudged it.

The forward wall of the ship rippled, the first indicator that we were in for a big change. The new version of reality was similar to what we'd left behind. There we were, a tiny yellow contact in the center of the big wall. But the gray disk that had been Venus, complete with some raised bumps of metal that represented a relief map of scorched mountains, had vanished. As far as I could tell, we were in space and there was nothing in the area except the ring and our ship.

"Where did we go?" Sandra asked in a whisper.

For the first time, hearing the fear in her voice, I felt bad. She was really scared, and I'd risked both our lives, not just my own. I should have reversed the ship and flown her home the moment I'd found her hanging on the ceiling of the observatory. At least, I comforted myself, she wasn't likely to try the stowaway thing again if we ever got home from this little adventure.

I pointed to the wall. "Venus is gone. We have to be somewhere else. I'm guessing a different star system."

Inside, I was filled with a mixture of panic and exaltation. We'd made it to another star? I wanted to whoop aloud! Even better, we seemed to be alive and intact. I would have relaxed and cracked open a brew, but I had a whole new set of knots growing in my gut. Where exactly were we? Who was detecting us even now and heading in our direction?

"Socorro, show me a scaled schematic on the forward wall of this entire star system."

The ship hesitated. "Requested job incomplete. Not all sensory data accessible. Some objects are suspected, but unobservable from current coordinates."

"Just show me what you can and use best-guess estimates for the rest."

The forward wall shimmered, twisted. Things bubbled into relief, expanding and contracting in size as we watched. I suspected I was giving the ship's processors a workout.

"Warning: the projected schematic includes incomplete—"

"I know, Socorro," I said gently. "Just complete the command as best you can, no warnings are required on incomplete data when I've approved their inclusion."

"Poor thing," Sandra said. "You're freaking her out."

The image became increasingly clear. As it did so, I squinted hard, my eyes flicking over every inch of it. This was vital data, something no one had ever seen before. There was a big disk in the center, presumably the star at the center of the system. There were smaller bodies floating around, more than a dozen of them.

"Kyle, open up the cameras," said Sandra. "Let me see out!"

"Just a second," I said, breathing hard. That star in the center looked kind of—big. Too big.

"Socorro, what is the class of the main star in this system?"

"The closest star is spectral class B."

159

I blinked in surprise. "A blue giant?"

"Can I see it?"

"Absolutely not," I snapped. "Socorro, increase the hull thickness. I need more anti-radiation shielding."

The ship hesitated. "Insufficient mass available."

"Increase the mass around the bridge, then. Thicken the walls and make the densest wall the one facing the blue giant."

"Specify mass increase."

"I want it thick enough to stop all radiation from that star," I said.

"Mass unavailable."

"Cannibalize the mass from the troop cargo hold," I ordered. "And from primary holds A and B. Begin shielding now. Get it as thick as you can with available mass."

"Working."

"What's wrong, Kyle?" asked Sandra leaning forward in her jumpseat.

I turned to her and gave her a shaky smile. I tried not to look as if I was sweating—but I was. "I should have thought of this. I should have thought of a lot of things. We came out near a blue giant."

"So?"

"So, they are big stars that pour out a lot of radiation. We could be frying."

"Wouldn't we feel that?"

"Probably not instantly."

Sandra stared at me and turned to look at the back wall of the ship. There, the wall was *bubbling*, as if it were a pot of mercury on a stove. I followed her gaze. The wall grew thicker as I watched.

"The ship is moving mass from other parts of the vessel to that wall, in order to protect us."

"Is it lead?"

I shrugged. "I don't know."

"Just talk to the ship. Keep me from frying."

I nodded and stared at the wall that bubbled up behind my chair. I imagined the ship had jettisoned all those seats I'd put in the back for carrying troops. So much for that idea.

Sandra made a strangled sound. I snapped my head back to her. Had she gotten a heavy dose? Had she felt it first because I had the pilot's chair between me and the blazing star behind us? I knew that blue giants could be twenty times as big as our sun, and worse, they could be 100,000 times brighter.

When I looked at Sandra, however, she was pointing at the forward wall. I followed her finger and saw red contacts floating there. Some of them were heading in our direction.

"Identify incoming contacts!" I ordered.

"They are Macro ships. Detailed identification pending. Six vessels are converging on our location."

"Maybe we can talk to them," I said, thinking aloud. I'd taken the time to transfer to my ship everything I could from the neural nets of the brainboxes I had available. We'd lost most of the Nano knowledge of the universe when the Nano ships had left us. I constantly berated myself for not having copied *Alamo's* big, experienced brainbox and kept it as a backup. What kind of a computer teacher couldn't be bothered to backup software? Fortunately, this ship had learned enough from the brainboxes that ran the factories on Earth to speak the primitive binary language of the Macros. With my edits to the communication script, we should at least be able to talk to them.

"We've got to run, Kyle," Sandra said.

"Running away may not be our best choice," I said. "I think they are programmed to be cautious when confronted by brazen behavior. That's worked so far."

"You are theorizing with my life."

"The stakes are much higher than that," I said. "I'm gambling with our entire species. Let me think for a second."

I looked at the trajectories of the ships. They seemed to be coming from various planets—one from each. Could they be mining ships?

"Are the incoming ships armed, Socorro?" I asked.

"Unknown."

"Do they have any weapons ports you can detect at this time?"

"Their range is too great for configuration data."

I narrowed my eyes. "How far away are they? How long will they take to get into our weapons range?"

"The closest is approximately three hours from longest effective range."

161

I relaxed a fraction. We had some time to think. I studied the schematic of the star system. "How long would it take to visit the closest of these neighboring bodies?"

"One hour."

I nodded appreciatively.

"No way, Kyle. Don't you even think about it," said Sandra.

"Socorro, put us on a course for the nearest planetary body," I said, not looking at Sandra. "Execute."

"Kyle, dammit, we should just run."

"Why? They already know we're here. We can scout a planet then come back to the ring and run before they can even reach us."

"You want to know why we shouldn't spend a few hours sniffing around in their territory? I can't believe you even have to ask, but I'll give you a reason: What if they turn the ring *off*, Kyle? Did you think about that?"

"Good point. But I still think it's worth the risk. We came here to scout the system. We've learned a lot—but I want to know more."

"Do you really want to restart the war?"

"If we've done that by coming here, then we need the intelligence all the more."

Sandra looked terrified. I began to worry about her health. This little adventure seemed causing her a lot of stress.

"When we get home, I think you need a vacation," I told her.

"Yeah. That's what I need. Let's take our next radiation bath on the beach."

For an hour, the red contacts grew closer. More appeared as well. There were nearly twenty by the time we reached the dark, gloomy rock we'd been flying toward.

"Socorro, move us behind the planet so the blue giant is on the far side."

We were whisked away to the night side of the barren, nameless world. Huge growths of crystal loomed toward us. I could only imagine the treasure trove of strange minerals they represented. Perhaps heavy elements that were fantastically rare on Earth would be commonplace here.

"Ship positioned," Socorro said.

When we were shaded by the planet, on the dark side of it and thus shielded from the radiance of the blue giant, we went into the observatory where Sandra had first stowed away. I scanned everything and took many pictures, storing them for the spooks back home to analyze. There were some amber contacts on this nameless rock with us. Ground-based machines, the *Socorro* told me. I had the ship take us to examine one of them close-up. It was busy sucking at the surface of the planet. Leeching valuable minerals. It was a mining robot, something bigger than any machine I'd ever seen. It was nearly a mile long and looked like a beetle with twenty spherical wheels. The wheels weren't normal either, being covered with vicious spikes. Each spike was fifty yards long. Some of the spikes were broken. All were gleaming and worn from stabbing into rubble.

"Kyle, that is about the creepiest thing I've ever seen," said Sandra after we watched the spike-wheeled robot churn and probe for several minutes. The machine ignored us completely as we glided around and observed it closely.

"Only another robot could love it," I agreed.

"The Macros must need lots of steel to construct more of themselves," she said.

"These machines aren't hunting for steel. Common elements like iron, nickel and carbon are easy to come by. I think they are hunting for heavy metals—radioactives and unusual alloys."

"Let's look at the stars from here. Maybe we can recognize some of the constellations and tell where we are."

"Excellent idea," I said. I had the ship turn us upside down. Standing on what had been the ceiling, we gazed upward from our tiny, cold observatory into an alien star system. Perhaps we were the first humans to ever have done so. I started snapping pictures. We moved the ship at various angles and shot thousands of images.

"Do you recognize any of the stars? There are some close ones, really big ones."

I eyed the sky in concern. There were other big ones, blue-white. We were probably in some kind of small cluster of new, young stars. Blues often were born in groups of superhot, short-lived clusters.

"I don't see the big dipper," I said, "or the seven sisters, or anything easy like that. I think that's the Milky Way, at least," I said, pointing to the band of brighter light that crossed the sky. "That means we aren't in the center of the galaxy, or another galaxy with a different configuration."

"But isn't the Milky Way brighter than it should be?"

"Definitely. But since this world has no atmosphere, I'm not sure if that means we are closer to the galactic center or not."

"I think it's *bigger*, too," she said stepping up and cocking her head. "Thicker."

I nodded slowly. I had to agree with her, and that gave me a chill. If we were close enough to the galaxy center that we could visibly see a difference in the size of it, then we were many light-years from home. Probably thousands of light-years away from Earth. I didn't mention this to Sandra, however. She was freaked enough as it was.

"We'll just take every reading and image we can home and let the pros figure it out," I said with a confidence I didn't feel.

"How long are we going to hang around?" asked Sandra as a few more minutes slipped by.

"We've seen enough," I said. "Socorro, move all the shielding to the forward wall of the bridge."

The process of shifting shielding from one part of the ship to another took several long minutes. We left the observatory and strapped ourselves back into our seats. The forward wall shimmered, bubbled and *thickened* while we watched. On the way back to the ring we would be flying toward the blue giant, so I wanted all our shielding in front of us, not behind us. This was another reason I'd come out here to this rock. It had allowed us to hide on the dark side of the planet to reconfigure the ship's mass without getting an extra dose of radiation. It was like stepping into shade to adjust one's hat and sunglasses. When the ship had finished moving all the mass we had forward to create a shield between us and the blue giant, we headed back toward the ring again. I made a mental note to bring extra shielding on future scouting trips—if there were going to be any.

"Now, cover all the cameras again, and accelerate at three Gs back toward the ring."

The ship did as I ordered. We both grunted in discomfort as the forces of acceleration pressed us back. I almost gave up my chair to Sandra for her comfort, but I figured if one of us was destined to pass out, it should be her, not the pilot. We were in a combat situation.

"Next time I'll set you up with a nice chair like mine," I promised her. "If there is a next time."

"Why wouldn't there be?" she asked. "Do you think they'll catch us and shoot us down?"

"Maybe, but there are lots of other things that could go wrong."

"Like what?"

"We'll find out soon enough," I said.

"Just tell me."

I sighed. "Okay. I'm worried about time-dilation."

"What?" she asked.

"It's a relativistic effect."

"A whats?"

I took a few deep breaths. Under heavy acceleration, just talking wasn't easy. "You know that we must be lightyears from Earth, right?"

"Sure."

"Well, I've done little bit of investigation on my computer. The closest type B stars I know of—blue giants—are Regulus and Algol. They are less than a hundred lightyears away from home, but still pretty far."

"So, you are saying we are at least fifty lightyears from home?"

"More than that," I said, nodding.

Sandra looked at me with big, brown eyes. Her skin suddenly looked a little green.

"Is this acceleration making you sick?" I asked.

"Just keep talking."

"Okay," I said. "You know that we aren't supposed to be able to travel faster than the speed of light, right?"

"Yeah, but we just did."

"Maybe."

She stared at me. "That trip didn't take fifty years!"

"Not to us, no. But maybe it did in reality. As you get closer to the speed of light, time slows down. It could be that we *did* spend many years coming out here and—well...."

"When we get back home everyone we know will be old?"

"Well, not exactly. You see, we have to travel back the same distance, for the same amount of time."

Sandra's pretty brown eyes focused on nothing as she grasped what I was saying. She looked even greener than before. "A hundred years. More than a hundred years. They'll all be long dead."

"Maybe," I said.

165

I watched her as the implications sank in. "That's why we keep running into alien machines instead of life forms, isn't it? They don't care about the time differences. They just keep going, more or less immortal."

"Yes, but don't freak out yet. It's just a nagging worry. I don't think time dilation fits all the facts. You see, the Macros responded to us very quickly by sending out more ships after we defeated the first one. If relativistic effects were in play, they would not have been able to react so quickly. They would not have known for many years that we had won and they needed to send more ships."

"That's a pretty thin thread, Kyle. They could have some technology aboard their ships we don't have. This is their ring. They know how it works. They could have something to counter the effects that we know nothing about."

I shrugged. "Yeah. Like I said, it's something to think about. We'll know soon enough."

Sandra was quiet for a long time while we flew toward the ring. The contacts slowly grew closer, but they could not catch us. I was increasingly glad I'd loaded this ship with engines and little else.

When we were a few minutes out from the ring, Sandra finally spoke up again. "What are we going to do if it's been more than a century?"

"We'll have each other," I said brightly.

She didn't look happy. In fact, she looked pissed. "Do you want to know what I'm going to do if we get home and everyone I've ever met is dead, Kyle?"

"No."

-30-

The *Socorro* had underestimated the speed of the Macro ships—or maybe they'd accelerated harder after realizing we were going to get away. In any case, three of them were almost in weapons range when we got to the ring.

I braced myself as we slid through it and shot out the other side.... But nothing happened. There was no shimmer. No feeling like a California trembler had hit. Most importantly, no gray disk of Venus reappeared on my forward wall.

"Socorro, where are we?" I asked, hoping she hadn't had time to update the forward screen. It was a faint hope.

"Unknown," the ship said.

"Is that the same blue giant on the screen that was there a minute ago?"

"Yes."

"They turned off the frigging ring," said Sandra through gritted teeth. "I knew it."

"Socorro, switch shielding to the rear wall. Bring the ship about one hundred eighty degrees, full deceleration on all engines—give us six Gs."

Sandra gasped and her body lurched. We were unable to speak for a time as the ship turned and shivered. Silvery rivers of metal flowed over the ceiling and the floor, knocking secured furniture around. The ship was transferring mass from one wall of the bridge to another.

"What the hell...?" asked Sandra, unable to complete the sentence.

"Maybe we went through the wrong way," I said, gasping.

"Put… stabilizers… next frigging… trip," Sandra managed.

"Agreed," I grunted back. I looked at her, she was bent almost in half by the sideways G forces. She was having a much harder time of it than I was with her jumpseat. It wasn't supportive enough for this kind of force.

"Socorro," I said. "Build a supportive wall behind Sandra's jumpseat. Turn it so she is facing the same way I am and form a metal shell pilot's seat that is a copy of mine."

The ship did as it was told. In less than a minute, Sandra was sitting on a molded metal copy of my own chair.

"I was going to pass out," she said.

"Yeah, I know. You would have already if it wasn't for the nanites in your body, compensating."

"Why didn't you think of this sooner?"

"I thought you looked cute there hanging on the wall."

She rolled her straining eyes in my direction and gave me a dark look. It was made even stranger by the forces that rippled her face and pulled back her long hair into a wavering stream behind her seat. "You left me there to keep me quiet, didn't you?"

I smiled. "How's curved steel for padding?"

"It sucks."

We had to decelerate very hard indeed to counter the forward motion of our ship. When traveling through space at several hundred thousand miles an hour, you didn't just turn around on a dime. Even applying twice the thrust we'd used coming from the planet to the ring, it would take us about half an hour to reverse and shoot back through.

"Socorro," I said, gritting my teeth. "Estimate time back to the ring."

"At current thrust: fifty-six minutes."

"Time until the Macro ships are in weapons range?"

"Twenty-four minutes."

"That's it then. Reduce thrust to two Gs, Socorro," I said.

"What the hell are you doing now?" demanded Sandra.

"We can't escape," I said. "We have to talk our way out of this. Acting like we are desperately running for it isn't going to make them more trusting."

"But what if the lead ships are unarmed and we are just waiting around for the other, armed ships to get to us?"

I shrugged. "Could be. But I doubt the whole business of flying through the ring the opposite way is going to work anyway."

"You think they turned it off?"

"Probably."

"If they kill us, we've had our last team-shower, Kyle," she said.

"I'm thinking."

And I did think. In my experience, the Macros were not sophisticates. They were aggressive when they sensed weakness and cautious when they sensed strength. The best strategy when dealing with them was therefore bold, brash action. Keeping that thought in mind, I soon came up with an angle to pursue.

"Socorro, open a channel to the nearest Macro ship. Use the root binary language scripted for Macro communications."

"Channel requested... channel accepted."

Silence. I'd expected some kind of warning or accusation, but nothing came from the Macro ships. Was that good or bad? I suspected it was neither. They were willing to listen, but they still approached doggedly. Would they fire when they got into range? I suspected they planned to.

"Socorro, relay what I say to the Macro ships unless I tell you to cut the channel."

"Ready."

"I am Kyle Riggs, Commander of your allied forces from Earth."

No response. Perhaps, like the Nano ships, they hadn't yet heard anything that required a response. These machines didn't have the best diplomatic manners.

"I'm here to inform your Macro Command that our cargo will be ready for pickup on time in the Sol System," I told them. "Acknowledge receipt of message."

I heard some binary chirruping. I heaved a sigh. At least they were talking.

"Incoming Message: *Transmission received*," said Socorro.

"Macro Command, we detect incoming Macro ships. What are their intentions?"

"Incoming Message: *Forcible dismantlement*."

I glanced sidelong at Sandra. I shouldn't have. She looked terrified and I found the look distracting. I'd forgotten she hadn't been with me when I'd first dealt with the Macros. They could be—difficult.

"Negative, Macro Command. We are a friendly ship. We are a Macro-allied ship. Do not force us to destroy incoming allied vessels."

There was a long pause. Possibly, the ships were discussing the matter. We were far enough out that it took several seconds for radio transmissions to be relayed between vessels. I wondered about their command structure.

"Cut transmissions, Socorro, but leave the channel open. Can you tell me which ship is transmitting the incoming messages? Light it up with a circle on the forward wall when transmissions are received."

"Options set."

"Now, reopen the transmissions," I said.

The pause in the conversation went for nearly a minute. Sandra finally couldn't keep quiet any longer. "They are going to blow us up, Kyle. Stop talking and start running or shooting!"

I put up the palm of my hand toward her, then pointed at the forward wall. One of the ships had a ring around it.

"Incoming Message: *You are not permitted to fire on Macro ships.*"

"We are only permitted to destroy enemy ships," I said.

"Incoming Message: *You are not permitted to fire on Macro ships.*"

"Macro ships that fire on any friendly ship are automatically reclassified as rogues. Rogue ships are enemy ships, and therefore will be fired upon."

Another pause. This time I didn't look at Sandra, but I sensed she was having some kind of fit in her seat. She probably wasn't comfortable with the fact I was threatening them.

"Incoming Message: *Your ship has been reclassified as a rogue.*"

"Explain your reasoning for this reclassification."

"Incoming Message: *Earth-system vessels are not permitted to leave Earth-system.*"

"I have reviewed the terms of our treaty. No such terms have been stipulated, or agreed to."

"Incoming Message: *Agreement modified.*"

"The new terms of our agreement are accepted. Now, allow us to exit this system so we can comply with the new agreement."

"Incoming Message: *Exit the system immediately. Session terminated.*"

"Socorro, cut transmissions. Close channel."

A loud expulsion of breath came from Sandra. I wondered how long she had been holding it. "Kyle, you crazy macro—"

"You have to talk to them like that," I said, cutting her off gently. "They are like predatory beasts. They come at you, planning to eat you, but a brave front may make them uncertain. In this case they turned around."

"Maybe," she said eyeing the big screen in front of us.

I followed her gaze. None of the ships had changed course.

"How long until they are in firing range, Socorro?"

"Two Macro ships are in range now," said the ship.

I nodded. No one was firing. "Macro speed and course?"

"They are decelerating, but the course of each vessel remains unchanged."

"Will they get to the ring before we do?"

"If deceleration continues at present rate, four of them will reach the ring within one second of our arrival."

"They mean to escort us back to our system," said Sandra.

"That's very thoughtful of them," I said. I smiled at her.

She shook her head. "That was totally amazing. You've regained your co-shower privileges."

"Is that all?"

"What more do you want?" she asked playfully.

Sandra could turn a scowl into a flirt in ten seconds flat. I loved that about her. "Do you have a twin sister?" I asked.

She looked for something to throw at me, but couldn't find anything, so she crossed her arms and pouted in her chair for a while. I could tell she wasn't really upset.

I ordered the Socorro to turn us around again and gently brake the rest of the way to the ring. The Macro ships shadowed us. They meant to meet us and head through together. I sensed they weren't in the mood for any more funny business. Machines are sticklers for their rules.

I climbed out of my pilot chair with difficulty. I took careful steps under what felt like one G of steady, crosswise force. I used my chair to support myself, and when I'd gone as far as I could that way I sprang from the seat to hang onto a set of handholds I'd placed here and there around the ship. The handholds were rungs in the walls, like cheap towel-racks, but much stronger. I grunted as I worked my way to a spot in the wall and touched it. The metal melted at my touch.

"Where the heck are you going?" Sandra asked finally, watching my efforts to enter the kitchen area. "Don't tell me you are hungry now."

I came back out after a minute or so of struggling against the acceleration to get the fridge open. A G of sideways force would have been even more difficult to deal with if my muscles hadn't been enhanced. As it was I felt heavy, as if I were in a diving suit at the bottom of the ocean.

I came back to the bridge and jumped back to my command chair. I handed Sandra a can of beer then popped mine open. It bubbled weakly. At lot of the stuff in the fridge had been bashed around, but cans always seemed to hold up well under G-forces.

"A celebration," I said.

"What are we celebrating?"

"Life—while we're still breathing."

"I'll drink to that," she said, and she tipped her can back. Streams of beer flowed over her cheeks and wet her hair. She patted at the mess and complained. Drinking when G-forces are pushing you back in your chair was an art form she hadn't yet mastered.

"It's warm," she said after a quiet minute. We were close to the ring now.

"Yeah. I think it's the radiation from the blue giant. The kitchen isn't shielded."

"Is it okay to drink this stuff?"

I finished my beer, then tilted my head to one side and crushed my can. I kept crushing it down until it was about the size of a sugar cube. Can-crushing had become a habit of mine.

"Don't worry about the radiation," I said. "We'll have the nanites do a rework on us at the cellular level when we get home."

"Will that hurt?"

"Hell yeah."

Then we flew into the ring, and everything changed.

-31-

I hadn't slowed the ship down enough to safely reenter Venus' atmosphere. We'd been decelerating, but there was no speedometer on my Nano ship, and using imprecise verbal commands such as *take us in slowly* proved too vague in this instance. The ship had no scripts or experience to safety-check my decisions when going through a ring. Things went badly.

When I later regained consciousness, I estimated we went through the ring at about Mach 1. That's a very slow speed in astronomical terms, but when hitting a thick, soupy atmosphere it was much too fast. What passed for air on Venus was similar to water on Earth. Hitting it at speed was like plunging a jetliner into the ocean. We didn't even slide along the surface, we dove smack into it.

I think what saved us was the thickening of the hull around the bridge. Other areas of the ship were wrecked. When I woke up, drifting over Venus in my crash seat, the forward wall was dented in and blank.

"Socorro?" I asked.

"Responding."

I felt a moment of relief. At least the brainbox had survived.

"Where are we?" I asked.

"Unknown."

"Why is the forward wall blank?" I asked. As I looked at it, I became increasingly alarmed. It wasn't only blank, it had big creases in it, lines that poked in toward us menacingly.

"Emergency procedures have reprioritized nanite formation settings. Resetting to standard settings."

"No," I said hurriedly. I didn't know what the emergency priorities were, but I figured they were a good idea right now. "Maintain all emergency priorities."

"Acknowledged."

I tried to unbuckle myself with my right arm, but my hand didn't work properly. I felt bones grind. I figured out my right thumb must be broken. I sweated as I pulled it straight and set it with a click. The nanites in my body would have to work on that one. I used my left hand to unbuckle and levered myself painfully out of my chair. I checked on Sandra next. She was hurt worse than I was, and I felt more guilt than at any point on the trip. She came around at my touch, moaning.

"Are we home?" she asked me.

"Almost. Just relax, you've got a few injuries."

"I don't care," she said, keeping her eyes squinched closed. "Just tell me what year it is."

"Everything's fine. It's the same day we left," I said. I had no idea if I was lying or not.

Sandra smiled with the half of her mouth that still worked properly. Blood ran from her left eye down her neck. Her eyes stayed shut. "Good," she said, and passed out again.

I gently eased her back into her seat and made her as comfortable as I could. Rivers of nanites flowed over the walls around me in veins that grew, pulsed, and then shrank away to nothing. I knew the ship was reconfiguring and repairing itself as best it could. I questioned *Socorro* about the status of the ship. We had no communications, no sensors, and only one engine. Worst of all, my flatscreen had a big crack in it.

I checked every camera in turn, and eventually found one that still worked. I managed to get it to feed images to the cracked screen. I had my ship limp back to the ring. The Macro ships were gone. Had they escorted us here and left? Were they up in Venus orbit now, or heading to Earth to check up on things? I had no idea and no way of finding out.

I ordered my last camera covered with a protective nanite dome again. I might need it. I ordered the ship to ease us up out of the atmosphere. The worst part was the high-velocity winds in the acid-clouds. I flew the *Socorro* through them, then dared to uncover my last camera again. Fortunately, it still worked. Without sensors and with no replicating mini-factory aboard to build new equipment, we might have been unable to navigate home.

We spent the next week limping home, taking sightings on Earth with the camera and realigning our course to glide after her. Like all planets, our world was a moving target, and we didn't have as much power as before. But we made it home before our food supplies ran out. By that time, Sandra and I had healed up completely and were bored out of our minds. Even acrobatic freefall-sex had worn thin.

It was with great relief that we drifted down out of the sky over Andros Island. I headed for the main base, figuring I had a lot of debriefing to do. We still didn't have any working communications, so they didn't know I was coming. Using my lone working camera, I guided us in, giving verbal commands to the *Socorro*, as the ship was flying blind. The beam turrets homed in on us and followed us down ominously. They didn't fire, which at least indicated they recognized us.

We landed and a dozen marines rushed out to circle the ship. They were wearing their full kit, with hoods down, reactors on their back and beam projectors held across their chests. I swiveled the camera and began to frown.

"What's wrong?" asked Sandra. "Why is everyone running around like that? Don't they know us?"

"Something has them worked up, that's for sure."

I knew I should go out there and talk to them, but I hesitated. I licked my lips, and felt Sandra staring at me.

"Something is horribly wrong," she said. "It's time-dilation, isn't it?"

"Nah," I said. "It looks like our time. The beam turrets have just been built. The camp looks the same as the day I left."

"Don't go out there, Kyle. Something's wrong, don't you sense it? Let's just fly up and away, gently."

I looked at her. "Why?"

"This might not even be our world. What if we came back to the right time, but not quite the right place?"

I paused. That was a new and frightening idea. "A parallel universe? I don't buy that."

175

"What else would make them act so differently if we've only been gone ten days?"

"Maybe it's been a year. Maybe there has been a coup of some kind, and I'm not as welcome as I once was."

"Two more reasons to back off. If we don't make any surprising moves maybe they won't fire on us."

I nodded. "Socorro, follow Sandra's orders if I'm out of contact."

"Sandra is command personnel?"

"Yes."

I kissed her. I had to pry her fingers away from my neck, then I went outside.

The men were indeed nervous. When the hatch melted open and I stepped out, they didn't point their projectors at me, but I felt them twitch as if they wanted to. I stepped up to the duty Sergeant. I thought I knew him.

"Santos?" I asked.

Santos opened his mouth, closed it again, then opened it again. He heaved a huge sigh. "Yes, sir. Good to see you, sir."

"What's going on?"

"We've got orders to escort you to the command center, sir. On the double."

I looked around at them, they looked serious—and nervous. I nodded.

Mentally, I contacted the *Socorro*. The ship still sat grounded behind me. Her bulk blocked out the sky. *Socorro, seal all entrances.*

Acknowledged.

I'd figured it out. I was pretty sure this was a coup of some kind. Crow or one of the other officers had made a move and grabbed power. I thought about trying to dodge back aboard my ship, but I didn't figure I'd make it past a dozen armed men. The best move was to bluff it through, as I'd done with the Macros.

I turned and walked toward the command center. The men followed me. Sergeant Santos hurried to keep up.

"Uh, sir?" he said in a hushed voice.

"What is it, Sergeant?"

"Do you know what the hell is going on?"

I gave him a half-smile. "I was about to ask you the same question. Don't worry Sergeant, just back me up and I'll straighten it all out."

The man looked relieved. I felt relief myself. Maybe I could turn this firing squad into an honor guard. Whoever had organized this coup didn't have full control yet if these men didn't know what was up. If they hadn't decided whose side they were on—well, I'd make sure they were on my side.

"Give me your sidearm, will you, Sergeant?" I asked.

"Uh, of course, sir," he said, handing it over.

I walked up to the command center. We'd long ago fixed the window the *Alamo* had broken by plucking out the irritating General Sokolov. I threw open the door, ushered Santos and two of his nearest men into the building, then slammed the door behind us. It shook the glass in the window.

There was Crow, standing over the big, pool table-sized planning computer. I walked up to him. I was big on the direct approach.

Crow turned and saw me, and his brows knit into a fierce frown of determination. His lips curled back into a snarl. I nodded to him. If that's how this was going to go down, I was ready. He stepped up to me and reached out his big arms, teeth bared.

"What the hell did you do up there, Kyle?" he asked.

Both of us registered surprise. I'd been expecting something along the lines of, *You're finished here, Riggs.*

Crow's surprise was of an entirely different nature. He looked down and found a pistol probing his belly.

"What the hell is this? Put that away, man. We have an emergency," Crow said. He batted away the pistol, and I let him. He pointed toward the big computer table. I followed his finger warily. I was confused.

"They came down three days ago. At first, they were just wandering around, scanning everything I suspect. We tried to talk to them, but they mostly ignored us. Then the Chinese made a bad move."

"The Chinese?" I asked.

I looked at the computer table. It glowed with a sweeping map of Eastern Asia. It was dotted with icons representing bases, population concentrations and military units.

"What the hell is going on, Jack?" I asked. "Pretend I have no idea what you're talking about."

"It's the Macros, Kyle. They came back and the Chinese shot some missiles at them from their silos in Tibet—the ones around Delingha. Apparently, they had some new ground-to-space weaponry they wanted to try out. Now, the Macros are bombing them. They are killing millions."

-32-

I almost puked. The guilt welled up in me, the horror of knowing I'd screwed up monumentally—even if unintentionally. As I raced back to my ship I wondered if drivers felt this way when they plowed into a group of school kids in a crosswalk.

It couldn't be a coincidence. The Macros had followed me back through the ring. They'd wanted to come scout our system, even as we'd done to theirs. It was a response that was almost human, and I was sure that I'd awakened that response. What was the old adage about letting sleeping dogs lie?

They'd followed me back through, decided to check out their new ally Earth, and things had gone badly. The Chinese had made the next mistake—I couldn't shoulder all the blame for that one. They'd panicked. They'd seen four Macros cruising over their nation in orbit, and had taken a poke at them.

Obviously, they'd developed new weapons. Of course they had. Every nation on Earth with half a military was madly developing space-warfare capabilities. They didn't have fusion technology or nanites, but they had old-fashioned electronic computers, ballistic know-how and nuclear warheads. They'd become paranoid when the Macros came into orbit over them, not wanting to become the next South American wasteland. They'd fired—and to their credit, they had managed to take out one of the four Macro ships.

But at tremendous cost. The three remaining Macro ships now sat over their patch of land and had by all reports unloaded nearly a hundred nuclear strikes. They had not targeted population centers, but had wreaked their cold revenge solely upon military installations.

Still, it was China. There were people everywhere, and fallout traveled. The casualties were already in the millions and millions more would die in the weeks ahead due to radiation and general chaos. Those predictions only held if the bombardment stopped now, however.

I raced into the ship in a nanite-charged blur of motion. Sandra followed me and climbed into her seat, strapping in. I ordered *Socorro* to lift off before either one of us had finished fooling with our buckles.

Sandra looked at me, eyes dark with worry. "What happened?" she asked, her voice small.

I told her about China in a few short, clipped sentences.

"It's not your fault, Kyle," she told me.

I thought she might be crying, but I didn't look at her. My entire face hurt as my muscles twitched and bulged.

"What are we going to do?" she asked.

"We go to the factories first. We need a few things."

We flew to our not-so-secret base and I took a quick stock of things. There was a spare engine ready. I also cannabilized a new sensor system and a communications module. With a human vehicle, the repairs would have taken days to complete. Since each Nano ship was essentially made up of billions of workers, I was able to load the systems into a hold and immediately take off. The ship would do the rest, placing the systems, molding itself around them, and getting them operational. We were headed for China within fifteen minutes.

I spent the time getting briefed by Kerr on the China situation and talking to Crow about our fleet strength. I also uploaded all my data files and vid clips to Kerr's spook outfit. He had plenty of brains at his end who could analyze it all better than I could.

"I decided against flying our fledgling fleet up against the Macros when they first arrived," said Crow, sounding apologetic on the channel. Even he could feel shame when millions of people he'd sworn to protect died.

"Did you fly up there at all?" I asked.

He hesitated. "No. I kept the fleet grounded."

"You probably did the right thing," I said. "Maybe for the wrong reasons, but the right thing, none the less."

"Talk to me," he said.

"We have a new protocol worked out with the Macros. Anything that fires on either side is immediately reclassified as a rogue."

"So, the Chinese forces are rogue now?"

"Yes. And had you been there, you would have been required to fire upon them with the Macros, defending their ships."

"I would never have ordered that!"

"Of course not. But then, you would be in violation of our treaty with them. That might have broken the deal and the war would have restarted."

"What's the difference?" interjected Sandra. "If they are killing millions of us anyway, we might as well be at war."

"We are in a very delicate situation," said Crow, answering her before I could. "The Macros have the strength to crush us at will. We can't let this alliance crumble, even if it is a sham."

"So why are we flying up there Kyle? What are you going to do?"

I didn't respond for a while. "Whatever we have to," I said at last.

Crow and the others gathered behind my ship. There were exactly twenty-nine of us altogether. "Give me operational control Crow," I said over our private channel.

"You know what the bloody hell you are doing this time, Riggs?"

"I don't have time to talk you into anything. Every minute we wait, people are dying. Do you have a plan?" I asked him. "Tell me how to save China."

"I have no damned idea, you know that."

"Then give me operational command and shut up."

It took him a few more seconds, then he grumbled and ordered everyone to follow my orders for the duration of the engagement over China.

We reached orbit in minutes and glided up over the Atlantic, then Africa and the Mideast. We became weightless for a time, drifting in freefall. I hadn't had time to replace our cameras, but the one we'd used to guide us home still worked. I had it zoom in on the Far East.

"Look," I said to Sandra.

She sucked in her breath. Night had just fallen over Eastern Asia. The normal lighting in the cities was missing. The nation was dark, except for dozens of hot spots. Trailing with the winds, long plumes of smoke and ash drifted across the continent into the sunlit world of Siberia, Mongolia and Nepal.

"It looks like volcanoes have risen up," she said. "We can't live with these machines slaughtering us whenever they feel like it, Kyle. You have to stop them."

"I'm going to do what I can," I said. I thought to myself I should have left her home, but I hadn't thought of it until now. She'd been onboard the ship so long now, it seemed natural to have her along.

"Socorro, is our main battery operational?" I asked.

"Yes," said the ship.

"Group-link all ships' batteries. I want them to fire in concert at my order."

"Group-link established," Socorro said after a few seconds.

"Activate main batteries."

We heard a humming sound. Something shifted overhead, where the ship's sole turret was located.

"We can't destroy three Macros with twenty-nine ships," Sandra said.

I didn't look at her. I didn't think she was going to like my plan. I thought about asking her to go into our bedroom and wait there, but I knew she wouldn't do it, so I didn't bother.

On the forward wall, the three red contacts had appeared. They were set up in a perfect formation. You could have drawn a flawless right triangle between them. Each ship was big—huge. They were thirty times the size of my tiny vessel. As we approached, I knew their weapons systems would be tracking us.

"Socorro, light up military targets on Earth under the Macro ships. Show them as yellow contacts."

A hundred moving beetles appeared like freckles on the wall.

"Turn them red, Socorro," I said. "Now, remove moving targets. I only want to see stationary vehicles and buildings."

The screen shifted. Fully two-thirds of the contacts vanished. Those that remained were mostly tiny squares representing radar installations, barracks, communications centers and the like.

"What are you doing, Kyle?" asked Sandra in a harsh stage-whisper.

I kept my eyes on the big board in front of me. "Socorro, have all ships accepted the group-link?"

"Yes."

"Disable their resets," I said. "I want the group-link locked until I countermand it."

"Permissions set."

I eyed the targets below us. We were over China now, decelerating. So far, the Macros had not changed their formation. They remained on course, drifting over Asia. They weren't firing missiles at the moment. Perhaps they were determining a new, juicy target. Or maybe they were manufacturing fresh missiles as fast as they could. The fact they had not yet withdrawn or moved to a new part of the globe was ominous in any case. It indicated their mission here was not yet finished.

"Socorro, invert the fleet into firing position."

Our ships all had their turrets on top of each vessel. In order to fire directly downward, we had to be upside-down. This wasn't a problem for the crews, however, as we were all weightless anyway and concepts such as up and down were all just a matter of perspective in space.

"You're going to do it, aren't you?" Sandra asked me in a dead voice.

"Uh, you might want to go into the other room."

"No."

I drew in a breath, and ordered our ships to fire on the Chinese military. Big green beams stabbed down from space and burnt away trucks, tanks, planes and hangars. Bunkers were exploded to rubble. Missile launchers, abandoned in streets and deserts, melted to slag and I imagined flared into mini-mushroom clouds as their fuel ignited.

Systematically, I disarmed China's conventional military.

33

"Socorro, disable channel requests from Star Force," I said, growing tired of denying beeping calls from every ship in the Fleet. "Open channel to the Macro command ship."

"Channel request accepted."

"Send them this: All Earth Rogue targets will be destroyed."

"Incoming message: *Yes.*"

I thought about that one, rubbing my chin. What would get them to go away so I could stop firing?

"Request operational command for removal of rogue targets."

There was a long wait on that one. I wondered if the Macros had ever faced a similar situation. Perhaps other races had never been so eager to destroy themselves at their whims.

"Socorro," I said, noticing the firing had stopped. "Retarget larger installations that have not been completely destroyed. Fire on one every minute."

"Acknowledged."

The ship shuddered again as the turret moved and my ship's beam cannon stabbed down at Earth, punching through the atmosphere. There were enough clouds and smoke now that they obscured the beam, but I was sure they were still effective.

"Incoming message: *Rogue targets must be completely removed.*"

"Agreed," I said quickly.

"Incoming message: *Operational command given to indigenous forces.*"

With that, they moved on. Maintaining their triangular formation, they drifted slowly over Japan and out over the Pacific.

"Socorro," I said quickly, "Retarget only empty, destroyed facilities in remote locations."

"Retargeting complete."

A dozen sites were still on our forward screen. I left them that way. In rotation, we would pointlessly pound buildings that we'd already destroyed. I suspected that from here on out, the loss of life would be minimal.

After a few more hours, the Macros had completed two, slow patrolling orbits over the globe. No one else fired on them. The earthers had at least learned that was a bad idea. We continued to sit over China, beaming dead horses tenaciously.

Without further communication, the Macros left orbit and headed back toward Venus. I kept up the pretense of bombarding China for many hours, until the Macros were out of sensor range and the bulk of our planet was between their retreating ships and the crippled nation.

By that time, Sandra had calmed down. She was horrified, naturally, but she didn't seem to blame me any longer. She looked drained and tired. Gone was the easy smile and manner of the college coed I'd fallen in love with. I hoped she would bounce back one day soon. This war was taking a toll on everyone's spirit.

"You had to do it, Kyle," she said after she brought us a round of drinks. They were soft drinks, this time. I'd long since run out of beer and I hadn't had time to restock during our brief pause at Andros.

"Thanks for understanding," I said. "Socorro, open a broadcast channel to all Star Force ships."

"Channel open," said the ship.

"I'm sorry you all had to experience that engagement," I said. "For many of you, it was the first time you've fought in this war. Keep in mind, we are *still* in a war. We have a treaty presently with the Macros, but it is more to our advantage than to theirs. We had to fire on Earth forces to maintain that treaty. We are not yet ready to fight them on even terms. From their point of view, the Chinese military went rogue. If we had attacked the Macros, even if we had destroyed them all, we would have surely doomed Earth and our entire species."

I took a sip of soda. I looked over at Sandra. She gave me a flicker of a smile, the best she could do.

"Socorro, open all channels for requests," I said. "Close ship-to-ship group-link."

"Permissions set."

Crow was the first one to call me. He was in a petulant mood. "You could have told me what you were about, mate," he said.

"Be glad I didn't," I answered. "Do you really wish you had okayed that order?"

"You did the right thing—I think. But you should have told me. Crow out."

I huffed and ordered my ship to return to Andros. We still needed a number of repairs. I didn't even look to see if the others followed me. They could do as they pleased for now.

Sandra surprised me by climbing into my lap and putting her head on my chest. She didn't say anything.

I didn't want to blow it, so I just patted her awkwardly. I'd thought maybe she'd want to break up after this expedition, but instead she appeared to understand I'd made the best of a horrible situation.

Kerr called me next. "The Chinese want blood, Kyle," he told me. "Fortunately, they no longer have anything to avenge their dead with. I know what you did took huge balls, and maybe it had to be done. But I wouldn't open any fortune cookies for the next century if I were you."

"Thanks for the advice," I said.

"One more thing," he said. "We've got a fix on the second ring—or at least the spot we suspect a second ring exists."

"I'm listening."

"Have you ever heard of Tyche? It's a theoretical planet out in the Oort cloud."

"Let me guess, it's right where the rest of the Nano ships flew out and vanished?"

"You are a prophet. Yes, Tyche has historically been an explanation for an effect, an odd clustering of comets and other crap out in the farthest, darkest regions of our star system. People thought a big dark planet might be hidden in a far orbit, disturbing the ice chunks that fly around out there. But now with new evidence, it seems that it must be another of your rings, like the one you found on Venus."

"The Venus ring has its mysteries as well," I said. "For example, I don't know how we could have missed it all these years."

"I shouldn't be telling you this stuff," said Kerr.

"But you're going to anyway, because I gave you a wealth of free data. And because I'm one of the few people who can actually make use of your intel."

"Yeah, something like that. Venus has a thick crust, about thirty miles deep. We don't think the Venus ring came down from space and sank into the planet. Instead, our theory states it was already *inside* the planet, and it was recently pulled up out of the crust into the open."

"Huh," I said, thinking that one over. It would explain a lot. "Any clue as to who built these rings or when?"

"They've been around for a long time. Maybe it was the Blues. Maybe it was someone else we've yet to meet."

"Encouraging, given the friendly nature of everyone we've met out here so far. What about the atmosphere of Venus? Why hasn't it all escaped into the void on the other side of the Venus ring, where the blue giant reigns?"

"We are still theorizing on that point. I suppose for now, it's enough to know that only a cohesive moving body like a ship can activate the ring and be transported to another star system."

"Yeah," I said. "As usual, we know how the tech functions, but we have no understanding of the principles behind its operation. Nor can we duplicate any of it."

I told him then of my theory we were like Plains Indians who'd learned to use rifles and horses, the tools of a more advanced enemy.

"At least we're still on our feet and fighting," he said.

"Right, but do me a favor."

"What's that?" he asked.

"If they come and offer us a pile of blankets—just say no, okay?"

187

34

China weighed upon my mind over the following days. Looking back at it, I'd taken risks and things had gone badly. Guilt hung around my neck, but I tried to shake it off. I had to keep reminding myself that although I'd provoked the Macros into cruising over the Earth, the Chinese had decided their own fate by taking a shot at them. They'd paid a grim price, and I'd added a little damage of my own, but in the long run I'd helped save their nation from complete annihilation. I'd also kept the Macros from nuking the rest of the world and kick-starting the war again.

Because I'd been gone for over a week and Barrera hadn't staged a coup, I made him a Lieutenant Colonel. Major Robinson looked slightly annoyed. Barrera didn't offer any expression at all. He was a stoic man—the quiet, effective guy every leader needs to back him up.

When I told Crow about the promotion, he flapped a thick-fingered hand at me. "Great, great," he said. "Why don't you give him a bloody medal for bombing China back into the Stone Age while you're at it?"

"I ordered that, not Barrera," I said.

Crow shook his head. "Don't tell anybody about that. The press isn't blaming you—don't change their minds."

I frowned. "Who are they pinning it on?"

"Me!" roared Crow, stabbing his chest with a thumb. He did it so hard he broke the skin. His tee shirt welled up with a stain and a thin jet of blood squirted out onto the tabletop computer between us when he pulled his thumb back out of the hole.

"Not quite used to nanite-muscles yet, are you Jack?" I asked.

Crow dabbed at his shirt in annoyance. "They blame me, Riggs, because *I'm* the Admiral. I'm supposed to be in charge of the Fleet."

"Why didn't you tell them I was in operational command?"

Crow grinned at me, but there wasn't any levity in the expression. "Don't you get it, Riggs? I was in overall command. It was my fault, no matter what. The press loves you and they hate me. Don't you watch the vids?"

I shook my head slowly.

"Figures," muttered Crow. He ripped off his shirt and dabbed at the blood that still seeped out of his chest wound. "The one guy they gush over doesn't even care. I'm blamed for fouling the nest and I couldn't even control my own ship at the time."

"Life's not fair, Jack," I told him. "At least you've got that sweet Star Force pension to look forward to."

Crow glared. I smiled and left. I had an army to pull together, and only three months left to do it. The butcher's order was up, and I would see to it that it was filled.

The following days blurred into weeks. I had the recruits, the weapons and the uniforms, but that wasn't all I needed. Most of the cargo weight was in the contingency items. When I'd cut the deal with the Macros, I hadn't had the foresight to ask what kind of world we'd be required to fight on. Were we going to the Garden of Eden or an airless rock? Was it going to be hot or cold? What kind of gravity should I expect? So many unknowns…. I was overwhelmed trying to produce a force that could be effective in any environment.

Robinson and I had many late night meetings about it. He was coming with me as my exec. He had some experience and had shown loyalty. I figured he might make Lieutenant Colonel after this little exercise was over, too. But I didn't tell him that. It was best to keep them hungry.

I put Barrera in charge of production. When we left, he'd be running the show for me back on Earth—and that included keeping a handle on Crow. That was the plan, anyway.

Robinson and I juggled the numbers extensively. We knew we had an unknown amount of reserved cargo space on a Macro ship. We knew how much the cargo was to weigh, but not the volume we would be allowed. I didn't feel like flying back out to the blue giant system again and asking them for any more details. For all I knew each question would cost us Canada, or Mozambique. I didn't want to make any more horrible mistakes, so I figured we had to take all of our water, food, air and even living quarters with us. What did a crowd of eighty-foot tall robots know about comfortable, pressurized cabins with bunks, showers and working toilets? Medical systems too, were at a premium. I put together a staff of doctors and nurses to help out with the early hours after an injury. The nanites could repair any wound over time, but they didn't always keep a man alive long enough to effect those repairs. We still needed plasma to replace blood lost due to hemorrhaging, and about a thousand other things.

"We can't do it all, sir," Robinson told me with seven weeks to go.

I looked at him. "We're going to complete this mission, Major."

"Yes, sir," he said. "But I don't see how we can adapt to every environment we might encounter. There are extremes we can't deal with. Such as a world with four times our natural gravity."

"We have to assume the Macros are not complete imbeciles. They know what we can do, and they hopefully won't waste our troops in a place where we are unsuited. I'm assuming the world will at least be somewhere we can function."

"What if we are forced to fight underwater?" asked Robinson. "Our weapons will not be terribly effective in a liquid environment. What if the enemy technology is high-level? What if they have shields, sir?"

I eyed him. He'd always been a worrier, but he had some good points. It was daunting to be heading to an unknown world to face an unknown enemy.

"We need flexibility," I said. "I can only think of one way we can gain that attribute. We'll take a set of factories with us. Then we can produce what we need when we get there. We can take raw supplies and build appropriately."

Major Robinson locked stares with me and nodded slowly. "Is Admiral Crow aware of this detail of your planning?"

I sat back in my chair and crossed my arms. The chair creaked ominously. We'd still never gotten to constructing furniture to hold up our nanite-laden bodies.

"We're taking hovertanks, you know," I said. "Some of them will be very well-equipped—*hovertanks*."

Robinson smiled. "How many specially-equipped *hovertanks* were you thinking about taking?"

"Twelve. With each puffed up into a rectangular shape for shipping, about the size of a railroad car and packed with raw materials. Another eight will carry more raw mass, but no factories."

Robinson, still smiling, worked on his tablet. It beeped and lit his face with blue light. We worked out that each of these special hovertanks would weigh in at a little over a hundred fifty metric tons. We could easily squeeze them into our roster.

Most of the weight ended up being the living quarters for the troops. We built modular units that were considerably smaller than a Macro robot, figuring that they would be easily loaded into one of their ships. Besides weight, there were volume concerns, but we calculated that since much of a marine's weight was liquid or metal, we were dense enough to fit into a fraction of the space one of the big Macro transport's cargo holds. We had decided to build modular units for barracks, which could be stacked like bricks and could interconnect if placed close to one another. They could take a lot of heat, pressure and were armored against incoming fire. With a team of worker units, we could deploy anywhere—on a sea floor or a mountaintop. If forced to, we could handle a nearly-weightless vacuum environment like an asteroid, but I hoped we would not have to fight under such conditions. I couldn't imagine a lifeform that needed removal from such a place.

When we were all done amassing our expeditionary force, we only had five thousand personnel, about a thousand of which were non-combat support people. I only took volunteers and I insisted everyone be nanotized.

I hired Sandra as my personal aide. There was snickering, but I did my best to ignore it. If I'd been in their place, I would have smirked, too. I set her up with a desk in my private office in the command module. She handled all my personal incoming messages, which were countless. She liked the job, saying it gave her a chance to delete all the sexting messages I received as fanmail before I got to see them.

The main camp on Andros had been transformed by the time the big day came. We had thousands of troops living in the expanded base area in their steel modular units. The men had taken to calling their modules 'bricks', but not without affection. Each housed sixteen to twenty people. They were comfortable and well air-conditioned, a real bonus in the tropical climate of the Bahamas.

There were bricks everywhere on the sands around Fort Pierre by the time the Macros were due to return. Many of them didn't house troops, but rather supplies and armament. Many were dedicated to reprocessing breathable air, waste, water and food. Some contained arrays of reactors to supply power. Each of the hovertanks had their own brick to stuff them into, like steel garages.

When the big day finally came it was blustery and clear outside. Everyone watched the sky and checked their handheld computers approximately every eight seconds for net-news of the Macro arrival. Even Crow seemed nervous. I caught him eyeing the sky at regular intervals.

Eventually, the sun set and disappointment set in with it. The Macros were late. The news was met with a mixture of relief and fresh worry. What did it mean? Were they coming at all? Was there a problem? Would they not be needing us for six months or more? How long did we all have to stand around on this beach, waiting for them like thousands of stood-up brides?

Days passed, and I saw my troops growing edgy. I announced major war-games. Thousands of men drilled and sweated in the sun and the surf. We practiced beaming sand into glass, trees into smoldering stumps and ceramic targets into slag. Constantly, we checked the sky over our shoulders.

After a week, we began to relax. I didn't allow anyone to go on leave, but I began rotating people on and off the rosters for various reasons. As long as we had all the equipment we needed, and all the troops stayed on high alert ready to scramble into their bricks, I figured we were as ready as we were ever going to be.

By the eighth dawn, rumors ruled every mind: The Macros had a different calendar, and a year to them meant a millennium. The Macros had really wanted a big cargo of rare earths, and they'd mined that from our asteroids months back, the whole thing about troops being the cargo was a communications foul-up. The Macros didn't have anyone left worth fighting against, and we might still be waiting for deployment a century from now. Macro ships were on the way, but they would take years to get here. The Macros had all been destroyed.

I didn't buy any of the rumors, the theories. I waited and watched the skies as tensely as the greenest recruit. Maybe that was because I had some inkling of what might lie ahead.

They arrived before dawn at the end of a black, moonless night. The Macros were eleven days late, and I'd wager by then half my men had managed to convince themselves the huge ship would never come for them.

Sandra shook me awake gently. She kissed me over and over while I sighed and stretched in our bed. We had an entire brick to ourselves, but only a small part of it was our sleeping quarters. Most of the module was designed to be my command headquarters.

"What is it?" I asked her in a whisper.

"They're here," she said.

My eyes snapped open. I lurched up, and if she hadn't had nanite-enhanced reflexes, we might have bumped heads.

"We've got contacts on the boards?" I asked, slapping the walls lightly to make the ceiling brighten.

"Yes," she said. "And we've got video coming in over the net, too."

Our 'bricks' were more than modular living quarters, they had more in common with a Nano ship than a traditional Earth trailer. The walls teemed with nanites and were programmed to be touch-sensitive. The interface quickly became second-nature to everyone who worked with it. A single tap turned up the lights. A double-tap turned them off. If you applied a steady pressure to a small area for about a second, a radial menu of additional options came up in full relief. Even if a trooper was blinded, he could feel his way over the relief surface of the menu and make his selection. To make the menu hotpoints easier to find through a thick glove, I had scripted them to shiver slightly when active. They felt like hard, quivering beads under one's fingertips.

I sprang out of bed and reached my 'locker' in a single stride. To open the locker I put my hand on an indented area of the wall and made a spreading motion with my thumb and forefinger. The metal surface melted away, revealing a storage area jammed with clothing and equipment. I was dressed in less than a minute. The seals were all automatic, every seam in the suit seemed to melt together and form a single mass as the nanite clusters found one another and made friends.

I spread my hand over the exit portal and stepped down a short hall. Along the hallway was a conference room, a restroom and medical/weapons locker. At one end of the hall was the portal into the command center. At the other far end, the end of the entire brick, was an airlock that led to the outside world. Right now, we didn't need an airlock, but I suspected we would in time.

I melted the door of the command center and stepped inside. Sandra stayed behind and retreated down the hall. We'd decided that she couldn't be in the command center with me. Not only would that smack of nepotism and be bad for morale, it would likely be bad for our relationship. Sometimes a commander had to be a real asshole in public, and it was best not to have your sweetie-bunkmate in the room with you at the time. She would work in my private office, handling high-level communications and correspondence. In effect, she was to be a combination of secretary and personal security operative. She liked pistols, and was a naturally suspicious person. I figured as long as I didn't try to cheat on her, my back was covered.

I wore a full combat suit of Kevlar. The hood hung down my back, but otherwise I was fully prepared for battle. We'd made many improvements to our suits over the last year. I'd renamed them *battlesuits*, and they were now as full of nanites as I was. Our battlesuits were redesigned to keep us alive in vacuum, as well as a hundred other hostile environments.

The command staff looked up as I walked onto what was to effectively be my command post for this expedition. Detecting worry on their faces, I put up my own calm front. It was an act, of course. How can one be completely unruffled when one knows a ship full of huge, killer robots has just arrived to take you away to points unknown? Everyone knew this could turn into the worst blind date in history.

"Where's Robinson?" I snapped, stepping up to the blue-glowing table that sat at the center of the room.

"He'll be here any minute, sir," said Captain Sarin, a staffer. She was pretty and moved like a nervous bird. I'd worked hard not to notice her too much.

It was easy to ignore Captain Sarin today. I didn't even look at her. I was too busy studying the screen that was laid out at hip-level. I could see the Macros on the screen immediately. There were six large, red contacts coming our way. They were already in Earth orbit over Japan. I reached out, touching the screen and dragging it toward me. I spread my fingers over the lead ship, the biggest one. The image zoomed in. A red vector graphic of the ship filled the area at my fingertips. We weren't close enough for a camera view, but we had enough radar pinging off the Macros to get a good idea of their configuration. It had a familiar, cylindrical shape.

"Looks like this one is the transport," I said.

"Yes sir, that's been confirmed by reports from telescopic intel."

I nodded. I wondered why I hadn't been automatically given that feed, but I didn't complain about it. Earth was still far from a homogenous entity. We still barely cooperated, even in the face of our extinction. Given time, I believed that would change, but old habits such as mutually distrustful national militaries would die hard.

"What has me curious are the five escorts. They look heavily armed," I said, zooming in and twiddling my fingers to spin around one of the escorts, drawn in wire-frame. The AI identified no less than four missile ports on each of the Macro killers. I shook my head, the Macros really believed in missiles. They never seemed to use beam-cannons for anything other than anti-personnel weapons. I suppose it was a matter of power usage. Nuclear missiles were a form of stored energy, and did not use power when they fired that could better be directed to shields or propulsion. Our design was quite the opposite. We were all about small beam ships, rather than large missile ships.

"We have designated them as cruiser-class vessels, sir," said Robinson, finally melting open the entrance that led to the hallway and stepping into the command post.

"Sensible," I said, spinning the Macro with my fingers. "Looks like they will still outgun our destroyers—when we have destroyers. What's this here?"

Robinson took his post at the far side of the computer table. He isolated a part of the big screen for himself with quick, deft hand-motions and linked his image to mine so he could examine what I was looking at.

"I don't know, sir," he said.

"Robinson," I said, "they are over Wake Island now, we don't have a lot of time."

"I know sir, but we haven't been able to examine their ships this closely before. The ones they sent to China, they didn't have a system like that."

"It looks like a cannon of some kind."

"Yes sir," he said.

"Are they copying us? Are they building beam weapons to counter our longer-ranged ships?"

"I don't know, sir," said Robinson, sounding stressed. "It could be some kind of long-range sensor."

Analyzing enemy ship designs was a function of Fleet, not the Marines, but at this point Crow had yet to get his act together. Fleet barely existed. Recently, we'd spent all our time building up the ground forces we'd promised the Macros and whatever material we had left had gone into building up our own defenses on Earth. None of us trusted NATO farther than we could throw them. In the absence of Fleet intel, I'd given Robinson the task of classifying and analyzing what we knew of all Macro capabilities. I'd figured he would be a useful resource, seeing as he was coming with me on this little jaunt into the blue.

I outlined the protuberance in question on my screen with a circling finger. It did indeed resemble a cannon. As I watched, it shifted and tracked something.

"It has a barrel, a turret. That is definitely a weapon," I said, "and we have no idea what it does?"

"Correct, sir. We have no record of that type of weapon on a cruiser. They might have been on the vessels you met when the initial Macro fleet came to Earth. But they were so far out we don't have any close-up recordings of ship configuration."

"Well," I said, "I suppose we'll have to wait until they fire on something, then we'll have some intel on these big turrets."

"I suppose, sir."

I turned toward Captain Sarin, who hovered nearby. "Get an ETA clock up on the board."

She jumped and went to work on her section of the big screen. I was annoyed, but I tried to hide it. She should have put up an ETA clock automatically. My entire command crew was very green. Here we were, facing an implacable enemy with unknown intentions, and we still had few procedures in place concerning the operation of our own equipment. I tried to cut them some mental slack, but I couldn't.

"Staff, I want to say something right here, right now," I barked, sweeping my eyes over the group. I noted that everyone looked ashamed. I supposed they all knew they were in for a spanking, for one thing or another.

"We've got to pull it together," I said loudly. I would have hammered the tabletop with my fist, but I didn't want to accidentally crack the ballistic glass that covered it. "This is it, this is the real deal. Drink some coffee or something, but wake up! Now, who has made sure that our defense turrets are off, so the Macros can come down without getting blasted?"

"Isn't that Fleet traffic-control's responsibility, sir?" asked Major Robinson.

"Yes, it is. But do you trust them so completely that you don't want to confirm it has been done?"

A hand went up timidly to half-mast. It was Captain Sarin, the same staffer I'd set on building my ETA clock. She was still working the menus with the other hand. "I confirmed it, sir," she said.

I nodded to her in appreciation. "You see? Captain Sarin has done some forward-thinking."

The ETA clock, when it was finally operating, counted down from twenty-two minutes. I tried to give them all something to do while we waited. Waiting was always hard on troops. I'd learned that during my one active-duty tour in the Gulf as a Lieutenant. When stressed, it was much better for the mind to be doing something—even if it was pointless.

There came a moment however, during the final three minutes, that we had nothing to do but watch the Macro ships. The five escorting cruisers sat up in orbit over the Bahamas. The biggest ship, the transport, lowered itself gracefully down toward us. Dawn was breaking over the ocean. The sky turned pink in the east behind the transport, turning the monstrous ship into a hulking, black silhouette.

We'd planned this out long ago. We'd scripted traffic-control instructions and now transmitted them to the Macros using their own binary language. We landed the transport out in the Caribbean itself, as there wasn't an area large enough on land. The huge cylinder was the size of a skyscraper. It was like watching three supertankers, all bundled into one mass, lowering out of the sky. The Macro transport had huge feet, but I doubted it would use them for much. Instead, gravity-repellers like the ones that moved our hovertanks kept the monstrous ship floating just above the cobalt-blue waves.

Nothing happened for a minute or so after the big ship sank down. I addressed the brainbox that ran the command brick. It had an interface like any Nano ship. I'd found it easiest and fastest just to copy the personality and knowledge of the *Socorro*.

"Command module: respond," I said aloud.

"Responding."

"Are there any incoming transmissions from the Macro vessel?"

"Negative," said the module.

"Transmit the following: We are ready to embark."

"Incoming Message: *Fulfill the terms of our agreement immediately.*"

I felt a tickle of sweat under my arms. What did the Macros want? Everyone had their eyes on me. I was the architect of this entire thing, and if I had monumentally screwed up by misunderstanding the terms of our agreement, the existence of my race was in question. I swallowed, and tried to look confident and tough. I thought about exiting the room and working from my office. It would be easier to think if I wasn't being stared at by a half-dozen scared people.

I drew in a breath. I decided to brazen things through. The Macros seemed to respond well to that sort of thing.

"We are ready. We have prepared the promised cargo. Now, open your cargo bay doors so we can load your transport."

"Incoming Message: *We measure insufficient mass. Agreed-upon terms have been violated.*"

Insufficient mass? I wondered if we had screwed up somehow. Had they measured tons in an entirely different fashion? Did they have scales from some tiny world where a single ton metal was the size of a mountain? Had we promised them troops in tonnage equal to the size of the Earth itself?

My head swam as I groped for a next move. I rejected the mistaken scaling concept. That didn't make sense, as their holds couldn't support much more mass than what we'd promised them. Something else was wrong....

"Maybe they think we meant tons of nothing but troops," Robinson said in a stage whisper, as if the Macros might somehow overhear. "Maybe they've counted heads, and know that our troops weigh far less than a single kiloton in bodies alone."

I stared at him. If he was right, we would have to renegotiate, or we were doomed. I thought about this delicate situation. I knew I didn't have too long to respond.

"Sir," said Captain Sarin, "the cruisers are reorienting themselves."

"Give me the visual."

The image, transmitted down from space, snapped up on the tabletop in front of me. The Macro ships formed a classic diamond pattern over our heads, one ship at the center and one at each point. I nodded, noting that they had formed a similar formation over China. Apparently, during planetary assaults, they tended to form diamonds or triangles.

"Those unknown turrets on the bottom of the ships, they are activating sir," said another staffer. "They are tracking."

"Tracking what?"

"They appear to be tracking this command module, sir. All of them."

I nodded. "Well, at least we know now what those turrets are. They're ground-assault weapons of some kind."

-36-

"Maybe we should just go for it, sir," said Major Robinson.

I looked at him. "What have we got?"

"Crow took the precaution of massing up the Fleet over the production base. They are drifting very close to ground-level, but could head up into orbit at a word from us. All we need to do is report that the agreement is breaking down."

"I'm not ready to do that yet."

"Sir," he said, leaning forward. "That is your call. It is my duty to inform you of our status for any contingency. I believe we could take out this fleet fairly quickly."

"You have thirty seconds to convince me," I said.

Robinson put both his palms on the table between us. A rippling effect on the screen outlined each hand. It was the screen's way of idly acknowledging the contact and showing it was awaiting an intelligible gesture.

"We have more ships than we did when they hit China," he said with intensity. "That's nearly forty ships."

"Closer to thirty," I said.

"Yes sir, but the fleet only represents a fraction of our firepower. The big advantage we have right now is our ground-based weaponry. Every Macro ship is in range of our land-based beam turrets. We have two hundred and seven guns we could target them with. We also have hovertanks, with a combined firepower greater than the fleet itself."

I thought about it. Essentially, we could hit each of their vessels in turn with around three hundred cannons. This was because they were right on top of us now. We could blast each ship in turn with overwhelming firepower and destroy them all, probably within a few minutes, and definitely before they could retreat.

I grimaced. This was not how I had envisioned my day unfolding. I had brought peace to Earth. Was I about to plunge her back into war? I felt like Admiral Yamamoto, eyeing the charts and plotting the locations of US ships around Pearl Harbor. I imagined he'd felt similar misgivings.

"The problem is, Major," I said, "they will be back in a month or two with a hundred ships, and next time they might not be so kind as to park themselves in low-orbit above the single heavily-fortified spot on our planet. No matter how many guns you place on it, the Rock of Gibraltar can't defend the entire world."

"It might be our best option, sir," Robinson said.

I looked into his eyes. He wanted to do it. Even if it meant this command module would be splattered into oblivion seconds after the order was given. Was that bravery, or simple desperation, I asked myself. Probably, it showed an impressive hate for the Macros.

"Tell Crow to position his ships in orbit behind the Macro formation," I ordered Robinson. "Tell him not to fire unless he sees things go badly."

Robinson nodded and stepped away to pick up a com-link and make a private connection with Fleet. I turned to Captain Sarin and gave her similar orders to relay to Lieutenant Colonel Barrera. He was in command of the laser turrets and the hovertanks. If he group-linked them, they could all fire in unison at designated targets.

"Tell Barrera to disperse our hovertanks—just in case."

"Yes, sir," said Captain Sarin. She seemed far less excited about her orders than Robinson had been. I didn't blame her.

"Command module," I said, "transmit this to the Macros: we have not violated the terms of our agreement. We have all the promised mass here to load aboard your transport."

"Incoming Message: *Insufficient mass detected. Our terms have been violated.*"

"Crow is lifting off, sir," said Robinson in my ear. "He'll form up behind them so our own ground-based beams won't cause any friendly-fire problems."

"Barrera is group-linking the ground forces," said Captain Sarin into my other ear. "He suggests you evacuate the command module. He's relocating to the new underground bunkers now."

Barrera was right, of course. If this thing was about to turn into a shootout, I didn't want my command staff caught in the middle of it. I should pull out of the module and move to a safer location. I thought of Sandra, sitting in my office nearby with no clue what was going on, no inkling of the weighty decisions I was making.

I thought next of Kennedy and Kruschev during the Cuban Missile Crisis of the sixties. I'm sure they had felt pressure like this. Here I was with my finger on the button, and I had no idea what the other side was really thinking, what they might be up to. I was sure of one thing, however: the Macros weren't freaking out inside like I was right now. Being a machine-based intelligence had its advantages.

"Command module, transmit this: Macro Command, measure the combined mass of all the bricks stacked in front of you. There are nearly five hundred of them. Their combined weight exceeds the promised cargo weight."

Nothing came back for several seconds. I had them thinking, conferring. Perhaps they were doing as I asked, scanning the units.

"Incoming Message: *Contextual definition required for the term: brick.*"

"Certainly. This command module transmitting to you now is one 'brick'. We have broken up the cargo into four hundred and sixty-six bricks of identical size and configuration for easy loading and transportation. These bricks are stacked all around us."

Another silence stretched. People's eyes wandered fearfully over the ceiling and walls. Were we about to be blasted into subatomic particles?

"Incoming Message: *Terms met. Load the cargo.*"

Whoops went up from the stunned staff around me.

Robinson stared at me. "That's all it was?" he asked, incredulous. "They were only measuring this one brick?"

I nodded. "Looks that way. The Macros have always been literal-minded in my experience. They are rogue robots, after all, following some program laid down by their creators perhaps centuries ago. They aren't very flexible in their thinking. Maybe when they load a transport, they always do it with a single, massive pallet."

"Sir, the whole front of the transport is opening up," said Captain Sarin. She sounded choked up. She cleared her throat.

"Display it," I said.

The screen swam and refocused. The dawn light had grown brighter and turned the pink skies orange. I could see the base, the palms and the wind whipping up the beach. The ship was huge, and the cargo doors appeared to be on a commensurate scale. One end of the cylinder now aimed toward our base as it hovered over the sea. The doors consisted of four triangular leaves that opened flat end of the cylinder. The leaves unfolded slowly. The bottom triangle crashed down into the seabed and became a ramp, sinking into the beach like a dragon's heavy tongue. The side doors swung wide with tremendous groaning sounds on hinges each of which was as big as one of our bricks. The top triangular door lifted up to block out the sky overhead. Inside this yawning maw the ship was dark and empty.

"We can get aboard now, sir," said someone.

For the first time since I'd stepped into the command center today, I grinned.

"Relay a stand-down order to everyone," I barked. "Let's not blow this because one jumpy pilot takes an early shot. Get Crow's Fleet down on the ground again. Put the beam turrets back on standby and get the hovertanks that aren't coming with us back into their garages."

Everyone reacted with great energy. The loading process began in earnest.

It took even longer than I had imagined. We, as the command module, were one of the last bricks to be loaded aboard the Macro transport. I wasn't sure if I would be able to communicate with the base once I was inside the massive ship, so I had the trundling worker-machines with their whipping black arms pick us up last.

During the intervening hours, several people contacted me with final well-wishes and instructions. Sandra had been putting them on hold while I pondered starting a new interplanetary war, but now that we were loading they became insistent. She relayed them to me on a private com-link channel one at a time. The first in line was Crow himself.

"I'm sorry to see you go, mate," he said. "I honestly didn't know if they would actually come and take you."

"Keep building ships, Crow," I said, "and keep training new pilots. I hope to see the skies dark with Star Force ships when I get back. After you have about two hundred of these light craft, start building—"

"Yeah, yeah," said Crow. "I'll have a nice row of destroyers waiting for you when you get back, I'd wager. No worries."

Our destroyer class, long ago scripted, required ten times the mass, time and effort to build as the one-manned workhorses we'd been using up until now. They would not look much larger than our puffed-up little frigates, but would have ten times the firepower and double the effective range due to their larger beam-cannon mounts. A crew of six would operate them, mostly working as gunners to prioritize multiple targets.

"I've got plenty of worries," I told Crow.

Crow chuckled harshly. "I can understand that. But she'll be right. We'll keep building troops and ships in your absence."

"Wish me luck, at least."

"Luck, mate. Crow out."

I didn't get to take the com-link from my ear. Sandra had Kerr on the line.

"Why General," I said, "I didn't know you cared."

"Stay out of trouble out there, Riggs."

I snorted. Then the snort turned into a full-blown gust of laughter. I looked at the screen, where a steady line of trundling robots hovered along in teams of two, carrying bricks full of equipment and humanity aboard the alien transport. In order to keep from flipping over, the hovering bases of the worker units had to tuck themselves underneath the bricks. Their long arms reached up to the carrying handles on top. Cable-like fingers gripped the handles and held the bricks aloft, swaying and creaking.

"Such a thought at such a moment. I'm in deep here, Kerr. I'm in so deep, I'm never going to dig myself out of this monumental pile of trouble. Not this time."

"What I mean is, don't bring it back home this time," Kerr said.

My laughter stopped. "I get it. You are slapping me for China again. Listen, if France takes a shot at these ships as we leave orbit, I'm not going to be able to do anything about what happens afterward."

"No offense meant, Riggs. But you do tend to get ideas. Try not to get any on this trip. And have a good time."

"Sage advice, sir."

I couldn't press the disconnect button fast enough on that one. I had to ease up so I didn't break it.

Next in line was Barrera. As the link clicked in my ear, I heard loud rumbling sounds outside the module. Metallic clattering and rasping came from the roof. The hands were wrapping themselves around the carrying handles of our module.

"Talk fast," I said.

"Everything is in place, sir."

The floor heaved up under me. Everyone in the command post reached for the cable loops on the walls. The robot arms rippled and lifted. For a moment or two, we swung in the air as the two worker units automatically sought a good balancing stance underneath us. I felt like a rat in a cage.

"Mind the store for me, Barrera. When I get back, I want to see a Star Force Fleet—and Star Force Marines."

"I'll do my best, sir," he said evenly.

We disconnected. I noted that he was the only one who'd never wished me well. I wondered if that was due to an overabundance of confidence in my abilities, or simply a character flaw. I suspected the latter. Barrera was all business.

37

We had some difficulty with the natural contour of the Macro ship's hull. The transport ship's 'floor' was curved, not flat. The entire ship reminded me of a giant jar with a top that opened in flaps. We had suspected such an internal structure having observed these ships on several occasions. We had magnetic clamps installed on every module. Each brick clung to the floor—which was made of a ferrous alloy. Tubes extended between the bricks interconnecting them. We'd planned for all of this ahead of time, as we couldn't be sure the Macros would bother to pressurize the interior of their cargo hold while traveling. With the bricks interconnected like a miniature city, an individual could travel to any brick without having to exit into the hold itself. They would have to go through a lot of airlocks to do it, however. We'd designed every brick to maintain its own integrity. If a brick caught fire or lost pressure, the damage could not easily spread to the rest of the pile.

We were finally aboard and our command module was stacked atop the heaping pile of bricks. The modules were stacked three to five units high. The entire pile was ten modules wide and sixteen deep.

"What's the first order of business, sir?" asked Major Robinson.

I thought about it. We had a very long list indeed. We'd been flexible in our planning for this stage of the operation. We hadn't known how smoothly the loading process was going to go. We had tried to build the bricks to be compatible with the Macro ships, but until we tried it, we couldn't be sure. Now I was sure, and it was time to move on to bigger things.

"I think we're in good shape. I'm going to contact the Macros and try to get some information out of them."

My command staff eyed me. They looked apprehensive. I frowned, feeling a moment of irritation.

"Don't worry, I'm not going to upset them," I said.

"Ah…" said Major Robinson, his mouth hung open for several seconds.

I could tell right away he was choosing his words, trying to say something annoying without annoying me. I knew he was going to fail at it.

"Just talk, Major," I said.

"Sir, maybe we should wait until we are underway before we contact them. I've had a prior discussion—"

"With who?"

His eyes slid around to some of the command staff, who tapped at reports and screens, looking busy. "With others, sir," he said. "Anyway, as your exec, I think we should wait until we are out of the system. We nearly had an incident before we even loaded the bricks—"

"I suppose that was my fault too, is that it? Notice, Major, no one died today. Not yet, anyway."

"Yes sir, we've made excellent strides."

I grumbled and poked at the computer screen. "Maybe we should at least turn on the active sensor array."

"Oh—ah, is that a good idea, sir?" said Robinson.

I looked at him. What had so frightened this man? I dialed up the sensor array interface on the computer in front of me. I didn't look at them, but everyone was staring at me, I could feel their scrutiny.

My hand hovered over the big screen. We had our passive systems on, but we were already blinded by the hull of the Macro ship. Being inside the Macro hold had unsurprisingly shut out emissions around us. But if I turned on our active systems and started pinging everything, that might upset the Macros. That's what had my staff on edge. I sighed and put my hand back on the black steel border of the big screen.

"One brush with the Macros has turned my entire command staff into a flock of chickens, is that it?" I asked.

"Yes sir," said Captain Sarin.

I looked at her and chuckled. "At least you have the guts to admit you're scared... if that makes any sense. These are scary things, these ships, aren't they? But we have to take decisive action where it is warranted, people."

"No arguments there, Colonel," said Robinson. "But we just want to be away from Earth, so only *we* suffer from any—missteps."

I nodded, understanding at last. They figured I was going to cause some horrible misunderstanding and somehow sink Cuba, for example, under the waves.

"All right," I said at last. "We will role-play the part of happy, quiet cargo for a while."

Everyone breathed a deep, relieved breath.

"But I'm going to discuss one or two things with them first," I said, ignoring their newly shocked expressions.

"Command module, respond," I said.

"Responding."

"Send this transmission to Macro Command: All bricks are loaded. We're ready for transport."

For some reason, I'd expected a verbal response. Maybe a *welcome aboard*, or some other acknowledgement. But the machines said nothing.

"Sir, they are closing the doors!" shouted Captain Sarin. She selected our direct, external cameras and channeled the transmission to the screen we huddled around. She made a swirling motion with one finger, causing the camera to pan rapidly. The dark walls of the Macro hold swept by with sickening speed. Soon, blinding white light flooded the camera. The camera automatically dampened the brilliant image, but it left all of us blinking.

"Take a good look," I said. "Say good-bye to our world and our star."

Fixated, we watched as the four great leaves swung shut. The beach looked so inviting. The trees were tossing wildly now, the winds had increased in intensity as dawn shifted into morning. I could tell after a year down here in the islands that a tropical storm would blow up later today. Soon, it would be overcast, and the silver-lined clouds would turn into gray skies. Sandra and I had often enjoyed walking the beach in mild storms. I would miss the drumming sensation of warm rain on my face.

"Command module," I said, "send this: What are the stellar coordinates of our destination star?"

The speakers were silent. My staff held their breath. We still watched the big doors closing as we waited. Before an answer came, the last brilliant, white cross of sunlight shrunk to nothing. With a deafening clang, the doors shut completely. We all knew we had been entombed.

"Incoming Message: *Cargo is not permitted interrogatives.*"

I grunted. "What the hell does that mean?"

"I think they mean they don't want us to ask any questions," said Captain Sarin.

I glared at her. "I know that. I mean I don't like the implications of their statement. Some alliance this is. I'm feeling unappreciated."

The floor rocked a tiny bit. It was an odd sensation, like that of an earthquake. Unsurprisingly, the interior of the hold was pitch-black. There were no windows or lights. Now that the great doors had clanged shut, it was as quiet and cold as a grave.

"I think we've lifted off, sir," said Robinson.

"No kidding. External floods on," I ordered.

Captain Sarin manipulated a radial menu. I could tell she had dialed down the lights, muting them so as not to upset our hosts. We had flood lights mounted on every brick. On the screen, the big halogen bulbs snapped and we could see again.

"Roll the camera around. Let me see if they have anyone in here with us."

She rolled the camera in a three hundred sixty degree spin, then I had her check the ceiling.

"Ah, there we go," I said.

Everyone stared. There, on the roof of the hold, were two worker units. They had the familiar metallic, headless-ant look. They had beam weapons mounted where their heads were supposed to be.

"Workers," I said thoughtfully. "Outfitted with military kits. That must be some kind of portal behind them. They don't seem to want us going into the ship."

"I get that feeling, sir," said Robinson.

As we watched them, another worker came up from the dark portal between the first two. Then a fourth arrived, and the Macros took up a common diamond formation, all clinging to the ceiling directly overhead.

My command people watched the Macros intently. I knew none of them had ever been this close to a real live Macro before—if you could call them *alive*. For some reason, most of the veterans who'd fought with me in the South American Campaign had not volunteered to head out to the stars in the belly of a Macro ship.

I looked at the robot guards thoughtfully. "You know, those are probably the Macro equivalent of shipboard Marines. Even if there are a thousand more of them up forward, we could take this ship easily."

Robinson appeared nervous again. "But sir, the five cruisers escorting us might object."

I smiled. "Now we understand the reason for the escorts. Whoever said these machines were dumb?"

38

The whole business of not being allowed to ask a question ate at me. Keeping us sealed in a dark hold like mushrooms I could understand. But I needed *some* information. Even mushrooms are fed horseshit now and then.

I decided to solve the impasse by playing their game. I wouldn't ask any questions. After all, the Macros never did. Maybe they just didn't like questions. I would make imperative statements rather than interrogative questions. Just the way they always did.

"Command module, relay this message to Macro Command: In order to achieve maximum effectiveness, Macro Command is required to provide intel on our target enemy."

"Incoming Message: *Enemy species is biotic. Enemy species is space-faring. Enemy species must be eradicated from target system.*"

I took a victory lap, eyeing each of my chicken staff in turn. I wanted to say: *see, and no one even died yet.* I decided not to gloat, however. It was time to mine every detail I could out of the Macros and analyze the information later.

I almost asked a question then. I paused—it was like playing Jeopardy, you had to word things just right. I chose my words with care. "Command module, relay this: In order to adapt our equipment for the coming assault, we need to know gravitational pull of the target—environment."

"Incoming Message: *One point eight one Gs.*"

I winced. "A high-gravity world. Robinson, pass that down to supply. We'll need to get everyone set up with a light kit. Hopefully, it will be enough firepower, or we'll have to have three-man teams to drag heavy beamers around."

"I'm not sure we have a light projector and reactor for every man in the unit, sir," said Captain Sarin, working with a data cube interface on her section of the big screen.

"Then we'll make more. That's why I brought the factories."

I thought about what I could deduce so far. If the world was big enough to generate that much gravity, it would almost certainly have an atmosphere. The enemy was described as a biotic, which further supported the idea of an atmosphere. If it had been a gas giant, that would have meant a much higher gravitational pull, so the logical world to expect would be a solid, rocky planet with a thicker atmosphere than Earth.

"In order to adapt our equipment for the coming assault, we need to know the target planet's surface conditions. Temperature, pressure and atmospheric composition."

"Incoming message..." Macro Command proceeded to answer my queries concerning the target world. As long as I worded each question as a demand and gave a reason why they must answer, they seemed willing to tell me anything about the planet we were heading toward. They would not answer questions concerning the location of the world, or the star system, or the enemy strength.

After an hour of demanding information, we'd pieced together a fairly-detailed idea of the enemy we faced. They were larger than humans, maybe twelve feet in length. They were short, however, standing perhaps three feet tall. The average adult weighed in at about a thousand pounds by Earth standards. They were considered highly dangerous.

Their atmosphere may or may not be breathable. It had oxygen and nitrogen, but with measurable levels of argon, krypton and carbon monoxide. It was this last gas that worried me, as it was dangerous to breathe in any appreciable amounts. I couldn't get the exact percentages out of the Macros. I suspected they hadn't bothered to make a detailed analysis of exact levels of trace gases as they didn't need to breathe. The atmosphere was thicker than Earth's, about three times the pressure at the surface—which was hardly surprising given the higher gravitational pull.

I couldn't get much out of the Macros concerning the mission itself, or the weaponry of the enemy. They were technological, and I

213

had to assume they had given the Macros a hard time so far, or they wouldn't have called us in for this mission.

After about an hour of demanding information, something triggered in the Macro software. I suspected they had an algorithm running in their system software that detected the repetitive demands. Maybe it had counted the number of times I'd said *we need to know*. Whatever the cause, the Macros refused my demands after that.

"Incoming Message: *Session timed out.*"

I tried several more times, then decided I'd pushed things far enough. My nervous crew seemed to think they were on the edge of jettisoning us all into space.

A few more days rolled by, and they were filled with frantic activity. We had an idea now of what we were up against, and we had to gear our troops to face an environment where the air was unbreathable for extended periods, the gravity was nearly twice as strong as on Earth, and a very vicious enemy had to be eradicated.

I often overheard my people talking about what kind of creatures they thought we would be facing. The type they least wanted to find was some type of insect. That didn't align with my thinking. I rather hoped they *were* giant bugs. It would be easier to slaughter giant bugs than a race of big-eyed bunny rabbits, for instance.

On the third day, according to our chronometers, I felt a small shudder. I was in my quarters at the time, trying to talk Sandra into a team shower. She wasn't overly interested as the shower stall was cramped even for one person. My talk of conserving water wasn't flying either, as she knew as well as I did that we had plenty in the storage tanks and our nanotech systems were very good at recycling the basics.

"Did you feel that?" Sandra asked me. Her eyes were wide and dark.

"Yeah. That felt like we went through a ring."

"Could we have gotten there so fast? Wouldn't we know if we had reached Venus?"

"No, maybe not," I said. "We've got no way of knowing what is going on outside this tin can. And it has gravity-stabilizers. We aren't feeling the acceleration and deceleration the way we did on the *Socorro*."

"I want you to put them into your ship—if we ever get home."

"Agreed," I said. I put my shirt back on. Somehow, I'd managed to get it off, but hers was still on. My efforts had been dogged, but had yet to bear fruit. "I've got to go check things out on the command deck."

Suddenly, her arms encircled my waist. "Do you have to go? You smell so good."

I looked down at her in mild exasperation. "Now you tell me?"

I shook her off and tapped my way through a few melting doors. I soon stood on the command deck, tucking my shirt into place. Captain Sarin gave me a strange look with raised eyebrows.

"What?" I asked.

"Nothing sir."

"We just went through the Venus ring, people," I announced loudly. That got their attention.

"How do you know?"

"I've been through it before. Twice," I told them.

"That little shiver? The feeling like you were falling sideways for a second?" asked Captain Sarin.

"That was it. Now, we are in orbit around the blue giant, if the ring works consistently. I need radiation readings. These bricks should keep everything out that can leak into the hold, but I want to make sure."

"What kind of radiation levels are we talking about? What did you experience?"

"We really don't know. When we came back, we took a few handfuls of potassium iodide. No clue if that stuff helped. We didn't have dosimeter badges out there or a Geiger counter. We know we got a dose, but we had nothing handy to measure it with."

"You seem healthy, so what is there to worry about?" asked Captain Sarin.

"We arrived pretty far out from the blue giant, and we flew away from it to a nearby planet. But this time we are probably going to another ring in the system—something that links this world to the next one. That could mean we pass right by the blue giant."

Captain Sarin nodded slowly. She had a large graphic up on the computer now. I studied it in detail.

"Nothing?" I asked.

"Nothing. No radiation at all."

I rubbed my chin and frowned. Either the Macro transport was highly resistant to radiation, or things weren't as bad as I'd figured they were.

"Dammit," I said. "I wish I had a sensor array up. Our passive sensors still aren't picking up anything?"

"Nothing, sir."

"Prepare to turn on the active systems," I said.

Everyone in the room tensed up. Captain Sarin's hand strayed to the computer. I stared at her.

"That's not the sensor control system, Captain," I said.

She jumped. "No, sir."

I stepped beside her. She had sent a message to someone.

"Who are you contacting?"

"I had that messaging system up before, sir," she said. "I was just closing it."

Her forefinger stabbed the 'X' in the corner of the application. It vanished. Quickly, she dialed up the sensor controls.

The door opened behind me. I turned to see who showed up with interest. It was Major Robinson.

"What's up?" he said, looking from face to face.

"A minor conspiracy, by the looks of it," I said sternly.

Major Robinson paled. I waved away my own words and called him over to look at our supposed location in the universe. We had a chart up of the blue giant system. We'd taken it from the memory of the *Socorro*. All of the sixty-odd planets and other bodies were displayed in their relative orbital positions. We'd been there long enough to track and plot their paths and had programmed the system model into the tabletop computer. Overall, even though the nanite brainboxes were smarter and more flexible, I still preferred the interfaces of our own homegrown, electronic machines. They certainly were easier on a man's vocal cords.

I crossed my arms, put my butt against the tabletop and leaned against it. "I hate this blindness. I'm going to turn on our active scanners."

"Sir," Robinson said, "As a marine officer, I have to warn you that is strictly against protocol for any insertion mission. In our own military forces back on Earth, you don't start pinging when you don't even know what is outside the ship."

"That's the whole point of pinging, Major."

"But sir, we don't know the tactical situation. We can't do something like that unilaterally. The enemy might be listening for just such a signal to locate this convoy and destroy it."

I cleared my throat, knowing he was right. "Okay, I'll talk to the Macros about it."

Robinson gave me a look that indicated he didn't think much of my chances, but I ordered the command module to open a channel to Macro Command anyway.

"Relay to Macro Command: We would like to turn on active sensors."

The answer came back immediately, and it was definitive. "Incoming Message: *Permission denied.*"

"Why not?" I asked. I closed my eyes and sighed the moment I'd spoken the words.

"Incoming Message: *Cargo is not permitted interrogatives.*"

"Yes, right. Send them this: provide us your passive sensor feed so we can monitor our approach to target."

"Incoming Message: *Request denied.*"

"Then at least allow me to place my own passive sensors on the ship's hull!" I shouted.

There was a long pause. Everyone looked at the walls around us.

"Incoming Message: *Permission granted.*"

"Ha!" I hooted and clapped my hands together. "We'll be able to see what's around us in an hour!"

Everyone tried to look happy for me. It took a moment to notice they looked a little green, too.

"What's wrong now?"

"Who's going to install the sensor array, sir?" asked Captain Sarin.

I suddenly understood her concern. "Send two of our best techs."

Everyone in the command brick relaxed a little. They were all happy they didn't get the assignment.

39

We watched on the cameras as two suited men strapped sagging tool belts around their waists and lifted a barrel-like container between them. They were unarmed and anxious. The weightless environment made things much easier. They simply walked out onto the top of a brick in the maintenance and supply area and jumped toward the ceiling. They did a slow spin and landed on their magnetic boots. They were about thirty yards from the four Macro guards. They stepped toward the guards, who didn't move except to swivel their weapons systems. They tracked the approaching men flawlessly.

I frowned. "They could at least move out of the way," I said.

My marines took ten steps closer, then twenty. They walked slower as they approached. They tried waving at the Macros and gesturing for them to move aside. One of the machines twitched its gun-mount, tracking the gesturing hand.

One of the staffers in the command module waved to me. He handed me a com-link unit. "It's the two engineers, sir. They don't like it."

"I don't blame them," I said. "Just tell them to standby. I'll talk to the Macros. Maybe they don't quite get that we have to enter their ship in order to do the job. Damned machines."

"Command module, relay to Macro Command the following: Allow my technicians to pass your guards and set up the sensor array."

A few seconds passed. I watched as the two men stood there, moving uncomfortably.

"Incoming Message: *Give us your location.*"

"We're right there, standing in front of you."

"Incoming Message: *Give us the location of Kyle Riggs.*"

"Me? I'm right here. I'm in my command module, my brick, just where I've been every time I—" I said, then suddenly I halted. Something was wrong. "No, wait I—"

But it was too late. The four Macro guards in their diamond formation were carefully placed. All of them had a free field of fire and could burn down my men without injuring one another. Two of them fired on each of my unarmed engineers. The men were cut in half by the initial blazes of energy. They hadn't even had the chance to scream. But the Macros weren't done yet. They kept firing on the floating pieces until nothing bigger than a burnt finger drifted around in the hold. A mass of vapor, much of it atomized particles of my marines, floated in a steamy haze that obscured the Macros. The four machines still twitched, as if looking for fresh targets of sufficient mass to warrant further blasting. I noticed the sensor unit was still there, magnetically attached to the roof of the hold. They had not damaged it in the slightest.

I ripped my com-link off and threw it onto the table. "Dammit!"

The link beeped and I snatched it up again. A familiar voice spoke in my ear. It was Sergeant Kwon. I'd placed him on operational security. Apparently, he'd watched the fiasco on the ceiling.

"Sir, I'm requesting permission to burn down those machines."

"No. Request denied."

"Sir, I won't lose a single trooper doing it."

"I know you won't, Sergeant. But I don't need to compound this misunderstanding."

Two seconds of silence followed. "Yes, sir. Standing by."

I took a deep breath and looked around at my stunned command staff.

"Are we prisoners, sir?" asked Captain Sarin.

"What did we *misunderstand?*" asked Major Robinson.

I looked at them both. "The Macros are very literal. They gave *me* permission to install the sensor. That's because, as I recall now, I demanded they allow *me* to install it."

Major Robinson got it first. "Ah... so they figured out it wasn't you standing there at the exit when you contacted them."

"They confirmed I wasn't one of the engineers, yes—and then they burned down two perfectly good men because they were too close to the portal," I said. I was angry with myself and the Macros. I stepped to an emergency locker and broke out a combat suit.

Major Robinson came around to talk to me quietly. "Sir, you don't have to go out there."

I looked at him. "No. But I'm sick of sitting here in the dark. Don't you want to know what this ship looks like? Don't you think it would help our assault if we could see the world we were landing on?"

Tight-lipped, he nodded and backed away.

"You're in command while I'm out of contact, Major," I said, slipping on a hood and tapping to activate the nanites. They sealed the hood into place and I touched another contact to pressurize the suit.

I left them there, at the command table. I walked out into the airlock and jumped to the ceiling. I was glad for every zero-G training exercise I'd participated in. I did a somersault and landed on my feet on the roof of the hold. Clanking along, I soon stood amongst the burn marks that represented two of my men. I eyed the Macro guards with disdain.

"I'm Kyle Riggs. Let me pass."

After a few tense seconds, they broke formation and revealed a dark hole in the ceiling between them. I released the magnetic clamps on the sensor array and picked it up. The sensor array was about the size and dimensions of a trashcan. It was bulky, but weightless, as the Macro ship was now coasting.

I entered the portal and awkwardly levered the sensor array in behind me. Once through, I found myself standing in a dark, tube-like corridor that ran length-wise down the ship from bow to stern. I snapped on my suit lights and did a com-check with my command post. The signal was there, but it was sketchy. I looked up and down the tube, which was festooned with hanging cables. Some of the cables were semi-opaque hoses that ran with slow-moving, gelatinous liquids. Pinks, golds, blues and mauves slid this way and that toward unknown destinations. Other cables carried wires that showed bare metal. These were twisted-pair sets with only a tray-like guide of thin shielding between them. I suspected these were low-voltage data cables, but I couldn't be sure. I worked to avoid contact with all the cables, in case they carried a jolt that would blow my magnetized boots off.

I flicked on every recorder my suit had, relaying the recordings to the command brick where it would be digitally stored for posterity. As I roamed the dim tubes I took passages that led upward toward the outer hull whenever possible. The plan was simple: I would plant the sensor array as close to the outer skin of the ship as I could. The unit should operate through anything solid up to a foot of thickness, depending on the composition of the hull. The best spot I could find would be a simple window, but I doubted I was going to see any of those. The Macros didn't strike me as star-gazers.

After traversing two upward shafts, I lost contact with the command brick entirely. It was an odd, lonely feeling, moving around like a secret mammalian spy in the midst of the Macro stronghold. I felt like one of those squirrel-rats that used to sneak around in the nests of dinosaurs. In this environment, I was the alien.

I finally reached a tight tunnel with a lower ceiling than the rest. The hard, flat ceiling bent my back and made me drag the sensor array behind me, bumping over the uneven surfaces. This had to be it. I had to have reached the outer hull. I reached up and touched the smooth, solid surface overhead. Beyond this wall was the vacuum of space.

I searched for and found an alcove and tucked the sensor unit into it. I activated the unit and had it run a self-diagnostic. I should be getting readings soon, and these would be transmitted along a self-adapting wire made entirely of chained nanites to the hold below. The sensor array had its own internal reactor, so there wouldn't be any power problems.

I watched as the sensor-nubs self-modulated and scanned their environment. The final verdict was a yellow bar—not great, but much better than nothing. We would no longer be flying blind if I could get this signal down to the command post.

I flipped a valve open. A trail of gleaming nanites, looking like a mercury spill of deadly proportions, slipped out of the opening and snaked toward the nearest exit on their own initiative. Like a trail of ants, I knew they would find their way back home to the command brick. The nanite stream thinned until it was almost unnoticeable, no thicker than a human vein.

I stood up, pressing my back against the low ceiling. I followed the shiny nanite strand with my eyes until it disappeared. This place was oppressive, and I felt an urge to get back to the command brick. I turned my helmet right and left, looking up and down the remote tunnel. I'd only seen a few of the Macros, and they had been much further down, closer to the level of the hold itself. I bared my teeth, debating my next move. My mouth suddenly felt dry.

In the end I figured, *why the hell not?* When else was I going to get the chance to roam on an alien ship while it was in full operation?

I didn't follow the winding stream of nanites back to safety. Instead, I turned and crawled farther toward the stern, deeper into the Macro ship. The recorders were still on, and there was plenty of storage space on my suit's data-meter. I figured I might as well take the opportunity to do a little spying.

I picked my way toward the stern, heading in the direction of the engines and whatever passed for the crew quarters on a Macro ship. It was the opposite direction from the one the nanites had taken. I was moving farther from the hold and the rest of the humans on this ship. In my head, I could see Sandra gritting her teeth and asking me if I was insane. Fortunately, she wasn't around.

-40-

Much of the ship was repetitive. I hadn't been expecting a Van Gogh on every wall, but this was positively boring. Then I reached the central nexus of the ship.

As best I could figure, I was behind the hold, between the engines and the big empty space that contained my comrades in their stacked, steel, coffin-like bricks. This was where the Macros *lived*, so to speak. There were many strange rooms with no obvious propose. There were machines that churned and clunked independently, making air, weapons or replacement Macros—I wasn't sure which.

But when I found the laboratory, I knew what it was. There were tech Macros in there, workers with a dozen mandibles that moved with motions so fast they could not be followed by the human eye—like a hundred flashing knives being juggled at once. I knew the type: they had built the nukes that had annihilated the domes back in Argentina and taken a lot of my men with them.

It was the thing on the table that made me forget all about the Macro techs. It was a living creature—a big one. It was long, and definitely worm-like. It had legs, however, about fifty of them. I wasn't sure if it was a centipede, or a snake with a lot of legs. It spotted me with a jewel-like black eye. The creature opened its mouth and sort of yawned in my direction. I heard a high-pitched, singing sound. Was it trying to communicate?

The techs had it clamped down to a table with seven thick, metal hoops. Blood-like fluids ran down the sides of the creature from a hundred wounds. Suction tubes gargled and slurped up the fluids that ran from the wounds. The tech Macros' knives flashed, sliced and diced. They were *sampling* the creature, working it over with their fine instruments. I suspected they were dissecting it—alive.

I should have just turned around and walked away. I knew that, but somehow, I couldn't. I lifted a boot and placed it into the laboratory. The Macro techs reacted as if I'd touched one of their steel feet with a hot wire. They turned and the flashing mandibles froze in place.

I touched a button on my wrist. It was something we'd come up with for moments like this. A small nanite brainbox was located in my suit, like a CPU, monitoring pressures and the like. We'd allowed our larger nanite minds to teach them to speak a little of the primitive binary language of the Macros. They couldn't give speeches, but they could translate a few words for us.

I held the button down now, which would cause the system to transmit my speech in binary. "Identify," I said, pointing to the monster on the table.

The Macros stared at me for about three seconds. It was long enough for me to start sweating. Suddenly, under their cold inspection, my suit felt hot inside. Were they calling a combat squad with beamers? I had no way of knowing.

One of the techs extended a multi-jointed, bright-metal arm and stuck the spike at its tip into the side of the creature on the table.

"*Enemy,*" it transmitted back to me. The tiny brainbox in my suit did the translation. I had the feeling he'd said more, but that was all my system could translate. It was enough.

I've often been accused of impulsiveness. I can understand how people might see things that way—but I preferred to think of myself as an opportunist. I lifted a thin beam-pistol and burned a dime-sized hole into the spiny oval that served the monster on the table for a head. I held down the trigger for about two solid seconds, long enough for the beam to hiss out the far side of the creature and burn a tiny dark dot on the far wall of the laboratory behind it. The struggling monster immediately stilled. I slipped the gun out of sight.

Mandibles moved in what I thought was a confused, surprised pattern. Could they be gesturing? Were they asking one another: *Who the hell does he think he is? ...*or some Macro equivalent?

"Enemy," I said, holding down the translation button again. I pointed at the mess on the table. A wisp of steam looped up toward the ventilation grilles from both ends of the creature—from both the entry and exit wounds my beamer had created. I hoped the worm wouldn't ignite and start a fire… I'd given it quite a jolt.

"I kill enemies," I transmitted.

I left them there, twitching their flashing metal mandibles. Out in the corridor, I allowed myself a smirk. The Macros weren't the only ones who were literal-minded and who might have translation-based misunderstandings.

I made it back to the portal over the hold quickly. There was some excitement going on in the corridors. A few Macro warrior-types scuttled by. I hoped they were on some kind of drill—but I suspected they weren't.

When I appeared before the four guards, I had a scare. They stood their ground and leveled their weapons at me. I held down the translation button with excessive force.

"I'm Kyle Riggs," I said.

They appeared unimpressed.

"My mission has been accomplished. I will now prepare my invasion forces."

Several long seconds ticked by. I was now in net-range of the command module's smarter translation boxes, and when the response came from the Macros the translation was more complete.

"*Biotics are no longer permitted outside the hold,*" came the translation-box voice.

I grunted. They stepped aside, breaking their formation. I vaulted through and did a dive toward the command brick. A dozen of my men stood among the bricks, watching me. My helmet buzzed with calls as the word went out that I'd returned.

"How'd it go, sir?" asked Major Robinson, using his officer's override to cut out the lower-ranked calls.

"Just fine," I said, "but I think I need a drink."

"A drink? Are you dehydrated, sir?"

"Yeah, you could say that."

I reached the command post, broke the nanite seals around my neck with a combination clicking-ripping sound and pulled off my hood. Two people handed me a squeeze bottle of water. Sandra was there, third in line. I took what she offered. It was a squeeze bottle of beer.

"Thanks," I said.

Sandra gave me a suspicious look that I tried to ignore. She could tell I'd had more of an adventure than I wanted to let on to the others. Maybe it was all the sweat cooling on my forehead and neck.

I briefed them slowly, waiting until Sandra had gone back into my office to tell them about the lab, the creature on the table—and my rude intervention. They all looked shocked when I got to the part about my mercy-killing of the creature on the table.

"Do you think that thing was one of the enemies we are supposed to fight against?" asked Captain Sarin.

"Yes. I believe that's exactly what it was."

"Killing their prisoner was a dangerous move, sir," said Major Robinson. "It could have been misinterpreted."

"No, I think they got the message," I said.

"Sir, the nanite chain is complete. The sensor array is active," said one of the techs, interrupting. His name was Lieutenant Raphim Shrestha. He was a thin, quiet man. Now he sounded happy—as the sensor guy, he'd had precious little to do so far on this trip. For days, we'd kept the man sitting at a board in the darkest corner of the command center. Now he finally had something to do.

"Do we have video, Raphim?" I asked.

"No sir," he said. "just spatial relationships calculated from gravity-pulls and radiation sources. But we've pinpointed a number of bodies around us."

"Put it up on the big table," I said.

The first elements of the star system we occupied came up in the form of two large spheres on the computer table. I looked at it, and I frowned. The longer I looked the more I frowned.

"What are those?" Captain Sarin asked.

"Stars," I said.

"Where's the blue giant?"

I shook my head. "We're in a different system."

"Could we have jumped again and not felt it?" asked Major Robinson.

"I doubt it," I said. "Even if it happened when most of us were asleep, someone had to be on watch. Everyone knows the sensation now, someone would have reported it."

There were two stars in the center of the system, both about the same size and orbiting one another very closely. There weren't any planets around. This didn't surprise me. Most star systems had multiple stars, and those that did were less likely to have planets. The uneven gravitational pulls from the star tended to pull planets into the stars themselves or tear them apart over the many long years it took a star system to form. As I watched, a smaller body showed itself, very far out from the two stars.

"Is that a gas giant?" I asked, pointing at it.

"Too much mass," said Captain Sarin. "I think it's a third star. A small one."

I looked at the system and slowly, it dawned on me. "This might be Alpha Centauri. It's a three-star system. The configuration looks right. I'll bet that small star out there is Proxima Centauri."

The staff agreed in a murmur.

"But then what happened to the system with the blue giant?" asked Captain Sarin. There was a hint of fear in her voice. Up until now we'd all believed we were traveling through the same star system I'd scouted months earlier. But now it was sinking in that we'd been dead wrong.

"We don't really know how the rings work," said Major Robinson. "Maybe the Macros can set them to transport a vessel to different receiving rings."

"Or maybe we didn't go through the Venus ring at all," I said. "Maybe we went through the other one, the one out in the Oort cloud."

Robinson brought up a calculator app and pecked at it. "That would explain why there was no turbulence or vibration when we went through the ring. We should have felt some kind of effect after flying through Venus' thick atmosphere. I'm doing some calculations, sir…. The speed the Macros must have reached in order to get out to the Oort cloud in just a few days is alarming."

I nodded in agreement. "But with good gravity-controlling stabilizers, we would never have felt most of the acceleration. The Oort cloud ring is about six light-hours out from earth—maybe sixty AU. I'm sure our small Nano ships couldn't produce that kind of thrust. It seems like the Macro technology is in some ways superior to the Nanos. At least, they can build bigger engines."

"Can we be sure we flew through the second ring, Colonel?" Captain Sarin asked me.

"No. It's just a theory. We've got very little to go on. Possibly, there is a third ring we didn't even know about hidden somewhere in our system."

"But sir," Captain Sarin said. She looked at me strangely with wide, dark eyes. "If we don't even know how we got here—how are we ever going to get home?"

I shrugged and turned back to the big screen. She had me there.

-41-

For about a week we sailed across what we presumed to be the Alpha Centauri system. Some people whispered that perhaps we'd traveled here in some other fashion—that perhaps the Macros could jump between star systems at will. But I didn't buy any of those rumors. If they could do that, they would have brought their big battlefleet to Earth faster. They were using the rings, I felt sure. That meant it took time to fly from star to star, but it could be accomplished in days or weeks rather than years. Most of the travel time was taken up flying from one of these rings of collapsed matter to the next. Going through the ring itself to another system seemed to be instantaneous.

The team of lab coat-types we'd brought along to figure out just such phenomena were as baffled as the rest of us. Oh, they talked a good game—theorizing about hyperspace, stable wormholes and the like, but they really didn't have a clue. I didn't try to figure it out myself. I'd only taken two physics courses in my undergrad years, and I'd gotten a 'B' in both of them. I resigned myself to using alien technology without fully understanding it—probably for the rest of my days. Like every monkey we'd ever sent on a rocket ride in the fifties, I was only interested in when the damned thing was going to land.

On the second day, I decided I couldn't stay in the command brick forever, waiting for something to happen. I figured it was about time to participate in the training I'd ordered for the entire unit—high-gravity training.

I didn't tell Sandra about it, but the second I entered the airlock to exit the command brick she appeared. She pressed her way in, past the stuttering airlock doors, which wanted to close on her like a hungry elevator.

Sandra slipped into the airlock with me—a tight fit, I was happy to note. I pressed up against her freely.

"You're doing that on purpose," she said.

"I'm just happy to see you. How did you know I was leaving the brick?"

"I put a bell on you."

I frowned. A *bell* was tech slang for a tracking device. Most of the personnel carried them. They were small, and if you were tagged with a tiny transmitter you could be tracked by anyone with access to a computer. I reached up to my neck, but nothing hung there.

Sandra smiled and dug into my pockets, and I smiled back. I reached around her to return the favor, but she lightly slapped my hands away from her shapely hindquarters. She pulled something out of my front pocket. It was my portable com-link.

I looked at the com-link. It had a ring through it and she dangled the ring from one of her fine fingers.

"I get it…" I said. "You traced my com-link. That's a violation. I'm your superior officer."

"I'm not a marine."

I reached for her again, but the airlock dinged and kicked us out. It had long ago equalized the pressure, and now it had reached some timing limit and lost patience. It opened the exit door without being touched. A maintenance man in coveralls eyed us in surprise. We disengaged and struggled to get out of the tight squeeze with dignity. We failed.

Sandra followed me past the smirking maintenance man to one of the target-practice bricks. We waited for a fireteam to finish, then took a turn inside. The interior of the brick was dimly lit. We were issued two practice hand-beamers at the entrance by the duty sergeant. I thanked him and handed one to Sandra, who hefted it experimentally.

"You want to team up?" I asked. "I'm dialing an honor-level run."

"I've done this before."

"Not with the system set for one-point-eight Gs."

She frowned slightly. "I didn't know we could do that."

"I had a few Nano gravity stabilizers installed in these training bricks. Normally, their function is to lessen the effects of acceleration G-forces to allow for greater acceleration. We simply reversed the principle and had the Nano factories build us one that *increased* the gravitational effects. You still want to do it?"

She nodded.

"Just don't shoot me in the butt," I told her.

We stepped inside. Immediately, I felt *compressed*. It was hard to breathe, hard to move, hard to think. It wasn't exactly like carrying a heavy pack on one's back—it was worse than that. The very blood in my veins was heavier. My heart had to work harder to pump liquid up to my brain. Fortunately, the nanite-enhancements including a heart capable of pumping harder than normal human hearts. I could feel my heart rate and blood pressure increase. I took gulping breaths. I could tell right away that a double-gravity world was going to suck in combat.

We started the simulation, firing at nanite-generated targets that danced into and out of visibility. The lighting strobed like an electrical storm. The targets were all computer simulations, but the obstacles were real enough. After we'd cleaned out the first three sets there was a pause, then the lights went out entirely. I tripped over a simulated boulder and went sprawling. Falling in high-G is very different than falling on Earth. The floor came up with incredible speed and smashing force. My reflexes and strength kept me from dashing my brains out on the floor, but I did see a new set of stars in my head.

Sandra knelt over me, firing at the targets that took the opportunity to rush us. Using what intel we had on the enemy, we'd programmed the attackers to look like giant bugs. They fired back, screeched, chittered and rushed in. I didn't have time to get up off the floor, there was only time to aim and shoot.

In fact, I rather liked it down there. It was easier to think in a horizontal position with more blood pumping to my brain—and it was nice to have Sandra kneel over me. I fired methodically and we drove the phantom enemy back. The lights went up, and the score printed out on the ceiling. We'd killed thirty-nine out of sixty targets and survived.

"Not bad," I said, getting up.

Sandra smiled.

"You did okay," I said. "Very good accuracy. But now let's try hand-to-hand. We'll put away these beamers and trade them in for combat knives."

She looked less than pleased, but she was still game for more. I took our beamers and traded them in for dulled knives. We'd designed combat knives with a diamond edge, the blade specially-grown by nanites. They'd aligned the carbon atoms in a molecular line that was unnaturally sharp and strong. The knives had been created especially for situations like the one we were about to face. For the most part, we planned to rely on our beamers. But these knives didn't run out of juice, they weighed virtually nothing, and in close combat with another biotic they were extremely deadly.

We ran the course again with nothing but knives. This time, we were overwhelmed. We killed only about a dozen attackers with jewel-like eyes and snapping mandibles before the computer judged us as pulled down and dismembered. Sandra had been the weak link in this fight, and it showed.

When we exited the training brick and let the next fireteam shuffle in behind us, Sandra pinched my butt.

I turned around with a half-smile. "Is that a proposition?" I asked.

"You did that on purpose. You put us in there with nothing but knives because you wanted to beat me."

"Not exactly," I said. "I wanted you to understand your limitations. You are quick and accurate. You know how to use a gun. But you don't know anything about close fighting. Your muscles, while enhanced, are not comparable to any marine in this unit."

"Thanks for the lesson," she said.

"No charge."

"I want another shot at it," she said.

I knew that stubborn look in her eye. I'd seen it often enough. "Okay. We'll go again when these guys are done."

We ended up running each of the simulations six times. We beat the shooting match every time except for the last one. The hand-to-hand matches were all losses. We got better at first, but after the fourth round I could tell Sandra was slowing. Our score for the sixth round was the worst yet, only eight kills before the enemy pulled us down.

"I'm tired," Sandra finally admitted.

"I know."

"I'm not used to this."

"You did very well," I told her. "You might be better than the very worst marine in my outfit."

"Really?"

"Nah. I was just trying to make you feel better."

Sandra hissed and slashed at me with her plastic knife. I caught her wrist and kissed her. We half-wrestled and half-made out until the duty Sergeant cleared his throat. I looked up.

"I suppose you'll be wanting these," I said, handing over the practice weaponry.

"Thank you, sir," the Sergeant said, trying not to smile at us. He failed and grinned hugely. I couldn't blame him.

42

The next ring surprised us. We'd been floating along for nearly a week, crossing the breadth of the Alpha Centauri system—if that's where we truly were. Suddenly a new contact appeared on the big table, a tiny flickering oval shape on our projection of the star system. It wasn't near any planet. It could have been a station, or a larger ship. I was summoned to the command brick the minute the staffers saw the anomaly.

The first thing I noticed was the binary star clump was on the opposite side of the table. The second thing was that the velocity meter on the board was half what it had been the last time I was in the command brick. We'd been taking measurements of distance and position continually to every celestial body we had contact with. By measuring their relative distances to our position, we could tell we were now moving more slowly.

"We've changed our attitude?" I asked.

"The Macros flipped the ship around, sir. They did a one-eighty and they have the engines pointed in the opposite direction. We're decelerating hard," Major Robinson confirmed.

I put my hands on the big screen and drew them apart with a spreading motion. I zoomed in as closely as I was able with our imperfect sensory apparatus.

"It could be a ring," I said, staring at the oval thing.

The rest of the command staff huddled around us. "What should we do, sir?" asked Major Robinson.

I looked at him. "Do? We aren't flying this ship."

"I mean, should we ask the Macros if that's a ring?"

I thought about it and shook my head. I figured the Macros were only good for so many questions disguised as demands per day—per year, maybe. I'd never gotten the feeling they liked us, and they certainly didn't like talking to us.

"To the Macros, we are wild beasts, Major," I said.

"Sir?"

"I mean, we are something they plan to let loose upon their enemies. But they don't want to pal around with us. They aren't our friends, our teammates. Every time I communicate with them, I increase the relative cost and risk of associating with them. They think of us as cargo, remember? I plan to be good cargo for the rest of this trip. Good, quiet cargo."

"That doesn't seem like your style, sir," remarked Captain Sarin.

I looked at her with raised eyebrows and she looked down, embarrassed.

I nodded and grinned. "You've got a point there, Captain. But I want to make it home again. The only way we're going to achieve that, I figure, is by keeping the Macros happy."

No one offered any more arguments. We approached what we calculated must be the next ring. Over the next three hours, a slight curve began shaping our course. We continued to decelerate.

"It looks like we are going to fly right by it," I said.

"The opening in the center of the ring isn't quite lined up with our angle of approach," said our navigator. He was another fellow who had had little to do on this trip. Finally, his hour had come. "You see, to shoot through the ring, we have to change our trajectory, curving into it at an angle. That's probably why we are slowing down, too."

"We might be slowing down because there's an atmosphere on the far side," suggested Captain Sarin.

"I doubt that," I said. "We are still going too fast to hit a planetary atmosphere. We'd burn up if there was a wall of gas to run into on the far side. What's our current velocity? About two hundred thousand knots?"

"More than that, sir. Even after many hours of braking," Major Robinson confirmed.

The braking and the gentle curving of our course continued for another hour. It was hard to leave the bridge. I had my staff calculate the point when we'd hit the ring and they put a timer up on the

235

boards. I had them relay that timer to every screen in every brick. When we had less than half an hour left, I got out on the PA system and spoke to my troops.

"Marines, this is Colonel Riggs. You might have noticed the timer on the overheads. In twenty-eight minutes, we believe we will blink to another star system. That star system may well be our destination. I want everyone safely strapped into their assigned brick with every stick of equipment stowed and secured by the time that timer hits zero. Riggs out."

The twenty-eight minutes crawled like twenty-eight hours. But finally, the last seconds ticked away. I felt a tiny shudder. I knew, before the screen in front of me went blank, that we were in a different place now. We were somewhere new.

A big star grew to my left on the screen. It kept growing as the computers measured its gravitational pull and radiation emissions, adjusting their estimates. It was a *huge* star, bigger than the blue giant had been. The circle looked the size of a hubcap lying on the computer table. There was only one of them, at least. As we watched, more contacts swam into place. Planets. The first ones to appear were the largest of them. The gas giants, I figured. The planets kept popping up like bubbles as they were sensed and positioned. Things kept moving on the table, too, reshuffling. I knew that part of our sensory algorithms required the ship to move, so we could take readings from multiple locations and thus have a better conception of the environment.

"It's a red giant, sir," said the navigator in a hushed voice. "Another new system. If only I could *see* where we are. I wish I could just get someplace and look out a window."

I chuckled. I looked at the navigator in sympathy. He was a tall, thin fellow with hair that was naturally brown at the roots and the color of honey at the tips.

"Flying blind in these ships can be maddening," I said. "I've done a lot of it."

"Sir, look," said Captain Sarin, pointing to the screen. There was a small planet growing there as the sensors worked out its location and mass.

"We're almost in the planet's far orbit now," said Major Robinson.

We felt something new then. Something we'd never felt on this long journey, something we'd always expected, but never experienced. The ship itself vibrated and a deep thrumming sound could be heard.

Everyone looked at the walls.

"Crash-straps, deploy!" I ordered. Almost immediately, nanite arms reached down from the ceiling and grabbed each of us by the hooks that ringed our belts. More arms looped down and attached to our wrists and ankles. These arms would allow us to move freely, but not suddenly. Any sudden motion would be instantly restrained by the thin, black arms, preventing injury. They were scripted to react to shocks the way a shoulder harness did in a car back home, tightening when forces were applied that might throw us off-balance.

"Report, Major. What was that impact?"

"Felt like something big, sir. Sensors, Raphim?"

"Ah…" said the sensory officer, flustered. "It wasn't the Macro engines, sir. Something hit us."

"I think this is it, gentlemen," I said, raising my voice. "We have reached a hot enemy system. Sensors, zoom us in. I don't care about the red giant or whatever else is floating around farther than a million miles out. Give us only local contacts."

"Working on it, sir," Raphim said.

The image on the screen wavered, then faded away. The planet loomed now, large and to my right. Behind us was the ring. It slid away astern quietly, gently. Five smaller contacts surrounded us, they had to be the cruiser escorts.

"I don't see any enemy ships," I said.

"Maybe the planet is firing at us, sir," suggested Captain Sarin.

"How are we getting hit by the planet?" I asked. "A missile couldn't get up here this fast. We just arrived in the system."

Another shudder rocked the ship. This one was much worse. The nanite restraints tightened to keep me from being thrown across the computer table.

"Sensors? Talk to me, Raphim."

"No enemy ships. No enemy missiles. I'm not sensing anything moving or emitting, other than the Macro vessels."

"What hit us then? Replay that strike recording. Where was the energy released? Is there any radiation?"

Raphim was quiet for a second. I would have yelled at him again, but I could see his long fingers working swiftly on his board. "Radiation, yes. Gamma. And it was pretty close, sir. I'd say it was a nuclear warhead."

"Missiles, then," said Captain Sarin.

There was another less violent rocking sensation. One of the escort cruisers blew apart. The contact separated and flickered out. Everyone watched and breathed hard.

"Any incoming missiles?"

"Nothing sir," Raphim said. "No heat signatures. No motion sensors are being tripped. If they are missiles, they might be too small to detect, or they might be coasting in, cold. I don't know sir."

"Mines," said Captain Sarin suddenly.

I looked at her and nodded. "Makes sense. The enemy laid mines in front of the ring. They knew the Macros had to come this way, so they set up a trap for them—for us."

"The Macros are adjusting their formation, sir," said Raphim.

I watched the screen. The Macros seemed to have figured out the mines, too. They put every cruiser in a column, with us at the rear. The ships now followed one another in single file.

"At least we know they care about us," I said.

We all watched tensely as we arced down closer to the planet, decelerating into orbit. Two more cruisers vanished by the time we reached a stable orbit.

"Contingency plans?" I demanded.

"What plan, sir? What can we do?" Major Robinson asked.

"I want *you* to tell *me*," I said.

"You mean in case this vessel is hit? I don't know. We could try to bail out."

I stared at him. "We'd have to blast the rear doors down."

He nodded. "We could do that, then release the magnetic clamps on the bricks, letting them fall out the rear of the ship."

I pointed at him. "Good idea," I said. "We can get out a few of the tanks and take out the back door when the last cruiser is destroyed."

"Won't work," said the navigator.

"Why not?" I snapped.

"We are still decelerating, sir—flying backward," said the navigator. "With our engines forward and our noses aft. Even if we blast the doors wide open, we won't fall out. The G-forces will push us back into the Macro transport, not out of it."

"We could pump gas into the hold," Captain Sarin suggested. "Then there would be a pressure release when we blast the doors. Wouldn't the escaping gas propel us out the back?"

"Maybe it would at first," the navigator said, tapping out calculations. "But as long as the ship's engines are firing we'll be thrown back into it."

I heaved a sigh. "Set it up anyway. Deploy two hovertanks for the job. Maybe the ship will swing around into an attack posture soon. I at least want the option."

"If we are hit while the men are rolling out hovertanks…" said Major Robinson, shaking his head.

"Marines aren't people who want to live forever," I said. "Besides, I'd rather lose ten men than thousands. Relay the order."

Over the next hour, we reached a stable orbit and watched as the cruisers steadily fired those big belly-cannons we'd spotted back on Earth. Whatever they used for ammo, each salvo went down as a radiation-emitting fireball, pounding the planet. For the most part, they shot at the mountains. I suspected enemy bases were in those areas. Strangely, no counter fire came back to greet us.

We'd almost relaxed when one more cruiser was destroyed by what appeared to be a mine. The last cruiser survived, however. We breathed more easily after we'd made two full orbits around the target world without being hit. We figured that by then, the Macro ships had cut a path around the planet that was free of mines—even if they'd done it by hitting every mine in orbit. The cruiser had stopped firing by then. I suspected it had run out of targets. In the end, I never had to give the order to blast down the hold doors—or the order to take the Macro ship by storm.

"You know," I said to Major Robinson, "the mines were a pretty good idea. Very effective against the Macros. They tend to fight to the death once they decide to go for it. That's a weakness in my opinion. After losing the majority of a force, most human commanders would pull out. But the Macros don't like to retreat once they engage."

"The Macros are our allies, sir," said Major Robinson with mock severity. "Didn't you get the memo?"

"I wrote the memo," I said, smiling with half my mouth. "I'm just thinking of the future... I'm thinking we could lay a few of our own near the rings to keep out intruders. We could nail a lot of them early without losses."

Robinson stared at me and grinned. "One more piece of critical intel gathered on this mission."

I nodded. "One more reason to make it home."

We watched the image of the planet's surface, which now showed some details. With our passive sensors, it took several passes to piece together the landscape, to determine what was land and what was sea. The world looked huge, rocky and dry. There were oceans, but they were small and deeply sunken into holes—like dried-up mud puddles. I imagined the Earth might look like that if had been punched a few times to puff up some higher crags and to make the deeper holes. Then, if you dried up about half the oceans and drained the rest down into the craters... it might look something like this place.

"Inviting, isn't it?" I asked no one in particular.

"Maybe it's green and idyllic on the surface," suggested Captain Sarin. "It's hard to tell from up here with nothing more than a relief map to go by."

"An optimist, huh?" I said. "But let's hope you're right. We'll find out soon enough."

We spent three more hours orbiting. Occasionally, the big belly-cannon fired. This became increasingly infrequent, but always seemed to happen at the same point of our orbit.

"They are down to pounding that one spot, the base of that triple-peaked mountain," I said.

"It could be a major base," said Robinson. "One of their seas comes up to the root of the peaks. Let me check something."

He put both hands on the screen and worked with the image, turning it and zooming in. He put a scale graphic up next to it and whistled. "Look at this, from sea-level to the tallest peak—that's measuring over fifteen miles. It's eighty-thousand feet high."

I nodded, impressed. "That's taller than our system's highest, Olympus Mons back home on Mars."

"Let's hope we don't have to climb it," Major Robinson said.

I looked at him sharply. "Are we descending?"

Robinson nodded. He adjusted the visuals, allowing the screen to snap back into normal mode. I could tell immediately we were lower. We were coming down, and we were going to land.

43

Klaxons sounded. I ordered all my marines to prepare for ground assault. I ordered the crash-straps to resecure everyone in the command brick who'd escaped them over the last few hours. Outside our brick, hundreds of marines loaded into hovertanks near the big rear doors. They would be our first wave, rushing out when the doors opened. We had no idea how hot the landing zone would be. We hoped we'd be granted a safe LZ, but who knew how the Macros thought these things should go? The tanks would sweep the area, supported by infantry. Once they had given the all-clear, we would begin unloading the bricks.

I looked at my com-link thoughtfully. I hadn't spoken to the Macros since I'd placed the passive sensor array and fried one of their test subjects. I'd not wanted to push my luck. But specific information on our mission goals was required now.

"Command module," I said aloud, "open channel with Macro Command."

There was a delay. It was longer than usual. Maybe the Macros were preoccupied with the landing. Or maybe the original Macro commander had been blown away by an enemy mine and now I was being rerouted to the backup.

"Channel open," said the command module at last.

"Translate and relay: I am Kyle Riggs, Star Force Marine Commander. I need to know our mission goals."

"Incoming Message: *Destroy resisting indigenous biotics.*"

I sighed. Were we supposed to kill every bug we found on the planet? "Give us the coordinates of the enemy's most vital area."

A series of numbers came back. I waved my hand at Captain Sarin and our useless navigator. They worked quickly on the big board and pinpointed the spot. I was alarmed when I saw the goal coordinates.

"We have to get to the top of that eighty thousand foot peak?" I asked.

"No sir," said the navigator, working his fingers on the screen. The image quickly shifted to a side view. "The actual location is underneath the big mountain, at about sea-level. It's miles deep inside the mountain itself."

"Great," I said, getting the picture. We were going to have to dig them out. Suddenly, I understood why the Macros had brought us here. Their big machines weren't capable of going down narrow tunnels. Maybe the enemy were strong enough to fight off their smaller, worker-class machines.

"I get it," I said. "They can't get into the tunnels. So, it's time to send in the marines."

I felt everyone staring at me. I ignored them. "Command module, relay this: If we reach this goal spot and destroy all resistance, will we have completed our mission on this world?"

The answer came swiftly this time. "Incoming Message: *Send transmission when goal reached.*"

I disconnected with Macro Command. I soon felt gravity again. We were coming down into the atmosphere. "This is to be an underground campaign. Regear all our troops accordingly. Order supply to prep scripts for extra lighting, climbing equipment, suit-tethers and the like. We put this option on the menu, I remember the meetings."

Major Robinson worked his screen quickly. "It wasn't one of our top possibilities. But we can do it."

"Not even one of the top five maybes? We know this is a job the Macros wanted us for, specifically. We saw the enemy images a long time ago. They are stretched-out bugs. No one thought of tunnels?"

I looked around at my staff. They shrugged and pecked at their screens. I felt a shouting outburst coming up from my lungs, but I fought to hold it back. I forced myself to remember how green we all were. We had the finest tech humanity had ever wielded in a single force. But we had never done this before. This was our first invasion of an alien world. Theory was meeting up with reality, and there were bound to be mistakes.

"It's okay," I said, forcing down the tirade that bubbled within me. "We'll get through it. We'll learn from this. Now, give me a force-list run-down. Give me the bad news first. Let's recalculate our effectiveness unit by unit and come up with a plan to improve it."

This got them working again, instead of sulking. We'd drawn up plans for many different goal environments. Now that we had finally arrived, ninety-five percent of those plans were useless. I consoled myself with one thought: at least this wasn't an *underwater* campaign.

I took the time to study the looming mountain, zooming in to run a camera over the terrain. "See those blast marks?" I asked Robinson, tapping on the screen.

"They look like recent hits," said Robinson. "There are a lot of them. I'd say they are the result of the Macro bombardment. Maybe that's why we aren't under any kind of barrage yet. They probably took out their missile and artillery emplacements."

I nodded. "Sounds right to me. Now, give me the bad news. What can we do to adapt to an underground campaign?"

"The hovertanks will probably not function underground as currently designed," Robinson told me. "They are built for wide open spaces. I'm assuming the tunnels will be too small for big Macro machines—and that's why they brought us."

"Their ability to apply logic is certainly stronger than our own," I said, trying unsuccessfully to keep bitterness out of my voice. Why hadn't I put this possibility higher up on our list? It seemed so obvious in retrospect.

"Yes, ah—the hovertanks are built for long range, for flying fast over open terrain. Their beam turrets are high and not built to run into rock ceilings. We will have to do a full redesign to make them effective underground."

"Okay," I said, "what about our troops?"

"We have decent gear for this environment. We've been emphasizing lighter, lower-powered equipment to reduce the weight of each marine's kit. Our marines should do fairly well even with the high gravity. To prepare for underground operations, we'll use the factories to produce more effective tunnel-rat equipment."

"Good. What about our mobile base?"

"Not good," said Robinson. "If the hovertanks won't fit into a tunnel, then the bricks certainly won't. They can't be significantly reconfigured. This means when we set up our base, it will have to be out in the open. Our supply lines for men, machines, ammo and medical will all have to trace down into the tunnels. The deeper we go, the longer and more vulnerable these lines will become."

I crossed my arms, closed my eyes and thought hard. I couldn't see a way out of the scenario he was painting. Tactically, we should win in the open, if they faced us here. But once underground, every foot we went deeper into their lairs, they would have the increasing advantage.

As I tried to think I realized the heavy gravity was setting in, forcing my heart to pump harder. My body and mind felt sluggish. I opened my eyes again when the floor rolled under my magnetic boots. We had landed.

"It's go time!" I shouted, clapping my hands together. "Tell the hovertank pilots to rev up. Put a fireteam of four into each vehicle. We'll send out six of them, and if they survive, then six more."

Everyone took up their com-links and began talking at once, relaying my instructions.

"External cameras, I want a feed from the hold. Aim it at those big doors."

My staff soon had the image on the screen. The big floods were on. The floor of the hold was buzzing with activity. Marines scuttled to the back of the hovertanks and were swallowed by them. They each carried lighter rifles, similar to the ones I'd first built for the failed attempt to hold back the Macros in Brazil. The heavy beamers were just too much weight for this world. They also carried gleaming combat knives and light beam-pistols like the practice units Sandra and I had used in the training bricks.

I watched the men with a surge of pride. I'd help build them up, and they were rushing eagerly to invade a world we'd never even seen up until this moment.

The big doors at the back of the cylindrical Macro transport split to form a cross of lurid red light. The cross widened and yawned as the four leaves spread open. We'd been hiding in this tin can so long, everyone was blinking at the unaccustomed light.

The mountain was directly ahead of us. I could see only the base of it, filling my view of the world. It was like a reddish-brown wall of crumbling stone. A wall so tall it had to have been built by the hands of gods.

"The bottom leaf has touched down, sir," said Captain Sarin.

"Go! Hovertank group one: Go, go go!" I shouted into the com-link. Every hood in the taskforce buzzed with my words.

The first line of hovertanks surged forward as if goaded. They swept out of the hold and immediately separated into two groups of three, heading off to either side of the transport.

"Should we release the second squad, sir?" asked Major Robinson.

"Let me see the feed from the hovertanks first," I said.

We watched the screens. Three hovertanks split into two groups and vanished. The view from the command tank was relayed to a window in front of me. I dialed for clarity. The image was jumpy as the tank swept around the Macro transport in a widening circle. I saw and heard laser fire.

"What are they shooting at? Turret view!" I said.

I caught a glimpse of a dead bug, a worm-like thing that closely resembled the creature I'd killed on the dissection tables. Its back was burned away and steamy vapor rose from the carcass. It appeared to be unarmed.

I heard more turrets firing. Red digits floated above the various hovertanks on the screen, rapidly flipping to new values as the computers recorded and displayed their hit-miss ratios.

"Reset those turret scripts. Put them on defensive-fire, not aggressive-fire. Our mission here is to destroy resistance, not perform genocide."

I flipped through the different views. "Who set those tanks to autofire?" I asked.

Major Robinson lifted a hand—the hand transformed into an accusing finger which pointed at me. "It's still your basic script, sir. Those things aren't human, they tripped the software as enemies. Just as you would have wanted if they had come up on the beaches of Andros Island."

I hissed a long breath through my teeth. He was right. If those things didn't qualify to my AI as alien and possibly hostile, I didn't know what would. I recalled back on Andros Sandra had freaked me out a little bit with her idea of having kids plant bombs at the base of my beam turrets. Taking an approach of letting the other guy shoot first was too dangerous, I'd realized.... I had written the turret scripts to identify suspicious alien attackers and to fire *first*. At the time, I'd been thinking of Macros sneaking up on my laser turrets, but now these seemingly harmless locals had set off my software.

"Okay, mistake number forty-two. Someone write that one down, please."

Running this high-tech army was a lot like programming, I realized. Except that with each error I made, things died.

44

We had all our hovertanks out and positioned, forming a circle around our perimeter. I made sure the Macro transport ship was inside the perimeter and made it clear it was a priority for defense. Without that ship, none of us would be going home.

About half my marines were on the perimeter while the rest worked on unloading. Within two hours the landing site had transformed into a semi-fortified encampment. We used the nanites to turn the ground under us into a barrier by weaving themselves into the soil. We'd practiced this anti-tunneling nanite script back home. I'd come up with it after the Brazil campaign, but at that time I'd been thinking about slowing down the Macro burrowing machines. The effect of the nanites was to harden the soil into a pad beneath us. It wasn't as tough as concrete, but it was fast and took virtually no effort on our part. Onto this pad of woven soil, we began the lengthy process of unloading nearly five hundred huge bricks—each of which was about twice as heavy here as they had been on Earth.

We used about a tenth of our bricks as walls, forming an inner security zone. This wall had gaps, and didn't go all the way around the Macro ship. We placed and locked our bricks together, connecting several rocking outcroppings into what was roughly a hexagonal pattern. This was the core of our safe zone, and we stacked the rest of the bricks inside it, three layers deep.

The surface temperature in daylight was around a hundred and forty degrees Fahrenheit. Our suits had air conditioners and the nanites did their best to reflect the heat, but everyone was sweating within twenty minutes of our arrival.

I stood on top of a pile of boulders that made up one corner of the wall of bricks. Around me, a dozen marines aimed their rifles into the desolate terrain. Captain Sarin had been wrong—this was no garden of greenery. Everything was washed out with reddish light, making all colors blur into shades of orange and brown. There was vegetation—mostly stumpy growths that looked like they belonged at the bottom of an ocean. There were ugly, gray sponges and even uglier bulbous, tan things that resembled mushroom caps the size of pickups. And there was moss everywhere. Lots of moss.

"Sir?" asked Sergeant Kwon, crunching up to me. I noticed his feet sank deeply into the moss and the soil beneath. We were all twice our normal weight, and that put Sergeant Kwon into the seven hundred pound range, plus gear. He bore it all naturally, however. He looked right at home on this heavy world. His thick, layered body and round bear-like features seemed natural here.

"Good to be on solid ground again, isn't it, Sergeant?" I asked.

"Yes sir," he said, looking around and frowning.

He didn't look terribly happy to be here. "What's the matter?" I asked him.

"This place, sir. What do we call it?"

"Doesn't have a name."

"I know. But it should. No man should die in a strange place that doesn't even have a name, sir."

I looked at him. I nodded, finding his logic unassailable. "Right you are, Kwon. Do you have a name in mind?"

"Never went to school much, sir," he said.

"How about Helios?" I asked.

"What's it mean?"

"Helios was big in ancient Greece. He was the Sun Titan—sort of an early sun god."

Kwon looked up at the huge, red star. It was dimmer than ours; you could stare right at it without burning your retinas out of your head. But it filled about three times more of the sky than our brighter yellow star did.

Kwon nodded. "Helios. Okay."

I watched him stump away. I wondered how many of us would die here, and if any of the dead would feel any better about it now that the place had a name. Maybe Kwon would.

Our next surprise came when the Macro transport quietly lifted off. Some of my men had to leap for their lives off the ramp, which closed slowly like a giant lamprey's mouth. They scrambled off the triangular wedge of metal and gaped up at the ship as it closed the hold in which we had spent many long days. Once the great doors were closed, the ship rose slowly into the atmosphere and went to join the last cruiser in orbit.

"Guess we're stuck here now, sir," Robinson buzzed in my ear.

"Yeah. I think I'll build a summer cottage in those hills to the west."

"Do you think they'll come back for us, sir? Once the mission is finished?"

"Sure they will, Major. They won't waste good troops. It would be... *inefficient*. All we have to do is finish the mission."

"Yes sir," the Major said.

I raised my eyebrows, surprised my glib argument had worked on him. I had no idea if the Macros would come back. I supposed that had always been the job of mission commanders, to provide confidence to subordinates. I wondered whose job it was to blow sunshine into my ears.

When the third hour passed, the sky fell suddenly and intensely dark. Helios had a short rotation period of only nine hours. This made the transition from day to night three times shorter than what we were used to. Accelerating the effect was the looming mountain nearby which blocked the massive, red star before it went down completely. Once night had swept over the alien landscape, the darkness was more complete than it normally was on Earth. The planet had no moons. There was only starlight overhead, and the thicker, hazy atmosphere blocked much of that.

The temperature dropped dramatically—going down with the sun. Like any desert, the days were hot and the nights were surprisingly cold. Fortunately, our suits were more than up to the task of adjusting for the variance. We'd planned for much worse conditions.

We were still interconnecting the bricks when the enemy hit us. It turned out the bugs—or *Worms* as we came to call them—were smarter than I thought. The best time to hit a beachhead was as soon as possible with massive force. The goal was always to knock it back immediately. Any invasion is at its weakest at the moment of arrival.

We hadn't set up. We hadn't had time to dig in. We had very little ground covered. We were new to the territory. We hadn't had time yet to scout the area. We had barely begun to set up our fortifications.

"Sir," my com-link buzzed. "This is Major Yamada. I've got contacts."

"What are your tanks telling you, Major?" I asked. I stopped walking around on my pile of boulders and listened intently. Yamada was the commander of my hovertanks. They were my primary defense during the fortification effort. Most critically, they had the only sensor arrays currently deployed, one of the garbage-can like devices was a central component of every hovertank. Until I had stationary sensors and beam turrets set up, the hovertanks were my eyes as well as being my primary defensive units.

"Mass contacts, coming in columns," Yamada told me, "But we've scanned the plain around us with infrared visuals. We haven't spotted anything."

I nodded. "That's probably because they are tunneling underneath us. We have to think in three dimensions here, Major. Prepare for battle. I don't want to see any of your pilots leaning against their machines taking a piss. Patrol the perimeter. Don't let your tanks get caught as stationary targets."

"Roger that, sir," Yamada said, breaking off.

Within moments, the entire hovertank group lifted and began gliding slowly around our cluster of stacked bricks. Their beam turrets swiveled independently—aiming primarily at the ground.

"Men," I said, addressing the entire unit via my com-link override. "We are about to make contact with the enemy. An attack in imminent. Take your posts and expect the unexpected."

Although Helios had fallen into a pitch-black night, lamps had been set up to keep the camp brightly lit. These lamps beamed down from atop every brick we'd placed and locked down. I watched as my troops got my message and digested it. The effect on the marines was intense. They had been glancing around in concern, watching the hovertanks begin to move, but now they were openly alarmed. Men ran and sprang into foxholes.

I cursed as I watched this last. It was a natural reaction. Now, I wished we'd never dug a hole in the camp. I reopened the channel.

"Marines, everyone get out of those holes. I don't want to see any boots on flat ground. Get up on top of the bricks or find a boulder to hug. Move."

Men scrambled like rats, adjusting equipment, shouting. The Worms didn't give us much time. Unsurprisingly, they came out of the ground. What did surprise me were the machines they rode upon. I should have expected a mechanized attack, I realized that the moment I saw it boiling up out of the crunchy soil of Helios. I'd known they were technologically advanced. But somehow, I'd always thought I would see these Worms as naked beasts. I should have known that if they'd been able to plant thermonuclear mines in space, they wouldn't be coming at us with nothing more than pinchers and garden tools. But I'd always envisioned this as a bug-hunt. I'd figured I would be fighting hand-to-hand with a knife in each palm, slashing my way through piles of charging Worms.

But things didn't start off that way. They came at us riding in machines. Their strange vehicles resembled tubular sleds of ribbed, flexing metal—reminding me of the duct behind my electric Whirlpool drier back home. In the dark, all I saw at first was the brilliant flaring of the beam units the sleds had clustered at the nosecone. I realized instantly the beams were primarily for melting away the soil in front of the tunneling machine, but they could also be used as weapons. Then the full length of the rippling metal machines came into sight, flowing up out of the ground and charging at our hovertanks and the square of bricks behind them. The Worms themselves rode in these sleds, leaning out of openings in the flexing metal that allowed them to rear up in a pose making them resemble striking snakes. They looked around and worked rifle-like weapons of their own. They had no hands, but they had plenty of small legs and mandibles around their jaws. They used these appendages to operate their weapons, which were harnessed to their bodies. More and more tunneling sleds crested and burst out of Helios' alien ground all around us. The Worms fired from their sleds reminding me of ancient charioteers.

Our men and hovertanks let rip with a massive barrage of laser-fire. My autoshade goggles blacked out completely at times, but I could still see the intense streaks of released energy. In flashes, I saw Worm sleds scar, blacken and finally explode as they were lanced with hundreds of beams. Worm troops rolled out of their burning sleds and slithered closer, only to be shot a dozen more times before their smoking bodies stilled.

"North flank!" I heard over the command channel. "North flank, they are breaking through!"

I had my light rifle out and trotted to the opposite side of my rocky outcropping. I was on the northwest side of the camp. A knot of marines who'd been stationed here grouped up with me. I halted, waving to half of them.

"You men hold here. Hug a separate boulder each. Don't lose this high ground. If they take this outcropping, they will be able to fire down into our camp center. The other half of you follow me."

One half scattered, the second group—seven men—crunched behind me. We reached the northern side and saw the problem immediately. On this flank the Worms had bored out of the ground closer in. They were between the hovertanks and our outer line of bricks. In many cases, they had come up right in the middle of the hovertanks and gutted them, getting in close with those nosecone beam-clusters. Our hovertanks had run right over the beams and been sliced open like horses running over blades. Three of the hovertanks were smoldering wrecks. The last one had halted and was encircled by Worm sleds.

"Focus fire on those sleds!" I shouted, kneeling and taking aim. "Let's save that tanker."

We fired with deadly accuracy. The men along the bricktops nearby saw our streaking beams cutting through the night from the enemy flank and joined in. After less than a minute, we had driven the surviving sleds back to their holes.

The battle was far from over, however. There was a lull, but it was measurable in seconds. Reports began coming in then.

"Infantry wave incoming!"

"Worms are boiling up out of those holes!"

I scanned the lumpy, desert-like landscape. Then I noticed the beam-fire of my own men. It was coming from *inside* our encampment. The troops around me looked nervous. I took a full second to think. If the Worms were inside our perimeter, did we rush to support the camp center or did we stay at our post in case another wave hit the outer walls? At that moment, I wished I was inside my command brick, seeing the whole battle, rather than running around out here on foot.

"Major Robinson?" I called, selecting his direct channel. "Are you at your post in the command module?"

"Yes sir," came a harried sounding voice.

"Give me a quick report, what's happening?" I asked.

"I think our underground nanite-net has slowed them down, sir. But some of the enemy have breached into the central compound. Men along the perimeter are reporting big waves of enemy troops coming out of the holes their machines dug for them."

"Okay, keep coordinating the action until I get there."

I never made it. Firing began all around me. What looked like a thousand Worm warriors came at us in a humping mass from every direction. We sprayed them with beams and they melted, slagged and caught fire. They kept coming, however, their numbers increasing. I finally had the opportunity to see the Worm warriors close-up and in action. I didn't relish the experience.

Harnessed onto two sides of every Worm warrior were ballistic weapons. The Worms believed in guns. These short-barreled weapons required no heavy power-packs, however. They fired chattering bursts of pellets that exploded upon contact. The bullets weren't like Earth weaponry. They were not high-velocity, solid lead projectiles. Instead, each projectile was hollow and lighter—more like paintball pellets full of nitroglycerin than bullets. Each of the pellets was covered in a chitinous, brown shell and had a liquid center. We suspected they were partly or entirely organic in nature. I supposed, as I watched them spray my men down around me, that the weapons made sense. They were light-weight and the pellets were light, too. Heavy bullets wouldn't have much range on a high-gravity world like this. Besides, if you did most of your fighting in tunnels, range and accuracy weren't important. What you wanted was overwhelming firepower at close range.

The pellets fired with popping sounds and each round *cracked* as it exploded on impact. It was like being shot by a thousand firecrackers in a steady stream. Our tough, nanite-impregnated suits and skins could take a surprising amount of punishment, but if a Worm got in close on a man and sprayed him with those twin fire hoses of explosive pellets, that man went down and his belly was quickly transformed into a smoking crater.

I ordered my squad—which had shrunken to a four-man fireteam—to pull back to a cluster of big rocks. We squatted in there, breathing hard and firing at anything that humped or squirmed past.

"Okay," I said. "If they get in here, I'll switch to my blade. Who else is good with a blade?"

They all looked at me. These were not the kind of marines, I realized in an instant, who would volunteer for things like anti-Worm knife-duty. Those men had probably already died.

I slapped the head of the nearest PFC. "You're it. When they get in close, we kill them. The others keep firing, or we will be overwhelmed as they keep coming in."

It didn't take long to test my plan. Two Worms made it into our midst almost at the same time. They had been behind other Worms, who now twisted and writhed in their death throes. The PFC I'd tagged didn't have any choice about following my orders, as the first Worm practically fell on him. It flipped over the top of our sheltering rocks and dropped in our midst. Screaming, the PFC had his blade out and slashed at it wildly, taking off an entire row of those churning little legs.

I let my rifle drop from my grasp, knowing it would dangle by the black cord that led to my power-pack. I snatched out my knife and the fine edge gleamed green, reflecting the laser fire that flared all around me as the others kept their suppressing fire up in every direction. Before I could even take a step toward the PFC and his thrashing Worm, the second one joined the party.

I lunged at the second one. It was about to take out one of our gunners, who was directing his fire out into the oncoming enemy waves. I plunged the slightly curved blade into the monster's tail, getting its attention.

It doubled back on itself, hissing. An alien face came at me very quickly. I saw those multifaceted eyes and a maw yawned widely, full of dribbling spikes and sharp, horn-like ridges that probably served to ingest food. The maw was big enough to swallow my head, so I slashed at it defensively. It was a lucky strike. The thing's face exploded. Yellowish, semi-opaque liquids gushed over my goggles, which I was very glad to be wearing. The Worm wasn't out of the fight yet, however. Pinchers clamped onto my arms and tore holes in my suit at both shoulders. I brought my knife in low, where I hoped it kept its throat. More liquids splashed out of it.

I could feel those pinchers cut into my shoulders. Blood ran down my sides, pooling up in my boots. My right arm was pinned now—the monster had figured out which of my limbs was causing the damage. I strove with the Worm, and despite my nanite-enhanced muscles, its power was unstoppable. It was like wrestling with a thousand-pound python.

I felt myself going down, and a second later I was on my back. All I could see was Worm. It had markings on it, I saw then. Blue tattoos depicting strange, cursive symbols. For a disconnected second I wondered if the tattoos indicated its rank or identity. Was the alien atmosphere that now leaked into my suit causing my mind to wander?

I managed to switch the knife from my pinned right hand into my left. Tearing my left free for a moment, I reached up and slashed across both those big, jewel-like eyes. That did the trick. The thing let go of me and reared up. Blinded and mad with pain, its mandibles activated the triggers on both twin, short-barreled cannons and sprayed everywhere in a circle. Before we killed it, the thing managed to blast the leg off one of my men and accidentally killed the other Worm, who had by now pinned down the PFC I'd placed on knife-duty with me.

When we'd gotten control of the situation again, I crouched with my remaining marines. "Okay," I puffed. "New plan. We are fighting our way down to the bricks."

This seemed to brighten their moods. I was injured, but not badly. I and the PFC who still clutched his knife, but had lost his other hand to his Worm, both grabbed and lifted the worst injury, the man with a missing leg. The five of us charged then, firing as we went, running downslope toward the bricks.

The men on top of the bricks and the remaining hovertanks saw us and provided covering fire. A hundred Worms tried to get to us, to stop us, to pull us down. Only one of my men didn't make it. The PFC with the knife. A Worm sprang out from behind one of those big, squatty toadstool growths and rode him down, guns chattering, pinchers flashing in the black night. A hundred beams took the Worm apart, but when we dragged the PFC's body into the protective square, he was already dead.

Handing over my wounded to a corpsman, I brushed off his attempts to patch up my injuries and trotted to the command brick. I slumped into the airlock. It seemed to take forever to ding and allow me through. Part way through the process, sheeting antibiotic mists and beams of lavender radiation sprayed me. We couldn't allow any form of contagion to enter the command module—I knew this intellectually and had approved the scripts myself, but it was still maddening to experience the delay.

At length, I dragged myself into the command post. Everyone threw me a quick salute and turned back to what they were doing, except for Robinson.

Robinson turned to Captain Sarin. "Get a corpsman in here, we have an officer in need of care."

I waved a hand at him and leaned the other heavily on the computer table. "I'll be okay," I said. "I've just had the wind knocked out of me."

They ignored my words and brought in the corpsman. I was surprised to see it was Sandra. She had taken the training, I'd known that. And it made sense that she was the closest certified noncombatant.

"Hi hon," I said.

Sandra made an exasperated sound and went to work on me. It wasn't the first time she'd performed emergency first aid on my sorry ass. I suspected it wouldn't be the last. I tried to ignore her as she pulled my torso out of my suit and dabbed, probed and ripped lengths of tape. She whispered things to me, while she worked. Threats about what she would do if I ever got myself torn up like this again. These sorts of threats only made sense to Sandra.

"Give me the big picture, Robinson," I said.

"We're winning, sir."

"Losses?"

"Five hovertanks were destroyed, but less than one hundred KIAs. The Worms surprised us, but they ran into our surprises as well. I think they meant to hit us from underneath simultaneously, timing it with the perimeter attacks. But our nanite-woven shielding under the base slowed them down and channeled their attacks into three breach points. We were able to burn them before they could get the interior assault underway."

I nodded. "What about the big waves from outside?"

"Your position was hard hit. They did manage to take the rocky outcroppings, and the northern flank in general was overrun, but I pulled troops from the other walls where we'd repelled them and sent reinforcements to the breach points. We pretty much slaughtered them."

"Enemy casualties?" I asked, wincing as Sandra jabbed me with something sharp. I heard a clicking sound, and realized it was as stapler. We didn't bother with sutures these days, the nanites took care of the fine work. Rapidly stapling up a wound and wrapping it tightly to prevent blood loss worked best. The nanites would automatically push the staples out after awhile when they were no longer needed.

"The computer has done a recognition sweep with all the sensors. Over nine thousand Worms died, sir."

I looked up at him, impressed. "We did slaughter them, then. You did well."

"Yes sir," Robinson said proudly. "Clearly, they miscalculated."

"Maybe. Or maybe they were desperate. I believe they are smarter than they look. I don't think they expected to win, but thought it was worth a try."

"Sir?"

"I want you to recalibrate and redirect our sensors downward. I don't care about the sky or the surface of this rock. I want to know what they are doing under our feet."

Robinson paused and frowned. "You don't think this is over, sir?"

I snorted. "If the Worms had landed in Central Park and smashed back our first assault, do you think we would quit?"

-45-

The Worms hadn't given up. They were hard at work underneath us, tunneling deeply.

"There's something big, sir. Metallic," Captain Sarin told me, flipping images on the screen. "It's about a thousand feet down in a soil substrate. I think the ground there is softer, maybe easier to dig through."

The big screen showed crawling, finger-like traces heading in our direction. They had converged and were aiming directly toward our position. I stared at them in growing concern. It was obvious where the tunnels had come from. Tracing backward from its current location led directly to the huge mountain.

"We'll keep an eye on things, sir," said Major Robinson. "At this rate, the Worms won't be under us for hours."

I continued to stare at the screen, not saying anything. I didn't like this new, gathering assault.

Behind me, a small, strong hand plucked at the staples holding together my injuries. I knew it was Sandra, letting me know she wanted me to come to our quarters with her and take a break. She wanted me out of the command post and under her not-so-gentle care. But she wouldn't speak, I knew that too. She had no official capacity here, and knew enough not to interrupt a command discussion.

I turned to her and tried to smile. I think I failed. She frowned back. She could tell immediately I wasn't going to do what she wanted. "Sandra, thanks for the field-dressing. Excellent work as always. Could you return to your post in my office now?"

Sandra nodded, but gave me a small, pursed-mouth glare. She didn't bother to help me pull up my suit and help me reseal it. She turned around without a word and left. The spring-loaded door prevented her from slamming it behind her. I watched her shapely form exit—somehow, when she was angry, she managed to look even hotter.

The command staff tried not to appear embarrassed as she left and I stared after her. The whole thing was unprofessional, but I hardly cared. Dying in a firefight with alien Worms on a newly discovered planet—all in the name of service to machine overlords—didn't fit the norm, either. We made our own rules in my outfit. I pressed my own suit into place, activating the nanites via proximity so they linked up and sealed the fabric.

Once she was gone, I turned to my officers and tapped on the screen where the contact blinked. The tapping caused it to zoom in closer. There was no more detail to be seen, however. Only a wireframe cube drawn in warning yellow.

"What if this is one of their thermonuclear mines?" I asked, voicing the thought that had been on my mind the entire time.

"They haven't hit us with anything big like that yet," Robinson argued. "I figured maybe they don't want to set off a big radiation mess right here so close to their stronghold."

"Yeah, but maybe we just changed their plans for them. Maybe after we skunked their assault team, they've decided they will just have to live with a little radiation."

Robinson sighed. "It could be, sir. I don't like any of this. We've yet to gain the initiative on this mission. We've been reacting to enemy attacks since we entered the system."

"Well, let's change that. Send out hovertanks with sensor arrays hugging the dirt. I want to see everything that's underground between us and this advancing force. Have the tanks stop, turning off every system except the sensors and then set them active. Ping away at the enemy. When the tanks detect something, they can relay the findings."

Robinson didn't follow my orders immediately. Instead, he stared at me in concern. "We've already lost a quarter of our hovertanks, sir, and they are the units that did the most damage in the last battle."

"I don't care. The enemy won't find our tanks easy to sneak up on with their sensors active and directed downward. These Worms won't come at us in the air or over the land. They will dig to us. That's how they operate. If we can see them coming, we'll have the advantage. We can move over the surface faster than they can maneuver underground."

In the end, the objections stopped coming and my staff did what I wanted. We deployed our hovertanks between the base and the massive mountain that loomed in the dark nearby. I knew Sandra was waiting like a spider for me in my office, so I didn't go near it. I sent for food and drink, and received a tuna fish sandwich that wasn't made with tuna fish. I swilled it down with a squeeze bottle of water. At least the water was cold and tasted fresh, despite the fact it was heavily recycled. Nanites made great filtering agents.

The hovertank scouts didn't take long to pinpoint the enemy. In less than an hour, we had a fix on them.

"They are about a mile down, sir," said the Navigator. He'd been recruited as our underground tracker in this environment. "But they are coming up now, toward the surface."

"Let's do a little projecting," I said. "Show me where they should be in another three hours."

The Navigator created a cone of probable outcomes. The top of the cone struck several of the existing, shallow tunnels that we'd mapped, the ones the Worms had used to attack us the first time.

"Here," I said, tapping at an area on the upper edge of the cone. "They'll come out here."

"That leads dead center toward the camp," Major Robinson said. "They don't really have to be so direct."

"I'm not seeing a lot of subtlety so far with these Worm folks. We'll meet them at this tunnel junction."

Everyone looked at me. "Meet them, sir?" Major Robinson asked.

"What did you think this was all about, Major? We're going to have to go down there and stop them from lighting off this nuke and destroying our new base and all our shiny steel bricks."

"Is that really necessary, sir?"

"What else do you suggest?" I asked.

"We could collapse the tunnel on them with our own explosives from above."

"That's like trying to drown a catfish. They are *Worms*, man. They will dig their way out."

"We could at least try…."

"No. I'm not fooling around with a thermonuclear mine."

"What if they set if off in our faces?"

"Then we won't need a funeral, because we'll already be buried," I snapped. I was getting edgy, and all these petty worries didn't help things. Certainly, we might fail. I knew that. We all did. But that was all the more reason for fast, aggressive action. We didn't have anywhere on this world to fall back to. We didn't have a country of our own. We had to hit them, and keep hitting them, until we won or they did.

I realized, staring at the screen, that the Macros were the smart ones in all this. Here we were, two biotic species fighting to the death while they waited quietly above the fray in orbit. What did they care if we won or lost? They could come back next year with another of our legions, or with someone else's.

The more I thought about it, the more my hate for the Macros grew—which was saying something, because I'd never liked them to begin with.

Over the next hour, I decided to lead the expedition myself into the tunnels. When I told Major Robinson, he looked miffed. I knew he wanted to lead the expedition. We'd often talked about his need for field experience with Star Force troops and equipment. Not sending him was tantamount to a slap in the face. It suggested I didn't trust him to do the job. And I didn't. The stakes on this one were just too high. The Worms had to lose this fight, quickly and decisively. I didn't want them to think about sending in forces from different directions at us the next time—if there was going to be a next time. I shuddered to think what we would have to do if we had multiple angles of attack incoming right now. There would be no defensive action possible other than trying to lift our five hundred bricks and run, and we couldn't outrun them in that case, not even on the surface.

"I want you right here, running this big board. You are good at the big picture, Major," I said, blowing praise at him in hopes it would stick.

"Better than you, sir?" he asked.

"Don't push, Major."

"Sorry sir. How many of our troops do you plan on taking on this safari?"

I glanced at him sharply. "Do we have a problem, Major?"

"I just want to set up the duty roster, Colonel."

"I'll take three companies. There are three spots the Worms can breach into, allowing them the use of their existing tunnels to speed up their approach. I'll lead the middle group, where I think these unsubtle invertebrates are most likely to come up."

Major Robinson studied his portion of the big table, tapping at it and making swirling motions with his fingers to alter the orders for three companies of marines. "Anything else?"

"Yeah. We'll go in silent and dark. We'll have suit lights and receivers on, but I want the transmitters switched off. I don't want the Worms to know what they are digging into."

Robinson continued to slap at the table. I could tell he was irritated.

"Major, come to my office for a chat, will you?" I asked.

"Certainly, sir," he said, straightening and walking past me. He never met my eyes as he did it. He didn't look surprised.

I followed him to my office. Sandra greeted us like a girl exploding out of a cake. Fortunately, she was fully dressed. She popped up out of her seat, lips formed into a wild greeting. She stopped short, seeing Robinson was with me.

"Sandra, could you excuse us for a second?" I asked.

Sandra nodded and slid by me, running her fingers across my chest as she did it. I marveled, watching her slink by. She could turn me on with the slightest touch. She had a gift for it.

I turned back to Robinson, who watched me smugly.

"Shouldn't you be heading out, sir?" he said.

"What's your problem, Robinson?"

"No problem, sir. Sorry if I—stepped on your cape, so to speak."

I stiffened. "Superman wears a cape, Major, not me."

"Exactly, sir."

I glared at him for several seconds. "You really want to do this, Robinson? This will be your first field combat assignment."

"Not so, sir. I fought in North Africa—"

"Cut the crap, man!" I barked. "We aren't talking about a bunch of half-starved militia with Kalashnikovs, here. We are talking about

263

fifteen to twenty foot long Worms in a dark tunnel. Worms with bad attitudes."

Robinson shrugged and headed for the door.

"You aren't dismissed yet, Major."

"Request permission to return to duty, sir," he said, standing there, still not looking at me.

I frowned, sucked in a huge breath, then let it out. "You take the men down. But don't screw the pooch, Major."

He looked at me in honest surprise. "I didn't think you'd give it to me."

"So, the spoiled brat routine was all a show?"

"No sir. I'll take the mission."

"Get out of here. And make sure you come back."

I watched him trot to the airlock, a changed man. He hadn't fought the Macros. He hadn't fought the Worms—not up close and personally. He was excited and happy. I stared after him like a worried father. I felt like I'd just given a teenager the keys to my Ferrari.

-46-

I went back to the command post and leaned on the screens. I told myself there were plenty of good reasons to send Major Robinson. For one, I needed the time to work on new programming for our factories. We'd just set them up and they were churning out fresh nanites to make thicker, wider pads underneath our base to keep the Worms at bay. I knew there were a dozen other, better uses for the factories, which were in many ways our most powerful asset. One plan was to keep producing nanites, enough to weave a tough net of soil deep beneath the baked surface of Helios. I didn't have much hope for that one. The Worms could break through any such net, given time. Besides, the underground net would have to be huge. If they began using nuclear mines, they didn't have to get very close to wipe us out.

I had a better idea. I needed a new type of vehicle. One designed to tunnel into the heart of an eighty thousand foot high mountain. The trouble was, I couldn't be sure the enemy was going to give me the time I needed to design and build these new machines. The Worms clearly had an agenda of their own, and they weren't out of ideas yet.

I watched via base cameras as Robinson gathered his three companies and equipped them sparsely for light, fast maneuvers. When dawn broke with alarming suddenness, sending the surface temperatures upward ten degrees in ten minutes, he led his troops out of our base of steel bricks and marched them toward the black, hulking mountains. His three companies didn't have to go far to

265

enter the Worm tunnels. The nearest mouth was only fifty feet from the camp perimeter.

Each of the three targeted tunnels quickly swallowed an entire company of my marines. I watched them go, flicking my fingers one against another. I cracked my knuckles. Each one individually. Captain Sarin winced at the popping sounds, but I kept going until two joints on every finger had clicked. After that, I noticed the men had vanished as if I'd already buried them. Oddly, I felt better.

"Pull in the hovertanks," I ordered. "We'll let the enemy think we are withdrawing to await another assault here in our base. Leave only two out there. Turn off the active pinging, have the last two sit and listen passively. Tell them to be quiet, too. I'm sure these bastard Worms have good hearing."

After that, we waited. There were no transmissions coming from the three companies of marines. We didn't want the Worms to know they were there, waiting in ambush.

"The Worms are still coming, sir," Captain Sarin murmured.

I smiled at her. "Don't worry, they can't hear us in here."

"Sorry, sir," she said.

"How long have we got?"

"Robinson and his men will be in position in eight minutes."

I looked toward the door. Beyond it was the corridor, my office, and Sandra. I didn't really have time to go in there and tell her I'd sent Robinson rather than risking my own skin this time. I pulled up an app and sent her a private text.

I sent Robinson.

A moment later, the answer came with a tiny ding. *I know, babe.*

Frowning, I checked my person for a new bell. I found it in my suit. She had planted a little transmitter in my back pocket while she had patched me up after the last fight. I flicked it off and put it back in my pocket. I eyed the thing, shaking my head.

You've become sneaky.

The app dinged again. *I always was.*

"Sir, something's happening," said Captain Sarin. "The contact is turning. They are coming up toward tunnel three."

Robinson himself was waiting in tunnel two, the central tunnel. His company formed a cool green glow of massed contacts, waiting underground for the digging machines to arrive. I studied the screen.

"Should we alert Robinson, sir?"

I shook my head. "To get a signal down there we'd have to beam it directly to them, which would tip our hand—or send down a nanite strand, which would take too long. Dammit, I wish we'd waited to see for sure where they were going. We could have put all our assets into ambush at the right spot."

It was hard, waiting out the next few minutes. "If they set that thing off right where they are, what will be the estimated damages?" I asked. I had to ask. It was my job—but I didn't really want to hear the answer.

"The company in tunnel three will be lost. No chance of survival. Company in the central tunnel will probably die as well, due to shocks and cave-ins. Company one and the base itself should be fine—that's assuming the charge is the same size as the mines we met flying into the system."

"How long until the Worms reach our men waiting in tunnel three?"

"About seventeen minutes, sir."

"Captain Sarin, you are in operational control. I'm going to lead two more companies down tunnel three."

She looked shocked. "Why, sir?"

"To make sure the Worms don't have time to set off their bomb."

"But sir, in that case we'll lose three companies instead of one."

I was buttoning up, sealing nanite lines and pulling my hood into place. I spoke through the hood to answer her, which muffled my speech. "Those calculations only hold if the enemy bomb is a small one. If it's bigger, we have to stop it or we all die. I'm not going to take that risk."

I left them then and slammed my way out of the airlock. I wondered as I ran to form up two companies behind me how long it would take Sandra to figure out I'd gone down into the tunnels afterward. I figured she probably already knew. She was a smart girl.

The jog to the camp perimeter turned into a dead run once we were outside the limits of the camp. Kwon himself had answered the call for fresh, ready troops. He caught up with me before I reached the tunnel entrance, puffing in his suit.

"Crazy moves, sir," he said.

"What's crazy?"

"You love fighting the Worms, don't you?"

"Oh, that part. No, I don't. I would hate losing to them, though."

267

We dove into the darkness then. It swallowed us up. The first dozen steps were taken in almost drunken staggers along the ribbed, crumbling tunnel floor. Compared to the blazing red sky outside, the tunnels were intensely dark. The ceiling wasn't high enough to stand upright, either. I had to run in a crouch, bent at the waist. My powerpack scraped the ceiling of the Worm tunnel, causing loose rock and sand to sift down onto my back. A choking cloud of dust arose as we went deeper, sliding down mini-dirtfalls of loose soil. I knew, if I hadn't been wearing the suit with its filters and recyclers, I'd be choking and coughing by now.

We went down a hundred yards, jogged forward another two hundred, then slid downward, spiraling further still into the depths. At the end of the next slide, huge boots crashed into my back and rammed me into a tunnel wall.

"I'm so glad they regrew your lost foot to its full size again, Sergeant," I said.

"Sorry sir. They were too big when I was seven."

I nodded and climbed back up again and ran farther into the tunnels. Behind me, Kwon came on, puffing like a bear in a plastic suit. A hundred men followed him, then a hundred more after that.

I paused when we reached the last downward junction. "The Worms should have come up by now. I don't hear anything."

"We got here first, Colonel," Kwon said.

I blinked inside the blackness of my suit. Cool air whispered across my body, drying sweat and making my eyelids itch. One of the worst things about these suits was the impossibility of scratching one's face through them. I wondered vaguely if I could script a bead of nanites to do some scratching for the comfort of my men in full environment suits.

"I don't like it. Kwon, send a squad forward."

There was a brief spate of shouting and arm-waving. Soon, troops ran past me.

"Keep a sharp eye," I told them.

The squad leader nodded to me, and then vanished into the blackness ahead. I looked back up the tunnel, where my men thronged the tunnel in a long line. Suddenly, I thought this entire venture had been a very bad idea. This was Worm territory. This was their home ground. They could walk through these walls like ghosts, while we were strung out and blinded.

A sound came from the tunnel ahead. It was an odd sound. It was something like—crackling bones. An image was conjured in my head of my squad crushed to jelly, every bone in their bodies broken all at once. I crouched and unslung my rifle, waiting and peering into the dark, listening. Around me, a dozen men did the same. The eerie sound was not repeated.

We got a signal, however. "Gone sir..." came crackling words. "I... all of them...."

I lost the transmission. Kwon lifted his com-link to respond, but I slapped his hand down. "We're maintaining radio silence."

"If they are listening and heard that transmission, they already know we are here now, sir," Kwon said reasonably.

I heaved a sigh and lifted my own com-link. "Report your location and your unit."

Nothing came back. I looked ahead, deeper down the tunnel into the darkness. There was no sign of the squad I'd sent down there behind their confident gunnery sergeant, nor of Robinson's Company Three, which we'd sent earlier. There was nobody home.

I stood up. "Everyone retreat. Pull back out of this hole."

They tried. They did it in unison, and with relief and speed. But it was already too late. Probably, if I'd given the order the moment we arrived, it would have been too late. The Worms had no intention of letting us out of their trap.

The floor collapsed under my troops. The middle of the tunnel gave way and fell, taking about a hundred of my men down with it. The hard, ribbed tunnel surface sunk about a foot, then paused for a fraction of a second before yawning open. An abyss was formed. A drop of unknown depth. Men fell scrabbling and sliding down into the dark. Bolts of energy flashed, burning the ceiling, the walls, the feet of fellow troopers. Fifty yards back I could see the remainder of my troops, crouching in the same tunnel we did, cut off from us. A wild melee began down below in the collapsed section. I couldn't see it, but I could hear it.

"Suit lights on!" I roared.

We couldn't see much more with the lights on. Dust roiled up. I caught a glimpse of a silver suit, of a beamer flashing. I saw the hump of a Worm's back. They were about thirty feet down. They had dug out the tunnel under us and ambushed us, even as we lay in wait to ambush them.

"Damn the dust. Don't shoot unless you have a clear target."

A few beams spat out from the men who still crouched in the upper tunnel, but only a few. Below us, men fought in the loose earth. Knives flashed. We heard screams and roars of rage. Worm-guns chattered, their streams of explosives popping with orange fire.

"Focus on the gunners," I told my men. I aimed my beamer down and fired. A Worm blackened and twisted in a death coil. I'd gotten lucky. I could have just have easily hit one of my own men—if any of them had survived this long.

I turned to Kwon. "We're trapped at this end of the tunnel. We might as well join in the mess down there."

He hesitated, but only for a half-second. His big head dipped. "I've always hated worms, sir," he said, and slid downward into the madness below us, roaring.

I bared my teeth and followed him. More men and boots rained down behind me.

I found myself on my hands and knees in a mass of soft earth. It was like mud-wrestling down there. I pulled out my knife, letting my rifle dangle. I slashed at anything Worm-like and crawled out of the way.

I got to my feet when I could and glimpsed a new kind of Hell.

-47-

There was more room down here than I'd expected. The Worms had been busy. They'd carved out a horizontal space in each direction—or maybe the region was a natural gap, a cave in the layers of rock and earth. I couldn't tell which right now, and I didn't much care.

I moved toward a wall. There was less confusion there, and the odds of being hit by my own men firing down from above was less.

"Form up against this rock wall, men!" I shouted.

A few of them heard me and put their butts against the wall. Occasionally, a Worm rushed us and we burned it down.

"Don't trust your footing," I shouted. "There may be more traps—more layers below us. Turn your beams into the larger area of the cavern and fire at anything that squirms."

I took my own advice, peering through the dust, confusion and darkness. Columns of earth stood everywhere, blocking a clear line of fire, but I managed to squeeze off a shot every so often. The men around me did the same. Collectively, we stemmed the tide of Worms that rushed forward to kill the men who still struggled in knots in the pit. Twisted limbs, corpses and dirt choked the collapsed area.

It didn't take long for the Worms to notice their new, organized attackers on their flank. They formed up a unit of their own and pressed forward, about twenty of them. They reared up and let their chattering guns stream fire into my group. We had no cover, and I directed my men to advance and hug columns in groups of three.

Both sides were exchanging fire at close range now, about a dozen yards apart. On each side, troops momentarily revealed themselves, fired and ducked back. Sometimes, the incoming fire from the other side overwhelmed one of my men. Two went down in less than a minute, then a third slumped, his head missing.

I activated my com-link. "Forget about radio silence. Everyone down here knows the score, this is a pitched battle. If you are up top, I'm talking to you now. I want the last Sergeant in line to stay up there with three fireteams. Keep sniping down into that hole and keep them off our wounded. The rest of you, come down. We'll provide covering fire. Move north into the columns and hug the walls."

I signaled my remaining men. There were less than a dozen who could fight. "When they start sliding down, we all cover them with everything we've got. No grenades, though. I don't want this ceiling collapsing on us."

It wasn't long before more boots came sliding down with men behind them. My men roared around us and we all came out of cover at once, firing at the Worms.

The enemy recoiled, then returned fire. I was hit with a half-dozen exploding balls, and my left side was numb afterward. I drew my hand beamer and burned Wormflesh wherever it showed itself.

The men sliding down came in ever growing numbers. They picked themselves up, advanced and soon we had two fronts for the Worm ambushers. After another minute or two of fighting, the last of them died or retreated down black holes in the floor.

They'd killed half my men, and we'd never seen a sign of the bomb they supposedly carried. Maybe the whole thing had been a feint. At the moment, I found it hard to think. I panted and tried to push ribs back into my skin by kneading them through my suit.

"Sir, we've lost contact with the forward fireteam and Robinson's Company Three," said Kwon, hulking over me. "I think the Worms were waiting for us, sir."

"No shit," I said.

"Why didn't we see them? With our scanners I mean, sir?"

I paused for a second, wishing I could scratch my face. It itched with sweat and droplets ran down from my buzzcut into my eyes to sting them. "I think we were only detecting the metal in their machines—their drilling sleds. I guess when their infantry digs, we can't see them. Either that, or these tunnels were all here already, and they just slithered underneath us and dug until the soil was weak enough that it collapsed."

"So, they could ambush us again? Anywhere?"

"Yeah. Pretty much," I said. I crouched down on my heels. The idea of sliding down deeper into the depths of Helios didn't fill me with confidence. It made me want to walk in a crouch and feel every step of the way.

"Orders, sir?" Kwon asked.

I tried to think for a second. "Send one scout down each of these tunnels. They are only to go about a hundred yards out, then come back and tell us what they find. If they make contact with the enemy, they are to retreat immediately."

Kwon stared at me. "Should we maybe try to use ropes to get back up to the main tunnel, sir?"

"No. The Worms and their bomb are below us, not above us. We're going to take them out."

Kwon straightened and shouted for volunteers. He slapped the nearest four men who didn't stumble away fast enough. These *volunteers* separated and headed for the darkest, narrowest Worm-tunnels we'd seen yet.

Two of the volunteers never came back. One did with a Worm on his tail. We hammered the monster down with a dozen shafts of hot energy. The last man crawled back a full six minutes after we'd sent him down.

"There's a bigger tunnel down there, sir," he told me.

"Did you see any Worms?"

"No, but they are around. I could hear them. It sounded like they were driving a tractor or something."

Kwon and I eyed one another. "Show us the way," I told the scout. We followed him back down a narrow shaft into utter darkness.

The shaft ended as a hole in the roof of a much larger Worm tunnel. This one was horizontal and the ribs of earth on the floor and walls were thicker, as if a giant Worm had made it. Perhaps it had.

We gathered in the tunnel and counted noses. I had about sixty effectives left. I got out a computer and did some triangulating. According to my best calculations, this tunnel led from our base directly under the Worm mountain. I turned and headed in the direction of our base.

"What if the Worms are in the other direction, sir?" asked Kwon.

"I hope they are behind us. I hope they light off their nuke now, this far from our base. Then they won't kill everyone—just us," I said.

"Very reassuring, sir."

"That's what I'm here for, Sergeant."

We trotted down the tunnel, making good time. We figured out five minutes later that we'd guessed right. When we caught up to the enemy, I think the Worms were more surprised to see us than we were to see them. We came up right behind them without them sensing us, because they were driving a sled the size of a diesel truck and it made a lot of noise.

"Grenades first, then we beam them until nothing moves," I told my troops.

"Won't that set off the nuke?" asked Kwon.

"No, at least not in an effective way. If we light the explosive shell around the warhead's nucleus, it should cause an explosion, but the compression from the explosion won't be evenly distributed enough to cause critical mass."

Kwon said something else, I think, but I was already winding up with a grenade. I threw it—but didn't quite land it under the big sled. It hit the ceiling and bounced down under some Worm tails that slithered along in the rear of the formation. Other grenades flew after mine, and then the tunnel rippled with concussive explosions.

I didn't wait until I could hear or see right again. I had my rifle up in my functional arm and I squeezed off one-second bursts, firing at the big drilling sled where I figured I might do the most damage. I marched forward as I fired and a pack of marines advanced with me. Everyone on the front line was blazing and it felt good to be tearing them up for once.

We killed every Worm and their machine without a loss. It felt good to win one cleanly. I noticed that most of these Worms were different, as we picked over the bodies. They were smaller, and had different tattooed symbols on their skins. Were they females? Civilians? Scientists or sappers? I didn't know, and I barely cared. We'd stopped them.

We found the device, riding in the center of the machine. I counted myself lucky they hadn't thought to set it up with a dead man's switch. I had no idea what the yield was, but I was sure I was looking at enough kilotons to take out our base.

We slagged the box-like device with our beamers until radiation registered on our suit warning-meters. We all got a dose, but our suits stopped most of it. I knew from experience that radiation poisoning was like getting the flu when you had a body full of nanites to rebuild the tiny holes the subatomic particles blew through your cells. We'd live.

Finding our way out to the surface wasn't easy. About half-way up, we met with a rescue effort, which came in a strange form. A silver thread of nanites, like a mercury rope, trickled down to us from above. I connected my com-link to it with an accessory cable, and was rudely surprised when the com-link blew up in my face. A wisp of blue smoke drifted in the dark Worm-tunnel.

"Gah!" said Kwon, backing away. "Did they take our base, sir?"

I looked at him. "What?"

"The nanites. They've turned on us."

"No, no," I said, pulling out my suit's power cable and plugging it into the nanite stream. The liquid metal rippled as I pushed copper prongs into it. The nanites had a gelatinous consistency. "This is a power line. I tried to plug my com unit into it like an idiot."

Kwon watched dubiously. "How do those things keep the positive from the negative? And how do they not ground out when they touch the earth?"

I shrugged in my suit. The crinkling fabric rustled. "They seem to form tubes of conductive nanites sheathed by others with a non-conductive coating," I explained. "As far as we can figure out, they detect which prongs of an intruding plug need current, then reshape the tubes of conductive nanites into the right configuration."

The men around me hunkered closer. Several drew out their suit docking cables.

I smiled at them. "I can tell some of you boys are getting low. Who is down to a quarter charge or less?" I asked.

About ten men raised their arms. "Okay, you are first up. Ten of us shouldn't draw too much. Just ten now, I don't want to overload the stream."

We all gathered along the nanite stream, like hunters clustering around a fire. Our suits had fusion reactors, but they need fuel, fresh nanites and a full battery-charge. This nanite stream provided all of the above.

I slapped a PFC who hadn't needed to recharge yet and gestured for him to hand over his com-link. He did so reluctantly. "Private, find yourself another com-link on a dead marine."

He looked down the tunnel behind us, doubtfully. "Do I have to go all the way back down there alone, sir?"

"Of course not. I just gave you permission to rob the next man who dies. Think of it as your inheritance."

"Thank you, sir..." the PFC said doubtfully.

I took the new com-link and configured it to transmit over the power-line. It took a few minutes and was scratchy, but I finally got through to the command post. I was relieved and a bit surprised when Major Robinson answered.

"Kyle?" he said, sounding even more surprised than I was to hear him. "Colonel Riggs?"

"Yeah," I said. "We're still breathing."

"Unbelievable. About a dozen of your men came back out of the tunnels, saying you'd vanished with most of your troops into an underground trap."

I thought about ordering the men to be arrested for desertion, but decided to forget about it. I could understand that some of my marines had panicked and retreated back up that tunnel. Maybe their Sergeant had ordered them to withdraw to the surface. If I'd been on their side of the collapsed tunnel, I might have given the order myself. In the confusion, it was hard to tell if anyone was going to get out of there alive.

"We did fall into a trap. But we reversed things on the Worms and managed to find the device."

"You took it out?" he asked.

"Yes. But we're low on power, oxygen and radiation pills. We need to get out of here."

He was quiet for a second. "You just had to go down there yourself, didn't you, Riggs?"

277

I grinned and snorted inside my hood. "Someone had to do it. You were in the wrong tunnel. How did you get out so fast anyway, Major?"

"There was no party down there. The Worms went the other way, as you said. When you made contact, Captain Sarin got a message down to us that we had staked out the wrong tunnel. I got back to the surface and spent the rest of the time trying to figure out what happened to you."

"Are there any more incursions? Ones that we can detect, I mean?"

"No, not at the moment. If the Worms are up to something, they are being quiet about it."

"All right. Get me out of here, Major. I think we might have the initiative for the first time in this campaign. I don't intend to let a pack of invertebrates get the jump on me again."

It took several hours, but we managed to follow the silver trail of nanites up to the surface. We met with various rescue troopers along the way. We never found anyone from the company Robinson had sent down here ahead of my group. I hoped they weren't captured or lost and screaming down underneath us somewhere in the dark.

It was day outside, and the huge, red sun was glaring down on everything. My porthole-like goggles were blacked out due to the autoshading effect. As soon as I came out of the tunnel and walked to the perimeter of the camp, I was greeted by a smaller marine in a suit. As I got closer, I saw the feminine form through the bulky shape of the suit.

"Captain Sarin?" I said.

She walked up to me and took a swing at me. Her fist came up with shocking speed. I was surprised, but not enough to let her land the punch. I caught her wrist. Her other hand came up next, and I caught that one too.

"You bastard!" she breathed.

"I didn't know you cared so much, Captain Sarin," I said, grunting as I struggled with her. I watched her boots closely. She looked as if she might kick me, and I was all out of hands.

"It's me, Sandra, you idiot," she said. She wrenched her hands away from me, breaking the grip I had on her wrists.

"I know," I said. I sensed this was a bad time to laugh.

Sandra took two steps away, turned her back on me and hugged herself with her arms. I stood behind her, wondering if I should keep walking into the base. I needed a shower. Men tramped by us out of the tunnels in a steady stream, tired but amused. They stared and slapped one another, pointing out the scene to anyone who might have missed the action. There wasn't much privacy on an extra-solar expedition like this.

"What's the matter?" I asked.

"You snuck out on me, that's what."

"I've got responsibilities. You have to understand you can't come first. Not out here," I said. I started walking then, right past her. I entered the camp, squeezing between two bricks. There was a pool of shade there and the cool gloom of the spot felt momentarily good.

"Where are you going?" asked Sandra from behind me. I realized she had followed me.

"I need a shower," I said.

"What are you going to do after that?"

"Count our dead. Plan our next battle."

"Do you need any company in that shower?"

I thought about it. I didn't look at her. "I don't know. It's a pretty small shower."

Sandra kicked me then, in the rear. I laughed finally, reached back and grabbed her boot. Sandra was good with a gun and okay with a knife, but she wasn't so good at hand-to-hand. I levered her up and over. She did a flip and landed hard on her face in the dirt. I knew that fall had to hurt, nanites or not. A falling body sped up much more rapidly on Helios. The planet's gravity had a way of grabbing you and slamming you down when you fell. Tripping and falling on your face felt like you'd jumped off a roof. I helped her up, still laughing.

"Get your hands off me," she growled.

I thought about letting her fall on her face again, but didn't want to push things too far. I probably already had.

"Why did you do that?" she asked.

"You mean, why did I let you kick me in the ass?"

"No, I mean—" she broke off. "I was just so worried, Kyle. I hate the feeling—you know that. You snuck out on me. You should have told me you were going to go fight Worms at the bottom of

279

some hole. For hours, I thought you were *dead*. Did you know that? For *hours*."

"I thought I was dead, too," I said.

Sandra trudged beside me, brooding. I was relieved when she stopped talking and didn't give me a longer lecture. That was one thing about her I appreciated. She was a very physical girl. If you pissed her off, she didn't make a speech—but you might have to duck.

"If you ever flip me again, you'll wake up without any hair," she said.

"Better count your fingers first. I bite."

When we got back to the command brick and to our shared quarters, I stripped down and climbed into the shower cubicle. It was one of the few units in the entire base that wasn't publicly shared. Rank had its privileges.

About half-way through, when the cubicle was nicely steamed-up, Sandra joined me. She didn't talk at all. Her body was firm and insistent. The cubicle was really too small for that sort of thing—but we made do.

-49-

I spent the next two of Helios' day-night cycles working with the factories. They were fully set up now in the midst of the base. I scripted them to produce new, large-system components. Starting with the base design of a hovertank, I made many alterations. My plan was to mimic the drilling-sled structure of the Worm-machines. These new drilling tanks would be long and cylindrical. They would have their lasers at the nose, with a very short range, high-powered beam unit.

The required systems list was kept to a minimum. They needed grav units and reactors, of course, just to be able to move. Normally, all of my Nano machines had a rigid external shell. These machines would be different. In order to scoot through rock and soft earth freely, they would have a more flesh-like exterior. They would be able squeeze through tight spots of hard rock—much like a native Worm. The body contours and flexibility were provided by balloon-like masses of nanites. I worked with chains of nanites, forming a bubble-like skin that was flexible and gave to the touch. If you pressed too deeply or suddenly, however, the skin would snap taut, becoming rigid. In the case of a cave-in, they would not pop like soap bubbles. They would turn hard like turtle shells, protecting my marines.

Captain Sarin interrupted my scripting and testing as dawn rose on the third 'day'.

"Sir? The Macros are calling. I think they want to talk to you."

I blinked and rubbed my eyes. "Patch them through."

"Can we listen in?" she asked.

281

"Be my guest."

"Patching."

I waited for a dozen seconds. *"Identify yourself."*

"This is Kyle Riggs, commander of allied Earth forces," I said.

"You have exceeded your allotted mission time."

I raised my eyebrows. This was news to me. "We were not given a specific mission time-constraint."

"That is irrelevant. You have exceeded your allotted mission time."

I sighed. Snide comments churned in my head. I pushed them aside. Getting snotty with the Macros never helped anything. "We request aid," I said, "to help us get on schedule."

"Specify."

"Use your ground-bombardment cannons to reduce the enemy stronghold to a crater."

"Salvo reserves are at minimal levels. Enemy mound-shell is prohibitively resistant. Request denied."

My mind echoed the words: *enemy mound-shell.* Interesting. Equally interesting, the Macros must have limits to their firepower and supplies, just like everyone else. The only bad news was they had apparently grown tired of watching us sit in our base and defend against Worm assaults.

"We will attack in sixteen local days," I said.

"Unacceptable. You have exceeded your allotted mission time."

"Yeah, I got that. We request a time-extension."

"Granted. You must attack within two local days."

I thought about that. Eighteen hours? I tapped at my computer slate. I wasn't sure I'd have a single drilling machine ready by then. "I'm not sure we can do it so soon. Explain the consequences of a failure to comply."

"This fleet unit will perform a strategic withdrawal in two local days."

"Clarification of your statement is required: You will pick us up and retreat from the system in two days."

"Negative. Failed experimental ground forces will be left in place."

I felt cold inside. Helios forever? "Tell me when you will return to pick us up."

"Target worlds are placed upon a priority-queue. When this target returns to the head of the queue, Macro fleet units will return."

"Specify the time span."

"Unknown."

I was breathing faster. I couldn't help it. 'Unknown' sounded like it could be a very long time indeed. "We will attack within two local days."

"Accepted," said the sexless Macro voice.

"How will you know we have achieved our objective?"

"Macro Command must be linked to the goal point."

I frowned, not quite sure what to make of their requirement. "You want us to contact you when we reach the center of the mountain?"

"Macro Command must be linked to the goal point."

I grunted, somehow I'd missed their point. They wanted to be *connected* to the goal point. Well, the only way I could think of would be to drag a nanite strand down there with me. Radio wasn't going to penetrate miles of rock. "We'll take a nanite strand with us into the mountain. When we reach the goal point, we will make contact."

"Accepted. Session terminated."

The channel closed and I was left staring at my computer slate. I tapped at it quickly, pausing to think now and then.

Another incoming channel request beeped. It was Major Robinson—he and the entire command post staff had been listening in. I tapped at a screen and the channel opened.

"Sir," Robinson said, sounding jittery. "We can't possibly be ready in eighteen hours."

"We'll be ready, Major," I said.

"How, sir?"

"We'll use the existing hovertanks. We'll refocus the existing heavy lasers, turning them into new, nosecone drilling-units. Underneath, these planned drilling-sleds use the same components as the hovertanks."

"Underground hovertanks, sir?" asked Robinson, sounding incredulous.

"You're right. It is a weak-sounding name. Let's call them *drill-tanks*. I like the way that rings."

"Let's suppose for a second we can build these things—and that they work," he said. "How can so few of them carry enough men down into the tunnels?" he asked.

"We'll puff the nanite skins up to carry every man we can. When we get to the mountain, we'll dump the men out and let them follow the drill-tanks into the tunnels on foot."

Robinson was silent for a few seconds. "That will pretty much leave the base defenseless, sir."

"Hopefully," I said, "the Worms will try to stop our attack, rather than counterpunch against our base."

"Do you really think the Macros would pull out and leave us here? Is that their style, to just give up and run? Maybe it's all a bluff, sir."

"In my experience Major, computers rarely bluff," I told him. "Besides, there is more at stake here in any case."

"How so?"

"What if that priority-queue includes Earth as a target? Our failure may well constitute a breach of our arrangement with the Macros, in their eyes. Perhaps we will have outlived our usefulness in such a case. Earth might be reclassified as a target again."

"May I state for the record that I'm less than satisfied with your plan, sir?" he asked.

"Your objection is logged and filed, Major Robinson," I told him in my most officious voice. "Riggs out."

The next eighteen hours went by quickly. In the end, we had eleven ungainly-looking drill-tanks ready to roll when the deadline arrived. We'd unshipped with twenty hovertanks, but seven had been lost in the first Worm attack.

The last two hovertanks I'd left unaltered. They still carried their long range weaponry. They had the mission of escorting my redesigned taskforce to the mountain. I was worried about getting hit on the way to the target. The two hovertanks, still carrying their long-range heavy beam turrets, could protect us as we skimmed over the surface of Helios, exposed. Afterward, they would return to base-defense duty.

I had bloated each machine to hold as many troops as possible, but we could only take six hundred troops with us. When we reached the mountain and folded the tanks down to fit into the tunnels, the marines would have to jog after the tanks. The balance of our infantry forces would stay behind and garrison the base. I set their factories to spilling out new, stationary beam turrets of the sort we had on Andros. Given enough time, they could build themselves an impregnable defense.

With so many men aboard the drill-tanks, the machines whined and growled, straining to lift the weight. Occasionally, they touched down and scraped over the surface. The high gravity caused the tail section of each vehicle to drag and bang over spots in the landscape that thrust up. Rocky outcroppings and bulbous growths were scarred and pitted as we passed over them.

We approached the Worm stronghold with sensor arrays fully active and pinging. I half-expected to see the ground beneath us churn and collapse, a thousand white-skinned Worms revealed and seething. It didn't happen. They watched and waited, biding their time. I could feel their alien senses tracking us.

As we approached their stronghold, I studied the mountain. The blackened craters that had scarred the rocky walls where the Macros had bombarded them seemed faded. I wondered about that. There hadn't been any noticeable precipitation. No snow, rain or sleet. What had cleansed the black marks off these mountains? The damaged areas had been huge. I zoomed in with my goggles, but the mystery wasn't solved. I didn't see any worms up there, smoothing over the surface. And yet the surface had changed. I thought about what the Macros had called the mountain's surface: *mound-shell?* What did that mean, exactly? I could have asked them, but I had been too busy trying to negotiate a way for my marines and my entire species to survive. When I talked to the Macros, I always felt it was best to keep the conversations as brief as possible. That way, the odds I would screw up horribly were reduced.

I felt the heavy atmosphere hitting me as I rode in the open back of an altered hovertank. In order to maximize seating, my drill-tanks had been opened up like yawning clamshells. We'd spread the nanite skins to their limits to fill them with troops. This left everyone open to the thick gusts of Helios. The planet's high-pressure atmosphere resisted our passage more than it naturally would have on Earth, just as slogging through water was harder than walking through air. Driving at fifty miles an hour, the wind resistance was harsh and buffeting. It roared and tore at my suit with clawing, invisible fingers.

I'd ordered the pilots to take a curved route to our destination. In case the Worms had dug massive tank-traps beneath the surface, the indirect approach should circumvent them. I was wary of taking expected paths after my experience with enemy tactics underground.

As we drove on toward the mountain and it loomed ever larger, until it dwarfed the land like an endless wall of dark stone, I began to doubt the wisdom of my attack. We had superior technology. We had just taken the initiative by launching this assault. But once we entered their domain I thought the advantages shifted to their side.

I tried to think of an alternative, but could not. And so we kept going, heading for the looming wall of rock on a wide, curving path. The mountain fortress had more than one cavernous entrance. We did not head toward the largest entrance in sight, but rather one that seemed out of the way. Tactically, this might mean the entrance didn't lead to a tunnel that would take us all the way into the heart of the stronghold. I figured if we hit a dead-end, we would employ our drill-tanks and continue that way.

When we reached a range of a mile or so, we met our first hints of resistance. From high-up on the mountain, probably from alcoves and cave mouths that were barely noticeable from below, long-range rifle fire rippled down upon us.

The incoming fire was quite a bit different than it would have been on Earth. First of all, we could see it coming. Each projectile came down as an orange spark like a tracer round. I doubted the bullets were designed to behave like a tracer, but because of the increased thickness and the composition of the atmosphere, the bullets were actually burning up as they came. Another difference was the fire wasn't straight, even though they weren't more than a mile off. The rounds came in a dropping arc, like artillery fire, due to the tremendous gravitational pull of Helios. Despite the thick air, and therefore increased air resistance, the gravity caused the bullets to fall harder at the end of their trajectory. The bullets sped up a fraction as they came. They rained down on us like falling meteors.

I was impressed most of all by the Worms' skill with their weapons. They dropped those bullets into our midst with precision. They did not seem to be picking out individual targets, but instead landed their fire in the middle of my sitting marines. I never saw a single shot miss my tanks entirely. To do that took great skill, I knew, as we were moving at high speed and they could not sight on us directly the way a sniper could on Earth.

Bullets punched into the curved metal surface of our yawning drill-tanks. Near me, a man was hit in the shoulder. He spun around and fell into the lap of a second man. Then the bullet popped inside his body—it must have had a timer. The marine howled and writhed. Blood poured from the wound.

I could order the tanks to button-up, but doing so would require that my men disembark and run after the tanks. That would leave them moving slowly and more exposed than they were currently. I reached for my com-link, but paused. The two escorting hovertanks had already begun to return fire without orders.

The enemy snipers had no doubt thought they had the clear advantage. We were exposed and they were well-covered, invisible to the naked eye from this distance. What they had not calculated upon was the precision of Nano sensors and Nano brainboxes, which unerringly swiveled, locked and spat back gouts of energy. Almost as soon as each turret fired, it swept a fraction to one side or the other and fired again.

I zoomed in with my goggles, watching the enemy die on the mountain walls. I saw burnt, twisting Worms falling from their perches, struck dead. Within thirty seconds, the incoming fire faltered, and a minute later stopped entirely. Even using the technique of slipping forward, taking a quick shot and retreating wasn't enough to escape our defensive fire. The brainboxes tracked them and remembered them—even timed and predicted their next exposure. They were burnt the moment they revealed themselves.

I smiled tightly. My scripts were slaughtering the enemy. It was a good feeling, but a grim one. Somehow, it was hard to enjoy watching artificial systems slaughter biotic troops—even when I was on the winning side. The Worms were, after all, defending their home.

We reached the mouth of the target tunnel without further incident. In a way, the fact the Worms had given up so easily was disconcerting. I knew they were inside their massive stronghold, waiting for us. What did they have planned for us once we'd entered their domain?

I reviewed our plan as we massed around the tunnel entrance. The more I thought about the plan, now that I stood there at the foot of the vast monolith, the less I liked it. Heading into the Worm tunnels seemed the height of folly. The trouble was, we didn't have any other options. Not if we wanted the Macros to give us a ride home.

I took a deep breath as we climbed out of the shells and scanned the area closely. This was it. This was go-time. There was no turning back, no hesitation. We were here to do or die.

The scanners showed nothing obviously threatening. I'd worried about the enemy setting mines around the outskirts of the mountain. Perhaps a certain level of damage would be worth it to them to stop us early, right at the doorstep. One well-placed, nuclear mine could blow us all off the planet surface and even though it might grievously damage their home, they would be rid of us as an effective force.

"Sir," said a sensor officer, Lieutenant Chen. She had a precise step and physician's attitude. I'd met her before. I considered her a sharp-troop.

"What is it, Lieutenant? Do you have contacts?"

"Yes, thousands, possibly millions of them."

I stepped up to the scope and peered inside. "I don't see that many."

"Look at the glimmers, sir. The trace contacts."

"You mean—under us? Are they down below? They are registering as cold and motionless."

"Yes. They're dead, sir," said Chen.

I looked at her, then looked back into the scope. There was a three-dimensional image inside—or what appeared to be inside, but which was artificially generated. I knew I really looked into a small box that simulated depth and registered interesting objects the scanner had picked up, displaying them with symbolic shapes and colors. My troops were bright blue circles. I could see a few Worms, they were—worm-shaped and bright yellow. Very faintly glowing green contacts were everywhere, however. There were indeed thousands of them. I waved my hands near a pickup, and caused the point of view of the scope to drive deeper, into the landscape. There were layers and layers of worm-shapes beneath us.

"They are all dead?"

"Yes sir. We are standing on a vast graveyard. The piles are thousands of bodies deep—below our feet, sir."

I looked at her. She looked back at me, evenly. I nodded. "Thanks for telling me. Keep me informed about anything else that strikes you or your team as odd, Lieutenant. But I'm primarily interested in live Worms."

"Of course, sir," she said.

I stepped away from the scope, uncertain of what to make of this development. Maybe the Worms had been burying their dead out here at the edge of the mountain for generations.

I stopped worrying about dead Worms. I had plenty of live ones to think about. I had the Macros on my mind as well. I set up a communications box at the tunnel entrance and buried it under a light layer of loose dirt. With luck, the Worms wouldn't destroy it. I attached a nanite strand to the unit. We would pay out the strand behind us as we advanced into the mountain. My officers liked the idea, figuring we could use it to communicate with our base. Heading into a mountain with no way to communicate to anyone on our side was a frightening prospect. What I didn't tell them was I did not intend to chit-chat with Robinson on this system. Sending signals with it would only alert the Worms to its existence. I had set it up to follow the Macro instructions. When we got to the heart of this mountain we'd use it—not until then. Even if we never got out of the mountain again, maybe the Macros would count our mission as accomplished and at least pick up Sandra and take her home.

The drill-tanks finished reconfiguring themselves after a few minutes of making sounds like rusty hinges. I ordered the first tank to enter the cavern, with a company of marines behind it. I held back the second machine for a full minute. If the Worms destroyed my first group, I wanted reserves with which to respond.

Nothing happened to my scouts, so the rest followed. I was in the middle of the column. As the cavern blocked the big red sun of the surface world from view, I found that I missed it. The tunnel walls were about a hundred feet apart and were ribbed, like the smaller tunnels we'd found near our base, but on a much grander scale. The huge tunnel could have held a train, and I was reminded of the Atlanta subway system, much of which is carved from solid rock.

We marched forward into the gloom. Soon, we had to switch on our suit lights and every man had his light beam-rifle in his hand and at the ready. No one looked happy to be here.

"Kwon," I said, speaking on a private channel.

"Sir!" he said, hustling up in the long line to march at my side.

I'd put Kwon in the unit I marched with. I could have ridden inside one of the drilling machines, but I wanted to see and hear what my troops did. I didn't believe in leadership from air-conditioned comfort. Especially not when walking into a den of traps.

"What do you think we should do, Kwon?" I asked the Sergeant.

"Sir?"

"Just tell me."

"We march into the heart of this mountain and kill whatever we find, then go home."

"Clearly stated, Sergeant," I said. "Do you think following these tunnels is going to work out for us?"

"No sir. The Worms will dig underneath us and trap us. Just as they did before."

I nodded. "Column, halt!" I ordered.

Everyone looked surprised. The drill-tanks glided forward another few paces, then stopped. Their nosecones twitched from side to side. It was an affectation of their past designs. They still sought distant targets, even though they had very limited range now. I hadn't had time to rewrite all their scripting.

We were close to taking the first big bend in the route, which would swing us to the east. I looked back down the tunnel behind me. Out there, in the red glare of the sun, things looked a lot safer.

"Drill-tanks, turn west. We'll plow right into the walls here. Let's have a look at what's on the inside."

Autoshaded goggles flipped to black all up and down the column, on the faces of every marine's hood I could see. Then my own went dark, and the big, short-ranged lasers flared up with blooming light. I closed my eyes, but still the glare was painful. I dropped my rifle, letting it dangle from the power cord and put my gloved hands to my face. I ordered everyone else to do the same, using the command override channel. I didn't want to be blind, or even have splotchy vision, when these tanks finished chewing holes into the walls.

Eleven big, smoking holes were drilled into the stone wall. The main tunnel we were in filled with gray vapor. Atomized rock roared around my suit. I felt the air-conditioners kick on as the temperature soared. The fans quickly ran up several octaves to high.

Then the light leaking past my fingers dimmed. I dared to peak with my left. The drill-tanks had inched forward, sliding into the holes they'd bored. The tanks farthest back, however, hadn't moved in yet. I frowned at them.

"You three in back, stop drilling. Forward tanks, keep going," I shouted. I trotted back toward the last tanks in line. Their drilling nosecones glowed a deep cherry-red with intense heat.

"Nothing sir," said the nearest pilot as he climbed out of his tank and came down to stand next to me.

We examined the wall together. We were only a few hundred yards from the entrance at this point. The stone was blackened, but seemed almost impervious to our drill-heads.

"This rock isn't the same as the stuff farther in," said the pilot. "It's a lot tougher closer to the exit.

I nodded. "Bring your tank in deeper. You can follow another unit that has had an easier time of it."

I trotted back to my unit and thought about what I'd seen. Perhaps the dead outside and the density of this outer area were connected. The Macros had indicated that the mountain had a tough shell, and that blasting at it from space had not been effective. I suspected they had done so previously, and at length. Perhaps that explained the dead Worms outside. Maybe, like a giant anthill, they had died in their thousands and their millions, but their mountain had withstood the assault.

I came up to the first drill-tank that was making progress. It had fully half its length inserted into the hole it had burrowed. I judged the process as too slow, however. We would never be able to drill our way into this mountain's heart if it took a full minute for every yard of progress.

"Sir, up here!" said Major Yamada, my tank commander. "Lead drill-tank, reporting a sudden change in rock-density!"

"Talk to me, Major."

"If you get in about thirty feet, it gets a lot easier, sir. A *lot* easier."

I slapped Kwon's chest as I ran by him. He caught on and trotted after me, as we ran toward the front of our long line of drill-tanks and men.

My celebration was short-lived. The Worms chose that moment to make their objections to our presence in their territory very clear.

-51-

"Worms, Colonel Riggs! Zillions of 'em!"

I heard the override shout in my headset, it came in over the command channel without the speaker identifying himself. It had to be one of my drill-tank pilots, I figured. This calculation proved correct, as I heard the drill-tank farthest up the line, the one I had sent into the tunnel first, begin firing. Rather than the steady pulsing beam of the drill, which was built to burn rock a few feet from the nosecone of the tank, the beam unit could be focused further forward to be used as a short-range weapon.

"Report!" I shouted, running now toward the front of our column. Heavy footsteps behind me indicated Kwon was right on my heels. "Is that you, Yamada? Specify enemy contact."

More firing erupted ahead of me. I thought it was coming from the second drill-tank in line.

"Broken through—into some kind of chamber," came the response. His labored breath blew over the microphone. "This is Major Yamada, lead tank, reporting."

"All tanks, stop drilling," I ordered. "Withdraw into the main tunnel. We've made a breakthrough."

"They've got something big they are rolling up, sir. I can't focus that far back."

I grimaced. Out of range? That indicated Yamada had opened up a seriously large chamber. The tank's nosecone weapon should be able to effectively strike at a range of at least two hundred yards.

I arrived, puffing and pushing past a clot of marines. They were trying to support the drill-tank, but couldn't get around it in the narrow, freshly-bored tunnel. Yamada was backing out, and marines were dodging to get out of the way. He never made it, however. I heard a heavy *thump*, then the front of the tank exploded. It had been hit by a shell of some kind and knocked out.

My little Nano tanks were deadly at range, but they were not heavily-armored. I'd always known that if they were hit by something serious, their two inches of front-facing nanite armor would fold inward like cardboard.

"Yamada?" I shouted, but there was no response. He was probably dead in there.

I switched my voice-out to local, and shouted at the men around me. "Grab this thing and pull it back. We can't let them have time to organize and attack."

A dozen powerful hands gripped the tank anyway we could. Normally, Nano machines were smooth and rounded in every dimension. This one had been hit, however, and looked like a splashed mass of metal. Frozen with flanges sticking out in every direction, I could tell the brainbox had been hit. The nanites had no instructions, and so held their chains where the enemy shell had left them.

Another thump sounded. "Duck!" I shouted.

The second shell struck the mass of the drill-tank. The dead hulk bucked backward, pushing me off my feet. More nanite metal splashed everywhere, some of it burning. Whatever they were firing at us, it was incendiary. Gouts of molten metal twisted in the air and crawled on the tunnel floor as if alive—in a way, I supposed that it was. The squirming metal rained back into the tunnel where the marines and the surviving drill-tanks had assembled, pooling up into beads on the floor. The nanite droplets fell amongst us and sounded like handfuls of thrown coins.

"Heave!" I shouted, climbing to my feet, grabbing the wrecked tank with both gloved fists and pulling hard. More marines helped, including Kwon with his ham-sized fists. The tank moved. A grating sound indicated some success. The metal flanges scraped the smoking sides of the tunnel.

"All together now," roared Kwon, "On three—one, two, THREE!"

We all heaved and the tank ripped loose like a bad tooth. Screeching, it came out of the tunnel like a nail being pulled out of a board. Roaring, we kept pulling, dragging it rapidly. Within thirty seconds, we had it out in the main tunnel, and we could see what it was we faced.

I saw nothing, at first glance. The tunnel was pitch-black. There were no Worms, or anything else. *Great*, I thought. They were resetting their ambush.

Pulling my head back so a sniper couldn't take me out, I signaled my men to take cover. We stood on either side of the tunnel, hugging the walls. I breathed hard for a few seconds, trying to think. All we'd managed to do is open up a flank for ourselves. We had over five miles to go to get to the center of this Mountain—and that was only counting straight, horizontal space. We were in a three-dimensional fight now. We could go up or down, and so could they. I had no doubt this mountain was riddled with traps and tricks and the Worms were busy making more every second, now that they knew which direction we were coming from and where we were headed. They would whittle us down, making us pay for every advance. At this rate, it would be a month and countless dead before we could reach the goal. The trouble with that was, I didn't have countless men—I didn't have a month, either.

I looked ahead down the main tunnel. Should I just press ahead and fight our way through whatever they had planned for us on the main route? Or should we fight our way into this narrow side passage and try to do the unexpected? After about a minute of hard thinking, I decided to punt and feel my way through the situation. We'd give the Worms something to think about and see how they wanted to play it.

"Drill-tanks, I need two more units up here. Drill me two more holes, right next to this one. I want you hiding on either side of this shaft. If the Worms rush through to this tunnel, you will break through and hit their flanks."

The drill-tanks rolled up and began working on the walls. I called for my sensor unit officer. Lieutenant Chen came up, dragging her wheeled equipment behind her. She set it up at a safe distance, aimed the pick-up nubs at the walls and worked the interface.

"I can't see past these thick walls. The material is very dense."

"I gathered that," I said.

"The density drops off, however, about fifty feet in. I can't tell what's there, only a few shadowy contacts are registering. But the echoes indicate lower density. It could be a cavity, or low-pressure material. Something about as thick as sawdust."

"Or Worm-meat," I suggested.

Chen nodded after a moment. "Could be."

"Sir," said Kwon, lumbering up to me. "There's something going on inside the drilled tunnel."

I trotted to the mouth of the tunnel that led, reportedly, to a zillion Worms. I waved my hands for quiet and ordered the drill-tanks to idle. Steam wisped and churned. A choking cloud of vaporized rock clung to the ceiling. We waited, quietly.

I heard something then, after turning up the exterior pickups on my suit. Kwon voiced my own thoughts, having heard it as well.

"Something—slithering, sir," he said behind me.

I waved for him to shut up. For once, he did. We all waited. Something slithered closer.

The unseen Worm made a final rush as we held back quietly. I was stunned when I saw it come out of the tunnel. It was huge. This was no twelve-foot baby Worm. This was a granddaddy, a titan of a Worm. It reared immediately and the two guns on its sides spoke. Marines tried to scatter, but it was too late.

Double thumps sounded—except at this close range, they were booms not thumps. Incendiary shells fired independently into my clumped together troops at close range. Blood, bone and scraps of gear exploded, leaving black marks on the hard, ribbed floor of the great tunnel.

We lit it up, of course, with a hundred burning beams of light. Our lasers lanced the beast, hissed into thick skin, blackened it, and then bored deep into the monster's flesh. Men held down their triggers, screaming in rage or fear or both. Beams shot through the great tube of squirming meat and burst out the far side seconds later.

It did not die easily, however. The twin great cannons on either side of it chugged, reloading themselves. I fired at the mechanism, hoping to disable it before it could get off another shot. The Worm turned in my direction. Could it have realized my plan to destroy its armament? I'll never know. It lunged forward with one heaving motion, struggling to function now, due to the vast number of wounds in its body. The great head dipped down, and to my horror Lieutenant Chen was swallowed almost in her entirety. The strange, horizontally opposed jaws opened and shut, chopping her off at the feet. Two boots and gray-white shinbones were left, sheared off and still standing on the tunnel floor.

We kept beaming, and it sagged down, convulsing and thrashing. Men were tossed about in wild confusion, dodging the monster and beaming it until it was only a quivering, steaming mass of meat.

Long before it stopped shivering, however, a new wave of Worms arrived. Nowhere near as big as the monster we'd just finished, but large enough to ride bareback, this wave seemed endless. They were unarmed, fortunately. They had only their snapping jaws and mandibles.

We backed up into a circle and burned them as they came by the hundreds.

"Drill-tanks in the side tunnels, break through!" I shouted, and heard the big boring lasers fire up.

The Worms kept coming, ignoring the sounds in the newly bored tunnels on either side. I was very glad I could not smell the burning gore or feel it, slick and greasy on my hands.

The two drill-tanks ended the rush of Worms. We slaughtered them. Hundreds, perhaps thousands died. I had to give them their due, they didn't mind dying for their home. Not for the first time, as I stood slipping on the wet floors, I doubted the ethics of our mission. Was Earth so worthwhile that we should wantonly destroy other species on other worlds to ensure our survival? How many other worlds would my boots tread upon, how many mass-murders would I be responsible for, following the heartless orders of the Macros?

I pushed these debilitating thoughts aside and tried to focus on the goal. If we could get to the heart of the place, hopefully killing as few Worms as possible, we could be done with this mission and out of here. I suspected the strategic value of the mountain's heart was industrial. Perhaps it was the last factory they had that could produce nuclear mines. Maybe, if we took it out, the Macros would leave the rest of the Worm population alone as they could no long obstruct the rings and disrupt Macro fleets. I told myself that whatever it was, all of this would soon be over with. I don't like to lie to myself, but sometimes, it's necessary.

The tunnel we'd bored through first was so choked with Worm bodies, I ordered the drill-tanks in the side tunnels to make new passages. When they broke through, a rush of men followed them.

We entered a vast underground chamber. It had artifacts, here and there, the first Worm artifacts I'd seen.

"What the heck is this?" asked Kwon, stumping up to me with an oddly-shaped lump of resin in his hands. The thing looked like a melted tree-branch, or a bone made of candlewax.

I took the object and examined it closely. I had no concept of its significance. It did not look like a natural formation, however. Someone had created this on purpose. My men were wandering the chamber, using their suit-lights to examine the walls. They pointed and poked at the artifacts they found. There were ovals on the walls, with dark reliefs formed inside the ovals. These reliefs were delicate, and when my men reached out and poked at them, they broke and crumbled.

"I bet they make these," said Kwon, "with spit or something."

I looked at him sharply, then looked back at the walls and the ceiling. I ran my suit lights over a dozen ovals and sculpted shapes that stood apart here and there, rising up from the floor like stalagmites.

"Hands off, everyone!" I ordered. Men moved quickly. They backed away from the walls and pulled out their weapons. Beamers glowed, their targeting dots shining red on a hundred spots.

"No," I said, "they aren't dangerous. These are—pieces of art. This is some kind of gallery, or museum. Don't damage anything further. No souvenirs."

A few men dropped twisting sculptures of brown resin. Kwon came up to me and leaned close.

"This don't look like art to me, sir," he said, using his usual, overly-loud whisper. He reached out to touch a flaky sculpture with his thick fingers. Pieces of it crumbled as he poked at it.

"I know. But a lot of what I find in museums doesn't look like art to me, either. To a Worm mind, maybe this is priceless. Maybe that big Worm was the librarian, and the others were on a field trip from school."

Kwon gave a halting, honking laugh. I didn't bother to argue my point further with him. Few of my men seemed to be troubled by the fact we were invading the city of another biotic species and wrecking the place. The Worms were just too different, I supposed. For most people, they engendered no sympathy.

"Enough dawdling. Let's move out. Wounded get to ride in the drill-tanks. No faking. Kwon, get my team moving. Put anyone who breaks more stuff in here on point."

My last order got a response from the men. No one wanted to be on point. Kwon, shouting and slamming his great hands together to make booming noises, got everyone moving again. We found a tunnel out of this place and set a drill-tank to digging right through the wall of it. I aimed it as straight as I could. No more fooling around, we were going to bore our way to the central chamber—whatever it was—and get this mission finished. A few of the frescoes and reliefs broke as the drill-tank fired up. I gritted my teeth and felt slightly sick about it. What would a pack of humans at the Smithsonian look like to an army of Worms? Would they be capable of respect and mercy? I couldn't be sure, but I figured any beings that valued art must have some kind of higher aspirations.

52

Once we broke through the relatively thin walls of the art chamber and plowed deeply into the dirt beyond, the drill-tanks began to speed up. I was surprised to see they were soon moving at a slow walking-pace. At this speed, we could reach our goal in few hours.

I had a new sensor officer assigned by now—a non-com corporal named Jensen. "Jensen, get over here," I shouted.

"Sir!" he yelled and trotted up, dragging the unfortunate Lieutenant Chen's array behind him. It was gouged and heavily-stained, but was still operable. Jensen bounced the unit over every hard rib of dirt on the tunnel floor.

"Take it easy with that thing. Treat it like a rifle."

"Sorry, sir," he said, standing nervously beside me.

I watched him fidget for a second or two. I wondered if he thought I'd somehow given Chen an assignment which had led to her gruesome death. He could be right. Maybe these Worms, especially the big ones, didn't like our actively pinging sensor arrays. Maybe it made big Worms grumpy to get hit with sonar echoes. Well, that was just too bad.

"Don't piss yourself, marine," I said. "You've got a sweet gig here. All you have to do is switch that thing on and feed me the density readings while we follow this tank to Hell. You are my sensor-operator until you're dead, or I find someone better."

"Thank you, uh, sir..." Jensen said. With diffident fingers, he worked the sensor array's interface. He set it for a thirty yard range—unreasonably short for most purposes, but enough to answer my question.

I snorted as I watched him dial down the range even further. I knew why he did it. He suspected that the active pinging of the sensor unit was what had drawn that big Worm and caused it to eat Chen. Maybe he didn't relish the idea of ending up inside the next big one's belly.

"Well?" I asked.

"This is very soft stuff, sir," he said. "It's softer than normal dirt back home. It's not even dirt, really. It's more like—sawdust. Full of cellulose and resins. It is structurally sound, however. It doesn't seem to crush down easily, or we would sink in it. Another point is the heat we are using to make our own tunnels, we are melting the material and making it stiffer."

"All right," I said, considering his information. "You're going to walk right behind the lead drill-tank from now on. Keep that thing dialed up another notch or two for range. I want to know if there are any cavities around us, any openings. They should be easy to spot now, with thin walls and even thinner stuff on the other side. Make sure you don't let the roof collapse on us, or let us sink through the floor into some water reservoir."

"Right. Yes, sir," Jensen said. "Ah, how far out do I have to scan, sir?"

"Thirty yards. Every direction. And don't let me catch you dialing it down any closer, either."

"No sir," said the Corporal. He made a spinning motion with his finger on a blue screen. The device pinged with greater enthusiasm. Jensen himself looked slightly green to me. I bet he was thinking about Chen again. Who knew? Maybe that sensor unit sounded like a mating call to a Worm. Jensen began trailing the drill-tank with the sensor bumping behind him. He reminded me of a golfer with a wheeled golf bag, lost in the rough. I smiled inside my hood, behind my goggles. This had to be worst *rough* any golfer had ever experienced.

Our system worked for quite awhile, making relatively rapid progress. We avoided neighboring tunnels whenever we detected them by changing course. We went up, down, left, right—any direction to keep away from existing tunnels. But always, we drove closer to our goal, the heart of the great mountain.

As we passed through the soft interior I picked up handfuls of the crumbling stuff. We didn't have a full lab with us, so I couldn't do a

301

chemical analysis. After looking at it and experimenting, I had to agree with Jensen. The material was not the normal contents one expected when venturing into a mountainside. If I squeezed the earth in my hand, it compressed somewhat. It looked like dirt, but *fluffed up* dirt, the kind you get when you freshly plow a field and don't wet it down afterward.

"Kwon, come up here," I said waving to my Sergeant. He never seemed to be far from my side. I wasn't sure if that was because he wanted to protect me, or if he thought I frequently needed help. I didn't bother to ask which it was.

"Sir?"

"What do you make of this? You grew up on some kind of farm, didn't you?"

"We cut down trees and bred koi, sir."

"Yeah, a fish-farmer. I've worked with soil for years myself. What do you make of this stuff?"

I placed a handful of crumbling dirt into his glove. The lump of earth looked small in his big paw. He squeezed it and let it sift through his fingers. He seemed to take my instructions very seriously.

"Seems like dirt to me, sir," he said.

"Just normal dirt?"

"Nah. It's Helios dirt. Not the same. Its half Worm-shit, sir. Good, fertile dirt."

I nodded. "Yeah, that's what I figured. Have you noticed that there aren't many rocks down here? Don't you think we should run into a boulder now and then?"

Kwon looked around at the walls. Our drill-tanks made a different ribbed pattern in the walls of the tunnel than the Worms themselves did. The laser drills left the walls hot and steaming, with shiny melted glass patches.

"No rocks?" Kwon asked.

"Not really, no. Nothing big."

"That is strange. I've dug into caves, into mountains. There are always rocks, sir. Big ones."

"Yeah," I said. "I think I know why."

Kwon turned his hood to look at me.

"We aren't in a mountain, Kwon, not really. This is an artificial mound. A hive, or a nest. Kind of like a termite mound. They get pretty big in Africa, you know."

"Eighty thousand feet?" Kwon asked dubiously.

"No. But these are really big bugs. And they are sophisticated—intelligent. I think this isn't a hollowed out mountain at all. I think they built this whole thing. The outer shell is tough, extremely tough and resilient. The mountain's skin is a half-mile thick layer as hard as steel. The Macros bombed them, hit them hard, but couldn't blast down this far. That's why they brought us in. To root the Worms out. Don't you see?"

Kwon scooped up a second handful of earth and crumbled it. "You could be right. The inside of big anthills look like this. The dirt they stack up is broken down into crumbs. It gets soft like—like a ground coffee crystals."

I snorted. "I didn't know you were a poet, Kwon."

"A what?"

I shook my head and waved his question away. Once in awhile, I ran into an English word that Kwon didn't know. One of them was apparently *poet*. I wasn't surprised.

"Why did you join up, Kwon?" I asked him suddenly. Men in Star Force rarely talked about their old lives. As in the French Foreign Legion of centuries past, it was considered rude to ask. The stories, when they were told, were never happy ones.

"Me?" he asked, surprised I would take an interest. "I joined up to fight the Nanos."

"The Nanos? Not the Macros?"

"Yeah," he said. "The Nanos killed my sister, see. One of those ships picked her up like a tick and squished her, dumping her out again a minute later. She fell right through the roof of a smokehouse on the farm. I wasn't there, I was in the army at the time. But when I heard about Star Force recruiting to fight the aliens, I joined up."

"Then you found out we were fighting the wrong aliens, right?" I asked.

"Yeah. Funny, huh?"

"Hilarious," I said. "If it's any consolation, I don't like the Nanos either—or at least I don't like whoever sent the Nano ships out. I call those guys the Blues."

"Are they blue, sir?" Kwon asked.

"No," I said shaking my head. "The only color I'm sure they are *not*, is blue."

"Okay...."

"But maybe Sergeant, if we live long enough, we'll get our chance to explain our feelings to the guys behind the scenes—whatever color they turn out to be. Maybe we'll get to see what color they are on the inside, too."

"I look forward to that, Colonel."

We made it pretty far before the Worms caught on. I wondered if they had laid in ambush for hours, suspecting we would show up at any moment, walking along one of their big, roomy tunnels. No doubt, they had a dozen traps set up, and were busy arranging deadfalls and cave-ins. But at some point, some bright Worm commander must have noticed that we were coming, that we weren't following their twisting, looping passageways. We were off the track and digging our own way in.

The first sign they'd figured it out came from my men at the rear of the column. I saw, rather than heard, the first evidence. Flashes of light bloomed up from far behind me. At this distance, the autoshades were slow to react to laser fire. Magenta afterimages splotched my vision. But the glassy walls of the tunnel had reflected it back up to me.

One of the odd things about laser-fire, as compared to ballistic weaponry, was how quiet it was. The weapon itself did little more than hum when it went off, unlike a gunpowder weapon, which boomed. Sometimes, depending on what the beam hit, the target exploded with a considerable sound, but that was the exception. My marines made most of the noise in battle, rather than the beamers themselves. Often, combat was fought in relative silence except for a few shouts and the screams of the wounded. I suspected that even ancient battles, when men hacked at each other with swords, had been louder.

Everyone stopped and craned their hooded heads around. We saw the green flashes, and now my autoshades were working, dimming the view of everything around me. The dimming effect was an odd one, making me feel as if I sank into deep water—or maybe a lake of ink.

"Rearguard company, report," I said into my com-link.

"Enemy sighted, sir!" came back a young tanker Captain's response. Roku, I thought his name was.

"Are they advancing?"

"Negative, sir. We saw them pop out of the tunnel walls way behind us, and we took some shots at them. They seem to have retreated, sir."

"How many?" I asked.

"No more than three confirmed," Roku said. "Request permission to pursue. They might be scouts and thus give away our position."

I was impressed by Captain Roku's brave offer. "No, don't pursue. They've found us. It was bound to happen. I'm not going to lose any men in their tunnels. They will have to fight in our tunnel, now."

"Orders, sir?"

"I want your platoon to hold your position for five minutes, then withdraw to catch up with the rest of us. Burn any Worm-noses you see poking through. And watch the walls for more breakthroughs."

I hailed the drill-tank pilots next and ordered one of them to reverse and babysit Roku's group. I also ordered a second drill-tank to come up and join the first one at the point of our column. I wanted two of them to drill forward from now on, side-by-side. We would make a wider avenue for our people, allowing the drill-tanks to maneuver. With a wider passage, my marines wouldn't be strung out into such a long, vulnerable column.

We were about three miles from the marked heart of the mountain when Corporal Jensen waved for my attention. I could tell from the urgency of his gestures, something was wrong. I grunted and hustled over to look over his shoulder.

He was tapping at his sensor screen dubiously. "Sir," Jensen said. He appeared worried, as always. "Sir, there's nothing up ahead."

"That's good, isn't it?" I asked.

"No sir, I mean there's *nothing*. We're drilling into some kind of void. Some kind of big, empty space."

I pressed the com-link override, broadcasting to everyone. "Column halt!" I roared.

But it was already too late.

53

It was the loose soil that got us into trouble. Anyone who's ever tried to dig a hole on the beach knows the story: the sandy walls cave in on the sides of the hole, filling the bottom. We'd been drilling along, making our tunnel and hardening up the walls with the heat of our lasers. We were creating a tube-like structure of stiffer material as we went through the mountain. But when we reached an end-point, a spot where the light dirt had somewhere to go when we drove into it, the dirt fell away from our tunnel in a rapid, sloughing motion. Our tunnel and its glassy walls were exposed to open space. The ceiling cracked and earth poured in. The dirt below us shifted too, and sent us down into the void we'd reached. The dirt above came down after it, pelting us. Within seconds after I'd called the halt, my forward team found itself helplessly sliding down into a pile of soft earth, tumbling at a forty-five degree angle a hundred feet or more downward.

I went down with the rest of them, trying to bodysurf and failing at it. I went under, and dirt buried me. I reached up with my hands as I realized I was being buried alive, trying to keep them up and visible. I wondered, as the dirt first roared, then finally pattered over my head, if my suit would keep me alive for days, and if I would ever be found and dug out. Something heavy hit my hand, cracking my fingers. I winced, hoping another drill-tank hadn't just rolled over my hand. I wiggled my fingers experimentally, they hurt, but I thought they were all responding to my brain's commands.

I tried to operate my com-link with my chin, but it didn't work. I had no way of trouble-shooting it. Maybe the unit had been ripped loose during the fall. Life-giving air still hissed out of the rebreather into my suit, however.

Something grabbed my fingers after I'd spent about a minute down there. Something that pinched horribly, pulling them out of their sockets. I would have pulled them back under the ground, if I could. The pinch stopped, for a blessed moment. I felt the walls pressing in on me, suffocating me with the weight. Many people who died in avalanches died because the pressure compressed their lungs and would not allow them to breathe, even if there was an air pocket available. Here on Helios, with the nearly double gravity to contend with, the earth weighed a lot and my lungs labored to suck in each gulp of air.

There was a fluttering sensation around my upraised glove. Was that a Worm? Were they rooting around up there, looking for good morsels amongst my men? The sensation of movement around my exposed hand increased, and for a moment, I wished I'd never put it up there, like a flag on a sand castle.

Another crushing grip closed over my hand. Wrenching force was applied. I felt my shoulder give first. It slipped out of the socket, and I screamed in my enclosed suit, the sound of my cries was muffled inside my crumpled hood. It sounded as if I were screaming underwater.

I squeezed whatever had me and held on. I was hauled out of the dirt like a carrot, dribbling brown earth everywhere. When I was half-exposed the horrible ripping sensation stopped. My arm flopped down at my side. I used my other hand to smear dirt from my goggles.

I was still buried up to my waist. Standing over me was Kwon. He had both hands on his rifle now. He was twisting this way and that, shouting something. My com-link still didn't work, and I couldn't make out what he was talking about.

Then the autoshades triggered as light-weight beamers flared around me. The men were firing at something. Painfully, I extracted myself from my early grave and got to my feet.

Kwon looked me over. He reached toward my head with those thick, ungentle fingers. I flinched, but let him do it. He fumbled with something near my ear. I heard a click, and suddenly my head filled with sound. My com-link had become disconnected in the fall.

"—we've got at least thirty down, Sergeant," I heard someone say.

"Worms north and east. They are staying in the growths."

"—sniping at us!"

I looked around, staggering, holding my wrenched shoulder. I tried to take stock of things. Men were everywhere on the slope, nearly a hundred of them. There wasn't much cover, but we were in a depression of sorts, and if the Worms were to the north and east, they didn't have a good firing position on us. My own men, I realized, were up on the rim of the mound formed by the landslide. They were the ones firing back at the snipers. Others worked to scrape out a trench for cover.

We were near the bottom of a fantastically large cavern. The ceiling appeared to be a thousand feet up in the gloomy distance. The floor of the cavern was covered with growths, things that looked like rubbery, slimy crystalline formations. I could tell by their flower-like structures were living growths, not some kind of mineral deposit. They reminded me of large fans of coral. It was as if I looked out into a drained undersea grotto.

I looked upslope. I could see the broken mouth of the tunnel. My men poked out with their lasers, looking down at us. No one seemed to be in charge.

I looked down slope. Tumbling wasn't good for tanks, I thought. One of the two drill-tanks I'd had leading the way had landed nose-down at the bottom of the slope. I could tell by the trail of dead, flattened marines that led down to its resting place, the machine had taken a few men down with it. The second drill-tank had fared better, it was upright and the torn skin of it was slowly reshaping itself. That meant the brainbox was still intact. The gun didn't have enough range when configured for drilling to hit the snipers. If the Worms tried to rush us, however, that tank would be a powerful defense.

I shook my head and tried to think. "Riggs here. Anyone got a fix on the snipers?" I asked on the operational channel.

A few men cheered. "Good to hear you made it, sir," said a familiar voice. I glanced down at the HUD readout. It was Captain Roku.

"Captain? Did our lead pilot make it?"

"No sir. That slide down the hill killed a number of good men."

"All right," I said, "Roku, you are in command of the remaining hovertanks. You are now second in command of this expedition."

"Ah, yes Colonel," said Roku, surprised.

He shouldn't be, I thought, he was next in rank. There were two other captains in the infantry, and they may or may not be senior, but I wanted one of my pilots in the lead if I didn't manage to dig my way out of the next hole I fell into. Knowing the chain of command was critical in a place like this, where deaths could alter the face of things at any moment.

"Captain, can you get your tanks down here with us safely?"

"With time, sir," he said. "We we can drill down in a spiral to your level and come out nearby, safely."

Kwon waved to me, pointing out toward the floor of the cavern. My vision had adjusted somewhat. The coral-like growths occasionally puffed smoke. The enemy was hiding out there, like crawling snipers in a forest. They were moving around on the open floor of the cavern to flank us. If they kept moving, they would soon have a clear shot at my men, with no cover between us and the incoming fire.

"Explain your current situation, Captain," I said. As I spoke, sniper fire spanged off a nearby dead marine's reactor unit. I wasn't surprised, the Worms tended to shoot dead bodies. They didn't seem to be able to tell the difference between a live man and a dead one. I ducked down to avoid further fire, and Kwon knelt beside me.

"I've backed the tanks down the tunnels about a hundred yards," said Roku in the calm voice of a man who sat confidently in his tank. "The last cave-in was caused by the combined weight of the two forward drill-tanks. If we drilled down and around—"

"Forget that, Captain," I said, cutting him off. "That will take an hour or more. We've been exposed to the enemy. They are already on the move, and more of them will gather every minute. Soon, they will probably hit you from behind up in that tunnel and assault us frontally in this ditch we've dug for ourselves down here. Somewhere in the middle of this cavern is our target. I need your tanks and men down here pronto, to help us finish this thing."

"Sir? How do I do that, sir?" he asked.

"You'll figure a way, Roku. I can't micromanage what I can't see."

"What if I can't do it, sir?"

"Then I'll be calling you Lieutenant from now on," I said. "I'll get my marines out of your path and take some cover in that coral forest looking mess on the cavern floor. We'll give the snipers something to think about while you get your asses down here. You have ten minutes. Riggs out."

I thought I heard him mutter something about *Riggs' Pigs* before he disconnected. I smiled, and slapped Kwon with my good arm.

"Thanks for pulling me out of there. I'm not sure I could have done the same for you."

"But you would have tried," Kwon said.

I nodded and crawled to the top of the trench line. Dirt popped twice around me, the snipers were getting testy. I ducked back down. "Let's get some suppression fire on those marked sniper positions. We've got about fifty men down here. I'll take the first half down to the forest. You cover me."

Kwon nodded. He turned toward the men we could see hunkering up in the tunnel mouth. As yet, none of them had moved. Whatever Captain Roku had in mind, I hoped he would get a move on.

"Listen up!" Kwon boomed up at them, dialing up his external directional speakers to an ear-splitting level. "Suppress those frigging snipers, NOW!"

"Well done," I said, gathering up a platoon's worth of marines. Their officer and the company's second sergeant had been buried along with a number of others. I went from man to man, tapping every other one and jerking my thumb. Soon, I had a pack of them following me.

My left arm burned and tingled now. I knew from too much experience that it would start working again soon. The nanites were almost magical, but they had a terrible bedside manner. They never cared much about the patient. Sometimes, they might build the nerve endings last, or cut them during the healing process. Other times, a marine might suffer in agony for a long while before an injury was healed. As part of their symbiotic relationship, they were capable of cutting nerve-damaged areas to prevent pain from becoming overwhelming and causing a marine to thus become ineffective, but it didn't always happen that way. When they were healing a man, they repaired whatever was the most expedient portion of flesh first.

Every man hoped they did the nerves last, but it was a matter of luck, really.

I took my team down to the site of the wrecked drill-tank first. I stepped on something hard that was buried under the tank. I reached down and smeared away a mass of dirt. I found the sensor array that Jensen had dragged down the tunnel with him. I eyed the cracked screen. I hissed in anger. He had dialed down the range to the minimum.

Moving around the base of the tank in a crouch, I found Corporal Jensen next. He'd been right up there with the tank, and it wasn't surprising he'd gone down with it. Half his head was missing. *Lucky bastard*, I thought. Now, I wouldn't get the chance to ream him for having disobeyed orders and leading us into this mess. If he hadn't been so worried about another giant Worm, he might not have taken those last few steps out into open space.

When we were gathered in the shelter of the wrecked tank, I realized we were never going to make it to the corral forest on foot. It was more than a hundred yards of open ground away, and the enemy fire was increasing by the minute, cover or no. Overhead, lasers flashed into the forest and Worm rifles puffed back. Sometimes a Worm thrashed in the coral-looking stuff, flipping and burning. Sometimes one of my marines pitched back, screaming. But they had us pretty well pinned down.

"Captain Roku!" I shouted into my command channel. "What do you have for me?"

"We've got a plan, sir."

"Talk to me."

"We'll roll each tank out of the tunnel with a rope—a nanite rope—attached to it. With our marines and another tank holding onto it, we should keep the momentum down to a slow roll. I should have the first tank down there in another few minutes."

I nodded to myself. He wasn't going to get down here within ten minutes. In fact, it sounded like it would be closer to half an hour. But I doubted he could do any better. "Okay, do it. But what is the state of this tank down here? Is your pilot alive in there?"

"Yes sir, he's injured, compound leg fracture. But you don't really need your legs as a tanker."

"Good point. Name?"

"Warrant Officer Sloan, sir."

I opened a private channel with Sloan. "Can you run your machine, Sloan?"

"Yes sir, but the enemy are out of range at the moment—"

"I don't want you to shoot. I want you to throw out your flanges. I want you to head right toward the forest and let us get behind you. Take us right into the forest."

"I'm on it, sir."

Within a minute, Sloan managed to glide his tank forward. I watched it transform, puffing up around the forward section like a cobra puffing up its hood. The tank listed noticeably to the right. I could tell his gravity-repellers on that side were shot, but he could still drive it. I ran behind the tank, and my troops followed me. This maneuver we'd practiced hundreds of times back home. First employed by the Germans in World War II, this tactical maneuver provided moving cover for infantry on an open battlefield. We hugged the spread shields of the slowly rolling tank, using the cover from enemy fire to the front. When we reached the enemy lines, we would spread out and mop up. As long as the enemy didn't have any heavy weaponry of their own, or outflank us, we should be able to take them out.

The first fifty yards went well. It was about then, I think, that the Worms realized what we were doing. They stopped firing at the tank, which was immune to their small arms. They began to dig instead.

"Watch for Worms," I said. "They might dig under our feet."

The big gun on the tank spoke then, flaring up with a tremendous glow of heat. Swathes of coral-like growth blackened and curled. Worms caught by the fantastic heat and power of the big, short-range cannon exploded into vapor and twisted remains. It was as if we'd applied a blow torch to a squirming nest of maggots.

When we were very near the coral forest line, we learned what the enemy had been up to. They'd dug tunnels in the earth in our path, right below the surface. When our tank glided over one of them, it collapsed and the right side of the vehicle sank down with a sudden, sickening lurch. The brainbox was inexperienced in actual combat. The stabilizers whined, overloaded. Like a panicked animal, the tank thrashed and overcompensated, trying to lift itself upward. As it was already weak on the right side, applying more thrust caused the entire tank to heel over onto its side. The big gun, still firing, exploded upon contact with the surface.

"That's our cue, boys! Scatter and advance!" I screamed.

I led by example, charging toward the corral forest past the burning wreckage of the drill-tank. Feet pounded behind me, but I didn't bother to look to see who followed and who didn't. A few men were sucked under by greedy Worms, who squirmed in the soft soil beneath us.

I drew out my hand-beamer, and burned anything that looked remotely dangerous. I let my rifle dangle, as my injured arm wasn't ready to handle it yet. My goggles flared and darkened in strobing, confusing pulses, *dark-light-dark*, as men fired around me. The goggles prevented blindness, but the effect was still disconcerting upon the mind.

The moment I reached the corral forest, I threw myself on my belly. I landed painfully on my damaged arm, which didn't quite cooperate and flopped down ahead and under my body. I sucked in a breath and let it out as a hiss, suppressing a scream.

Still hissing, I squirmed on my belly, like one of the Worm troops. When I had reached a decently covered spot, I chinned my com-link and called for Kwon to advance with his squad as soon as he was able. We needed a position staked out in the forest before the enemy could surround us.

"Push 'em back, men," I told those that joined me in our burning crystalline forest. "Everyone get under cover and burn everything that squirms."

I looked back at the ground between the wrecked tank and the forest line. I counted six dead marines and I mentally added Warrant Officer Sloan to the list. But then the tanker came crawling over and tapped my leg.

I grunted in surprise. "How the hell did you get out of there, Sloan?"

"These tanks can practically run themselves you know, sir."

"Yeah," I said, looking back at the burning tank. I knew all about scripts for Nano machines. Obviously, Sloan had given the vehicle its instructions, then slipped out the back and followed his own tank on foot with the rest of us. I thought about reprimanding him for abandoning his post, but really, it had turned out to be pretty good thinking on his part.

313

54

There were about twenty of us holed up in a circle of ground we'd taken in the forest. I worked toward an area with lot of scattered stones on the ground. This was the first spot I'd found rocks of any kind down here in Worm land. I realized this must be natural, real Helios earth, not the compressed sawdust and worm-shit we'd dug through to get here. In this spot, the enemy would have a tougher time undermining us.

It seemed to take a very long time for Kwon's group to press the attack. I realized, looking back, that they had their hands full. The tanks were rolling down one at a time. The nanite 'ropes' worked well. The tanks could glide over the rough terrain, but the downward angle was too great for them to negotiate without overbalancing in this heavy-gravity environment. I thought to myself I should have designed them lower to the ground, for more stability.

We held back the Worms with our superior firepower, but they were growing in numbers with each passing minute. It was only a matter of time until they brought in a super-worm with cannons to wipe us out, or overran us with sheer numbers.

Finally, after what seemed far longer than was reasonable, Roku had his tanks down out of the tunnel and onto the floor of the big cavern. He had the tanks extend their flanges and rolled them toward our position. Large groups of marines followed every tank, hugging the back of the machines for cover.

The Worms, seeing they were about to be outgunned, decided to go for it. They charged us from every angle, and some dug underneath, collapsing the soil under our bellies. My hand-beamer radiated heat right through my glove. Twisting, heaping bodies flopped everywhere, out numbering the strange, tree-like growths themselves. Finally, my beamer quit. My powerpack was still good, so I figured it must have been the lens. I reached for my rifle, but saw I'd lost it somewhere along the way. The thick, black cable ran down to a frayed end.

I ditched my powerpack it and drew out my knife, because about then, they were getting in close. I still had the power unit built into my suit. It was enough to run the air conditioners and the rebreather.

The man on my right suddenly sprayed blood. A fountain of it shot straight up. It was as if he'd discovered an oil gusher—a red one. He struggled, but without screaming. Maybe his throat was missing, I couldn't tell.

The Worm that had bit him surfaced then. The whole scene reminded me of a shark attack on a swimmer that I'd seen on a documentary back home. The Worm had come up underneath the marine, finding a spot where it could break through the stones we lay on. It had taken out a big chunk of his belly.

The Worm humped up out of its hole, glistening, and tried to finish the job. I crawled over to it and worked my knife. The weapon was astoundingly sharp. The Worm's flesh tore apart like wrapping paper. The next six slashes hacked off its head. The Worm choked out brown liquids from its maw. I wasn't sure if it was coughing blood, salivating excitedly or spitting at us out of spite. The three of us struggled, with gruesome results, until the Worm stopped thrashing and spraying.

I turned my attention back to the battle, but saw no new targets. The enemy were in retreat. All around me, men rolled onto their backs and gasped for air. Marines shouted for medics, but we'd only had one, and he was dead. We had to take care of one another now. I took it upon myself to help the guy who lay dying beside me.

After I'd unclamped the dead Worm's jaws from his guts, the marine ripped off his hood. He looked at me. I saw he wasn't bothering to hold his breath. He was past caring about the poisonous atmosphere of Helios.

I let him do it. If he wanted a fresh breath before he died, who was I to deny it?

"What's that air taste like, private?" I asked.

"Burnt pizza," he said in a raspy voice. "And you know what else, Colonel?"

315

"What?"

"It's really *hot*. Even down here, under all this dirt, in this gloomy hole, it's *still* hot. That just seems wrong, sir."

"Yeah," I said, "I'll get you a squeeze bottle of water."

I rummaged in my belly-pack, and found a bottle. But by the time I'd turned back to hand it to him, his eyes had glazed. I cursed and commandeered his weapon. I went back to firing at the retreating Worms. They were soon out of range and invisible in the strange forest.

I counted noses. I had nine effectives left. Several minutes later, Kwon rolled up behind a row of tanks.

"What's your rush?" I asked bitterly.

"Sorry sir," said Kwon. "You did a great job keeping the snipers off us while we brought the tanks down."

"We kept the enemy busy all right," I said. My tone dripped with sarcasm, but Kwon didn't seem to catch it.

We loaded the wounded into the tanks and formed up behind them. We set off marching through the crystalline forest, breaking every frond of pink crap we saw as we went. The men had passed around the rumor that this forest was the enemy's food-supply. They were intent on wrecking as much of it as they could. Maybe they were right, but I doubted it. Who knew? I thought about stopping them, but somehow I'd lost some of my compassion for our enemy as well.

I put two tanks on point and had my troops hustle up behind them. We didn't drive straight for the central point, but rather spiraled in, hoping to avoid traps. We stuck to ground that looked the most solid, but that was a tough call, too. From our vantage, in the middle of a thousand crackling pieces of alien vegetation, it all looked about the same.

Up ahead, I didn't really see anything special about the area that we were targeting. Could this be it? I dared to hope. Maybe the Macros had just wanted us to get this far, into the heart of the enemy. I wondered if they had just chosen the midpoint of the Worm mound and sent us here, figuring that if we made it this far, we must have done the enemy a lot of damage.

Kwon was having similar thoughts. "What are we doing here, sir?"

"I don't know. It looks different than the rest of this termite mound. Maybe this spot is some kind of shrine?"

Kwon snapped his fingers. I wasn't sure how he managed to do it through his gloves. He pointed at me. "Yeah. That's it. This is some kind of shrine. We are in a big, Worm sacred-place. A graveyard for heroes."

"I thought their graveyard was outside," I said.

"I bet they worship their gods here."

"Could be," I said.

"Maybe this explains why the Macros had us come here," said Kwon. "Maybe this is some kind of holy place for them."

Or maybe the Macros had no idea what's down here, I thought. *Maybe the machines just wanted us to drive our way to the center of this hellish mound, because it was big and in their way.* I kept these thoughts to myself, however. It wouldn't do my men any good to hear them. Troops needed a specific goal to keep them going.

We pressed the Worm defenders back, meeting only skirmishers. But we could tell they were building up for something big, gathering their strength. I came to appreciate that most of the Worms that had once lived in this vast place had to be dead. We'd seen millions of bodies buried outside, but only met thousands in the heart of the place. I wondered how many Worms could live in a place like this, a vast nest, if it were fully populated.

We reached a slope that went upward, and when we topped the rise, we met a surprise. It wasn't the surprise I'd been expecting—namely about fifty thousand pissed Worms. Instead, it was a depression of sorts, a bowl formed in the middle of the mountain. We were very close to the spot my maps told me the Macros wanted us to reach. Looking down the slope into the center of that dish of earth, the answer was very plain.

A ring sat there. A ring that was smaller, much smaller, than the ones I'd seen before. It was probably only two hundred yards wide. Half of it was sunk down into the earth. Looking at it, I suspected it had been buried, or had been constructed bit by bit from the bottom up.

There were Worms crawling over the ring and around it. The device was clearly made of the same sort of material the others I'd seen were made of. I hoped I would have time to study it, the information could be invaluable to our own nerds back home.

"Flip on every suit recorder we have," I ordered. "Roku, order your tanks to scan that thing continuously, and store the feed. I want every brainbox we have to bring home a record of it."

Seeing us, Worms began humping, crawling from all sides of the ring. They dropped the last dozen feet to the floor of the place and squirmed away. My men fired down on them, burning them as they ran. I ordered them to stop, as the enemy was unarmed.

"Where the hell are the Worm troops?" asked Kwon at my side.

"More importantly," I said, "how did the Worms get a ring down here?"

"Maybe they found it, and built this mound over it. Maybe it is their god."

I huffed. "I think the Macros fear this ring. The Worms have a plan, and the Macros sent us down here to stop them. Maybe this thing will transport a Worm army to the Macro homeworld. Maybe it will let them push their nuclear mines through to blast the Macros."

"Let's take it and find out," Kwon suggested.

I nodded. "Company Alpha swing left, Echo right. I want one tank leading each group. The rest advance toward the artifact. Fire only if fired upon. If they are surrendering and in retreat, maybe we can finish this without further bloodshed."

I figured I was dreaming when I described this final step as a cakewalk. But the Worms still managed to surprise me.

-55-

The Worm troops were hiding, of course. Not out around us in the forest of fan-like growths. They were right there, all along the rim of the bowl that surrounded their ring. They had dug in and laid waiting under our feet. By the time I'd advanced my forces to the ring and we were completely in the bowl, they exploded out of the ground and charged us, raging, from every direction at once.

I really wished, at that moment, that Chen or Jensen or at least one of their sensor arrays had survived the trip, but they had all been lost or destroyed along the way. We couldn't see what they had in store for us, and thus were taken by surprise.

Thousands of them. They came on, guns chugging out steady streams of popping balls. We burned them, and they blasted us. The bowl wasn't very large, and they were in close in less than a minute. The drill-tanks rotated their big weapons, spraying blinding heat into the advancing enemy like flamethrowers. Ranks of Worms turned into twisting, smoking bodies. Often, their magazines of explosive pellets were ignited, and the resulting explosion flattened everyone nearby.

We were killing them ten to one, but they still had the weight of numbers. Once in close, when it was down to knife-work, the Worm troops had the advantage. They were six times the weight of a man, stronger, and their jaws were deadly.

Kwon and I took up a stance in the center. The bowl-shape of the terrain helped us then. We had a free field of fire. Since the enemy were higher up than my marines, we could fire over our men and hit

319

the Worm troops that were still pouring out of the holes around the rim.

"Mark your target!" roared Kwon. "Don't burn one of my men in the back or I'll burn a hole in yours!"

I sent the center tanks to the front—which was everywhere. "Pull back Bravo and Delta," I shouted into my com-link. "I want a central reserve in case they break through our line completely. We'll give fire support from the base of the ring itself."

"Sir!" shouted Kwon, standing back-to-back with me. We both fired intermittently, steadily, out into the massed enemy ranks.

"What?"

"Sir, we have to get out of here."

"We're holding them."

"But we don't know what this thing is going to do," Kwon pointed out.

I glanced over my shoulder and looked up at the big ring that loomed overhead. It was mottled and craggy. It seemed weathered and ancient, rather than freshly built. But who knew with the Worms? Nothing they made had straight lines and smooth surfaces.

"You think they wanted us to hug this thing?" I asked.

"They gave us one surprise," said Kwon reasonably. "Why not two?"

"Yeah, why not?" I agreed.

Bravo and Delta companies had gathered in the center with surprising speed. No one wanted to be on the front lines, holding back the mass of charging Worms. There semed to be no end to them. The bodies were stacking up into steaming heaps. Some of the enemy troops were scrabbling over the bodies of their comrades or burrowing under to get to us.

"We're going to break out! Everyone push back the same way we came in. We know the way out if we head in that direction."

The men needed little encouragement. We marched southward, and the enemy lines folded away from us, falling back from our concentrated fire.

When I reached the rim of the bowl, I looked back and realized I couldn't withdraw entirely. We'd made it to our destination. We had to tell the Macros about it. I got out the special unit, the one that was tied to the glittering trail of nanites that wound back all the way to the outside world. I wondered how many times the wire had been broken. I'd seen it snap just from a marine carelessly treading on it. The wire had naturally repaired itself, being made up of billions of nanites. Miles of nanites, spun along a hair-thin path to the world of sun and wind. Just thinking about it made me homesick for an open vista. I'd even welcome the red, fluttering glare of Helios right then.

I pressed the button I'd never pressed until then. The one that opened up a channel to the Macro command.

"Identify," came the response, quickly and coolly.

I relaxed a little. I hadn't known if the thing would really work until then. "This is Colonel Kyle Riggs. I've reached the goal point. The mission is complete."

"The mission is incomplete."

I watched the pitched battle around the ring. In two spots, our lines had fallen back. They had not yet buckled, but I could do the math. With each wave of Worms that poured out of the holes, we lost a number of men. At some point, we would lose too many and the enemy would break us. We'd dissolve into pockets of struggling, encircled, desperate survivors. If they had enough troops and enough time, we would be slaughtered. There would be no surrender. No retreat. Maybe this is what the enemy had planned all along. Maybe Kwon was right, and they did worship here at this ancient altar. That made us a dramatic blood-sacrifice.

"What do I have to do to complete the mission?" I shouted.

"The nanite wire must touch the transport ring."

I stared at the shimmering strand of liquid silver that ran to my otherwise disconnected com-link. My eyes went back toward the ring which stood downslope.

"Standby. We'll do that now."

I grabbed Warrant Officer Sloan by the shoulder. He'd kept with me since the initial battle in the cavern. As he'd lost his tank, he'd joined my unit by default. I lifted a loop of the nanite strand and gave it to him.

"You want to end this whole nightmare, Sloan?"

"Damn straight, sir!"

"Here, run this down to the ring. Make sure it has a strong contact."

He nodded, grabbed it and ran. Like kite-string, it ran out behind him. Shimmering and whipping, it reformed itself as he went, trying to keep its structure even as it was stretched further.

The Worms showed no sign of easing up. Kwon and I used the time to fire in support of the men who were now beaten back toward the base of the ring itself. I watched my men stiffen their resistance there. Having a structure at your back—any structure, and troops on your flanks helped keep spirits up. But still, we were retreating. Men left behind among the Worms thrashed and were torn apart.

"I don't think they like us messing with their gods, sir," said Kwon. "The Worms are pushing hard now."

"I think they know what we're doing," I told him. "We only have to hold them for another minute or two. I want to see us make an orderly withdrawal toward the ring. Relay that to Roku."

Kwon bent forward over his com-link, giving my instructions to the tank commander. I noticed the signal light was blinking on my hotline com-device. I picked it up.

"Riggs here," I said.

"One minute has passed. The mission is incomplete."

"Yes, one more minute," I told them, setting down the handset again. Literal-minded bastards.

I watched as Warrant Officer Sloan reached the base of the ring. He took the wire and wrapped it around a jutting spur of the odd material. I thought to myself that if I had the time, I would go down there and investigate the structure carefully.

The signal light was blinking again. I picked it up.

"Connection detected."

"Yes, it's ready," I said. "You can come through now."

"Sequence engaged. Portal opening imminent. Withdrawal recommended."

"Yeah, we're pulling back to the ring now. We'll meet your big boys as they come through."

"Portal opening imminent. Withdrawal recommended."

"Okay, I—" I stopped. My mouth hung open in my suit. I watched the battle for a frozen second. Six Worms reached a drill-tank. They bit the metal hull and fired streams of bursting rounds into it. The metal of the tank withered, but the head-like turret continued to swivel, burning them.

Thoughts burst in my mind like enemy explosive pellets. Macros always repeated themselves when a miscommunication had occurred, I realized. They had told me to withdraw. When I said I was pulling back to the ring, they told me to withdraw again. I wasn't getting it. The only answer was they didn't mean I was to retreat to the ring, they were telling me to retreat *away from* the ring. What was I not understanding? Possibilities presented themselves inside my fertile mind. None of them were good. What if they weren't sending troops, but instead a bomb of some kind? A wave of sickness rolled over me.

"Everyone get away from the ring!" I shouted, keying the command override. Every headset rang with my words. I took a step forward, then two more. I screamed into the microphone, causing my voice to distort and break into a scream. "I repeat, move all units away from the ring! Head south, to me! Priority one! NOW! *Go, go, go!*"

The ring began to… *thrum*. It was gentle at first, but grew into an undeniable force, a sound that could not be ignored. Every skull felt it, whether they had ears or not. It was a deep, forceful, brain-shaking vibration.

I saw perhaps half my tanks shudder, halt, and reverse direction. Hundreds of marines looked around, confused. Their unit commanders reinforced my orders. I could hear them, yelling at the troops and waving for them to pull back. As the ring was at their back, they had no choice. They rose up and charged the advancing Worm line. The enemy met them eagerly, but recoiled in shock as beams, knives and howling marines ran upslope into their ranks.

I experienced a moment of hope. I felt maybe they would escape whatever was coming, but my elation was a very brief affair.

A strong breeze came up next. I took another five steps downslope, toward the ring, toward my struggling troops. Kwon laid a heavy hand on my shoulder.

"We gotta go, sir," he said. His words were gentler than his grip.

Maybe he knew what was going to happen. Maybe he'd witnessed the wrath of an alien god before. The breeze grew into a wind, then to a howling gale. My suit ruffled around me. I felt it move and shift.

"What are they sending through?" I asked.

"Nothing, sir," said Kwon.

I looked at him suddenly. I twisted back to look. I saw the first man lose his footing. It was Warrant Officer Sloan. He'd been standing at the base of the ring, closer than anyone. He lifted up, pin-wheeling his arms for balance. He lost it and landed on his face. His body, dragged by an unseen force, began to thump and roll toward the ring. He flipped over and over, tossed about like a leaf as the force of moving air grew ever stronger and then—then he was gone. He slipped into the span of emptiness that was the gap in the arch of the ring and vanished. There was a spot of color on my vision, where it had happened. I'd never seen something go through the ring like that—not this close. It was like an... an *event*. A sparkling change to reality.

I knew, in my heart, that Warrant Officer Sloan was somewhere else now. Most likely, he floated in space. Perhaps he orbited a world no human had ever laid eyes upon until this moment. Or perhaps he was on the surface of a neutron star. He might have been instantly burnt to a vapor, or crushed to the size of a flat coin by unimaginable gravity. Or he might be simply floating somewhere, calling *mayday* to no one in a heartless void without even starlight to accompany his ending.

I grabbed up the com-device that connected me to the Macros. I could see by the glowing green LED the channel was still open. I almost broke the device in my fury and desperation.

"Turn it off!" I shouted.

"*Mission accomplished. Return to base for pickup.*"

"You are killing my men! Turn it off now!"

"*Mission accomplished. Return to base for pickup.*"

"Fucking machines!"

"*Mission accomplished. Return to base for pickup.*"

I destroyed the com-device. I smashed it through with my fist, and I enjoyed the sensation immensely, despite my agony of spirit. Kwon pulled me away, and I let him drag me toward the rim. We stumbled along until we caught a passing tank. Several of the drill-tanks had escaped. They were heavier than my troops, and denser. They were able to resist the hurricane force of suction that now drew everything up into a swirling tornado in the area around the ring. Worms twisted in those winds, hundreds of them. My troops drifted between the Worms. They still fired off and on, burning Worms who came too close with pencil-thin beams of brilliant light.

Kwon dragged my fingers to a handhold on the hovertank. There were plenty of handholds around the base of every tank for soldiers to hang onto. Kwon crushed my fingers around one of these loops of metal. I would have shouted in pain, but I didn't care about pain jus then. Kwon then used one of his ham-like fists to grip another handhold himself and placed his second hand on the back of my neck. I kept hold of the grip he made for me, but he still held me by the scruff of the neck, as if he didn't trust me and I thought I might let go.

There were marines around me, inside and outside of the tank, but not many of them. I craned my neck back to watch as we raced away, half-dragging marines and smashing down coral-like growths.

I looked back and watched hundreds of marines and Worms, swept high up in a maelstrom. Many of them embraced. Knives and beamers flashed, maws snapped. By ones and twos and clusters of up to a dozen struggling forms, they were all sucked together into nothingness.

I wondered if, when they reached the far side, they continued fighting to the bitter end. I suspected—knowing both my men and the Worms—that they did.

-56-

When we reached our base of bricks, the Macro ship had already landed. Ice crystals, formed no doubt in this strange planet's upper atmosphere, crackled and fell away in blue-white sheets. I assumed they were formed from water vapor, but I couldn't really be sure and didn't care to ask.

The base itself was a mess. They'd suffered a Worm counterattack—possibly one motivated by revenge. I leapt off the tank I'd been riding upon, one that was positively roomy now that we'd lost three quarters of our troops. I sprinted into the bricks, leaping atop the first one I saw. The command brick, which had been situated upon a stack of others in the central compound, had been knocked over. It lay on its side, canted downward so one end was thrust into the ground. The airlock was up high, stuck up into the air. Bodies were everywhere. Most of them were Worms, but one in ten was a marine.

I ran up over a steaming pile of corpses and leapt to the top of one brick, then another. I went to the command brick airlock, and ripped at it.

A hand fell on my shoulder. I whirled. It was Major Robinson. I could tell from the look of him that he'd finally gotten his chance to prove himself in combat. He had a fist-sized hole in his side that was black and oozing. The nanites were working on it, showing silver in the wound.

"She's not in there, sir. We evacuated the command post where the Worms flipped it."

"Where then?" I said, panting from my run and my panic.

Robinson pointed out toward the limits of the camp, to the north. I saw a figure sitting out there on the top of a brick. I ran to her, but didn't sweep her up in my arms. She had a knife in her hand, and it was covered in gore.

"Sandra?" I asked, kneeling beside her.

"You came back," she said. She didn't look at me.

"Yeah. I'm back."

"I didn't really think you could survive walking into their nest."

"Most of us didn't. But we have to prep up. We have to go now."

"I killed them. Lots of them. Some were our own men."

I looked at her and eyed the knife in her hands. Some of the gore on it was dark red, not the usual brown that filled the Worms. I wasn't sure what to say. Had she lost her mind?

"I'm still not very good with a knife," she said.

"What happened?" I asked.

Sandra shook her head, and drew her knees up to her chest. She rocked slightly while she told me about Worms tearing holes in the suits of men and injecting them with some kind of bio-poison. They'd died slowly after the battle, beyond the help of nanites or corpsmen. They had screamed and raved and begged her to kill them. In some cases, she had done as the marines had asked.

I waited until she was done, then she hugged me, and I comforted her as best I could. Despite everything, she felt good in my arms. I could feel the shape of her, under the bulky suit. Something tight in my belly relaxed a notch. At least I hadn't lost Sandra.

"Are you going to tell me all the shit you went through in that mountain, now?" she asked.

"No."

"Thanks," she said. "Don't ever tell me, okay?"

"I won't."

The Macro ship came down a few minutes later. There was no time for rest. The Transport opened its yawning maw to swallow us all whole again and take us away from Helios, and I for one would be glad to see the last of this world.

We gathered everything we could and began loading. Before we were half-finished, an earthquake shook the planet. The arid, cracked surface of the land split. Movement caught my eye, something huge shifted. I looked up to the north and my jaw sagged down inside my suit.

The mountain, the home of the Worms, had collapsed in upon itself. It took a long time to fall all the way down. The shoulders fell first, then the cone-like top crashed down. A vast plume of dust and debris shot up into the sky, blotting out the red sun, casting our tiny base into shadow.

I felt cold inside. We'd done the Worms more harm than they deserved. And although the creatures were viscous and disgusting, it was I who'd led an army onto their land, not the other way around.

We had righted the command brick on top of the growing stack inside the hold. Around us, the rest of the bricks began to appear, one by one. Our last operating loading machines were performing their final duties. Theirs was the long labor of stacking all the bricks into the Macro transport's hold again. It went much more slowly this time, because most of our loading machines had been destroyed.

"Colonel, sorry to interrupt," said a voice in my ear. I tried to ignore it, but it wouldn't go away.

"What is it, Major Robinson?" I asked in resignation.

"Well sir…there's something—ah, I think you'd better come to the op center, sir."

I frowned, not liking the worry in his voice. "I'll be right there."

I had to take Sandra's hand from my sleeve, where it had landed the moment I took the call. She'd gotten more clingy today. I tried to do this as gently and quickly as I could without hurting her feelings. Naturally, I failed.

I left her pouting on top of a brick and trudged into the command module. Captain Sarin was there, I was glad to see. There was no sign of the rest of them. Even Major Robinson had left.

"What's up?" I asked with simulated alertness and interest.

"A new contact, sir. Something big."

"Big? How big?"

Captain Sarin shook her head and played with the screen controls. Our big screen had three long cracks in it now, but it still operated. The lower left corner was dark, however. It looked as if someone had thrown black paint over that section.

I watched the screen as the underground tunnel complex came up in wireframe. We'd mapped much of the underworld in the area o our base. We'd come to understand there were more events going on underneath the dirt of Helios than there were on its surface.

I caught sight of what she was talking about almost immediately. There was something there, a long, blue thing. "That's a new tunnel? Where did that come from?" I asked.

"No, sir," she said. "I don't think it's a tunnel."

As I watched, it *moved*. The entire length of it, maybe a mile or more, of what I had assumed to be a stretch of tunnel... *moved*. That's when I caught on.

"It's a granddaddy Worm, isn't it?"

"Yeah, we think so."

I leaned over the table and stared at it in shock. As I watched, it inched forward a few more pixels. It had to be driving through the earth beneath us as fast as a dog could run. I tapped at the screen, reading the estimates of diameter and length. I nodded my head.

"I'd been wondering, the whole time I was down in the Worm mound, what Worm had made those big tunnels. Now we know."

"We've got about eighteen minutes at its current approach velocity," said Captain Sarin. She sounded as drained and defeated as Sandra had when I'd found her.

"Let me guess where it came from, and where it's headed," I said, doing the math. The tail of it pointed toward the mountain. The head of it pointed directly at us.

"What can we do, sir?" Captain Sarin asked.

"Don't worry," I said. "We'll beat it."

"You really think we can kill something that big, sir?"

"No. But maybe we can outrun it."

One would not think a loading process could be sped up dramatically, but we did it. In such situations, it's all a matter of priorities. I threw every moving marine I had under the weight of bricks, straining and heaving to help the loaders. We took the essentials first: our air purifiers, water units, generators and the factories. A lot of the sleeping units would have to be left behind, which made up half the bricks we had. I had a lot fewer marines to put into them now, anyway.

I didn't bother reconfiguring the last five drill-tanks I had. We just put them into service, opening them up into clam-shells and put brick on the back of each. Then we set a lot of men to shoving until the revving drill-tanks slid, scraped and bumped their way up the ramp. The bricks were unloaded into the Macro hold by unceremoniously dumping them out. We didn't even bother to stack them, we just turned on the clamps and went for the next brick.

By the time the giant Worm was about a minute from arrival, and had begun to dig upward toward the bottom of our base, we'd managed to get around a third of our bricks into the hold. I decided it was high time to contact the Macros and tell them to lift off.

"Macro Command, this is Kyle Riggs. Respond."

"*Unnecessary communications are wasteful of system resources.*"

"Right you are, but this is not a waste of time. Close the transport doors and lift off."

"*All ground forces are not aboard.*"

"You are incorrect, Macro Command."

"*All ground forces are not aboard.*"

"Sir," said Captain Sarin at my side. "I think they mean the bricks and equipment we left behind."

"Macro Command, we are abandoning a portion of our equipment to escape the incoming mega-biotic enemy," I said, realizing I'd coined a new word: *mega-biotic.* I hoped it wasn't going to be one I would be using often.

There was a hesitation. That was all the time our Worm friend needed, however. It broke through our thin shielding of nanite-woven materials, lifting it up like a sheet of paper. Bricks heaved and were tossed twirling like matchboxes. A gout of dirt, rocks and debris flew into the hold itself. Men scrambled for cover.

The Worm itself was tremendous. I'd spent too much of my youth watching movies about giant creatures destroying cities. Here was one worthy of the task. Its maw flipped open, tossing out gouts of brown liquid. The orifice was big enough to swallow one of our bricks whole, without chewing.

The creature did not roar, but the ground at its base did Everyone was showered with clods and wet clumps of unidentified matter. A tossed brick, falling end over end, crashed down upon the Macro ramp with an ear-splitting crash.

The sky lit up with a hundred beams of energy, darkening my goggles. Major Robinson had set up a number of automated mini turrets using the heavy beam packs my troops had given up in favor of their lighter kits. He'd added a brainbox to control them, and fastened them atop the outer ring of bricks that formed our base wall. These turrets fired now, cutting dark lines in the endless mass of flesh that towered a hundred feet up in the middle of our wrecked base. More small turrets were manned by marines. These needed only a tripod, a beam unit and a generator. Too heavy to be carried on this world, they could still be operated by a marine as a stationary gun emplacement. Robinson himself set one of these up as I watched on top of a brick in the hold. He and a dozen others fired at the giant Worm that shaded us from the red sun with its bulk.

The Worm shuddered in reaction. I could tell it had never felt the burning sensation of our weapons before. Unfortunately, the output of our weapons was nowhere near enough to kill it. Enraged, the Worm began to thrash and struck down with its countless thrashing feet, each bigger than a man. Bricks tumbled and crashed. The beams kept flashing, cooking Wormskin and the wet meat beneath.

"*Abandonment of equipment without cause weakens the value of the ground forces,*" said the Macro Command voice calmly.

"You've got to get us out of here, sir!" said Captain Sarin, screaming to be heard.

I thought hard, my eyes wide. "Marines, you may fire at will!" I commanded.

More beams leapt up, stinging the monster. We only managed to anger it further. Mad with pain, it writhed and snapped with greater energy. I realized, as it destroyed my encampment, it was only a matter of time until the Worm turned toward the Macro ship. With the hold doors open and with us inside, it would no doubt come in here for a snack. I knew from experience the big ones didn't die easily. And this one looked to be about fifty times the size of any I'd seen before.

I decided to give Macro Command one more chance to see reason. "We have no need for the abandoned equipment," I said, shouting into my link to be heard over the crash and roar of the great Worm. "Fighting this biotic would cost us more in terms of effectiveness than leaving the equipment will cost us."

Another hesitation. It seemed to be a very long one, but perhaps that was only because the Worm was twisting about, looking for fresh prey. Then the head turned, and lunged directly into the Macro hold.

"Abandonment of equipment without cause weakens the value of the ground forces."

"Sir!" buzzed Major Robinson in my ear. "I think we can take it down, sir. You brought a few hovertanks back from the mountain. If we concentrate their fire at the head—"

"No," I said. "Man your post."

"Why not, Colonel?" Robinson demanded in exasperation.

"Because the Worm has already destroyed our last hovertanks. Only a few drill-tanks are left, and they haven't got the range."

The great head dipped down into the Macro ship twice more. Each time a beam turret, along with a marine and the brick he stood upon was removed.

"Macro Command, my forces are being erased. It is imperative that we take off right now."

"Abandonment of equipment without cause weakens the value of the ground forces."

"I assure you, we will still be an effective fighting force!" I shouted into my microphone. My words were relayed up to Macro Command.

More marines were devoured—their beamers and bricks all sucked into the monster's maw without a trace.

"Assurance accepted. Lift-off imminent."

I didn't have time to ponder exactly why the Macros changed their mind. I figured I would worry about that later.

"Everybody back away from the doors!" I roared. My men retreated deeper into the dark hold, firing as they went.

-57-

The Macros didn't bother to close the doors. It would have taken too long. They simply lifted the ship's nose—the cargo entrance—and applied thrust. The bricks didn't go flying, fortunately. Our magnetic clamps saw to that. Many of my men were not so lucky. As the floor heaved up under their feet, they stumbled at first, then flew tumbling into the stack of bricks behind them. Loose equipment and the surviving hovertanks slid along, revving hopelessly to stabilize themselves. Men were crushed and mangled. Many fell all the way to the distant back wall of the hold, where they lay in a tangle of broken limbs. Few of them died, however. My nanotized marines were beyond tough, and survived where normal men would have perished. Over the next few days of healing, however, many of them came to wish they had died.

The great doors at the front of the hold closed with agonizing slowness. When they finally clanged shut, cutting out the red glare of the giant sun, they left us in the cold and dark. Men groaned, hissed and sobbed. Some begged to be dug out of wreckage. Others shouted with glee to be off Helios and back into space.

All told, Riggs' Pigs had lost over two thirds our complement of human lives in the Helios campaign. We had a fighting strength of less than two thousand men. Very few of those I'd taken with me into the Worm stronghold remained standing.

We figured out later Major Robinson had been swallowed by the giant Worm, along with many others. One of the turrets the monster had decided to devour had been manned by the Major himself. Of my entire command staff, only Captain Sarin still lived.

"It's too bad we didn't kill that damned giant," Sandra said to me during the first quiet moment we had in our quarters.

"The Worms are going to need that monster to hollow out a new mound," I said.

"I'm surprised you care about them at all. What are we going to do now, Kyle?"

"We'll go home. We'll build up, and next year when the Macros come for another load of cannon-fodder, well, we might have a surprise of our own waiting for them."

"You're talking about starting the war again."

"What do you call this?" I asked.

"At least we won," she said.

"No," I said, shaking my head. "No, we didn't. The war never ended, and we just killed our own side."

Sandra folded herself in my lap. "I don't know what you're talking about."

"The Worms were on *our* side. I'm beginning to understand this universe now. We are organic life—and the machines are our real enemies. They are living death."

"I want all this bloodshed to be over," she said.

"Well, it's not over. We're in it deep. But I'm thinking about a new kind of war. A war of flesh against machine. This time, we won't be kissing any big, metal behinds. And we'll be fighting on the right side."

"Can you do one thing for me, Colonel?" she asked.

I looked at her. Our faces were close, but we didn't kiss. "Name it."

"Don't take me with you next time."

I huffed. "Then don't ask to come."

"I'll have to ask. Just tell me no."

I smiled. "You know I can't do that."

Sandra finally stopped talking and we kissed. For a short time life was good.

The End

Books by B. V. Larson:

STAR FORCE SERIES
Swarm
Extinction
Rebellion
Conquest

IMPERIUM SERIES
Mech
Mech 2

HAVEN SERIES
Amber Magic
Sky Magic
Shadow Magic
Dragon Magic
Blood Magic
Death Magic

Other Books by B. V. Larson
Velocity
Shifting

Visit BVLarson.com for more information.

19837199R00181

Made in the USA
Lexington, KY
09 January 2013